THE
GRASS
DANCER

SUSAN POWER

B

BERKLEY BOOKS, NEW YORK

This is a work of fiction. The events described are imaginary, and the characters are fictitious and not intended to represent specific living persons.

Portions of this book have appeared in
The Atlantic Monthly, The Best American Short Stories 1993, The Paris Review, Ploughshares, Story, and
The Voice Literary Supplement.

THE GRASS DANCER

A Berkley Book / published by arrangement with
G. P. Putnam's Sons

PRINTING HISTORY
G. P. Putnam's Sons edition / August 1994
Berkley edition / August 1995

ISBN: 0-425-14962-5

BERKLEY®
Berkley Books are published by The Berkley Publishing Group,
200 Madison Avenue, New York, New York 10016.
BERKLEY and the "B" design
are trademarks belonging to Berkley Publishing Corporation.

PRINTED IN THE UNITED STATES OF AMERICA

10 9 8 7 6 5

Acknowledgments

For generous support during the writing of this book, I thank James A. Michener, the Copernicus Society of America, the Mary Ingraham Bunting Institute of Radcliffe College, and the Atlantic Center for the Arts.

Heartfelt thanks go to my agent, Henry Dunow, and my editor at Putnam, Faith Sale, for their prodigious efforts on my behalf.

For warm encouragement and early faith I am deeply grateful to Connie Brothers, Frank Conroy, Margot Livesey, Tobias Wolff, and especially Lois Rosenthal—editor, mentor, friend.

I am thankful to the many dear friends whose support has meant the difference, and while I cannot list them all, I tip my hat to those who have been there so patiently, week after week: Lan Samantha Chang, Stephanie Griffith, Alyssa Haywoode, Beth Herstein, LeAnne Howe, Pamela Leri, Nancy Linnerooth, Meg Lysaght, Brian Ragan, Karen Straus, Rhonda Strickland, and of course, Bradley Pritchett (there since Ophelia days, sustaining me).

A special thank you to my relatives, particularly Jan McKinney, Douglas Power, and my aunts and uncles from the Standing Rock Sioux Reservation, and to those people who may not be related by blood but who are certainly family: Anne Collamer, Angeline DeCorah, Mary Green Deer, Irene Jaske, Anne Lim, Malcolm Robinson, Soiesette Robinson, John Salter, Jr., and Katharyn Yamamoto.

Finally, I am forever indebted to my mother, Maȟpiya Boǧawin (Gathering of Stormclouds Woman), who has brought me closer to my ancestors and who is always the inspiration and the source.

To my mother, Susan Kelly Power,
who told me the stories.
In loving memory of my father, Carleton Gilmore Power,
who read them to me every night.

And for the great ladies who gave me keys to two cities,
my grandmothers,
Josephine Gates Kelly and Marjorie Gilmore Power.

SHUSH, WE HAVE TOO MANY STORIES
TO CARRY ON OUR BACKS LIKE HOUSES.

Joy Harjo, *In Mad Love and War*

THE
GRASS
DANCER

Prologue

Crowns of Glass

WHEN HARLEY SAW HIS FATHER, CALVIN WIND SOLDIER, and his brother, Duane, in dreams, they were wearing crowns of glass. Drops of blood trickled down their foreheads, beaded on their black lashes, and slipped into the corners of their mouths. Four weeks before Harley was born, his father and his older brother were killed in a car accident. What happened was this:

Henry Burger's best friend, Lloyd, punched in the jukebox combination E-5 for the sixth time that evening. Patsy Cline was singing "Crazy" in that voice Henry recognized as sorrow become liquid, tears glazing her vocal cords.

"Will you give it a rest?!" someone shouted, but it was too dark in Border Beer for Henry to spot the patron.

Lloyd ignored the complaint, howled, "I'm cra-a-azy for lo-o-ovin' you-ou," half a measure behind Patsy, while squeezing the long neck of his beer bottle.

Henry reached over and grasped Lloyd's freckled arm. "Cool it, okay?"

Lloyd's jaws clamped together and he smiled with his teeth. He let go of the bottle. "Patsy's trying to tell you something, buddy. *I'm* trying to tell you something." Lloyd balled his right hand into a fist. "Jeannette," he said. He

3

held up his left fist. "Leonard." Then he popped them together, making an ugly sound.

Henry Burger shut his eyes. *I already know,* he thought. *And you know I know. This is revenge.* It had taken Lloyd just one week to get back at his good friend, Henry, for refusing to cosign a dubious loan. *Friends are friends, but finance is finance,* Henry had thought, though certainly not said, when Lloyd approached him with his latest scheme to make quick money. This time it had been a dream of reviving Buffalo Bill's Wild West Show, enlisting the participation of some of the natives who regularly passed out beneath Border Beer's sticky tables.

"They'll jump at the chance!" Lloyd had said. "How else will they ever get to see New York City?"

"What makes you think they *want* to see it?" Henry had asked, knowing it was Lloyd's fondest wish yet doubting very much the native population was so inclined.

"Well, just forget it. Be negative," Lloyd had said. But it was not forgotten, and he couldn't resist reminding Henry of his girlfriend's recent infidelity.

Until the evening when Lloyd, underscored by the vocals of Patsy Cline, publicly made reference to the affair, Henry Burger had been able to pretend it away. He wasn't blind. He could see Jeannette was growing tired of him. He wasn't smart enough, he supposed. She'd been to college in the East and had read more books than he'd set eyes on; her bookcase was so heavily stacked the shelves buckled.

"Any day now, I'm history," she often threatened, and Henry didn't know if she meant she would leave him or the Sioux reservation.

"What do you mean?" he had probed on several occasions. "Are you homesick? You want to leave North Dakota?"

Her usual response was a sigh, although one time she'd muttered, "God, yes."

He was quick to advise. "You haven't given this state a chance. You've been living on the reservation the whole time, and that's no kind of life."

Jeannette had erupted then, telling Henry he would never understand the glorious Dakota Nation and he should shut his trap. He didn't like to argue with Jeannette, to see her gray irises drain of color and her eyes crinkle until lines like spokes radiated from their corners. So he was quiet.

He tried to be understanding. To hold on to Jeannette McVay, the skinny blonde who could name the rivers of the world while kissing his shoulder, Henry even ignored her interest in other men, Sioux men. As long as no one threw it up to him, he could turn the other way and mind his own business. But Lloyd had ruined everything. Henry Burger proceeded to drink harder and faster than ever before in his life. He moved from beer to Scotch, until shot glasses slipped through his fingers and he could no longer bring them to his lips.

Henry left the tavern bordering the reservation for his home in Mandan.

"Give my regards to the little lady!" Lloyd called after him.

Henry made it to his pickup but forgot to turn on the headlights. He could sense something was wrong as he moved out of the parking lot, but he was too busy trying to locate Route 6 in the utter darkness to pinpoint the problem. Once he found the road, he was able to ride it from memory. He felt it roll smoothly ahead of him and heard the familiar sound beneath his tires. *Thrum-thrum-thrum.* It soothed him, and his eyes were about to close in sleep when he heard the first chunks of gravel hit the side of his truck.

On other nights he had been oblivious to the sound, more aware of the twisting shadows beyond the road. At such times he remembered stories from his childhood about vengeful Indians: fierce warriors who were always ready to die, and even a beautiful woman wearing a crimson flap of a dress, who lured men to their death.

This night Henry was blind, and his other senses took over. He could hear voices moving with the wind, mocking voices speaking a language unfamiliar to him. *Sioux,* he guessed. More gravel hit his truck, denting the sides and flying off the undercarriage. Henry Burger momentarily forgot his cheating girlfriend and the good buddy he'd left behind him, gloating at the bar. It was the old enemy rising up to challenge him.

Those goddamn Indians, they never quit, he thought. Henry rolled down his window and yelled at the Sioux ghosts he was certain were pelting his truck with rocks. "You shitheads don't even know me!" he screamed. He gave them the finger and rolled his window shut as quickly as possible, so the angry ghosts couldn't shoot him out of his pickup.

Moments later Henry saw eyes coming toward him, the roundest eyes he'd ever seen. Indian ghosts in the Badlands were trying to play with his mind, he imagined. They'd sent eyes to scare him out of his white skin, to watch him peel away from his soul. Dead Indians were trying to put one over on Henry Burger.

He wiped his sweaty hands on the lamb's-wool seat cover and took firm hold of the steering wheel.

"I'll slam you back to hell," he whispered to the eyes, heading straight for them. He charged his four-wheel-drive pickup into their strange light, blinding them forever.

Henry Burger became one with his steering wheel, and Harley Wind Soldier's father and older brother were sucked out of the windshield of their car, onto the hood, where they rested like ornaments.

1
Grass Dancers

(1981)

CHARLENE THUNDER HELD A MICROPHONE TO HER MOUTH and blew into its silver-mesh-covered dome. Feedback crackled from speakers, and it startled the people setting up concession stands and crafts tables into checking the sky for storm clouds. When Charlene's breath swept cleanly through the speakers, like ribbons of wind from the northern plains, she closed her eyes and listened. She pretended she was beside Harley Wind Soldier, blowing gently on his breastbone. She would cool him down only to heat him up. She would trace the outline of his ear with her soft fingers of breath, touching him without touching him. She would tease the hair at the nape of his neck, lifting a section with one long exhalation and separating individual strands with warm staccato puffs.

On the ground below the girl stood Chuck Norris, the kung fu dog. He carefully checked all four directions before peeing on Charlene Thunder's hand-tooled leather purse. He had been scouting her activities all morning, waiting for a vulnerable moment, the chance to make a statement. When Charlene had dropped her bag beside the emcee's platform, freeing her hands so she could help set up sound equipment, Chuck crept behind it, daintily lifted his good back leg, and released his hatred for Charlene in a thick stream of urine.

Chuck Norris could be spiteful. Some believed it was

11

because he could manage only one emotion at a time in his compact body, becoming wholly consumed by either affection or malice. He had the distinction of being the only Pomeranian pooch on the reservation, perhaps the only one in the state of North Dakota, and so was a bit of a local celebrity.

The Powwow Committee was busy preparing the grounds for a three-day dance festival, the Dakota Days Contest Powwow. Several young men, including Harley Wind Soldier and his friend Frank Pipe, were setting up tipis, weaving lodgepoles together and stretching canvas over the ribs once they had been locked in place. Harley was high above the ground, balanced on a friend's shoulders so he could reach up to secure the lodgepoles with ropes. The sky pressed heavily on his head, like a low ceiling suspended above the prairie, and he imagined that if he thrust his hands into the air he could easily snag several clouds.

"What's Charlene doing up there?" Frank called to Harley.

"I guess she's testing the mike."

"Why can't she just say, 'Testing, testing,' like a regular person? How come she's got to breathe all over that thing?"

Harley shrugged. Other people were probably wondering the same thing, but no one would interrupt Charlene. She could blow into that microphone until she hyperventilated, chatter into its black metal cone, or sing "The Star-Spangled Banner" if she liked. The reason no one would complain was parked in a wheelchair under a canopy woven of willow branches. The boys who were replacing old branches with fresh-cut switches and setting up benches in the circular powwow shelter had rolled the old woman into its shade.

Charlene's grandmother Mercury Thunder watched from her chair, shaking her large head at the girl's foolishness.

"Those Wind Soldiers are very bad news," she had warned just a week earlier. But Charlene ignored her.

"You can't help who you love, Unči," she had protested.

"Yes you can. You love yourself, you love your family, and you don't let your feelings run around and jump into someone else's hand." Mercury had made a fist. "You grab on to your own life and push it around where you want it to go."

Mercury believed she held her life firmly in place beneath her tongue, and she didn't spit it out here and there, in bits and pieces, diffusing its power. She had even taken a new name, changing it from Anna to Mercury after her granddaughter brought home a copy of the periodic table in the eighth grade and explained to her: "An element is a substance that can't be split into simpler substances."

"That's my story," Mercury had told Charlene, running her thick forefinger across the chart. "I'm all of a piece."

Charlene had opened her mouth to object, to explain that her grandmother could never be one of the chemical elements, assigned an atomic number and measured for atomic weight, but Mercury presided over the kitchen like a force of nature. Charlene's words were snatched from her mind before they ever made it to her vocal cords. She imagined they were pulled into the old woman's energy field, the electric air surrounding Mercury's body like her own personal atmosphere.

Mercury Thunder was the reservation witch. Had she practiced good medicine, people would have called her a

Dakota medicine woman and rubbed themselves against her at every opportunity. But Mercury practiced selfish magic, lived her own doctrine of Manifest Destiny, until her power extended across the Dakotas.

No one would chastise her granddaughter, for fear of waking the next morning with crossed eyes or a tongue twisted like a pretzel. No one would challenge Charlene and take the microphone from her hands to stop the hoarse windy noise, which was blasting through the powwow grounds like a gale. There was only one spectator brave, or foolish, enough to exhibit signs of displeasure: a small orange dog snarled at Charlene as she stood swaying on the speakers' stand.

Chuck Norris kept his eyes on Charlene as he moved backward in Harley's direction, his teeth bared and a growl grinding out of his throat. When he reached Harley he stood guard, snapping at the invisible breeze Charlene breathed from the stage. Even Chuck Norris could sense which way the wind was blowing.

An hour later the tipis had been erected, the sound system installed, and the Powwow Committee drifted across the open field, visiting with dancers and singers from all parts of the country.

Frank Pipe was resting in the shade of the dance shelter when Charlene found him. She crept behind him, grabbed his long braids, and twisted them across his throat in a playful stranglehold. He put up his hands as if to surrender, and Charlene lightly slapped his face with one of his braids.

"I want to know. Where is that beast?" she asked.

"Who?"

"Psycho dog. Look what he did." Charlene held her

leather purse away from her body, thrusting its urine-soaked flap under Frank's nose.

"Man, he really hates you." Frank laughed. He tried not to stare at the dog, who had ducked behind a garbage barrel to watch Charlene.

"It's mutual. I'm going to kill him this time. Tell me if you see him."

Frank nodded and watched Charlene continue her search of the powwow grounds for Harley's dog. She wouldn't sling her soiled bag over her shoulder, so it dangled instead from her hand. When Charlene wasn't looking, Chuck ran to Frank and lovingly chewed at the hem of his jeans.

"This feud has got to stop," Frank lectured Chuck. He ran his fingers through the ruff of fur that circled Chuck's neck like a bushy collar. Chuck and Charlene had been at war for two years, ever since Charlene fell in love with Harley during their sophomore year in high school. Chuck whined and rolled in the grass, exposing his belly.

"We'd better hide you in the truck for a while." Frank tucked the dog under his arm and carried him to Harley's battered pickup. Then, to keep him quiet in the cab, he bought Chuck his favorite treat—moist wispy cotton candy, which dotted the dog's face like random tufts of pink fur.

Pumpkin sat quietly in the backseat of Nathan Hill's rusted Pinto station wagon. The Hill brothers were settled in front, eating Fig Newtons, and Twyla John's head poked between theirs from the rear of the car, her finger pointing out the tape she wanted them to play. All the way from Chicago to Minnesota the Hill brothers had played powwow tapes, and now Twyla begged for a little Earth, Wind & Fire.

At eighteen, Pumpkin was the oldest occupant of the car and the designated chaperone. No one called her that, of course, but she understood her position, based on her spotless reputation in the Indian community. After all, she had been the only girl in her graduating class at Sand Creek High School in Chicago who wasn't pregnant, and she'd been chosen as valedictorian and delivered a speech titled "Exclusion: The Plight of the Urban Indian," which was well received by the predominantly Indian audience.

Pumpkin imagined that her appearance inspired trust as well, for she was considered not overly attractive, not the kind of girl to spark trouble. She had bright red hair and red freckles the size of ladybugs, which contrasted oddly with the dark skin she'd inherited from her full-blood Menominee mother. Her father, who was responsible for the red hair, given his half-Irish blood, had been the one to dub her "Pumpkin," a name that had stuck until everyone forgot she had another.

Pumpkin dragged her reputation behind her like a dead weight, conscious that it was one more thing to separate her from her peers. She had always been different, even when she tried not to be, unable to curb her curiosity, which led her to read great numbers of books. Her world was constantly expanding, until she could no longer fit herself into the culture that was most important to her.

I stand outside of it, she thought, then realized she must have mumbled it aloud, for her companions turned to stare at her, including Nathan, who should have been watching the road.

"It's nothing," she said.

"Flaky, flaky," Twyla teased, before returning her attention to the music wars in the front seat.

At least I'll get in a few powwows before I take off, Pumpkin thought. Just the idea of college made her nervous in a way that was both good and bad. She would leave for Stanford in the fall, able finally to indulge her academic side but fearful of moving from one culture to another.

This goes beyond leaving home and my parents, she had written in the essay required of all applicants. *I know I am committed to a college education because I am willing to go to great lengths to earn one. I will have to put aside one worldview—perhaps only temporarily—to take up another. From what I have learned so far, I know the two are not complementary but rather incompatible, and melodramatic as it may sound, I sometimes feel I am risking my soul by leaving the Indian community.*

Pumpkin was determined to make the most of the summer, hitting as many northern powwows as possible before returning to Chicago. She smoothed the Dakota Days publicity flyer on her lap, absentmindedly stroking the face of a dancer in a photograph that appeared below the print. The dancer was about Pumpkin's age, and although his face was covered with the makeup paint that men used at powwows, Pumpkin could see he was handsome. His hair swept to the sides from a widow's peak, and his dark eyes tilted upward at the edges like the eyes of a cat.

Pumpkin checked the program schedule. "We're going to miss the welcoming feast, but at least there isn't any dancing tonight. We should be all set for tomorrow's Grand Entry."

"If we ever get there," Twyla said.

• • •

On Friday morning Harley rose early to organize his costume. His mother, Lydia, had ironed the white satin shirt he wore beneath a heavy bone breastplate, and his black neckerchief. Silent as always, she handed them to him, her lips moving only to form a tentative smile. Her fine black hair was pulled back in a ponytail, but the wisps at her hairline escaped and curled across her forehead. She seemed very young. She could have been Harley's sister. He reached out and hugged her then—something he did only rarely since turning seventeen—because as he watched her, she blurred at the edges, looked to him like a person being slowly erased by some spectral finger. He wanted to feel her there, crushed against him, tall and slender, her face level with his own.

"It's going to be a good powwow," Harley said. He felt her head move up and down in agreement, and he released her. His mother drifted out of the tiny living room into the kitchen, the room where she spent most of her days. Silence trailed after her like a shadow, spread along the floorboards, and washed up against Harley's legs like a dense mist. Harley had never heard his mother's spoken voice, only the singing voice she sometimes set free at dances, to join in an old, particularly beautiful song. Ever since the accident that had claimed her husband, Calvin, and Harley's brother, Duane, she refused to speak to anyone, refused to form even a single word. Had it not been her choice to remain mute, Harley was convinced she would have discovered other means of communication, such as sign language. But she expressed herself only minimally, with nudges and shrugs, leaving an empty space between herself and her son, a deep cavity Harley had internalized.

Harley couldn't remember a time when he didn't feel

the black, empty hole squeezed in his chest between heart and lungs. It was solidly lodged there, sharp-cornered like a metal strongbox. When he was little he told himself it was only a matter of years before it filled up, packed with new experiences and sudden insights. When he drew pictures of himself with crayons, Harley always included the empty hole by drawing a black spot on his torso. Adults laughed: "You can't draw a belly button on top of clothes. See, your own navel is hidden under your shirt." His first-grade teacher had scolded him about it in front of the class, so he stopped drawing the hole, to please her. But he knew it was there. He could see it under the crayon-drawn shirt as if he had X-ray vision that burned through paper.

When Harley grew older, the empty box didn't fill itself in the way he'd hoped. It stretched to accommodate his new size. It grew as his bones lengthened and his heart swelled. It became elastic. So when Harley stood in front of the bathroom mirror, running a wet comb through waves of black hair, he recognized his face without claiming it as other people claimed theirs: casually, unconsciously, immediately. Harley slapped his comb onto the porcelain sink and jabbed the mirror with his index finger. He pointed at the face. The face pointed at him.

"Who do you think you are?" he muttered.

Harley reached inside the medicine cabinet for the makeup paints he would use to prepare his face for the dance. His fingers trembled as he touched the three stubby cylinders: the newer blue and black crayons and the worn chalky white stick. The markings Harley drew were ancient, passed down from father to son or, in his case, from mother to son. Wearing them was like slipping behind an ancestral mask. And as Harley painted, blotting sweat from his forehead and temples with a paper towel, he thought he heard the dead grandfathers' voices scratching the house with hoarse whispers, rasping like static from the radio.

We are rising, we are rising, the voices hummed. And when Harley's painted mask was in place, an angry magpie dive-bombed the bathroom window, screeching, *We are here, we are here.*

Harley and Frank pulled into the powwow grounds an hour later, and Chuck Norris was the first out of the truck. The two of them enjoyed watching Chuck bully the other dogs, so much larger than he. No one was certain how Chuck had subdued the tough reservation dogs, especially since he'd lost half an ear to them, but he'd managed it somehow. Now he led the pack across the field, scavenging for cotton candy and caramel corn to satisfy his sweet tooth. Harley nudged Frank when an old battle-scarred dog known to be part coyote found a half-melted candy bar and dropped it at Chuck's feet. The Pomeranian grinned and licked the old dog's face.

"He's a pirate," Harley said proudly.

"You got that right," Frank agreed.

Most people indulged Chuck because of the tragic circumstances surrounding his arrival. He had been abandoned, probably by tourists on their way to the Black Hills. He'd been in sad condition when he wandered onto the reservation: his fur was matted and filthy, and one of his back legs flapped uselessly behind him, completely shattered. Frank's grandfather, Herod Small War, caught Chuck in a pillowcase and patched him up, but the dog never regained control of his broken leg. When he was excited it shot to the side in a wild kick—which is how he got his name. Herod became attached to the dog and intended to keep him, but Chuck had other plans; he chose to live with Harley.

Chuck usually shadowed Harley, keeping jealous watch, except at powwows, where he could be persuaded to go his own way. So Harley was able to slip off to Herod's tipi without Chuck's running in circles around his feet or begging to be carried.

Frank didn't like outdoor powwows as much as those held in a gymnasium or community hall, because grass muffled the sound of his black cowboy boots. He felt his slight frame didn't take up enough space in the world, so he had taps nailed to the soles of his boots. This way his approach was signaled long before he came into view, his steps clinking like coins on the sidewalk.

Frank was small-boned, with delicate features, and women had fussed over him when he was little, calling him a ''beautiful child,'' which he detested. Like his grandfather, he rubbed sesame seed oil into his black hair until it was strangely iridescent; it was so long the ends of his braids brushed his knees. When he played basketball or anticipated a fight, he would twist his hair into a bun fastened by large hairpins and remove the two silver hoops piercing each ear. He was proud of the scar dividing his left eyebrow and the one resembling an arrow below his right eye, because they marred an otherwise smooth, hairless face.

''What a rugged Sioux,'' Harley teased Frank whenever he caught him fingering the scars.

After Harley left to change, Frank moved to join the three older men he spotted near the dance area. One of them was his grandfather, a Yuwipi man, frequently consulted on spiritual matters. Beside him stood Herod's old friend Archie Iron Necklace, pressing all his weight onto a

thick walking stick. The youngest of them was Harley's cousin Leonard Fire Cloud, who was dressed in a traditional costume, similar to the one Harley would be wearing. Leonard, a much-decorated veteran of the Vietnam war, had been given the honor of carrying the American flag at the head of the procession known as Grand Entry. He was looking around for Harley; his cousin was supposed to dance beside him, carrying the Sioux flag—a long staff decorated with eagle feathers.

"Where is he?" Leonard called to Frank.

"Running on Indian time," Frank said. "He should be here any second."

Herod held out a steaming plastic bowl, filled to the rim with *waštunkala,* Sioux corn soup. "You want some?" he asked Frank.

"No, thanks."

A shrill yip startled the group, and everyone looked down at the source of the noise. Chuck Norris moved through his begging routine: he lifted his front paws in supplication and then rolled over three times in quick succession.

"Okay, okay, I'm sorry I forgot to ask *you,*" Herod told him. The old man fished a good-sized piece of venison from the soup and gave it to Chuck.

"Don't you give him the good meat," Archie scolded. "I can't believe how you spoil that mutt. He's just a big orange rat, and if this leg would ever heal, I'd drop-kick him right out of here." Chuck growled at Archie, who poked him with the walking stick. "You be quiet, you *šiča!*"

"Here he comes," said Frank, as he noticed Harley jogging toward them, followed by a stream of little girls.

"Harley and his fan club," Archie said.

"You're just jealous," Herod told him. "You couldn't get a woman's attention if you paraded through here buck naked."

"Don't give me any ideas," Archie said. He wiggled his thick gray eyebrows.

"Let's go," Leonard told Harley. "We've got to get this show on the road."

Harley and Leonard left to collect their flags, and Frank stood quietly in the grass, his hands shoved in his back pockets. Grand Entry was about to start, and he watched the dancers separating into clusters according to gender and style of dance. Frank himself never danced, except for Honor Songs and the Rabbit Dance, which was ladies' choice. Dancing meant the responsibility of a costume, and Frank wanted to be free to leave at a moment's notice, unencumbered by feather bustles, deer-tail roaches, sleigh bells, heavy beadwork, or other dance accoutrements.

Frank watched as Leonard and Harley danced side by side, tall and straight as pines. Their faces were painted with black-on-white teardrops, and a blue vertical stripe was drawn from their matching pointed widow's peaks, down their strong noses, to the edge of their chins. As they passed, the heavy flags held out in front of them, little girls shoved each other and older girls voiced approval by trilling—le-le-le-le-le—in a high, ancient call. The women who had set their caps on Leonard, a longtime bachelor, commented boldly behind their hands or their fans made of eagle feathers, and giggled, scandalized at the things they found themselves saying about him.

Other dancers followed the lead men in pairs, forming a great circle, until every dancer was in the arena. Frank shook his head at the spectacle. He didn't mind the attention Harley received; what disgusted him was that Harley never seemed to notice.

Herod tapped Frank on the shoulder and handed him the bowl of soup. "I'll be right back. I've got to give the invocation." Herod moved to the speakers' stand to deliver a prayer so the powwow could finally begin. Herod thanked Wakan Tanka, the Great Spirit, for bringing them all together, representatives of several tribes and several states.

"We're still here," he said, and many of the drummers pounded their drums in approval. "Our culture is still thriving, and it makes me feel good to look around and see so many young ones taking part." He prayed for a successful powwow and for the safety of its participants. Herod believed in short prayers, and he quickly rejoined his grandson and his old friend to watch the first intertribal number.

"Look over there," Frank said. He pointed to a young woman in a grass-dance costume standing at the edge of the arena. It was unusual to see a woman in a man's costume, but the outfit suited her. Yarn fringe was used to represent long grass and fell from the girl's body in red and yellow waves. She was pinning her contest number to the front apron of her costume, smoothing the fringe so the number wouldn't be concealed.

Frank stared at her for several moments. He couldn't decide why he found her so attractive. She wasn't pretty in a conventional way, but it would be difficult to forget her face.

"Have you ever seen a girl grass dancer?" Frank asked Herod.

"No, I never did. But I guess it's about time. They have every right."

Frank looked at Herod in surprise. His grandfather wasn't known to be very liberal when it came to women.

"You have to remember, there's two kinds of grass dancing," the old man explained. "There's the grass dancer who prepares the field for a powwow the old-time way, turning the grass over with his feet to flatten it down. Then there's the spiritual dancer, who wants to learn grass secrets by imitating it, moving his body with the wind. I guess a woman should be able to choose her own style."

"Which is better?" Frank asked.

Herod laughed. "Archie, did you hear this one? *Which is better?* Both. Both. Wouldn't it be the best thing to learn to become the grass *and* learn to control the grass?"

"Let's see what this one does," Frank said. He collected lawn chairs from the back of Harley's pickup for his grandfather, Archie, and himself. Then they settled in the chairs to watch the girl dance.

When Pumpkin first noticed Harley in his black-and-white beaded costume, crying painted tears from forehead to chin, she recognized him as the dancer from the flyer. Her right thigh began to itch. The itch became a searing pain, shooting from the hook-shaped scar on the back of her leg a few inches above the knee. She wanted to put her hand there, maybe hold a chip of ice to the burning skin, but she knew it would be a useless gesture.

Her leg throbbed as Harley danced toward her, carrying the Sioux flag. He was tall and danced with a straight back. He didn't slouch. His eyes didn't cut to the crowd, measuring its reaction. He didn't seem to notice his surroundings, and his unfocused gaze fascinated Pumpkin. She was determined that he would notice her. The scar burned hotter, and Pumpkin was relieved to find her section of the line of dancers moving into the arena. Cool air stirred by movement soothed her pain.

She knew the ache signaled fear, but she was weary of her own terror. As a child, she'd suffered from panic attacks so severe that her parents worried she was epileptic. The summer she was thirteen she had lost patience with herself, and had both acquired the scar and put an end to the panic attacks.

Lake Michigan had tempted her. It was a clear emerald green, and she could see to the bottom. The sand looked soft. Her parents avoided the crowded beaches, preferring deserted stretches of the lake, unpatrolled by lifeguards. They jumped off boulders marked NO SWIMMING! NO DIVING! Pumpkin usually waited for them on a boulder, hugging her knees to her chest, fervently whispering prayers that they wouldn't drown. Her parents were far out, their heads little more than black spots bobbing beside the white buoys that warned boats away from shore. She knew they would hug the buoys for a few minutes, to catch their breath before the return swim.

Pumpkin looked into the water. It lapped gently against the breakwater of piled rocks, pulsing in and out, regular as a metronome. It had its own way of speaking, and that particular day Pumpkin heard its voice. *Cool water,* it bubbled. *Lovely, cool water.* Pumpkin dropped one foot over the side to feel the water against her skin. It was smooth, like pressed satin straight from the bolt. Her foot glided through it. Tears filled Pumpkin's eyes, and she shuddered.

"I'm sick to death of this. I don't care what happens!" she cried. She jumped into Lake Michigan feet first, even though she couldn't swim. As it turned out, the water was shallow and she could walk with her head above the surface. The lake was unusually warm, and its liquid absorbed her violent spasms of fear and carried them away.

She remembered it as the day she broke her fear apart. It was also the day an inexpert cast made by a fisherman on a nearby pier hooked Pumpkin in the back of her thigh. She hadn't felt it right away, only when the man pulled on the line. The hook wasn't deeply embedded, so she easily yanked it free, but the resulting scar would be livid in color and trouble her whenever she was afraid.

Because her fear was suddenly localized, she could choose to ignore it. The scar throbbed when she auditioned for a scholarship to attend an inner-city ballet school, it stung when she took the SAT examinations, and it burned like fire when she secretly applied to Stanford. Pumpkin was no longer immobilized by fear but rather motivated by the irksome pain in her leg. And so she was drawn to Harley because the attraction frightened her.

"Where's your contest number?" a powwow judge asked Charlene when she danced into the arena during Grand Entry. He marked down the number of every dancer present, as contestants were awarded points for participating in the specialty dances. She shook her head, and the judge smiled.

"That's good. It's good to see the young ones dance for fun and not for profit," he told her.

Charlene enjoyed dancing, moving so closely with the beat that she sometimes pretended she'd become the music, but it wasn't the reason she avoided contests. She no longer entered them, because she always won. Her grandmother Mercury would identify the competition and keep the rival dancer's image in mind as she prepared a gummy wad of bad-luck medicine. She chewed the gluey ball, consisting primarily of pork fat, until the competitor crossed her path, and then she spat it carefully onto the ground in the space that person had just vacated. Her magic never failed. The targeted dancer would sprain an ankle or succumb to a curious case of the flu before reaching the finals.

Under those circumstances Charlene hated winning a trophy and wouldn't wave it in the air during the victory dance, even when Mercury called from the stands: "Smile big. Smile big, now! Show off your prize!" She would gesture for Charlene to raise the trophy and face the camera. But Charlene slumped away from her grandmother, hoping no one had noticed Mercury's tricks, hoping no one thought she *wanted* Mercury to affect the outcome.

Charlene identified with Darrin from the television show *Bewitched*. He tried so hard to keep witchcraft out of his house, but his witch wife, Samantha, pulled him into the magic and rattled his mortal brain. Charlene sometimes talked to the TV set, addressing herself to the pretty blond wife with the twitching nose. "You'll give him an ulcer if you keep it up." And then Charlene would feel her own pain, the exploding headache spiraling from her eyebrows to the crown of her skull.

As she waited for the emcee to announce the Rabbit Dance, Charlene danced every intertribal number. She was going to ask Harley to be her partner. She noticed a young woman in a grass-dance outfit who looked vaguely familiar. She'd probably seen her at other powwows. Mercury liked to travel the powwow circuit during the summer, getting one of her young men to drive her and Charlene. They had gone to dances as far away as Chicago, Milwaukee, and Grand Rapids, comparing them, buying small souvenirs at each one. Charlene went up to the girl to welcome her; perhaps they could become friends for the weekend. Charlene usually wandered the powwows on her own, a little lonely, shunned by the others, who feared her grandmother. Perhaps this girl had never heard of Mercury Thunder.

"Hey, there," Charlene greeted Pumpkin. "What a trip, a girl grass dancer."

The two shook hands and, smiling at each other, exchanged names. They talked through one dance, and then Pumpkin pointed to the web of flesh between Charlene's thumb and forefinger. Stenciled there was a curious tattoo, a cluster of round black teardrops.

"What's the deal with these tattoos?" Pumpkin asked. "I've seen a bunch of Sioux girls who have them. Is it some kind of club?"

Charlene shook her head; she stroked the tattoo with her fingers. "No, it was my idea and they're just copying me. It's in honor of this guy," she whispered. "Wait till you see him. Then you'll understand." It took only a few moments for Charlene to spot Harley dancing past them. "There he is." She motioned with her chin.

Pumpkin didn't say anything for a while, absently nodding her head. Finally she said, "I know. I've had my eye on him too."

Charlene bit her lip. *Stay away from him,* she shouted in her head. *You can't just show up out of nowhere and make a move.*

Charlene attempted to sound nonchalant when she asked Pumpkin: "You must have a boyfriend in the city?"

"No. I think I'm too weird." Pumpkin laughed.

"Why? Because of the way you dance?" Charlene tried not to stare at Pumpkin, but she was curious.

"Because of the way I think," Pumpkin finally responded.

Harley had circled around the drum and returned to Charlene's view. She was no longer interested in the grass dancer. She wished for a quick moment that she had a little of her grandmother's fire so she could warn the girl away from Harley, spitting: *I have powerful medicine, and I can turn it on you like that!* Charlene snapped her fingers as if she had spoken the words aloud. Pumpkin peered at her.

"I'll see you around," Charlene said. She turned her back on the girl and walked over to the food booth to get a can of soda. She was so annoyed that she missed the emcee's announcement of the Rabbit Dance, and by the time she returned to the arena, the couples had already formed. The second couple, behind the head dancers, was Harley and Pumpkin. Charlene had to close her eyes for an instant because she'd been overwhelmed by the sight, by the gaudy flash of Pumpkin's red-gold hair, shimmering in the sun.

Dancers were more reckless and extravagant with their energy during the evening session because the sun was going down, cooling the exposed plain. Charlene was out of breath at the end of a fast song played by the Rocky Boy Singers. She gathered her shawl on her shoulders before sitting in a lawn chair behind the host drum. She wondered if Harley had witnessed her triumph at the end of the number, when she completed a one-legged spin to stop firmly on the last beat. She finished so perfectly it seemed her moccasins pinned the song's tail to the ground. Even sweeter than this, Charlene had seen Pumpkin overstep: she gave a tentative hop after the final drumbeat, as if she expected the song to continue.

Charlene gloated, shaking out her legs to relieve cramped calf muscles. She fell deeper into her chair, when, all at once, one of the vinyl strips beneath her ripped.

"What the—" Charlene leaned over the side to look under the seat of her chair. Chuck Norris grinned at her. He clenched the torn vinyl strip between his tiny crooked teeth.

"You obnoxious little shit!" Charlene hissed at him, batting him away with her hand. "Keep doing that and you'll end up in my grandma's soup kettle. Just a stringy little piece of meat."

Chuck Norris barked and lunged toward her before chasing after a group of children. Charlene quickly forgot him, as the host drum sang a song honoring veterans. It was a Dakota song, rather than the usual intertribal using vocables in place of words, and it dated back to World War II. The men launched enthusiastically into the chorus, and it took Charlene a moment to translate the lyrics into English; she was becoming less proficient in the Dakota language after so many years of school:

> They're sending Sioux boys to Germany—
> Hitler better look out.

She chuckled to herself. *Those macho Sioux guys,* she thought.

Veterans of the last three wars were dancing, wearing jeans and cowboy boots. They moved casually, with a double stamp, their arms dangling awkwardly at their sides or bent to hold an American flag draped across their shoulders.

The host drum segued directly into another old number, this one a love song in response to war:

As the young men go by, I was looking for him.
It surprises me anew that he is gone.
It is something to which I cannot be reconciled.

A high wailing voice broke into the chorus like a ghost
singer, lifting the song into the sky. It was Harley's mother,
Lydia, who hadn't spoken a word in seventeen years. Charlene noticed Harley slip beside his mother, dancing in
place. The two of them stood behind the seated drummers,
surrounded by people holding tape recorders to catch Lydia's famous voice. Lydia seemed oblivious to the crowd's
excitement. Her head was thrown back and her eyes were
closed as she bobbed in time to the music.

A competing voice suddenly rolled across the arena: a
flat, heavy voice, thick as tar, muffling all the others. Mercury Thunder wheeled herself to the drum and, after setting
the brake on her wheelchair, rose from its seat with majestic
grace. Her booming voice was violent, unlike Lydia's,
which quivered in lament, and since she couldn't bend her
knees to dance in place, she worked her fists up and down,
like a woman grinding clothes against a washboard.

On Mercury's right, Sonny Wilson held a plate of Indian
tacos he had fetched for her. On Mercury's left, Junior
Black Owl reached to support her as she stood singing, but
she shook him off without turning around to acknowledge
his presence. Both men were in their mid-twenties, unusually attractive, and both looked dazed and astonished,
as if they had just been clubbed. Their expressions were
familiar to Charlene. All of Mercury's lovers appeared addled, exploited by the magic she stirred with spoons. When
Mercury was finished with a man she would let him go, and
sense would come back into his eyes. He couldn't remember much about the affair, but sometimes he would

dream about Mercury and discover, upon waking, that he'd wet the bed like a little boy.

Charlene knew she could have Harley Mercury's way if she wanted. She could bring her grandmother stray hairs from Harley's head or feathers from his costume, and Mercury would burn them to a powder. She would make a love paste to be baked in brownies, or a love soup mixed with buffalo meat, and one meal later, Harley would be dazzled by Charlene. But it wouldn't be real. Harley's eyes would be empty and his efforts to please too desperate.

Charlene's knees dipped automatically in time to the old song, but it seemed to be breaking apart, it became hard to follow. She realized it was Mercury's doing. Mercury hadn't been able to drown out Lydia's singing, so she turned her attention to the drummers. She stared them down, one at a time, intimidating each to the point that his drumstick would slide off the drum and fall silently to the ground. Soon the host drum was dead quiet, and Mercury nodded her large head in satisfaction. But the song continued, undiminished. Lydia sang about love and loss, each note a cry swirling through the air. She sang to the end, and when she had finished she wiped her face with her apron and returned to the food booth. She hadn't once glanced at Mercury.

During the evening session Harley finally worked up the courage to approach Pumpkin. He had noticed her even before she asked him to be her partner in the Rabbit Dance. She was the best grass dancer on the field; she became a flexible stem, twisting toward the sky, dipping to the ground, bending with the wind. She was dry and brittle, shattered by drought, and then she was heavy with rain. Harley sat through two songs to watch Pumpkin dance. He walked up to her as she rested on the dancers' bench.

"You're a good dancer," he said. "I like to watch."

She smiled. "You too."

Harley brushed the compliment aside. "What made you decide to do grass style?" he asked.

"It's a challenge. I tried women's traditional and women's fancy shawl, but I was always myself out there. As a grass dancer, I'm trying to become something else. I step outside of myself. Do you know what I mean?"

Harley nodded. "I think so."

"Is that your dog?" Pumpkin asked. She pointed to Chuck Norris, who was watching the two of them, his head moving back and forth as if he followed their conversation. Pumpkin reached over and picked him up.

Harley moved forward, his hand out. "That's not a good idea. He can be pretty evil."

But Chuck Norris allowed himself to be cradled in Pumpkin's arms. "Hey, we match," she told the orange dog; she even kissed the top of his head. Chuck closed his eyes and relaxed; he looked ready to purr.

"That's amazing!" said Harley. "You don't know how unusual that is. He's taken to you right off."

Pumpkin and Harley sat on the low bench and talked about Chuck, about Pumpkin's attending Stanford and the powwows she would miss. Members of the Powwow Committee were beginning to move through the grounds with garbage bags, putting the area in order.

"You want to talk some more when the dancing ends?" Harley asked Pumpkin. "I know a place where we can go to get away. It's not far from here."

"Sure. But I have to tell my friends. Where should I meet you?"

Harley pointed out his pickup and took the sleeping dog in his arms.

At the conclusion of the evening session, he led the dancers from the arena and retired the Sioux flag. He changed from his costume back into jeans and packed his gear in the truck.

"You ready to take off?" Frank asked him. Chuck Norris was asleep in the cab, snoring loudly, his paws twitching.

"Actually, I've sort of got a date," Harley said.

Frank whistled. "I don't believe it, the hermit's got a date. Hey, I'm proud of you!" He clapped Harley on the shoulder. "I can get a ride with some Crow girls I met. They're staying near my place, and I think they like me." He winked at Harley.

Harley grinned in relief. "Could you take the monster?" he asked.

Frank lifted Chuck out of the cab. "Full report in the morning!" he called over his shoulder.

Charlene saw Harley leave the powwow with Pumpkin beside him in the truck. She tried to reassure herself. *It's just one of those powwow things,* she thought. But Charlene had never seen Harley take interest in a girl before. He kept to himself, and his many admirers consoled themselves with Frank. Charlene sat trembling in the grass. *She'll be gone soon,* she told herself. *That's a city girl. Pumpkin won't be around long enough to make a difference.* She willed herself not to cry.

Mercury was visiting with her young men, and Charlene spotted her wheeled beside the bonfire. Mercury's face glowed with perspiration. She was about seventy but looked years older. Her skin was so puckered it resembled smocking, and she had lost most of her teeth. Her white hair was short and wiry, springing away from her head. Charlene worried that she'd inherited Mercury's figure: broad shoulders and a thick waist, tapering to skinny legs.

Charlene often wondered what her parents had looked like, but Mercury claimed she didn't have any photographs of them. "They gave you to me," she had told Charlene, "and then they ran off to one of those big cities and drank their minds away." Mercury swore they had died within two months of one another, but she had never produced a death certificate or told Charlene where they were buried.

Charlene had fine brown hair she thought of as her mother's, a flat round face she believed was her father's, and a head full of Mercury's ideas. Mercury didn't believe in school, but she did believe in what she called Life Lessons.

"I should write a big book giving all the answers," she'd told Charlene one Valentine's Day morning. Charlene was ten years old at the time and still believed her grandmother owned the answers, had them sewn in a calico sack tied off at the top with a white shoelace. Charlene had spent years searching for the bundle, certain she would recognize its shape and weight, imagining the feel of all those answers running through her fingers like the kernels of sunflower seeds.

Mercury had been eating the chocolate turtles Reuben Broken Nose had brought her shortly after sunrise. She let Charlene pluck one from the box, but no more than that.

"After all, they're *my* winnings," she whispered in her granddaughter's ear.

Reuben Broken Nose leaned in the doorway between hall and kitchen to watch Mercury eat. He hadn't been invited to sit down. When Mercury sucked the last string of caramel from her broken wisdom tooth, she handed Reuben the Valentine's Day present she'd made for him. It was a turquoise cotton ribbon shirt, decorated with eggshell ribbons and silver studs. Charlene noticed that the hem and collar were slightly bulky, as if something had been stitched in the seams. Reuben put it on over his flannel shirt, and after he smoothed it once with his hands, he dropped into a kitchen chair, gazing blindly at Charlene.

"The wonders of sage." Mercury chuckled, shuffling to his side. "Lesson One!" she cried. Charlene bolted from her chair to stand at Mercury's elbow. "You see this man?" Mercury peered at Charlene until her granddaughter nodded. "I know you think he's something special. You're just like all the others around here who get gussied up to try to catch him." Again Charlene nodded, and she even stroked Reuben's inert hand with one finger. He was the reservation heartthrob, not so much because he was handsome—in a bland, mixed-blood sort of way—but because he was funny.

"Well, I'm telling you he's not special. Not like me and not like you. He's a dime a dozen."

But you can't make me laugh, Charlene was thinking.

"I don't mess myself with women, because you can't be sure about them. Sometimes there's a lot of power there, and you have to be careful. But most men I know go down like that." Mercury snapped her fingers. "You can use the easiest medicine, the oldest tricks. Powders that are so stale you think maybe you should throw them out because the magic's seeped away. I'll teach you to take control."

Charlene watched as her grandmother thrust her face inches away from Reuben's. She gave him a string of orders, a list of chores he would need all day to complete.

Then she straightened up and clapped her hands. Reuben
stood a little unsteadily and made his way to the woodpile
outside Mercury's trim house. Moments later they heard
the sound of wood being split into kindling. Mercury
turned to her granddaughter and held out her hands.

"You see," she said.

Harley still wore the mask of tears when he drove
Pumpkin to the deserted house surrounded by dried mud.
As they made their way on foot to the house, gray powder
dusted their boots and the dragging end of a blanket Harley carried over his arm. The structure was exposed like a
dollhouse, its eastern wall collapsed in a heap of rubble,
which Harley expertly climbed with the aid of a high-
beam flashlight. Pumpkin matched the placement of her
feet to his and balanced herself by gripping the belt at his
waist.

"After you," he said. He stepped aside so Pumpkin
could enter what had once been a fine sitting room. Beer
cans and bottles littered the splintered floorboards. Harley
kicked piles of debris into a corner and spread the blanket
in the center of the floor.

Graffiti covered the walls, and Pumpkin squinted to de-
cipher the ragged sentences. *Frank does it better* was written in crimson lipstick pencil and had sparked a debate. To
Frank's credit, he never wrote on the walls. But he was a
popular subject. The consensus was that Frank indeed did
it better, and his name was scrawled in so many hearts
Harley thought it would be difficult to count them all.
Frank's name was penned lovingly even on the sagging
ceiling, in a provocatively round script.

"Frank's a busy guy," Pumpkin said. She gestured toward the walls.

Harley smiled. "I think he has Olympic potential. I don't know how he does it. He has so many girlfriends, one after the other, but he manages to keep them all as friends."

"It's a gift," Pumpkin murmured. She pulled Harley onto the blanket, where they both sat hugging their knees and watching the black sky.

"What about you?" she asked. "Do you go from one girl to the next?"

Harley laughed. "Just check out the walls."

It was true Harley's name wasn't pressed into the flaking wallpaper, but Pumpkin had seen at least a dozen of the tattoos that honored him. *Why me?* she wondered. *What's so special about me?*

Harley reached for Pumpkin's hand, and she gasped at the touch because her scar ignited in pain, as if a blazing lighter had been held to her flesh.

"Are you all right?" he asked. Pumpkin nodded. She rubbed the tender area with her free hand.

The pain emboldened Pumpkin; she laughed suddenly, threw her head back, and undid her braid. She wanted to surprise herself, behave in ways she couldn't recognize, shed her reputation and the bright fear. As Harley watched, his eyes round with surprise, Pumpkin removed her clothes until she wore only a pair of white panties.

"I've never done anything like this before," Pumpkin told Harley, and he believed her.

"You aren't scared of anything," he whispered. He bent to kiss her throat, a fragrant pool of shadows.

Harley's hands moved gently and carefully along Pumpkin's body. She imagined he was sculpting her from clay: delineating her tapered ribs, pinching her hipbones into angular mounds, pressing her belly with his palms to make it concave. She realized her body was lonesome. She was seldom touched, even by her parents, who were so shy she wondered how they had managed her as an infant. Had they really held her, bathed her, spooned cereal into her mouth with their own hands?

"You have the body of a dancer," Harley murmured, softly twisting the knobs on her knees as if he could spin them like tops.

Pumpkin leapt to her feet. She wanted to show Harley how completely she owned her skin and muscles. She found the moldy western wall with her left hand and rested her fingertips against it for balance. Her right foot pointed forward in a tendu and then rose from the floor to chest level in a taut arabesque. Moonlight played on her arch, accentuating its crescent curve. She moved her leg to the side, keeping it high and straight. For a moment it pulsed an inch higher; then it swiveled to the back. She leaned her torso forward, and as she tipped toward the ground, her right leg continued to rise. She was nearly in the split position when she heard Harley whisper reverently: "You are so different."

It was enough to stir Pumpkin from her demonstration, make her bring her legs together like scissor blades. She flattened against the wall and shushed Harley.

"I didn't mean it in a bad way," he said. He held out his hand to guide her back to the blanket.

"I know." She slipped beside him. "But you can't *say* things like that. You shouldn't ever be too arrogant or too loud about who you are. I don't think I believe in God, but I believe in forces. And they're nosy. Don't tell them you're here. Don't light any bonfires. Walk in the shadows and you walk forever."

"Who said that? That thing about the shadows?" Harley asked.

"I did," Pumpkin responded.

Pumpkin kissed Harley to make up for leaving him so abruptly. The scar burned steadily, but she ignored it and held Harley closer. This time it was Harley who pulled away, extending his arms as if to catch his balance.

"Wait," he said. "I feel like I'm falling."

"I won't let you go," Pumpkin breathed in his ear.

He looked at her and thought she could be a red-gold Indian angel, with arms wrapped tight like ropes around his body, and skin soft as feathers.

"You can talk to me," said Pumpkin.

"There's nothing here." Harley took her soft hands and pressed them to his heart.

"You're wrong," she told him. "I can feel your heart in there, beating like a two-step."

"Nothing's here," he repeated. Harley stood and walked to the edge of the room, where the planks extended into open air. "My brother died a few weeks before I was born. Duane. He took everything with him."

Pumpkin shivered. "I don't understand," she said.

But Harley couldn't tell her more, even though he could see his mother standing beside the casket. She was big with Harley but carrying him indifferently. Her hands were busy with her first son, her sleeping son. She brushed his hair into place and tucked a star quilt around his shoulders. She wiped away her tears with squares of cotton fabric, which she slipped beneath Duane's satin pillow, but the traditional tear cloths weren't enough. Harley saw his mother press her belly, wanting something more to give Duane. He imagined she located her own spirit membrane, caught her fingernail under its edge and peeled it away from her unborn child. It looked like cellophane and crinkled when she pinched it into a small wafer the size of Father Zimmer's holy hosts offered at Communion. And so Lydia fed her sleeping son his brother's soul, forced it between stitched lips. Before they closed the coffin lid, Harley saw his mother kiss Duane, whisper a final message: "I'll give you my voice too."

It was as if Pumpkin could read Harley's mind, she was so perceptive. She knew what to do.

"Come here," she ordered gently, urging him to stretch out on the blanket. She straddled his back and pressed the heels of her hands against his tight muscles, releasing the tension.

"I'm your friend now," she told Harley as she massaged his neck and shoulders. "I have plenty of soul to spare. I'm rubbing it into you right now. Can you tell?" She was kneading his lower back with her knuckles, and Harley nodded because a warmth was spreading. Pumpkin was making her way into his heart, lighting the corners of his empty soul with a red-gold flame.

"You won't be alone now," Pumpkin crooned. "I'm a part of you, like it or not."

And Harley could sleep. He could close his eyes without spinning away in the darkness. He thought that sleeping beside Pumpkin must be better than Frank Pipe's crazy sex adventures, but he would keep her a secret. He would keep her locked in that little heart chamber she'd reached with her fingers through the very wall of his back.

When Harley woke at dawn, he felt as if his frozen body was welded to Pumpkin's. The temperature had dropped twenty degrees overnight, and a chill had worked its way so thoroughly into Harley's bones he was too stiff to shiver.

He jerked himself to his feet and tucked the blanket around Pumpkin's shoulders until she was rolled in a cocoon. Harley fastened the snaps of his jeans jacket and huddled against the southern wall. He turned his head because he didn't want to face the rising sun; its pink light washed across his profile and briefly painted the dead white trees, caught in a river of mud. As he looked back at Pumpkin he glimpsed the lady of the house.

He hadn't told Pumpkin the deserted house was said to be haunted. Its resident was an elderly white woman who defied all stereotypes. She wasn't heard to wail or moan, she wasn't graceful and elegant, she didn't wring her hands or skim along the floorboards. She was built like a wrestler, and so heavy, even as a spirit, that the floor creaked when she stamped through the house. She was always spotted doing chores: churning butter, darning socks, beating rugs, sweeping floors. One old drunk even claimed to have caught her nursing a ghost-child, and when she saw him in the corner of her sitting room, clutching a bottle of Thunderbird wine, he said, she offered him her other breast, which he declined. She had been photographed a number of times by tourists, her cloudy shape caught on film, and although her face was obscured by an opaque mist, one could clearly make out her strict bun and a scolding finger waggled at all the useless people wasting her time.

Harley had never seen her before. He held still, to keep her in focus, because from some angles she disappeared. The old woman wasn't hard at work for this particular visitation. She was on her plump knees beside Pumpkin, stroking the girl's shimmering red hair with a pale meaty hand. The old woman was crying silently, her dark round teardrops falling onto the floor. In a few moments she vanished, and Harley moved to kneel in her place. He brushed his hand across the stained floor, hoping to understand her inky tears.

Like many other powwow participants, Mercury Thunder preferred camping on the grounds even though she lived nearby. Charlene had slept in her grandmother's tipi, and early Saturday morning she discovered Mercury sleeping in her wheelchair before the fire, her fists full of ashes.

"Unči, how are you doing? You okay?" Charlene gently shook Mercury's shoulder. "How come you stayed out here?"

"I had important things I was thinking. I had business with the fire." Charlene decided this was something she didn't want to hear about, but Mercury continued. "You know what occurred to me? There is a devil-man, but there is no devil-woman. I could be a hot queen and blow fire kisses from the palm of my hand. I'd keep that old Devil Jack entertained, and if he turned on me, boy, wouldn't I toast his slippers!" Mercury licked her lips with a bright red tongue, which Charlene thought looked scalding-hot.

"That's going against Jesus." Charlene attempted to sound as confident as Father Zimmer did in his Friday-afternoon lectures at the high school.

"Get back with your Jesus!" Mercury spat. "You take him right back where you found him, and don't bring him to me. That one has too many faces. You don't know where you stand with him. Give me honest Jack anytime, because I know he wants to do me in, but I can see him coming a mile away."

Charlene was shocked. "Why are you so mad at God?" she asked.

Mercury sagged in her wheelchair and rubbed her sore knees. "You wouldn't believe me if I told you," she finally answered.

It was a rare moment for Charlene. Her grandmother appeared vulnerable rather than omnipotent. But she knew Mercury would recover, so she walked away. She wouldn't repeat the mistake she'd made six years earlier.

Charlene was eleven years old when the arthritis in Mercury's knees became so severe she was confined to a wheelchair. Charlene expected this would interfere with Mercury's love life, but the young men continued their visits, knocking timidly on the door and entering like sleepwalkers.

"Why can't you fix your knees?" Charlene had asked Mercury one morning as she helped her move from bed to wheelchair.

Mercury didn't respond until she was safely seated. "It doesn't work like that. I'm not a healer."

Charlene decided *she* would become the family healer, so she took her savings to town and bought a package of Silly Putty. Later that night she rolled the flesh-colored dough between her fingers and pinched it into her grandmother's round shape. She pressed a wad of Mercury's hair, taken from her brush, onto the figure's bald head. Charlene worked the putty doll's short, spindly legs, bending them back and straight, back and straight, to make them flexible. Then she placed the tiny figure in an empty matchbox and tucked a Kleenex around it like a blanket before climbing into her own bed.

In the morning Mercury couldn't stand, and she had Charlene bring her a cup of soothing horsemint tea. Mercury looked as close to tears as Charlene had ever seen her.

"It was the worst night," Mercury complained. "It's like I ran one of those crazy marathons."

"Your knees don't feel any better?" Charlene asked hopefully.

"Better!" Mercury spilled her tea. "Do they look better? They're awful!" She pulled the covers aside, and Charlene winced when she saw her grandmother's swollen knees, puffy and shapeless as dough.

On Sunday, the final day of the powwow, winners of the dance competitions were selected. Herod Small War was asked to judge the men's categories in the final session, and during the men's grass-dance contest he watched Pumpkin closely. Goose bumps rose on his arms and legs. He was watching not a girl, he thought, but the spirit of grass weaving its way through a mortal dancer. Pumpkin was the color of blazing grass: grass that is offered to the sky in prayer. When the song ended, Herod wasn't able to choose second- and third-place winners because he hadn't seen anyone but Pumpkin dancing on the field. Luckily there were three other judges to make up for the slip.

When the winners' names were called, no one was surprised that Pumpkin came in first. Her friend Rodney Hill came in second, so between them they netted two trophies and five hundred dollars. More than enough to get them to the next powwow on their itinerary.

Before Pumpkin and her caravan moved on, the emcee announced a special song to be performed in her honor. It was Harley's doing. He had told the emcee that Pumpkin would be heading for Stanford in the fall, which delighted the old man.

"Let's hear it for this little Menominee girl from Chicago. What an accomplishment!" he roared into the microphone. The audience clapped and whistled, the drummers pounded their drums, everyone was proud, everyone craned to catch sight of Pumpkin. The emcee called on the Chi-Town drum to sing the honor song. The people stood, and Pumpkin was pushed into the arena. She circled once on her own before others fell in behind her to dance their goodwill and best wishes. Even Charlene adjusted her shawl and joined them.

People of all tribes slipped Pumpkin money and shook her hand. Someone eventually handed her a basket she could use to catch the contributions.

Harley danced about halfway down the line of well-wishers so that when Pumpkin rounded a curve in the arena, she faced him. Her headband had a circle of red, orange, and yellow beads pressed between her eyebrows, and it looked as if a fiery sun were rising from her forehead. Her braided hair escaped in places, glinting as though it had been sprinkled with glitter. Harley recalled what Pumpkin had said about lighting bonfires and alerting forces. But he wasn't frightened for her, even though he imagined that every spirit, angel, and god for miles around must have picked up Pumpkin's frequency and wafted to the powwow grounds to witness her honor song. He had no doubt they would capitulate, scamper ahead of her to chew the ground, transforming obstacles in her path into pyramids of dust.

Pumpkin directed the Hill brothers to head for the Fort Berthold Reservation, about one hundred fifty miles northwest of the Dakota Days powwow grounds. They had heard that a warbonnet dance would be held there the next night. For the first half-hour of the drive, Pumpkin's friends had teased her about her absence the night before.

"You stay out all the time," Pumpkin protested when Twyla shook a finger at her.

"But that's me. That's everybody else. You're not everybody else."

Pumpkin clutched the powwow flyer with Harley's photograph printed at the bottom. His eyes stared at her, and she stared back for a long time. He'd written his address on the reverse of the page, and Pumpkin ran her finger over the letters, gently enough to feel the faint depressions scratched into the paper. She looked for a separate meaning, gathered from the words by touch. She wondered whether she had dreamed the night in the deserted house surrounded by mud. Had she really given Harley a sliver of her soul? Pumpkin wanted to savor the memory, turn it over and over in her mind until she understood what had happened, the strange and unexpected connection. But Twyla fidgeted beside her in the backseat, making it difficult for her to concentrate.

Near Mandaree, on the Fort Berthold Reservation, the flat plains gave way to steep hills, their sides painted with dark rings that made Pumpkin think of ancient times, when the area had been covered by deep water.

"This was all under water," Pumpkin murmured. The rings were orange, red, and fuchsia. Purple sagebrush sprouted on the hillsides, and the grass at the top was a lush green.

"Did you think it would be this bright?" Pumpkin asked, but no one answered. Twyla and Rodney were asleep, and Nathan was concentrating on the winding road penetrating the hills.

Pumpkin had heard about the seashells that scavengers could find in the grass, such as the cone-shaped dentalium shells that had been used to decorate many older Sioux costumes. The wind was like water, rippling through the car's open windows, and Pumpkin imagined she tasted the ocean. It was actually the smell of rain invading the car, powerful enough to wake Twyla and Rodney. The travelers drove into a downpour so heavy that Pumpkin worried it would crush the car. But the vehicle soared, picking up speed on the slick road.

"Slow down!" the passengers yelled at Nathan, and it was in the act of braking that the car shimmied out of control.

For the first time in her life, Pumpkin wasn't afraid, because the moment was so terrible it was exhilarating. The car shot off the ledge, wheels rotating like propellers, and Pumpkin was flying across the Badlands.

Rodney's trophy sailed from his hands out the open window, and Pumpkin watched it slip, end over end. She smiled and nodded, tossing her own trophy out the window, excess ballast heaved off a ship.

The car finally landed on its nose, collapsing like an accordion. But Pumpkin was still flying, shedding fears and insecurities like old skins, until she was distilled to a cool, creamy vapor. Pumpkin melted into the sky, and so she never came down.

Harley was stunned into silence by news of the accident. Herod, Frank, and Leonard brought the news to his house. They couldn't work their mouths very well; it took all three of them to stammer the story, one picking up where another's voice had faded into silence.

Their words made Harley feel rock-heavy. He imagined

sand bursting from behind his eyes, pouring through his body, and filling him from top to bottom, as if he were nothing more than a useless sack. Chuck Norris whined at Harley's feet, longing to jump into his lap and wash his face back to life, but Harley planted boulder fists on his thighs. Eventually the men left, and Lydia replaced them at the kitchen table. She was silent, as ever, but her presence seemed to warm the room.

Harley managed to rise a few hours later, and he thought his limbs would float away from him, the sand having poured from between his toes, spilling to the floor. *Empty again,* he was thinking as he made his way to the medicine cabinet.

The crayons were there, and he began to draw. He painted the tears that had rinsed through his heart, because he could not cry them. He drew more tears than he ever had before, layer upon layer of black drops, until they fused and his face looked painted for war.

A voice in his head whispered, *I'm a part of you, like it or not,* and Harley's sudden liquid tears cut tracks through the paint.

I would give you back if it would help, he responded. *I would give you back.* But his chest was warmed by a red-gold flame even his salt tears couldn't extinguish.

The night after the accident, Charlene dreamed that she and Pumpkin were finalists in a spelling bee. They were both about ten years old and dressed in navy blue pleated jumpers. The backs of Charlene's legs itched, and when she looked down at her feet she noticed that her loafers were scuffed. She couldn't stop shifting uncomfortably.

Pumpkin's red hair was French-braided, and orange

light shot from her green eyes like electric sparks. Charlene could see Pumpkin was going to win. Pumpkin's hands were laced coyly behind her back, and although she tried to keep her mouth in a tidy line, it trembled into smiles.

Mercury was testing the girls, wielding a baton from her wheelchair throne. She pointed to Pumpkin. "Spell 'grass,'" she said.

"That's too easy," Charlene objected, but Mercury quieted her with a wave of the baton.

"We're waiting," Mercury said pleasantly.

Pumpkin grinned, stretching her freckles, and raised her hands to her sides. She opened her mouth to spell the simple word, but there was no sound.

"Come on. That's a five-letter baby word. Just go ahead and spell it." Charlene thought Pumpkin was pausing for dramatic effect.

Pumpkin opened her mouth again, and a cluster of tiny black birds the size of thimbles fluttered from her mouth. They darted forward, only to slam against a pane of glass that was invisible even to Charlene. Each time Pumpkin parted her lips, birds spilled out, and smashed in waves.

"Stop!" Charlene was screaming for Pumpkin and the reckless birds. "Stop killing them!"

But Mercury had turned her back and was wheeling away, the baton caught between her teeth to free her hands.

Charlene couldn't remember the dream when she woke, trembling, but she was left with a question wrenched from so deep in her gut it made her heave. *Did Mercury do it? Did she do it for me?*

• • •

Herod Small War asked Harley and Frank to drive him up to Fort Berthold so he could visit the site of the accident.

"I want to say a prayer for those kids," he told the boys. "They come all this distance, far from home, and maybe their spirits will get lost in the hills, trying to find their way back to Chicago."

They passed dozens of white crosses along the route, each cross representing a highway fatality. So many Indians smashed themselves on the roads it was old news, but most accidents involved alcohol.

Harley hadn't intended to bring Chuck Norris along, but the little dog insisted, nipping at Harley's ankles when he tried to leave. Chuck hadn't let Harley out of his sight since the day of the accident. The cab of the truck was pretty crowded, so Chuck sat in Harley's lap, his front paws resting on the steering wheel as if he were the driver.

"Here it is," Herod said when they were close to Mandaree. Harley pulled the pickup to the side of the road, and the three men stepped out of the cab. Harley held the door open for Chuck, but he wouldn't jump.

"Are you coming?" he asked, impatient. Chuck backed away from the door, his head down and his legs shivering.

"Stay here, then," Harley said, slamming the door.

Herod seemed relieved to find the scorched earth surrounded by a wide swath of flattened prairie grass. He tugged on Harley's sleeve and pulled him closer so he could share the view.

"You see!" he cried. He pointed to the devastated ground. "Those rescue workers couldn't have done all that."

Harley and Frank were confused. They waited for an explanation.

"This reminds me of the powwow grounds from when I was little. Those old-time grass dancers did a good job of pounding the fields flat. They churned through waist-high stalks like they were wading into a river, and it went down like that. Just like that." Herod pointed again to the pressed plain extending beyond the point of impact.

"What do you mean?" Frank asked. "Who do you think did it?"

"Those kids. Those four Menominees. Now they're the true kind of grass dancers. Now they really know how to prepare the way."

Frank looked skeptical, but Harley believed the old man, because the last time he glanced over his shoulder before climbing into the truck, he thought he saw four figures, graceful as waves, dancing the grass into a carpet.

2

Christianity Comes to
the Sioux

(1977)

HARLEY WIND SOLDIER WAS SEATED IN A RIGID METAL chair that held him like a torture device. He leaned his elbows on the slim board bolted to his chair, which formed a makeshift writing table. Harley and his classmates were arranged in a circle, their eyes trained on the teacher, who sat cross-legged on her desk.

Jeannette McVay—the eighth-grade social studies teacher at Saint Mary's School—was the fairest person in the room, though she had spent the summer baking in the sun on a foil sheet. She addressed her Dakota students with what she hoped was cheerful compassion. "You're probably wondering why I moved your desks," she said. "I thought it only fitting to form a circle, because I know your people have a cyclic worldview. And since this is a give-and-take situation, where I plan to learn from you as much as I hope to share my own knowledge, I want to look at the world through your eyes for a change. Don't you think that's refreshing?"

Harley Wind Soldier shuffled his feet and stared at the big toe emerging from a hole in one of his high-top sneakers. He was only thirteen years old, but he grasped the woman's meaning. He thought she was *unšika*. Pitiful. He could see purple crescents blossoming beneath a wash of liquid makeup, fresh bruises on his teacher's face no doubt stamped there by her boyfriend, Virgil Ribs. There was a tiny cut below her right eye, which Jeannette was attempting to cover by resting her chin in her hand, fingers striping her face. But Harley glimpsed the scabbed seam. He hoped she fought back.

I bet she feels so sorry for Virgil, just because he's Indian, she cries over his split knuckles, Harley thought.

Jeannette McVay faced a room of sullen children, admiring their bronze complexions and straight black hair, although the girls had ruined their tresses, in Jeannette's opinion, by getting feathered cuts that framed their faces like black wings, in a Sioux version of the Farrah Fawcett look. She dyed her own hair a flat black, attempting to match her students' shade, despite Virgil's complaints that she looked ready for Halloween.

Jeannette often wondered what kept her in this isolated territory, where she feared she would always be a stranger. The answer that surfaced most often was: *The children. Who better than an outsider can make them understand the wealth within their poverty?* Jeannette doted on her pupils, considering them royalty in exile. On a little shelf built into the wall behind her desk, Jeannette had placed a set of the complete works of James Fenimore Cooper. She shared the books with her students, reading aloud, and didn't notice when they rolled their eyes at one another.

One day, after reading a particularly lengthy passage from *The Prairie,* Jeannette looked up to find Frank Pipe standing before her. He licked his lips and drew empty circles across the smooth surface of her desk.

"Yes?" she prompted.

Frank cleared his throat. "We were wondering." He looked behind him, seemed to find what he needed, and turned back to face his teacher. "Instead of this stuff, could you read some of that Vine Deloria?"

Jeannette picked up her pen and wrote the name on a tablet. "Now who is that?" she asked sweetly.

Frank looked directly into her eyes for the first time. "He's our cousin," he told her.

Since that day Jeannette McVay had plunged into a study of Native American literature, and the James Fenimore Cooper texts were taken to a Bismarck thrift shop. Jeannette became more Sioux than her Dakota students, no longer addressing them by name, which she read had not been common practice in previous generations. When she heard the children call to each other, carelessly spilling names off their tongues, she scolded them.

"Your ancestors didn't do that sort of thing. You should go back to the old ways. They're so beautiful."

Finally she organized the students into the circle of chairs to get their thoughts moving in the right direction. Perhaps her scheme was working, for Harley Wind Soldier no longer noticed Jeannette's injured face or the dim classroom. Harley's mind traveled to the muddy yellow Missouri River. He sat at the top of a steep embankment, settled in new grass. He closed his ears to the voice of his teacher, ignored her long eastern vowels, and listened instead to the song of sliding water.

Harley was remembering a walk he'd taken with his friend Frank Pipe and the boy's grandfather Herod Small War just a week earlier. Herod had led them to the river and pointed downstream.

"That's where Christianity came from," he'd told the boys. Harley squinted at the water, imagining Jesus poling upstream on a raft, His sandaled feet wet from the churning spray, or, if He was traveling when the river was low, stepping across the sandbars without leaving footprints.

"What do you mean?" Frank Pipe had asked.

"Well, I see it this way." The old man put his hands together and scraped his palms absentmindedly. Harley heard a dry rasp: the noise of crisp leaves. "A steamboat finally made it up the Missouri, using stilts to get over the sandbars. It brought the first piano to this area, the first one our people ever heard. They took to that music, I think, because it's dramatic, and you know how we are, always ready for a big show. That sound made them believe about heaven better than any priest's words. They could *hear* it, couldn't they? After that piano and all the church music hit this tribe, there were a lot of converts. A lot of new singers translating those hymns into Dakota."

Herod approached the water, said a few words too quietly for the boys to hear, and dropped a pinch of tobacco into the Missouri.

"What was that?" his grandson questioned when he returned.

"I was just saying to Wakan Tanka that I haven't forgotten Him. I didn't go the way of the steamer and the great piano. I listen for His voice and the music He makes in the water and through the wind."

Harley had stepped away from Herod and his friend so he would see nothing but the river. He watched and watched, looking for the steamboat, certain he would glimpse the piano on its deck and hear the rousing chords produced by a restless passenger. But the water flowed without traffic, and Herod Small War told Harley it was time to go.

"I think we should share a few stories." The voice of Harley's teacher drew him from the river. He returned to stale air and boredom.

Jeannette McVay presented her plan: "I'd like to hear from everyone over the course of the next two days. Each student in this room is the receptacle of ancient wisdom. I know it's there, in the deepest part of you. All the stories you've heard, prayers you've learned, customs you may take for granted. So what we're going to do is pull them out.''

Jeannette punched the air with her soft fist, then yanked it back. To Harley she looked like someone working a toilet plunger.

''We're going to tell our extraordinary stories and confirm our way of looking at the world. Your voices are valid.'' She painted circles in the air. ''Valid and necessary and, I'm sure, compelling. So here we go. You.'' Jeannette pointed to Frank, since she could not call his name.

Frank Pipe fussed with his long braids, poked his fingers through the interlocking strands and tugged, then twisted the loose ends around and around his index finger.

Jeannette made him stand in the center of their communal circle because, she said, ''this is the way your people's old-time council worked.''

Frank could see that his classmates commiserated and dreaded their own turns. He took a deep breath and launched into a story about Iktomi, the tricky spider who was both clever and imprudent and whose misadventures served to instruct. Frank thought of it as a baby story but knew his friends would understand how inappropriate it would be for him to speak publicly of his grandfather's ceremonies or reveal his heart for everyone to see. As he spoke, he was remembering a different story, which he might tell Harley someday after a savage basketball game, when they had both collapsed on the ground and were counting the rafters on the gymnasium ceiling.

It was a memory from his childhood, one of the first times he attended a Yuwipi ceremony conducted by his grandfather. Herod had been asked to solve a local mystery. Someone was killing the reservation dogs, an animal a week, strangling them and leaving their limp bodies in the owners' yards. The killer was also shooting coyotes, whose corpses had been turning up in sheds and root cellars. The Dakota people loved their dogs and had respect for the tough coyotes; they wanted the criminal found.

The ceremony excited Frank, although he was quaking against his mother for its duration. The lights were extinguished for much of the evening, as if in a blackout, and heavy blankets covered the windows. The spirits were noisy when they came, and mischievous: pulling someone's hair, shaking a rattle in another's ear, so close the person started.

Frank Pipe would never forget the sound of glass exploding in the dark room. Something had burst through the window behind him, and he was lucky for a hanging quilt, which stopped most of the spinning glass that flew through the air like shrapnel. In the sudden moonlight, Frank identified the creature as the largest coyote he had ever seen, tall as a pony. It lunged for one of the participants, and though hands stretched to hold him, the man was carried off like a bone, his head cracking against the window frame as the coyote leapt into the night with its victim. Leo Mitchell's body was found the next day at the foot of Angry Butte, punctured by incisors thick as pencils.

Herod said: "The spirits weren't satisifed with just identifying the person who did those terrible things. They wanted justice."

Frank never discovered why Leo Mitchell, a soft-spoken young man who was skilled at hoop dancing, had hunted the dog population, but he learned something about the swift retribution spirits were capable of working. He wondered what Jeannette would make of the story. Would she accuse him of dreaming? Would she consider him crazy?

Frank finished his tale about Iktomi and returned to his seat.

"Thank you for that fascinating parable!" his teacher enthused. And for a moment Frank wondered whether she was referring to the spider or the coyote.

"Who shall we call upon next?" Jeannette's eyes scanned the group and focused on Charlene Thunder, who was squeezed into a fussy old-lady's dress her grandmother had made. Tiny print daffodils were scattered across Charlene's chunky figure, a field of flowers straining against her abdomen. She thrust her hands into the deep patch pockets to hide her fingers; just a few moments earlier she'd been gnawing her cuticles so much they bled.

"Take your time," Jeannette encouraged the girl. "Just start when you're ready."

Charlene stood in the circle with her back to Harley Wind Soldier because he was her favorite. She couldn't bear to have him watch her, notice the scratches on her short legs, which came from walking through open country in skirts and no stockings, and see the battered slippers with heels worn down unevenly.

Charlene's voice was nearly a whisper. She told the class a simple story she remembered about a Dakota woman who was so unhappy when her husband brought a second wife into their household that she pouted until she turned to stone. Charlene imagined that the other students were smirking; they already knew her stories, too many of them—the numerous legends recounting Mercury Thunder's spells and conquests. These were events Charlene found difficult to discuss, so she murmured her tale of the punished woman, thinking all the while about her grandmother and how *she* would freeze someone *else* into rock, keeping her own flesh pliable.

Charlene was pulled into the memory of a winter three years past, when Mercury Thunder decided she would light her house so that it shimmered on the plains like an earth-bound constellation. A crust of ice lacquered her complicated two-story hipped roof, but Mercury was adamant, she wanted lights. After a serving of her delectable corn soup sprinkled with dried parsley from the garden, a young man named Luther Faribault could be cajoled into just about anything. He scaled Mercury's roof, the set of outdoor Christmas lights the old woman had purchased at a Bismarck dime store looped across his shoulder. Charlene watched in horror as his feet slipped and he clung to the surface by his fingers; then, at another step, his hands lost their precarious hold and only his well-placed toes, gouging ice, kept him from plunging to the ground.

Luther had gained the treacherous peak and was fastening the lights, when a slight miscalculation in the distribution of his weight sent him falling. He landed on his back and couldn't breathe for several moments. Mercury stood over him, her eyes blinking with curiosity, while Charlene knelt beside him in the snow, tears streaming down her cold face.

"I'm pretty lucky," Luther finally said.

"What?" The girl leaned closer.

"The snow saved my neck pretty good." Luther struggled to his feet and stamped snow off his boots. He looked unhurt except for his left shoulder, which was dislocated.

"You better go to Indian Health," Charlene told him.

Luther shook his head. "No, I'm going to give this one more shot."

Charlene appealed to her grandmother because she could see that Luther Faribault was lost somewhere behind his eyes, guided only by Mercury's desires. "Don't let him!" she begged.

The old woman placed her heavy hand on the crown of Charlene's head. "But it will be so nice," she said.

Once again Luther climbed Mercury Thunder's house, this time with the use of only one arm. *The spirits must pity him,* Charlene thought, when he somehow managed to complete the job.

"I think this legend's going to require some discussion," Jeannette told her class, startling Charlene.

Charlene wandered back to her chair. The image of her grandmother's twinkling roof burned her eyes.

"This is great," Jeannette continued. "The perfect material for a serious discussion." She slid off her desk and leaned against it, staring at her pointy boots. "I'd like to hear what the girls think about the woman's plight. What were her options with a second wife moving in?"

Jeannette tried valiantly to lead her class into a debate about the old Dakota practice of taking plural wives. But getting the students to express themselves was like heaving a thrashing lake trout out of the water. Some of them didn't care one way or the other, hadn't the slightest interest in what they considered the minutiae of history. Others felt their teacher would never understand the intricacies of tribal relationships, how a woman could seem downtrodden, at the mercy of her husband's whims, yet turn around and join him in battle if she desired, tell him to vacate the lodge, which belonged solely to her.

It's complicated, Harley Wind Soldier was thinking, unwilling to explain.

Things aren't always what they seem, Frank Pipe thought to himself.

And Charlene Thunder could see only her grandmother—a plump, majestic sage grouse, a robber fly, a towering hill—wrapping her long arms around the earth and squeezing firmly, her enemies whirling into lost space.

The next day Jeannette called on Harley to speak. He was the tallest of his classmates and stood in their midst like a stiff red cedar. He watched the floor and tried to generate some moisture in his mouth. Harley didn't know what to say. He hadn't been raised in a house of conversation; he couldn't produce stories his mother had told him. What Harley did surprised him. He made up a story. It was all about a lonely warrior who was an outcast from his tribe because of his penchant for telling lies. In the warrior's mind they were tales, but his delivery was so compelling that his listeners were taken in, time and again, only to discover at the end of the narrative that it had been fabricated. Soon no one would listen to him, and he wandered the prairies alone, telling his stories to the wind and the grass. The creatures who were not human, and didn't chase after the truth, appreciated his anecdotes and would follow him at a discreet distance so they wouldn't miss anything. They decided to thank him for the many hours of pleasure he had given them, and each night one of their species served as a guide and led him through their world. He scratched his back against trees with the bears, tunneled into the ground with the prairie dogs, coasted in the air with hawks, and raced the mule deer across flat stretches of grass. Finally he returned to his tribe and shared his experiences. The people laughed—his neighbors, even his cousins. His uncles told him: *You are embarrassing us.* The warrior was ridiculed until the creatures who were not human emerged from the countryside to surround him. An eagle landed on his shoulder and glared at the people, grasshoppers rode the arches of his feet, a gray kit fox lectured the gathering of humans with his short barks. The menagerie claimed the warrior and accepted him into their society. He left then and never returned, although some said he followed his own kind on occasion, lonesome for conversation.

Harley shrugged at the end and dropped back in his seat.

"How wonderful." Jeannette sighed. "How sad. Where does that come from?"

Harley scraped at a hardened wad of gum stuck beneath the seat of his chair. He shrugged again.

"Just heard it somewhere?" Jeannette asked.

He nodded in response because, in truth, he felt so empty he believed it must have come from outside him.

"So that teacher's been telling you stories?" Herod Small War asked.

"No, she's been making *us* say them," Frank Pipe answered.

Herod, his grandson, and Harley were cleaning the yard in front of the old man's cabin. When Herod's wife, Alberta, brought them lemonade, they took a break, lounging near the back door.

"I want to tell you something," Herod said to Harley. "I've been thinking about one of your ancestors nearly every day. He's probably tired of waiting for me to speak out, so now he's pestering my thoughts."

Harley sat on the ground, his back against the cabin wall.

"The one I'm referring to is your uncle, Ghost Horse. Actually, he is the brother of your great-great-grandfather. That's how far back he goes."

Harley nodded; he had heard the name before.

"This uncle of yours had a powerful dream, where the

thunderbirds appeared to him. You know what that means?"

"Yes," said the boy.

"Sure. He had to become *heyo'ka*. And that is hard." Herod ran his thumb in jagged lines across his arm. "He painted the lightning on his arms and legs and his face too. He did everything the opposite of the way it's usually done, and he said what he didn't mean."

Harley looked up. "He lied, then?"

"No." The old man shook his head. "He just said things in reverse. But everyone understood that, so they got the drift."

Harley trailed his fingers in the dirt, etching parallel streaks of lightning.

"That one was fearless and took many risks on the battlefield. Your father was that way too. You come from a long line of soldiers."

Harley's breath caught at the mention of his father, the man in a photograph who had never held him. "He fought?" Harley asked, unable to say "my father."

"Oh, yes. In Korea. And, some would say, right here." The old man coughed into his hand and stood up with difficulty. "Ghost Horse, you leave me alone now," he scolded. "I said your name to this nephew."

As far as Frank Pipe was concerned, his friend Harley Wind Soldier had become insufferable. He was copying his ancestor's contrary behavior. Frank resented not only the aberrant conduct but also the fact that Harley wasn't properly respectful, acting as if he were playing a game. It was the end of September and still quite warm, yet Harley went around in a windbreaker, shivering and blowing on his hands.

"So cold," he insisted. "Gonna freeze to death." He'd taken a ballpoint pen to his limbs, tracing lightning bolts that marked his flesh like blue tattoos, and now when he shot hoops, Harley aimed for the rim of the basket rather than the net, and cursed when the ball dropped cleanly through the hole.

"Play right," Frank said, annoyed. But Harley didn't seem to hear.

Finally, in the vast parking lot of a Bismarck movie theater, Frank lost his temper. The boys had come with the rest of their class to see *Star Wars*—a Saturday outing planned by Jeannette McVay and funded from her own pocket. The students were so transported by the film that they persuaded their teacher to sit through it twice. She observed their eager faces in the flickering light, and wondered what they were thinking. She watched her class rather than the movie.

Harley Wind Soldier stared at the screen with great intensity, imagining himself in that other time and other galaxy, a world where the forces of good and evil were clearly separate, no murky territory of ambiguity. He was currently obsessed with order, maintaining a psychic balance by discovering the opposites of his desires and voicing them. Harley was so uncertain of the positive space he took up in the world that he was investigating the negative. Although, when he thought about his changed behavior, it was in terms of ancestry. Harley imagined himself in a long line of men, erect soldiers who followed one another in perfect order. He wanted to stand behind them in his own allocated slot, looking straight ahead, confident, his eyes focused rather than flitting from side to side.

He charged from his seat when *Star Wars* ended for the second time, and hit the parking lot before everyone else.

Frank soon joined him, awed by what he had seen. He chattered about hyperspace and light-speed and a world with two suns.

"Wasn't that cool?" he asked Harley. He was frustrated by his friend's silence.

"No," the boy breathed, meaning yes. "It was the dumbest thing I ever saw."

Frank Pipe's fist shot straight out from his shoulder, surprising him even as it landed squarely on Harley's nose, breaking it.

The next Saturday, Harley Wind Soldier left his house early in the morning to visit the sluggish Missouri. He was no longer mimicking the contrary life-style of his predecessor Ghost Horse. He walked against the flow of water, in the direction of its source, soothed by its lush voice. He squatted on his heels, wondering what his tribesmen thought when they saw a steamboat for the first time. It must have seemed like a monster, chewing up their trees to power its journey. And then it must have struck them as a powerful spirit because of the wondrous music it introduced.

The water was full of dark chords, which Harley struggled to hear. *Would my father have enjoyed that music?* he wondered.

Harley Wind Soldier squinted at the Missouri, his eyes nearly closed. Within that strained vision he could see the figures emerge, stepping from the past to line the present river. His ancestors in their smooth buckskins streamed by him in a dignified parade. They were followed by their children and cavorting dogs, whole villages turning out to watch the eventful passage.

A ripple went through the crowd, which pulsed forward

for a better view. Harley was the last to see it, gliding toward him. The flat-bottomed steamer rolled across the water, spun forward by its great wheel. The boy searched the deck, and there it was, an elegant upright piano inlaid with mother-of-pearl. The pedals glinted in the sun, and the ivory keys were arranged in such perfect symmetry that Harley was reminded of the spine of a fish.

A young man in a bowler hat seated himself at the instrument and pumped the pedals as if to test them. His fingers drifted to the keys, and then the young man teased music from the wood-and-ivory table, his eyes closed and torso rocking: so intent on his performance he didn't notice the dense crowd along the shore and never guessed that he was ushering in a new religion.

3

The Medicine Hole

Herod Small War
(1976)

MY OLD FRIEND ARCHIE IRON NECKLACE WAS DELIGHTED to see me sleeping in the cabin pantry. His laughter woke me up, and when I turned my face to the back wall I saw his stubby fingers waving at me through the chinks between warped boards. Every night before I went to bed, I used chewing gum and wood chips to plug the crevices, but while I slept, the wind worked on my makeshift caulking, pried it loose, blew dirt and insects onto my blankets. That morning I woke to find grasshoppers nesting in my hair, a half-inch layer of grit covering my bed, and two bold deer mice sacked out in the bowl of my Stetson hat. The wind must have blown it right off my head and knocked it on the floor.

"Look at you," Archie teased. "Getting back to nature."

I dumped the mice out of my hat and flicked the grasshoppers from my hair. Then I grabbed one of my wife's heavy skillets hanging on the wall beside my bed and banged it against the back panel, close enough to Archie's thick fingers to make him withdraw.

"It's too early to be plaguing me," I growled.

"Oh, I'm sorry," he said. "I forgot, you're an old man."

That got me out of bed. I knew he could see me, so I ignored the pain in my hips and knees, pretended my joints were oiled hinges so I could rise like a young man. I was smooth.

"Don't talk 'old' to me," I said. "Didn't you use to scout for George Washington? Didn't you make cow eyes at Martha till she run you off?"

Archie just laughed. He liked to rub it in that he was two years younger than me, seventy-four to my seventy-six.

"I'll be right out," I told him. I had to go through the kitchen to get to the back door, and I passed my wife, Alberta, standing before the stove, cooking oatmeal. The way things were going in my house, I didn't know if she intended to eat the gruel for breakfast or slather it on her face as some kind of beauty treatment.

"Archie's here," I mumbled. She nodded. "I'm going out to see what he wants."

I found Archie squatting on his heels, his back against the pantry. I couldn't help but wince as I observed my new bedroom from the outside. It was a pitiful sight, a small attached room hanging off the back of our tidy cabin. It leaned precariously to the right, looked ready to collapse.

Archie jerked his thumb at the ramshackle structure behind him. "Was this Alberta's idea?"

I shook my head. "No, it was me."

Archie smiled, but I could tell he was disappointed. He'd spent a lifetime interested in my wife and wouldn't have minded seeing me fall from grace. I waited for him to explain his early-morning visit, but he sat silently on his haunches. I realized then that he was showing off, demonstrating how easily he balanced on his heels. He was wearing mirrored sunglasses to hide his small right eye, which was tipped upward at a sharp angle. He ran his hands through the two bands of white hair streaking his otherwise coal-black head, marking him like a skunk. He didn't speak, so I turned my back on him. I pushed my face into the warm wind, taking deep breaths, pretending to meditate. By then I was a pretty famous *Yuwipi* man, the one who finds things: misplaced objects, missing persons, the answers to questions. There were times when my reputation came in handy. I could clear my face of any expression, retreat into my thoughts, and the people around me would wait quietly, respectfully, convinced I was experiencing a vision. Sometimes their assumption was correct, but nine times out of ten I was just spacing out. Archie must have suspected this, because he interrupted my reverie.

"I'm waiting for a delivery," he said. "Wait till you see what I won at the bingo last night. Aljoe's driving it here from Bismarck in his pickup."

"So you've been playing bingo with the old ladies?" I couldn't help myself. I had to tease. I could just see him at the long table, too many paper cards to keep track of, his fingers fumbling with the red plastic disks he used as bingo markers. He probably knocked some to the floor and bumped the table when he tried to retrieve them. I bet the old ladies left an empty space on either side of him, he was so clumsy, endangering their own precious cards.

"If you were as lucky as I am, you'd be playing every night," he said. I couldn't ruin his mood. He was too satisfied with whatever it was my nephew Aljoe would be depositing in my yard.

While we waited, I pointed out my new neighbor, a magnificent Brahma bull purchased by the rancher who leased several acres of my land. He was eyeing us too, staring rudely right into our faces. He shook himself a couple of times, his muscles rippling, his nostrils flared. He was full of contempt.

Old biddies, his bloodshot eyes told me. *Come any closer*

and I'll snuff you out in one breath. The split-rail fence that
penned him in seemed suddenly flimsy.

"Kind of goofy-looking, isn't he?" Archie said. Those
mirrored sunglasses must have distorted his vision.

Just then Aljoe pulled into my dirt yard. His upper body
was hanging out of the open window. He raised his fist in
the air and whooped. For a second there he lost control of
the pickup, and I thought it was going to swerve into our
cabin and shear off the dilapidated pantry, but he slammed
on the brakes. Aljoe, my grandson Frank, and his friend
Harley spilled out of the cab and raced behind the truck. I
took my time getting there. I didn't want to seem too curious. The boys struggled with a dusty tarp that hid Archie's
prize, and when they finally ripped it back I bit down on
my lip. I couldn't breathe. In the bed of the pickup was a
black-and-silver Harley-Davidson, a heavyweight motorcycle with water-cooled engine and front disk brakes. It was
wicked and beautiful.

"Is this for me?" I teased. But I couldn't get a rise out of
Archie. He was preoccupied, his hands pressed solemnly
against the front wheel, his head bowed. He looked like he
was praying to that machine.

"Oh, man, I want some of that," Frank whispered.

"Not for a while," I said. After all, my grandson was
only twelve.

It took all five of us to get the bike on the ground. Archie
told us we better not scratch his baby. When it was safely
parked on its kickstand, he removed a red bandanna from
his back pocket and carefully wiped the shiny chrome, eras-
ing our fingerprints. Finally he straddled the machine and
gripped the handlebars.

"I'm ready," he said.

"You've never ridden one of these things," I told him.

He waved me off. "I've got nothing to lose." Before I could argue further, he revved the engine and took off. The spinning back wheel tossed dirt in our faces.

"Don't worry! I showed him how it works!" Aljoe shouted above the noise of the open throttle.

As my old friend Archie Iron Necklace raced his motorcycle up and down the dirt road, exciting the bull, and luring Alberta outside to see what was happening, I swelled with pride.

"Look at him go!" I hollered. He split the air with his sharp nose, and I could almost feel the wind rushing past my own face. I clapped my hand on Frank's narrow shoulder and sent a war cry into the exploding dust that whirled in the wake of Archie's rush. Archie had us spellbound, openmouthed with admiration. Any minute, we expected him to fly above our heads and circle the Sioux reservation, executing wheelies on the roofs of our houses. Even old men like us could steal a little thunder. It was a glorious ride.

But Archie was betrayed by his own heart, his fancy for my wife. When he spotted her beside me, he urged the bike even faster. It jerked forward then, slipped out from under Archie like a horse bucking him to the ground. It sailed a few feet in the air, over the split-rail fence, and landed at the bull's feet. Archie rolled in the dirt but was able to stand. He limped toward us, head hanging and hands stuffed in his back pockets.

"You okay?" I asked him. He nodded. "That was *some* ride." I glanced over his shoulder then, distracted by some activity beyond the fence. It was the bull, fiercely charging Archie's bike. He was doing a job on it, kicking it with his hooves, stamping it into the grass.

"He's going to kill it!" said Harley.

Archie ran to the fence, waving his arms, yelling, "Hee-ya, hee-ya, get away!" The bull paused, cocked his head to one side. He rolled his black eye from Archie, to me, to the bike. Then he raised his front legs and landed on the gleaming metal, using his weight to crush Archie's treasure beyond repair.

"You won," I called to the bull. He lowered his head and smiled.

"Is Archie crazy or what?" Alberta asked me later, during supper. I was mopping up chicken gravy with her heavy fry bread, but her comment stopped me. I set the bread in my plate.

"Don't get me started," I warned. "If anybody's crazy around here, it's Josephine Fredericks."

Josephine just happened to be my wife's best friend, and there was plenty of evidence to back up my accusation. An angry silence fell between us, and Alberta picked up the book she'd been reading all day, even while she cooked supper. I couldn't make out the title from across the table, but I could see slips of paper marking particular passages. I knew this was more of Josephine's handiwork. My wife read avidly, so consumed by whatever it was she was reading that I could stare at her unnoticed. Up until two months back, when her interfering friend decided to make her over, she had been beautiful. She didn't look seventy. Her face was round and uncreased except for laugh lines. She had a subtle overbite, and dimples in her cheeks. But now she looked unfamiliar, her thin lips drawn larger than they actually were and her thick brown hair set in tight curls she didn't comb out but left coiled like springs.

I cleared the table and washed the dishes. My wife usually stopped me before my hands got wet, but that night she let me putter around the kitchen. She was oblivious to her surroundings.

"Good night," I said as I made my way to the pantry and my hard cot.

"Mmm," was all she managed.

Once I was in bed I couldn't relax. I shivered under the blankets, even though it was summer and I was wearing long johns. In the Dakotas it can get pretty cold at night, but it wasn't just the temperature. I missed my wife.

Josephine Fredericks was right in the middle of our troubles, but she hadn't always been a bad influence. As a matter of fact, in the past I had preferred her to her husband, Lyle, who was a self-proclaimed elder—too noisy about his traditional upbringing, too ready to introduce strangers to our sweat lodge. While he was living, Josephine remained in the background, soft-spoken and hardworking. She dressed simply, in long cotton skirts and baggy tops, and wore her hair in braids. Not two seconds after Lyle's throat closed in reaction to a bee sting—Josephine liked to say he "died of bees"—that woman had cropped her hair so short it bristled like the guard hairs of a porcupine, and she'd changed her wardrobe to loud-colored pantsuits and chunky plastic jewelry. She organized women's meetings and lobbied for a bookmobile to be sent onto the reservation. Then she made her friends read.

I knew I was in trouble the night I came home from a *Yuwipi* ceremony to find my bedroom lit by dozens of votive candles and my wife's hair sprinkled with red glitter. She took me by the hand and led me to the bed.

"I want you," she breathed.

I jumped back and clutched the medicine bundle I had taken to the ceremony. I peered at her, wondering whether cruel *heyoka* spirits had taken over her body. My modest wife had never been this forward.

"Did I scare you?" She looked uncertain then, a little ashamed. When I didn't move or speak, she hurried to make things right. She snuffed out the candles and rinsed the glitter from her hair. I thought that would be the end of it, a moment of temporary insanity, a case of cabin fever. But Alberta only reread the manuals Josephine had recommended, books like *The Joy of Sex* and *Our Bodies, Ourselves,* which strengthened her resolve to convert me to her world of passion. A new vocabulary entered our home. Words such as "climax."

"I want us to climax together," my wife told me, and all I could picture was the two of us dragging our old bones up the side of Mount Everest. I was horrified by this sort of talk, which flew in the face of Dakota prudery. I refused to take her seriously.

"What has come over you?" I asked her.

She pointed to her books. "New ways, Herod. I am learning the new ways and have new expectations." She said this boldly, but I noticed that she watched the ground as she spoke.

Truthfully, I was more than a little afraid that I wouldn't be able to live up to her expectations, rise to the occasion, so to speak. At seventy-six I was in pretty good shape, but sometimes my body went its own way and wouldn't listen to me. So after a lifetime of nights spent beside Alberta's soft form, I escaped to the pantry, where the folding cot was hard and the wind played its tricks on me, but my wife's small hands couldn't tease my flesh.

I fell asleep in the chilly room, wrapped in my own lonely arms prickled with gooseflesh.

• • • •

The next morning I was awakened by the desperate clucking of a stout prairie chicken that had somehow managed to slip its sleek head through the chinks in my pantry wall, only to find itself stuck. I heard its feet scratching against the boards and its stunted wings flapping wildly in an attempt to extricate itself, and above the racket of the fowl I heard another noise, Archie's laughter.

"What we've got here is the makings of a reservation zoo," he cackled. He sounded like the chicken.

I rolled out of my cot and snatched the chicken's head, being careful of its sharp beak. "Ho, foolish brother," I said. "Settle down and we'll fix you up." The chicken relaxed as I spoke, enough so that I could push its head through the opening. Once the bird was free, I expected it to run off and return to the open grasslands. But instead it chased after Archie, pecking at his snakeskin boots. Fury plumped its feathers until it looked turkey-sized. Archie hopped from one foot to the other, shaking his legs and yelling at the chicken: "These are boots, not dinner, you dumb cluck!"

Archie finally made it to Alberta's Ford Pinto and hurled himself onto the hood, where he sprawled on his belly. The chicken paced in front of the car, reluctant to let him go. I didn't rescue my friend. I figured he had it coming. But Alberta chased the prairie chicken from our yard with a broom.

"You want some coffee?" she asked Archie. He nodded and followed her into our cabin.

"Well, are you going to come out and greet your visitor?" my wife called to me. I pulled on a pair of jeans and ran a comb through the white hair that spilled past my shoulders.

"Hey, Herod," Archie said when I emerged from the

pantry. He shook my hand, his dignity fully recovered.

"What did you win this time?" I asked.

"No, no, I come on business." He wasn't wearing his sunglasses, so I noticed that his little eye was squeezed even smaller, squinting at me. "I want you to interpret something," he said.

Alberta rattled the pots and pans as she cooked breakfast, to let us know she wasn't listening. Archie grabbed my arm and leaned closer. "I dreamt about the medicine hole. Don't you think that's some kind of sign?" He flashed a smile so broad I could see the gold tooth in the back of his mouth. He knew he'd done me one better, invaded my territory of important dreams and visions.

"Tell it to me," I said. And he did.

For thirty years Archie Iron Necklace had faithfully assisted me in the *Yuwipi* ceremony. He did the kind of work one usually delegates to a son, teaching the sacred ways so that they continue from one generation to the next. I had three daughters and no son, but I would have taught my girls a few of my secrets and allowed them to assist me, had they shown any interest. I was counting on someday being able to pass the traditional ways on to my grandson, Frank Pipe, but until then, Archie would have to do.

For the first time, we organized a Yuwipi ceremony on our own behalf. We took the question of Archie's dream directly to the spirits. We fasted, conducted a sweat, and gathered together the holiest, most traditional elders we knew. After preparing the bare wooden structure, little more than a hut, that was used for the ceremony, Archie removed my shoes and placed them outside the circle of tobacco offerings. But now his hands shook as he performed the duties. He tied my hands and feet with rope, covered my head with a star quilt and bound it to my body using leather thongs. I could smell the sage he tucked beneath the bindings, even through cotton batting and heavy fabric. He lowered me to the floor so I rested on my stomach, and then he blew out the kerosene lamp. In darkness, spirits came to tell their secrets, quiet at first, testing their voices, but becoming noisier. I'd placed gourds on an altar of sage, and spirit fingers snatched them from the ground, shook them until the air snapped, the shrouded windows rattled. In darkness they picked rope knots with sharp fingernails, releasing me, the rope in loose coils, the star quilt neatly folded.

Look, there are four of you, the spirits told me in Dakota, but they spoke individually, at their own speed, so their voices overlapped and rippled in echoes:

Iho! (Iho!) (Iho!) Topa. (Topa.) (Topa.)

They showed me Archie's dream, spilled images across the black walls, and I recognized the vision as a moment in history—events that had taken place in the hot summer of 1877, a year after the Custer battle, the only difference being the identity of the four young warriors who had played such a large part in the episode. The original warriors had been replaced by me, Archie Iron Necklace, my grandson, Frank, and his friend Harley. But we were not precisely ourselves; something was off kilter, and I realized that the boys looked a few years older, perhaps sixteen, and Archie and I matched their age. We were young again. Archie no longer resembled a skunk but had pure black hair trailing down his back, as thick as his Indian pony's mane. We rode bareback, our powerful legs gripping the horses to free our hands. We thought we were alone, so the four of us played like children, chasing after one another on our quick ponies, smiling and laughing. Archie laughed so hard he fell off his horse, and the rest of us circled him while he rolled on the ground, gently tapping him with our sticks as if to count coup.

"Behind you," I whispered. I could feel my wrinkled mouth move in the dark as I watched myself maneuver the pony with my knees, pushing him to run in tight circles. We were not alone but observed by soldiers who had been scouring the hills and grasslands for small hunting parties such as ours, their thoughts bent on revenge.

Perhaps the sun addled our brains or we were dizzy from lack of food, having eaten only one stringy jackrabbit in three days, but we showed lack of sense. We allowed ourselves to be caught in the bowl of a valley, surrounded on all sides by trained marksmen who shredded the air with heavy bullets. Fortunately the barrage fell short; we were just out of range. They could have taken us in one rush, but they toyed with us, deciding to camp in the rising hills. I think they wanted to shame us, starve us out, but we cheated them of victory. After several days our horses dropped to the ground, dead of dehydration, and when the soldiers investigated they discovered we had vanished. The superstitious among them claimed we must have flown away, transformed ourselves into eagles or prairie hawks and wheeled above their heads. Others believed we had painted our bodies with black earth and crept past them in the night, stealthy as ground fog, in that Indian way they'd heard so much about. They had it wrong. The spirits showed me, and I nodded as I watched. I had heard the story.

The earth pitied those four young warriors, the earth intervened on our behalf by splitting its skin at our feet. The medicine hole gaped open, leading to a deep underground tunnel that snaked like an artery beneath the earth's hide.

I watched as we crawled out of the valley on all fours, blind as moles, emerging from crumbling earth a mile beyond the steep hills.

After the earth saved us, it restored its flesh, sealed the medicine hole so the soldiers couldn't follow. Tears moved across my old face; spirit breath blew them gently from my eyes so they twirled in all directions, seeping into my hair, trickling into my ears, falling onto my hands. I watched myself run away. I knew the four of us would run for miles, our breathing even and our legs pumping as if they could go on forever. I reached out my hand to brush the image of my strong young back, and the vision disappeared.

The spirits gathered themselves, prepared to leave. Their last message to me was a curious song they trilled in a high voice, like a group of girls. *You will find the medicine hole,* they sang. *You will find it.*

"We're going to do this right," I told Archie, once the Yuwipi ceremony and the concluding feast had ended and the elders had packed their *wateča* pails with leftovers. The four of us would travel to the valley site on horseback, in search of the medicine hole. It took me a couple of days to round up the horses, borrowing them from my neighbors, and I had to tell my grandson and Harley about our plan. I don't believe they felt it was their sacred duty to oblige us as much as they thought of it as an adventure. I couldn't blame them. I think if I'd been young I would have felt the adventure too, but it had long before squeaked out of my bones.

Three days after Archie Iron Necklace told me about his dream, the four of us set off, our saddlebags bulging with bottled water and sandwiches. Alberta sat in a chair by the open back door. A hot breeze stirred the pages of the book she was reading. She watched our preparations closely, her small hand shading her eyes.

"Looks like a storm coming," she said.

The gray sky tumbled with clouds, but I couldn't bear to postpone the search.

"It'll be okay," I said. "We'll be back before it breaks." I kissed Alberta's cheek. I was struck by how smooth and plump it was, like a ripe grape bursting with sweetness. "What do you make of all this?" I hadn't thought to ask her before.

She looked me over, from my feet to the peak of my hat.

"You'd do better to find your juice," she said. She stood up and went inside.

I blinked and thought I heard the rasp of dry paper. I looked at my hands, expecting to see brittle flesh crackle in the scorching heat, curling away from bone.

"Hey, dreamer," Archie called from somewhere above my head. The others had mounted their horses and were watching me.

"We're heading out!" I called, pulling myself onto the remaining nag. I perched carefully, my feet plunged deep into the stirrups, because I felt it would take just one blast of wind to knock me down. I was empty as a corn husk doll, sapped of vigor.

The boys rode ahead of us, and it was comforting to watch their backs. If it hadn't been for their modern clothes—jeans and *Star Trek* T-shirts—they could have been old-time Dakotas, they maneuvered their horses so skillfully. Archie and I rode in silence. Our horses picked their way along the edge of a prairie-dog town whose residents had disappeared down their holes, and all there was to see were earthen mounds and short clumps of buffalo grass. As we approached the valley, which was only a dozen miles from my home, I noticed taller grasses, stalks of bluestem and wheatgrass. The sun emerged from behind the clouds, and the landscape burst into color, dotted with sunflowers, bluebells, blazing stars, and purple sage. Archie was smiling, and I was beginning to enjoy myself, when we came upon an abandoned homestead about a mile short of our destination.

One wall of the house was collapsed, and the stone foundation was crumbling like sugar. The creek, which wound its way around one side of the house, had dried up, and the structure was now rooted in mud that had baked to clay. Its gray powder dusted the horses' hooves. I hadn't visited this place for over fifty years. I had forgotten.

Archie pulled his horse alongside mine. "You going to be okay?" he asked. I must have told him yes, because he moved on.

I watched the house, looked for the one I knew couldn't be there. She was long dead. But the sun dazzled me with its powers. It restored the shimmering creek and the muskrat lodge tucked against the shore. I could see muskrats swimming with the current, their skinny tails arching out of the water. A trick of light brought Clara Miller back to life, planted her in the yard, where she sat before a gleaming metal tub, shucking ears of corn with her powerful hands. I was familiar with this place, having worked here in 1921. There was the chicken coop I was supposed to repair. There were the tools.

I dismounted, and if Archie called to me, I didn't hear him. I walked toward the quavering mirage, drawn to Clara's rippling, distorted features. When I reached out to her, the image broke apart and dissolved into the heat.

"We better get moving. We'll lose the boys!" my friend shouted to me. I was reluctant to leave this place, now that

I'd rediscovered it, but Archie looked so worried I swung onto the saddle and followed him into the valley.

Frank and Harley were already studying the ground when we caught up to them. They'd turned their horses loose to graze, and we followed suit.

"What does this thing look like?" Frank asked me, practical as ever.

"I can't say, but you'll know it when you see it."

"Don't let those gopher holes fool you," Archie teased. "Try to fit yourself in one of those and you'll be out of luck." Frank rolled his eyes.

I lined us up and marked the territory we should each cover. "Holler if you find anything," I said.

Earlier that day I had envisioned our search, convinced it would be successful. I'd imagined my grandson in the field, nearly hidden by tall grass, crowing, *"Tunkašida"*— grandfather—"I can see it! I can see it now!" We would stand at the edge of the medicine hole, all of us young, all of us strong—the earth crying for two old men, dried up and sun-withered, pitying us enough to restore us, in body or in spirit. The earth would provide a soothing ointment to take away the pain I felt with every movement. All this I had anticipated. But now I was distracted, may as well have been a blind man scrabbling through the weeds. I was not in the present but in the past. I couldn't see what was before me, only what was behind.

In a way, I did find what I was after, for the young man inside me rose up, bristling with anger. I had not felt his presence for a long time. He was so strong I could almost see him; he scowled, but the expression didn't wrinkle his forehead, which stretched smooth beneath shiny hair.

It was Alberta, he hissed in my ear. *You old fool, can't you see that? She caused the pain,* he told me. And so she had.

In 1921, I worked for Miss Clara Miller, performing whatever odd jobs were necessary to keep up her place. It was the only work I could get on the reservation at the time. I figured she must hate me, since her father was one of the soldiers killed at the Little Bighorn in Montana. His dress sword decorated her sitting room wall, and I wondered if she wanted to use it on me, carve me up and send me to my Sioux ancestors. But she was always polite, if a little distant, and spoke as few words as possible. She was in her fifties by then, a large woman with silver hair coiled in a bun. She had never married.

Those were lonely days for me. My wife often slept in our daughter's bed; she scolded me when I touched her. "What kind of Dakota are you? Can't you control your feelings?" She reminded me that our daughter was an infant, and Sioux way dictated that a child must be self-sufficient, about four years old, before another could be made.

"That was in the old days," I sometimes pressed. "When the soldiers chased our people." Back then we could not afford to have more infants than we could carry on the run. Things had changed, but my wife held me to her strict interpretation of our sexual code.

A permanent dull ache spread from my belly to my chest. I thought I could feel pinpricks of loneliness in the pads of my fingers, taste it in the back of my mouth. Clara Miller must have been lonely too, longing to be touched. One day, as she sat before her metal tub filled to the rim with sweet corn, she reached behind her head and unpinned her silver hair. It tumbled down her back like a creamy lace cloak. She hiked her skirts to her knees, and I could see she had removed her stockings. Her legs were heavy and milk-white, solid as columns. She hiked her skirts higher, until they bunched in her lap.

When I kissed the back of her neck she quivered, like the dying pheasant I'd shot and killed a week before. Her silver hair smelled like smoke. Clara and I tangled together like the bale of wire resting beside the unrepaired chicken coop. We were shameless, falling to the ground, wading into the creek, making our way to her bed.

"I forgive you," she murmured as she kissed my throat, my earlobes, the crown of my head. "I forgive you." When we had stumbled into Clara's house, the first thing she did was hide her father's sword beneath the sofa. She turned his portrait to the wall so he couldn't witness her betrayal.

I didn't want to be forgiven. I regretted being born too late to fight the cavalry, but I kept quiet because Clara Miller let me hold her.

For one week we kept each other company. But then Archie dropped by one evening to walk me home and discovered what was going on. He pulled me from the house and pounded me with his fists.

"You've got a *good* woman," he shouted. "You don't deserve Alberta!"

I thought he would break me into little pieces, but instead he folded, his long legs crumpling beneath him, angry tears rolling down his face. I never returned to the Miller place after that.

Now I staggered through snakeweed and cheatgrass, the medicine hole nearly forgotten. I was beginning to understand my self-imposed exile, the withdrawal from my wife. Fifty-five years later I could still feel Alberta's stiff hand against my chest, pushing me away when I tried to embrace her. I could see her in the kitchen, starching my undershorts and splashing them with holy water in an attempt to kill my young appetite. This was the reason for my bitterness, for purposely tamping down my desires, pinching them from stalks to seeds to husks to dust particles the wind snatched from me as I slept, and sprinkled across the prairie: a potent fertilizer.

It was you, Alberta, I whispered into my heavy hands.

"Look what I found!" Archie's voice startled me. I waded through the grass to see where he pointed. He'd uncovered a large hole dug into the hillside, but it was just a coyote den. The boys groaned with disappointment.

"It will be on the valley floor," I reminded them.

We were heading back toward our individual sections of land when lightning flashed in our faces. Thunder cracked, sharp as gunfire, and dark clouds scudded across the sky. At first the raindrops were large and warm, like ripe berries; they quickly changed to sharp cold pellets. The boys were chasing the horses, trying to grab the reins, but the terrified animals took off for home at a dead run.

"What'll we do now?" Frank shouted above the rising wind.

"Look for trees," I hollered. But there were no trees in that valley, or lining the hills. We were exposed targets.

"We can make it to the house!" Archie said. I shook my head. Suddenly I didn't want to go there.

"Are you afraid of the ghost?" Harley asked me. He looked surprised.

Before I could respond, Archie grabbed me by the arm and hauled me after him. The four of us stumbled through slick grass, and beyond the valley we fell in slippery mud, one after another, until we were coated with a gray paste. When we reached the house, Archie pulled me across the rubble heap of the collapsed wall. We climbed rotting steps to what had once been Clara's sitting room. I half expected to find her father's sword, rusted in its scabbard, but the walls were empty of decoration.

We huddled together in one corner, waiting for the storm to pass. We could have plainly heard one another, now that we were out of the wind, but we didn't care to speak. Harley's words came back to me. *Are you afraid of the ghost?* It took me a moment to make sense of them. I should have realized when I heard the stories that people were talking about Clara. They described an abandoned house, haunted by a sturdy white woman. She was all business, beating her rugs, sweeping her floors, catching up on her mending. Clara was trying to put her place in order. She had no one to help her.

As it grew late and the storm continued, I told the boys to get some sleep. "We'll walk home in the morning."

Archie seemed cheerful, untroubled by memories of what had happened in this house. He hummed an honor song— *"to appease the storm clouds,"* he said—and quickly fell asleep. I was cold, and the damp floor was hard. I settled on my side, then on my back. I thought I wouldn't get any rest. But I must have fallen asleep eventually, because I remember waking up. It was the warmth that roused me, the warmth of a body pressed against my flesh. My arm was wrapped around another person. I held her close.

"Alberta," I breathed. I nuzzled her neck with my cold nose. "I'm so sorry. I forgive you. Will you forgive me?"

Yes, she whispered. *I forgive you.* She pulled away then, drifting from my embrace. I opened my eyes and found myself looking at Clara. Her hands were full of the bent pins she used to fasten her hair in a tight bun. Clara blew me a kiss with her white fingers and floated upward to the ceiling. She smoothed her bib apron with a meaty hand and used its edge to clean the windowpane before gliding through it.

My tongue was locked to the roof of my mouth. As a Yuwipi man, I had heard spirit voices and encountered dead ancestors, but a white ghost was something different altogether. I glanced at the floor. Archie and the two boys slept soundly, shivering in their damp clothes. Their empty hands were curled into fists.

I went to the window and could see Clara hovering outside the house, separated from me by a splintered pane of glass.

"What about the medicine hole?" I asked her.

Clara was high above the ground, her long feet churning the air, and her dress lifted to expose a sliver of heavy milk legs. She smiled at me, lips pulled tight across her teeth. Clara brushed the window with her fingertips, then rapped it with her knuckles. The sound reminded me of spirit rattles. Images flashed behind my eyes: Josephine Fredericks riding in the back of the bookmobile; Archie on his rearing motorcycle, ready to take flight; my wife, Alberta, backlit by candles, her hair shining, red and gold and brown.

Before she disappeared, Clara pointed to the ground beneath her dangling feet. Four warriors on horseback sparkled in the red light of the new sun, their shoulders glistening with morning dew. They wore eagle feathers tied in their hair as a testament to brave deeds, but they weren't painted for battle. All four watched me. I heard the wind wrap itself around the house, but it didn't lift their hair or disturb the arrangement of their feathers.

I pressed my hands against the window and repeated the

question I had asked Clara. "What about the medicine hole? Will I ever find it?"

The spirit warriors smiled, and one of them raised his hand, palm outward; it flashed like a mirror.

You are the medicine hole, he said.

4

Moonwalk

(1969)

MARGARET MANY WOUNDS WAS DYING. THREE YEARS earlier she had been diagnosed as diabetic, and now, although she felt her health rapidly declining, she refused to go to the hospital.

"I am old anyway," she told her relatives. "Leave me be."

Early one morning she called to her daughter: "Let me have a mirror." Lydia fetched her mother a compact mirror, and removed the powder puff before she placed it in her hands. Margaret thanked Lydia and fluttered her fingers to wave her away.

Margaret peered at her reflection, moving the compact in a circle so she could see her entire face. She thought she looked transparent as baby crayfish in the Little Heart River. Margaret had never been a vain woman, one to consult each mirror she passed or smooth her hair as she caught her reflection in a storefront window. She simply wanted to make certain she was still there, still flesh and sweet blood and silver hair. There were days she was so light she couldn't be sure. She felt herself floating beneath the covers, held down by sweat and three-star quilts. She couldn't eat anymore. Tender meat was like gristle, dinner rolls like gravel, and the sunflower seeds she had once craved stony as cherry pits. But she requested a last bowl of *waštunkala,* Sioux corn soup. It had been a staple on the reservation but was increasingly a delicacy, as it required extensive preparation. Margaret's twin daughters were busy in the kitchen, fixing what might prove to be their mother's last supper. Evie soaked dried corn in water while Lydia cut venison into strips.

Evie poked her head into her mother's bedroom. "Will you be able to eat it once it's made?" she asked.

"The broth will slide down my gullet just easy," Margaret said, stroking her throat with emaciated fingers.

"It'll be a while," Evie told her, for the corn would have to soak overnight and the broth simmer for most of the next day.

"I know," said Margaret.

Evie was impatient. She wanted to serve it now and see her mother's dark brown eyes shine, flash once again with amber sparks. *This is just typical,* Evie thought. She believed reservation life was out of balance; here everything that was trivial took an inordinate amount of time, while the momentous things occurred with obscene rapidity. *It's why I left all those years ago,* she told herself. *And why I never came back. Until now.*

"What?" Margaret asked. She snapped the compact shut and placed it on her bedside table.

"Nothing." Evie returned to the kitchen, the central area of Margaret's small cabin.

"And don't you let that Father Zimmer near me!" Margaret called after her daughter. "All he wants to do is have the last word over my body and go fishing for my soul."

Margaret had spent many years as one of Father Zimmer's faithful. But in past weeks, bedridden and preoccupied with mortality, she had withdrawn from him.

"I'm not a sheep," she'd ranted late at night when everyone else was asleep. "There's still time to go back."

Margaret had recovered an old faith from her youth, from the days when there was magic, before the concept of sin had washed over Dakota people, just as the Oahe Dam had flooded their reservation with stagnant water.

I have been defeated by guilt, Margaret had decided. And that is when she had her grandson, Harley Wind Soldier, bury her cedar rosary in the dirt yard. "Maybe something useful will grow," she told him. She took to praying to Wakan Tanka, the Great Spirit of her childhood, who had not been a jealous God, she thought, but had waited patiently for her to honor Him again.

"Mama's sure down on the old padre," Evie said. Lydia nodded, cleaning the serrated knife she'd used to carve venison. "You'd think at a time like this she might want to hold on to him for comfort," Evie continued. Lydia shrugged.

"Well, *I* won't let him in." Evie wouldn't push Catholicism on her mother. She didn't like what she considered the powerlessness of faith, preferring the safety of a world she could see with her own eyes.

"I wonder where Philbert's taken off to," Evie said. Her husband had left early that morning in their dented Chevy.

"I'm off to rediscover warrior country," he'd told her, blowing Evie a kiss as he backed out of the cabin.

"He's probably discovered a six-pack and some no-good buddies," Evie muttered.

Moments later she heard a car door slam in the yard, and her missing husband, chewing spearmint gum to mask his beery breath, burst into the kitchen and caught Evie around the waist in a powerful hug, as if he'd been magically conjured by her thoughts.

• • •

Evie hadn't looked back after leaving the reservation and moving to Minneapolis seven years earlier. "You look back, you never get off the res," she told Philbert when he complained of being homesick. But Lydia's short note—*Please come, Mama's dying*—roused her.

Philbert and Evie drove to North Dakota in a day, stopping only in Bismarck to buy groceries. It was July 17, 1969, and all the way from Minneapolis they listened to news programs covering the Apollo 11 mission. Astronauts Neil Armstrong and Edwin Aldrin were due to land on the moon in three days.

"It's gonna be a miracle," Philbert had said at the conclusion of each special report. Upon hearing it for the umpteenth time, Evie glared at him. He was oblivious. He steered the car with his elbows, leaving his hands free to mop sweat from his forehead and upper lip.

"Wish we had some of that air-conditioning," he complained. He stuck his head out the window to catch a breeze but was whipped by sandy grit.

Evie thought Philbert looked like a bug. More like a bug each year, with his long, skinny arms and legs, loose as tentacles, and his stunted round torso. His head was shaved in a buzz cut because he was lazy and didn't like to comb his hair. Philbert was thirty, three years older than Evie, and currently retired. At the peak of his rodeo career as a champion bull rider, he'd been stepped on. The bull's hoof left a small V-shaped scar directly over his heart, and even though several doctors had declared him healthy, he said his heart couldn't take it.

"It won't let me do that anymore," he told Evie when she urged him to ride again.

Evie had no patience with Philbert's heart, but she didn't argue. She worked full-time as a secretary for a lawyer and cooked dinner for Philbert when she returned home at night. She supposed there were women in America who would chide her for such slavish devotion, but she knew something they didn't: She had never loved him. She had been drawn to him because he was a successful bull rider, because he was bowlegged and uncomfortable without his dusty cowboy hat jammed tightly on his head. In short, she was attracted to him because he matched perfectly the image of her father she'd developed in a cloud of ignorance. Spoiling Philbert was Evie's way of apologizing for her lack of sentiment.

During the tedious drive from Minnesota, Evie had time to anticipate her reunion with Lydia. The endless comparisons she'd once made between them had tapered off in the years they were apart, but Evie found herself resurrecting the habit as her husband fiddled with the car radio.

Lydia had always been the good daughter, sweet-tempered and incurious, never dreaming of taking flight. And Evie wasn't beautiful like Lydia. Her nose was too thin and her upper lip so narrow it almost disappeared when she smiled. Her hair was dry and frizzy from too many perms, and she wore black-framed glasses attached to a beaded daisy chain around her neck. But she won Philbert because she had inherited what he called her mother's magnetism—a term Evie hated.

All her life Evie had envied her sister's beauty and placid nature. Right up until Lydia's husband was killed in a car accident. Lydia was pregnant with Harley at the time, and Evie believed his existence was what kept Lydia alive. As it was, she had seen her sister give up pieces of herself, including her voice. Lydia hadn't spoken a word since the accident, although she did sing at powwows.

People said she had the voice of a ghost. When Lydia

sang, women would carry their tape recorders to the drum to record her, and men would soften their voices to let Lydia's rise, above the dancers' heads, above the smoke of cigarettes and burning sage, some thought beyond the atmosphere to that dark place where the air is thin and Wanaği Tačanku, the Spirit Road, begins.

When Evie and Philbert finally pulled up in front of Margaret's cabin, five-year-old Harley was playing in the dirt yard, arranging pebbles and abandoned keys in elaborate patterns. He watched solemnly as his aunt and uncle stepped out of the car.

"Grandma is dying," he said in a voice surprisingly deep and hoarse.

"I know," Evie said, moving past him to enter the house. Philbert remained behind to visit with the nephew he'd seen only in photographs.

Margaret's cabin was whitewashed and clean, but bare. There had been a dirt floor when the sisters were growing up, but now there were planks covered with red-speckled linolcum. There were two large rooms, and an outhouse in back. Lydia had placed cornflowers on the kitchen table and was cooking *wožapi,* a berry pudding, when her sister entered.

Evie wondered whether perhaps Lydia would finally speak after five years of silence to greet her, but instead she calmly set aside her mixing spoon and gave Evie a quick hug.

"Good to see you," Evie whispered. Lydia nodded and retrieved her spoon.

Evie looked in on her mother, who was so pale she was almost white. *She isn't dying, she's fading,* Evie mused.

When Margaret saw Evie, she said, "My girl," and lifted a creamy hand.

Mama looks like a white woman, Evie thought as she sat down on the edge of Margaret's bed.

"You were always my favorite," Margaret whispered to her daughter.

"No, Mama, this is Evelyn," Evie said in a loud voice.

"That's right. I know it."

Mama is confused, Evie decided.

"My girl, I've missed you." Margaret held Evie's hand. "I have just a few things to give away, so let me tell you what to do."

Margaret told Evie that a set of books including the complete works of Jane Austen should be given to Harley in ten years, on his fifteenth birthday. Lydia was to have her mother's wedding moccasins, which had been worn only the one time. They were exquisitely beaded: a background of white cut beads framing crimson beaded roses. Evie was to have a gold locket she never knew her mother owned. Margaret pulled it from beneath her nightgown. The case was big as her thumb, with the monogram *MMM*. Evie wondered what was inside but didn't ask.

For the next couple of days the sisters looked after their mother together and spent hours at the kitchen table playing gin rummy. Evie no longer enjoyed the game. When she was little all she wanted to do was beat Lydia, even if it meant cheating, hiding unmatched cards beneath sets she spread like a fan and set down with a flourish. Lydia never seemed to suspect Evie's string of wins but played round after round with dogged enthusiasm, as if she expected to win at any moment.

Evie no longer cheated but found herself winning just as regularly. It was too easy. Time and again Lydia gave up the cards Evie needed, and even when she passed them up to help Lydia win, inevitably the card she drew from the deck was equally valuable. She couldn't lose. But Evie continued to play, because the game made Lydia's silence less oppressive. As children, they had played quietly. Each understood where the other wanted to go, what she wanted to do, with one glance. Evie realized that the present suspension of speech was different, uninformed, but she found it comforting. It was how they had always played cards.

Two days after her prodigal daughter returned, Margaret requested the bowl of corn soup. It was good to hear the girls moving together in the kitchen. The soup wouldn't be ready until the next day, but already Margaret could taste it, could feel the warm broth in her stomach.

Later that night Lydia and Harley returned to their own house, a half-mile down the gravel road. Evie and Philbert made pallets on the kitchen floor, and Margaret could hear them whispering in the dark for a while.

Margaret tried to sleep, but she heard scuffling feet and smothered giggles at the foot of her bed. She saw people crowding her bedroom. They were sitting on little wooden chairs, facing her bed, waiting like an audience. She started to ask them who they were, and caught herself just in time. It would be rude. Dakota hospitality required that she welcome all visitors.

"Do you want me to tell you the story?" Margaret asked the dark figures. "It's been in my head for many days now." They all nodded. Margaret closed her eyes and pressed her hands together. She began to speak:

"Charles Bad Holy MacLeod returned to the reservation in 1912, when I was seventeen. He came back from the Indian School in Carlisle, Pennsylvania, wearing a white man's suit with a high starched collar. He came back with twenty books and a head full of education. He came back lonely and ignorant. He looked like a full-blood despite the way he'd parted his short hair straight down the middle, but he didn't remember one story about his own tribe. He didn't remember one honor song.

"We worked a trade to educate one another. He read to me until eventually I learned to make out the words. Our favorite book was *Pride and Prejudice*. I liked that little white girl, Elizabeth Bennet, because she had wit and a backbone. I thought she would have made a good Sioux. In return I told him all the stories and legends about where he came from. I taught him many songs. We liked the warrior ones best because they were so conceited. We would laugh when we sang the chorus: *I have arrived, the battle will soon be over.* I even took him to the Grand River one night so he could hear a ghost. It was the ghost of a chief's son who was a *winkte*—a man who loves other men— mourning the loss of a lover killed fighting the Arikara. You could still hear him singing where his people had camped along the river.

"I wanted to reclaim Charles Bad Holy MacLeod for the tribe and for myself. I pitied him because the reservation agent had taken him away at age four and let Pennsylvania keep him until he was twenty-one. I was grateful my parents had kept me so well hidden in the brush of Angry Butte, guarded by Šunka Sapa, Black Dog, each time the agent came around. Šunka Sapa would have eaten the agent's scrawny throat before letting him take me. But we always had the last laugh, because those Indians taken away to Carlisle would return to the reservation and make up for lost time. They would become the most fanatic traditionals. Even Charles would have given up his white-man's suit and learned to dance again if he'd been with me long enough.

"As it was, I made him learn my crooked ways. I shocked him. On our wedding night I undressed in the lamplight, folding each garment as it was removed, placing it on the back of a chair. I unbraided my hair and used it to wash my breasts. My mother would have been disgusted because I was so immodest. But I did it because the part in my husband's hair looked like a straight white road, the kind I would never travel. His body was brown, and I was relieved. I thought the tight clothes might have pinched him white, leeched the color right out of his cells. I had to undo all those buttons and release him, because he couldn't move.

"I had the two best years of my life then. Charles did the accounting for a shopkeeper who didn't mind admitting he couldn't figure numbers and an Indian could. We were delighted with one another. My mother thought we were too delighted. She wanted to know when she could expect a grandchild. It's funny I didn't become pregnant in the two years we were together. Maybe if I'd had the son or daughter of Charles Bad Holy MacLeod I would have managed better when he died of tuberculosis. I wouldn't have left so much of myself in his coffin."

Margaret's voice had awakened Evie and Philbert. They listened, transfixed, to a story they had never heard.

"Why is she doing this? Who's she talking to?" Evie asked.

"She's telling her life," Philbert explained. "Probably just trying to let it go."

"It isn't fair," Evie whispered angrily. "I begged her to tell me things when I was little, family history, all kinds of stuff. And she would just laugh. Tell me I had to find my own answers in the world.''

Evie was crying. Philbert had never known Evie to cry before, and he didn't know what to do. He wrapped an arm around her and pulled her close, but she held her body stiff as a statue, unyielding as the hard floor beneath them.

"I guess people change when they see death coming,'' Philbert told his wife. She was suddenly quiet, her weeping ended. Philbert believed she had fallen asleep, when he heard her sigh.

"I wonder what those astronauts are doing,'' she said.

In the morning Margaret waited for the sun to light her room, expecting to see the faces of her audience. But the figures and chairs were gone. Margaret heard a cough and looked toward the window. There they were, clustered around her cabin and peering in, whole families with children perched on their fathers' shoulders. She couldn't make out who they were.

"It's pretty hot for so early in the morning,'' Margaret said. The crowd nodded, and she saw a flash of white hankies drawn across moist faces.

I will finish the story, Margaret thought.

"In seventy-four years I had just two men. One was big passion and one was understanding. But that's lucky, don't you think? To have passion and understanding?

"I was forty-seven years old in 1942, when I came to be working in Bismarck. They called me a nurse, but I'd had no training, just a willingness to work with prisoners of war. About a thousand of them were in the Bismarck camp.

"I worked with Dr. Sei-ichi Sakuma, a surgeon from San Francisco. He'd volunteered to work at the camp after his wife died of food poisoning in Manzanar. Dr. Sakuma had brought his own surgical instruments with him, and they were superior to any in the camp. I thought those instruments were beautiful and terrible. They fit nicely in my hand; the weight of them was just right. I handled them efficiently in assisting the doctor. He would tell me about his wife as he worked. How she wrote limericks and how she loved to jitterbug. Her name was Evelyn. I remember her as someone I knew, although we never met. Dr. Sakuma said I looked a little like her, and he watched me closely. 'I never knew Indians before,' he said.

"In our loneliness we became lovers. 'I thought I'd never want anyone again. It has been thirty years,' I told him. But we didn't talk about it much. There wasn't time. There wasn't space either, so we had to use the medical supply room to have any privacy. Dr. Sakuma had thin hair and wore wire-rimmed spectacles that pinched his nose. He was strong, but the bones in his face looked delicate. When I kissed him I was gentle.

"My mother never told me you could do it standing up. We had no choice because the medical supply room was so small. Three feet by three feet, but most of the shelves were bare, so we could spread our hands across the wood, pressing for balance. We smelled like rubbing alcohol and had to swallow sounds to keep our secret. It became a test of will to see how quiet we could be—violent, reckless, but horribly silent.

"It sounds vulgar, but there wasn't a vulgar thing about it. Mostly we needed someone to hold on to, reassurance that we were alive and warm under the skin. For me, it was a thaw.

"I didn't worry about getting pregnant. I guess I thought I was an old lady. Then I dreamt one night that I had swallowed two marbles and could feel them in the pit of my stomach. They were talking inside me like little chatterboxes. 'Quiet, be still,' I scolded. Later I realized they were my twin girls talking to me in a dream.

"From the day I discovered I was pregnant I avoided the camp. I called the medical director to resign and never returned. This is a sin I haven't wanted to admit. I left Dr. Sakuma with no explanations, knowing he couldn't leave the camp to find me. When the war ended I thought maybe he might try, but if he did I never knew about it.

"You know, I've asked myself so many times why I did this. Maybe I was worried my girls would be teased because their mother went to bed with the Enemy. Maybe I was afraid people would call them 'breeds. Maybe I was afraid Dr. Sakuma would reject me once he found out.

"After Lydia and Evelyn were born I returned to the reservation with a big lie about marrying a Canadian Indian, who left me. That lie made me a member of the Church and my daughters full-blood Indians. But it has never tasted right, and maybe that's why I can't eat the food my daughters bring me. Maybe the higher powers are scolding me, telling me to let the lie nourish me as I have nourished it. But it's time for the lies to perish, don't you think?"

Evie was stunned and too angry to cry. She was glad she alone had overheard Margaret's confession. Lydia and Harley hadn't arrived yet, and Philbert had gone for a walk, followed by a flock of wild turkeys. Evie couldn't bear to look at her mother. She imagined she would see the words strung out across the room, suspended above her mother's bed.

Margaret had told her daughters their father was a Blood Indian from Calgary. A champion rodeo rider who had won the All-Around title in North Dakota the year Margaret was forty-seven and starting to get an itch. He had been ten years younger but crazy in love, taking Margaret home to Canada, where they married. Eventually he'd left her, and she made her way back to the reservation to have Evie and Lydia.

That was the legend. That was Evie's understanding of her own history. Margaret had kept his name secret, ostensibly to prevent the girls from trying to trace their father. The family name they used was Many Wounds, Margaret's maiden name. But Evie had come up with her father's name. In a dream she had seen him riding a Brahma bull, his left hand raised triumphantly in the air. She couldn't see him clearly because the bull leapt and twisted, but she heard the emcee call his name. "The best ride of the day! Let's hear it for Sonny Porter!"

All her life Evie had been the daughter of Sonny Porter. She'd married Philbert because he rode the Brahma bulls so much the way her father had. Evie had even phoned the Calgary information once, asking if there was a listing for a Sonny Porter. She'd had no luck but imagined he could be anywhere.

When she was eight, she'd drawn a picture of him with the silver All-Around trophy in his hand. His face was empty of features except for a great crescent smile traced above his chin.

She believed her father was passionate and adventurous. *I take after him,* she had told herself over the years, and the idea pleased her.

A hot breeze moved through the kitchen, and Evie held on to the table, half expecting she would drift out the open window.

She had composed herself by the time Philbert returned from his walk. She focused her attention on the simmering corn soup and a stream of radio reports about the moon landing.

Philbert had brought the television from Lydia's place to Margaret's cabin. He set it on her low bureau so she could watch it from the bed.

"What's he doing?" Margaret asked Evie.

"The astronauts are walking on the moon tonight. We thought you'd like to see it, Mama."

"I've been there," she told Evie. She watched Philbert struggle to reach the outlet behind her dresser.

"What do you mean?" Evie asked, irritated by her mother's remark.

"When I was little, my *tunkašida,* my grandfather, woke me up in the middle of the night. I was about your age," she told Harley, who stood directly behind Philbert.

"He carried me on his shoulders to a field of prairie grass as high as his waist. He showed me the moon, told me I could go there if I wanted to bad enough. And for just one second I really was there, looking back at the spinning earth, bright as a blue eye."

"Oh," Evie said. Years before, she would have treasured this anecdote, but it had come too late for her to enjoy or believe.

Philbert brought in kitchen chairs for Evie and Lydia to sit on while they waited for the astronauts to emerge from their lunar module.

Margaret paid no attention to the broadcast. "*Takoja,* come sit with me."

Harley sat on the bed with his grandmother. She stroked the back of his head.

"Someday when you're grown up, you should liberate my grandmother's dress," she told him.

"Mama, we can tell him about the dress later. Don't you

want to see the men *walking* on the *moon*?''

Margaret pointed at the television screen. ''Are they going to dance? Are they going to put on a show?''

''Yes,'' said Evie. Philbert stared at her. ''Never mind,'' she told him.

''My grandmother's dress was the most beautiful and unusual dress people had ever seen,'' Margaret told Harley. ''It took years to finish beading the top of it, from the collar, over the sleeves, down to the waist. The background was blue beads, and she beaded buffaloes and Dakota warriors on horseback running through the sky, pictures of their spirits, because so many of them were dead. She wore it to only the most sacred ceremonies, and when she danced at the edge of the dancers' circle, she said she was dancing them back to life.''

Harley could imagine a buffalo hunt in the sky. He pulled back his right arm and aimed an invisible arrow at the space module settled in lunar dust.

''Okay, it's any minute now. Look, Mama, the astronauts are getting ready to go out.'' Evie felt it was important for her mother to see. She looked to Lydia for support, but her sister stared straight ahead at the television.

''Someone got hold of that dress after Grandma died, and now it's in the Field Museum in Chicago,'' Margaret continued. ''The Plains Indian section. I was in Chicago just once, years ago, and that was the only thing I wanted to see. I stood there all day practically, trying to figure out how I could get that dress back.''

Harley took his grandmother's hand and gave her the rusty skeleton key he'd found in the yard. ''I'll get it for you someday,'' he told her, slipping off the bed to stand beside his mother's chair.

Evie was desperate for the astronauts to leave their ve-

hicle and walk on the moon. She wanted to see it happen
and know it was real: a scientific miracle worked out with
equations. "It will be history," she said aloud.

"It's all history," Margaret told her, working the skeleton key in her palm as if she was trying to find a way out
of her skin.

Evie and Lydia were making fry bread, waiting for the
corn soup to cool enough for them to serve their mother.
Philbert sat at the kitchen table, eating the bread as quickly
as it was made.

"Save some for Mama," Evie scolded.

She was in a sour mood. Her mother had been totally
unimpressed by the shots of men walking on the moon.
Evie had left the bedroom disappointed, convinced that
Margaret was so ill she couldn't understand the significance
of what had just occurred.

Even Lydia seemed unaffected, kneading dough as efficiently as ever. *She's getting more like Mama all the time,*
Evie thought.

Harley alone remained behind to entertain his grandmother. He saw there were two moons in the world: one
on television and one in the sky outside his grandmother's
window.

"Two moons," he told Margaret, curling his thumb and
forefinger into a telescope he peeked through.

"More than that," Margaret told him, "many, many
more. For every person who can see it, there's another
one."

Harley covered his eyes with his hands. The idea filled
all the skies he could imagine, and all the rooms, and the
spaces between trees, until moons like opaque marbles tum-

bled out of heaven to roll in a spectacular avalanche down the buttes.

"That way everyone has a moon of their own."

Harley extended his arm so his hand neatly blotted the moon outside the window. He was bending his fingers to encircle its white image, wanting to cup it in his left palm.

"Mine will be a yo-yo," he told Margaret as he tried to pluck it out of the sky.

"*Takoja,* come here. I will show you the moon."

Harley turned away from the window and stood beside Margaret's bed. She told him to close his eyes and pretend. She would pretend right along with him. He felt the moon enter the back of his head. It merged with bone and popped his ears. He felt an expansion, then an adjustment. Harley stood before his grandmother with the moon in his skull, eyes pouring cool light onto her quilt-covered body. Stellar wind rushed through the passages of his ears, wave upon wave like the undulating roar of a conch shell.

Harley could read his grandmother's lips but couldn't hear her. She was saying, "That is the moon. That is the way into the moon."

He shook his head because he didn't understand. So she pointed to the television screen, where the men walked in a floating manner that was both heavy and light.

"They can only walk on the surface," Margaret mouthed.

Harley couldn't think. His mind was squeezed, crushed close behind his eyes. The moon left him so suddenly he fell onto the bed. His small arms slammed across Margaret's legs, making them twitch and shudder. Harley began to cry.

"It's all right," Margaret told him. "It'll be all right. But remember that feeling. Remember what it's like to be the moon, and you, and the darkness and the light.'' Her hand moved in a circle.

Margaret Many Wounds decided to die early: before a last taste of *waštunkala,* before kissing her family good-bye, before Father Zimmer performed the Last Rites to purify her Everlasting Soul. She needed the extra time to work her own magic.

Do you have faith? she asked herself. She nodded and slipped into the water. It had been coursing around her bed for two days, parting at Evie's feet, lapping against Harley's sneakers, and splashing hot spray onto Margaret's face. But the water was cool now. She didn't need to breathe, and she was conscious of movement. *I am moving,* she thought, but she couldn't say in which direction. *I am I,* she thought with relief.

After the water, there was no water. Margaret stood in a light without color. She was alone. She couldn't feel her body, but it was still there, she could see it from the outside. She was wearing her grandmother's dress, with matching leggings and moccasins. The beads were brighter than she remembered; each bead sparkled, dazzling as a sun. *I remember the sun,* she thought. A single eagle feather was pinned to the back of her head, tilted at an angle to the right. Her belt was silver conches on black leather, with a trailer falling to her ankles, silver at its tip. Three sets of dentalium-shell earrings dangled from her ears, set in holes an inch apart moving up her ears. Her hair was plaited in two thick braids, weighted at the ends with hair ties made of bullets and bones. She tried to guess her own age, but it was useless. *I am beautiful,* she thought.

She looked out from her body. A figure stood before her.

It was Charles Bad Holy MacLeod, wearing his white-man's suit.

"I've been waiting for you," he told her.

"I'm glad to see you again," she answered, confused because her joy was so calm. "They let you dress like that?" Margaret had immediately noticed that his high collar, now a burning, blue-hot white, still bit into his throat.

"I was accustomed to it," he explained.

"I left home early," Margaret told him, and Charles nodded. "I have one last thing I want to do."

"That's acceptable to us," he said, and for a moment Margaret thought she heard the others. "Do what you have to and then join us at the council fire."

"How will I find it?" Margaret wished she could go there directly; she was eager to learn what the ancestors already knew.

"Follow Wanaǧi Tačanku to its very end. It won't take long. When you come to the edge of the universe you will see us by the fire. Push across the border. Five steps will bring you to us."

"Mama, your soup is ready." Evie brought the *waštun-kala* into her mother's room.

"She's not there," Harley said. He was sitting at the foot of his grandmother's bed, watching the television screen.

"Of course she's there," Evie snapped. The soup spilled a little and burned her hand. "Shoot." Evie placed the bowl on the bedside table, cooling her hand with her tongue. "Wake up, Mama, it's what you've been waiting for."

Margaret's body was warm, but Evie knew when she clutched her mother's shoulder that she was dead. Evie felt naked and afraid. "Can you see me?" she asked. "I can't see you. Maybe I'll never see you again." Evie sat beside her mother, holding her soft hand. She reached for her mother's white braid and brought it to her nose. The scent was the baby shampoo Lydia used to wash Margaret's hair. Evie kissed her mother's cheek.

She didn't cry until she fished Margaret's locket from beneath her nightgown. It opened with a click, and Evie had to clean the tiny photographs with her pinkie to remove the lint. Charles Bad Holy MacLeod was on one side, his black hair parted severely down the middle and slicked back on either side. A high collar choked him, and his eyes burned with intelligence. The other photo was of a balding, middle-aged Japanese gentleman. His smile was nothing but pain, his teeth hidden behind stretched lips. Evie recognized the smile and the gentle eyes. The expression was Lydia's.

Everyone had forgotten Harley. He dragged the cane-bottom chair in front of the television set and knelt on its seat. His hands rested on the bureau as he watched the black-mirrored surface of Neil Armstrong's face mask.

Behind him Evie and Lydia were washing their mother. They used the mildest soap and gentlest strokes. They washed her hair and spread it on the pillow to dry. It ran over the edges like a spill of white ribbons. Lydia painted Margaret's face the old way; she dabbed crimson lipstick on her forefinger and ran it down the part in her mother's hair. She drew a large circle above each cheekbone and filled it in. Lydia removed the old nail polish and put on a fresh clear coat. Then she and Evie dressed Margaret in the silky buckskin dress she had worn to powwows, and wrapped her in a dance shawl quilted with a thunderbird design on the back.

You will fly with powerful wings, Lydia was thinking.

You will never dance again, Evie thought.

They dressed Margaret in the wedding moccasins she had willed to Lydia. The soles were still clean on the bottom, and the sisters were startled when the slippers were in place, because it looked as if roses grew from the arch of each foot.

Father Zimmer sat in the kitchen over a cup of black coffee. He was inconsolable. Philbert stood across from him, hands plunged deep in his pockets, jingling change. Philbert thought the priest was going to cry.

"I should have been here to ease the passage," Father Zimmer said, stirring his coffee with a spoon, even though he'd added nothing to it. The rising steam was like the vapor of souls. He cried to think that Margaret's soul would hang over the buttes like fog because she had died without his blessing. He didn't want her to be caught between Here and There.

"I will say a mass for her," he said, and Philbert bowed his head.

Harley's knees were beginning to ache, but he continued to kneel on the chair. As he listened, the voices of Walter Cronkite, the astronauts, and ground control in Houston were sucked away. He heard the Sioux Flag Song pounding from the black vent on the television set, but when Harley checked over his shoulder, he saw that no one else seemed to notice.

Neil Armstrong and Edwin Aldrin were facing the camera, and Harley smiled because they reminded him of two white turtles standing upright. Armstrong was using an aluminum scoop fitted into an extension handle to collect samples of rock without bending over. Aldrin was using a set of tongs to pick up larger pieces.

Somewhere inside the music Harley heard a familiar voice calling, *"Takoja."*

Harley was no longer lonely or invisible on the chair. He saw his grandmother's figure emerging on the screen, dancing toward him from the far horizon behind the astronauts. He recognized her weaving dance as Sioux powwow steps, but her beautiful blue-beaded dress was unfamiliar to him.

He said to himself, *Grandma is young.* But then she smiled at him, and the smile was old. Her hair was black and her hair was white. Her progress was steady, and she didn't bounce like the men in space suits.

He waited for Armstrong and Aldrin to see her, but they must have seen only the ground. Finally she came upon them, and Harley caught his breath because Margaret danced through Neil Armstrong. The astronaut never ceased digging at the ground, leaving footprints like heavy tank treads, but his oxygen system quivered a little as she passed.

Margaret Many Wounds was dancing on the moon. *Look at the crooked tracks I make like a snake,* she thought. At first it seemed it would take her a long time to make the circuit. *Am I dancing or flying?* she wondered when instead she completed it very quickly. Names came to her, though she had never learned them. *That is the Sea of Crises,* she knew, *and that is the Sea of Serenity.* She crossed the Sea of Fertility and then backtracked to the Sea of Tranquillity. That was where she felt Harley's presence.

Takoja, she called with her spirit. *Look at me, look at the magic. There is still magic in the world.*

Margaret danced beyond the astronauts and their stiff metal flag. She kept moving forward until she came to the beginning of her trail, mired in the gritty Lake of Dreams. She raised a foot and found Wanaǧi Tačanku, the Spirit Road, rippling beneath her feet. She set off, no longer dancing, walking briskly toward the council fire, five steps beyond the edge of the universe.

5
Morse Code

Crystal Thunder
(1964)

MARTIN LUNDSTROM WAS WHITE, A NORTH DAKOTA Swede in the heart of farm country, but was nevertheless an outcast. He had not one cowlick but three, a trinity of bristling tufts of hair rising from his brown head like three horns. His face was attractive—*I* found it pleasing—nearly sharp-featured but softened by beauty marks at his temple and chin, and when he smiled, seldom though it was, a delightful dimple puckered his left cheek. The others called him Tiny Tim because he walked with a pronounced limp only partially corrected by a thick orthopedic shoe. When I say "the others," I don't mean the Indians, the Dakota students from our reservation. We were outcasts on our own turf and left the Germans and Scandinavians to torture one another as they saw fit. We avoided them as much as possible.

By the time I was a senior at Saint Mary's High School I was a misfit myself, shunned by tribesmen because my mother had too many boyfriends and was rumored to practice Indian medicine. Regina Red Horn became a rude, annoying shadow and would stare at me in the hall as she sucked on the end of her black braid. Her faction of wistful cheerleader candidates—pretty, athletic girls too swarthy to be selected but persistently hopeful—pointed at me as they whispered, until I felt speared in the back by their sharp fingernails. In exasperation I dug out the leather pouch con-

125

taining my old jackstones and rubber ball, and wore it to school. When Regina resumed her aloof surveillance I went up to her, clutching the pouch in my hand. I squeezed hard enough to feel the spiky metal jacks.

"I'll take your eyes," I told her, "and wear them in my bundle. You better aim them somewhere else." I heard her gasp, and very quickly Regina Red Horn and her graceful flock migrated to the other end of the hall. Their disapproval was so potent I could smell it, a metallic odor like scorched gunpowder, but after it passed in a smoky cloud all I smelled was the soap on their skin.

I admired Martin Lundstrom from afar, considered him a talented artist and coveted the sketches he scribbled in notebooks. He was forever ripping them out and throwing them in the wastebasket, where I retrieved them when no one was looking. I liked the way he drew horses, capturing the weary, cynical posture of stocky farm horses, their heads down and muscles straining, while his elegant, slim-ankled Indian ponies reared at the edge of the paper, poised to leap off. I followed a trail of these drawings straight to the source after weeks of collecting them, smoothing them out, memorizing their lines. I approached him in the school cafeteria, painfully aware that my footsteps echoed in the great room, which had once been a chapel. I looked up and up at the high ceiling, determined to keep my destination a secret until I arrived. Martin Lundstrom occupied the seat closest to the garbage cans. He was alone, as usual, staring at nothing as he ate a slice of yellow cake. I heard him say, with his mouth quite full: "She's coming over." I paused. I held the drawings too tightly, and they crumpled in my hand.

"She stopped," he said, speaking to no one. I closed the space between us.

"She's here," I told Martin Lundstrom, and he smiled.
"I'm Crystal Thunder. I think you can really draw."

He looked at me then, not staring exactly, but with concentration as if trying to decide the best way to sketch my features. I had a flat, pancake face and glistening eyes I hoped made up for it. I was all one shade, brown hair, brown eyes, dusky skin, the only spot of color being the odd crimson birthmark on my forehead, perfectly bowed in the shape of a horseshoe. At least I had coaxed my straight hair into a stylish shoulder-length flip. I thought he might be pleased to sketch those lines. Martin ended his inspection and gestured to the nearest chair.

"Have a seat." I was still clutching his discarded pages as I sat down, and he held out his hand for them. "So she likes my work?"

What was this "she" business? I wondered. He could have read my mind.

"I don't talk to people much," he apologized. "I tend to think aloud. I've fallen into bad habits." Martin plucked a stub of charcoal from his pants pocket and turned over one of the wrinkled sheets. "Hold still."

His eyes probed me like hooks, and I opened my mouth once or twice; I was a great gasping fish. To ease the tension I crossed my eyes and saw the steep ridge of my nose dividing a world consisting entirely of pairs.

"She shouldn't do that," Martin scolded, so I stopped. His eyes never left my face, I'm certain of it, though I noticed his hand jerking across the paper. What his fingers accomplished they did using their own vision. He finished as Sister Francis rang a small silver hand bell, signaling the end of lunch. He handed me the drawing, then quickly stuffed his hands in his pockets and lurched away. Surely this wasn't my face, which I well know is round as a griddle and near as flat. This face was lovely in its symmetry: cheekbones neat as equilateral triangles, a firm rectangular chin, perfectly matched elliptical eyes, irises glittering like faceted gemstones. Even the birthmark was transfigured, into the delicate lips of a rosebud.

Saint Mary's was scandalized by my relationship with Martin Lundstrom. When we walked down the hall together there was rustling on both sides, mouths working overtime.

"Sounds like a plague of grasshoppers chewing a wheat-field," Martin said.

Sister Nora asked me to stay after class one day to help her wash down the blackboards. As I applied a wet rag to the slate, I heard her wheeze behind me.

"You're a young girl to be so serious about a boy." Her congested lungs strangled the words.

"I'm seventeen," I told her. I wouldn't make it easy.

"Have you spoken to your mother about this?"

"Yes," I lied.

"Well, she can't approve. It's a delicate matter for a girl. Her reputation. Remember that." I nodded, which didn't satisfy Sister Nora. "Will you?" she pressed.

"Yes, Sister." But what I understood was something different. Most of my classmates were dating, pinned by college men or given a heavy ID bracelet to wear—a ritual I thought was like the tagging of cows. No one cared when Germans dated Swedes or Dakotas dated Assiniboins, as long as like courted like. So Martin and I moved in our own space and ignored the gossip whirling around us, spinning furiously as dust devils.

Martin's widowed mother worked as a phone operator in Bismarck. He said: "She listens in when she can, and gets involved in the problems of strangers. I think they're all she can handle, the ones at a distance."

We agreed to keep our feelings secret from our mothers; I was relieved to make the promise. My mother might not care that Martin was white, but I was certain she would resent his influence over me. She begrudged Jesus the space He took up in my soul, though I promised her it was only a corner. In my mind He stood off to the side and pinched one edge of my spirit between His cold fingers, as if making ready to fold it.

"So who should be inside there?" I'd once asked her.

"I am your spirit until the day comes when you understand me, and then you should take over."

If I lived to be ninety, I would never understand my mother, all her secrets and memories and desires. She was claiming my soul for all time.

A few weeks before graduating from high school, Martin bought himself a sleek black Thunderbird.

"The first one I've seen in these parts," he said. "A fish out of water."

It was true I hadn't seen another of its kind—this was pickup country—but it didn't look at all out of place. It was meant to swerve down gravel roads like a black snake and stalk its own shadow across white fields of needle grass.

"How'd you pay for it?" I asked him.

"I've had a job. No one knows but my mother."

It turned out he had been designing catalogue covers for the Oscar H. Will Seed Company since he was fifteen.

"Those covers keep getting more popular. They tell me sales are up," Martin said with a shrug.

I went to the library to look at past issues, and spread

them out on a heavy oak table. Martin Lundstrom's hormones were loose upon the land. The rural scenes he painted were sensual, pulsing with the desperate energy of puberty. On one cover two women were silhouetted against a lurid sun, carrying baskets of corn in their arms. Their upper lips were damp with tiny beads of perspiration, sweet as seed pearls, and long tresses of wavy hair clung to their bodies. In another drawing, a tower silo rose from the ground like a man's organ thrusting into the sky. I could sense the movement, feel the earth shake. It became clear why the pictures were so successful. I could just imagine an elderly farmer—one long considered a pillar of the community—carrying a rolled-up catalogue in his back pocket. Now and again he'd reach back to finger the tube, rub it like a good-luck piece. His dreams would be spiced for weeks, hot as chili peppers, causing him to blush through breakfast and reach more often for his wife.

Martin was cautious and gentle with me; he handled me like a wild horse. It wasn't until June that he risked a kiss on the mouth, and as our lips brushed, his eyes widened, alert for signs of distress.

"It's okay," I murmured. I ran my hands through his hair and paused to finger the cowlicks growing against the grain.

We were parked on a dirt road that bisected a flat plain of mixed grass. Martin had spread an old wool blanket on the hood of his car, and we curled there, gradually relaxing as the heat of the car's engine warmed the blanket and melted our bodies. The sky was a flat stretch of blue and white, a weightless spring quilt settled on our bed. Slowly we undressed, folded our clothes, tucked our socks in our shoes, and placed the bundles on the roof of the car. As we moved together I saw my face reflected in Martin's gray eyes, and it was nothing like glancing in a mirror. The beautiful girl from his sketch peered back at me, her eyes blinking and filling with tears. I turned my head to the side so Martin wouldn't see me cry, and I noticed a box elder, our sole witness, perched on a gentle slope. It seemed to be waving at me, branch arms raised high, its gray bark deeply furrowed with worry lines. It frightened me, and I clung tightly to Martin.

"Crystal," he moaned, and I wanted to hush him.

Don't speak our names aloud, I was tempted to warn. *We aren't alone.* But I could guess how foolish that would sound. Martin would laugh if I told him the bare truth: *That glaring tree is my mother.* She watched us from the slope, her hair wild and fingers snapping, her thick roots buried deep in the earth, so deep they reached that place where there is nothing but heat and magma—all the planet's churning anger.

When I was five I learned that my mother was different. Old Mrs. Elk Nation was kind and allowed me to trail behind her at powwows. Her spine impressed me; it was so straight I like to think she was born with a sapling backbone, a flexible whip that stiffened to an erect trunk by middle age. She was a good dancer, one of the best, like a tree with elastic roots springing up and down in time to the music. I perched on her lap with pride and enjoyed the way she smoothed back the loose hair at my temples. She must have thought I was hypnotized by the soft touch of her hands, or too young to follow her conversation.

"I feel for this one," she told Emma Two Bulls, a Pine Ridge Sioux who was visiting cousins on our reservation. "This one belongs to that Thunder woman."

"*Ohan*," said Mrs. Two Bulls. "I heard of her. She messes with things you should leave alone."

"Bad medicine," Mrs. Elk Nation whispered. I could feel her moist gossip breath slide across the part in my hair. "You check which dish she puts out for the feed, and don't you taste any of it."

I scooted to the edge of Mrs. Elk Nation's lap and slid off her clenched knees.

"Restless?" she asked me. "Ready to dance again?"

I told her I was hungry, which wasn't true, but it gave me an excuse to move away from those words. I even rubbed the top of my head to brush off any words that had caught in my hair with their mean little hooks.

Until that day I had never doubted my mother. I accepted her presence as easily as my own and hadn't missed a father. My earliest memories of her were warm. I could remember being an infant strapped to a cradleboard and tipped against the wall of her kitchen, where I could watch my mother do her beadwork. She used the lazy stitch, picking up nine beads at a time to decorate leggings, moccasins, the yoke of buckskin dresses, purses, pipe bags, and the tapered handles of eagle-feather fans. She had beaded the turtle amulet that dangled from the top of my cradleboard. Sometimes I reached for its stiff horsehair tail, and she would tell me: "No, don't touch." She gave me a small beaded lizard to squeeze in my hands, and I could play with it as long as I didn't pop it in my mouth. Later I discovered that my umbilical cord had been sewn inside the turtle's shell to bring me good health and a long life. The lizard amulet was a decoy for harmful spirits, meant to confuse them should they try to steal my protection.

Back then I didn't need amulets, only my tall mother with her beautiful lined face. I wanted to touch her straight nose and crescent eyebrows, run a finger along her chapped, bitten lips. But she was across the room from me, busy with her silver needle and nylon thread, her movements so quick she looked as though she were spinning a web.

Mrs. Elk Nation's words put questions in my head, and they became a nuisance. I thought I could hear them knock together, tumble and click like gambling bones tossed against the back of my cranium. I wondered who my father was, where he was. I wondered why no one on our reservation wore the garments my mother beaded. Her customers were white collectors or Indians of other tribes: Chippewa, Cheyenne, Crow—*never* Dakota. Click. Click. The questions accumulated, and there was no relief. I could not interrogate Anna Thunder, my tall mother who seemed to know everything in the world. I had seen her crush potato bugs and snap the delicate pods of sweet peas. She had never struck me, but I was in awe of her efficient hands.

As the years passed and my questions remained unanswered, there were too many to keep inside my head and they spilled out, raising a painful rash on my arms. I fingered the bumps and recognized them for what they were: evidence of my curiosity. Perhaps someone with sensitive fingertips, or someone familiar with Braille, the tactile language, could have read my arms like a book. My mother never trailed a finger along my broken flesh but covered the area with clean white rags, wrapping me like a mummy.

"She should marry me," Martin said that fall when my figure swelled and I had to sew elastic bands into the waists of my slacks.

"*Who* should?" I asked. I wanted Martin to be quite clear on this.

"Crystal Thunder should become Crystal Lundstrom."

Martin poked his finger through the coil of my flip and the starched hair curled around it.

"Please," he whispered. "Please." I placed my hands on his shoulders and felt him tremble. His shorter leg was planted behind him, and he leaned forward, his weight on the good leg. He looked ready for a fight.

"We'll have to tell our mothers," I said. I didn't ask him: *Where will we go? What will we do for a living?* I knew we could work and manage to rent our own little place. There were no obstacles for me but my fierce mother, Anna Thunder, who could stretch a hide with her sharp pegs and scrape it clean, then work it until the skin was pliable velvet. This was how she worked a person's soul, gaining entry through the eyes. She never blinked. Her wide owl stare penetrated, then smothered.

"My mother won't allow it," I said.

"How can she stop us? We're of age. Crystal can do whatever Crystal wants."

I shook my head, but I told Martin: "Yes. Yes, I will marry you."

He dipped toward me, wrapped his arms around me, and stroked my stiff hair. I wanted to make him happy this last time, give him the answer he wanted, and speak aloud my own dearest wish.

I discovered my mother beading a small amulet in the shape of a turtle. Its shell was a spiral of red, yellow, and blue beads. I stood behind her in the kitchen doorway, looking over her shoulder as the needle stabbed and disappeared and reemerged.

"You're carrying a girl," she said. She bit the nylon thread.

I stumbled forward and grabbed the back of a kitchen

chair. Its thatched seat was coming loose, straw poked in every direction. I dropped silently into the chair.

My mother pointed her needle at me. She said: "You've been messing with that lame Swede. I saw you. Now he wants you to run away." I looked at the needle and would not raise my eyes to hers. I wouldn't let her in, not this time.

"He isn't lame. He loves me," I said, in that ridiculous order.

Anna spat into one of the tissues she kept crumpled in her apron pocket.

"He loves you, as if it matters." Laughter rose from her chest. "His feelings are useless dust!"

"I want to marry him," I said, so quiet I thought she couldn't hear me.

"You do whatever you like. Run off with that lame Swede and bear him a dozen peg-leg brats with even less sense than you have. Waste yourself, go ahead. But don't you waste that child." She poked me in the navel. "A soul for a soul."

I was so cold my limbs clenched and shivered, my fingernails turned blue.

"I haven't begun to teach you," she said. "You haven't come into your power, girl, you don't know what you're capable of. You could have your pick of any man and wouldn't have to settle on just one. I have so much to teach you, ancient ways passed down from the dead to the living."

My teeth chattered, and I hugged myself. "I want to be Crystal Lundstrom," I forced between cracked lips.

My mother slapped her beadwork on the table and rose from her seat. "You will not waste that child," she promised me. "A soul for a soul."

• • •

I wrote to Martin Lundstrom, my intended, that I would join him once the child was born. I told him that my mother would help with the pregnancy, but only if I kept to the house and didn't see him until then.

Martin took to driving his Thunderbird right up to the back steps of Anna's square house. "Come to the window!" he would shout.

And I always did, but concealed by Anna's heavy drapes so my poor intended couldn't catch a glimpse of me. If he set foot on the stairs, Anna would open the door and fill its frame, her hefty arms crossed beneath the rock ledge of her chest. She never spoke a word to him; the most she would do was flick her fingers—the rudest gesture a Dakota Indian could make. Eventually Martin would withdraw, clumping noisily down the steps in his mismatched shoes. To my eyes, he was graceful as a goshawk, he floated. One time he sat in the car for a solid hour, and I stood just as long behind the curtain, watching his face, touching it, the best I could, with my eyes.

My feelings for Martin hadn't changed, they had just been set aside, somewhere to the left of my mother, who now filled the empty places in me. She had never been so patient and affectionate before. She was a dream mother come true. Each night she bathed me in her claw-footed tub, soaped my back and washed my hair, her hands moving in warm circles. She combed my hair with the stiff head of a prairie coneflower, one hundred tender strokes, and plaited it in two French braids. She took my feet in her lap and counted the bones, smoothing each one with her thumb. She fed me wild turnips and leafy kale, cabbage stew, fried potatoes, corn on the cob glistening with butter, and moist lemon cake sprinkled with powdered sugar. At night we slept on her wide brass bed so she could watch over me even then. I think she sorted out my dreams, teased the unpleasant images from the harmless ones so that I never waked until morning, and the first thing I saw once I opened my eyes was my mother's concerned face hovering inches away, her breath sweet as mint, moving against my cheek.

We passed the long winter indoors, snug beneath blankets of snow. I had my mother to myself; she had banished her boyfriends for the duration, although Roger Bonnin turned up now and again to shovel snow off the roof, clear the chimney, and plow a tunnel from the back door to the gravel road. I felt protected, hidden. I remembered stories the nuns had told my class about the catacombs constructed by early Christians. At first I didn't miss the sun, which blazed somewhere above the snow walls. By March, however, I had dark circles under my eyes, a permanent shadow I attributed to the gloom. I missed the broad sky and bright colors, craved the wind and fragrant grasses.

The first thaw came in March, a week before I was due. The snowbanks still rose on either side of the house, twenty feet high in some places. I could see only a channel of light above our tunnel, a slim band narrow as a bracelet. I was surrounded by colorless white and reluctant to step outdoors for fear I would be swallowed up in its nothingness.

"Mama," I called, my pleading voice high as a child's. "I can't *see* anything."

My mother helped me into bed and told me to take a nap. "I'll handle it," she said.

I awakened late in the afternoon, and my mother was there, as if she had never stepped away. There is a song called "Stairway to the Sky," and I have seen religious paintings of pious Christians climbing a stairway lit by

God's finger, but none could compare to the steps Anna Thunder carved out of a snowbank, using an ax and a shovel. Her dress was soaked through from the effort, and her palms were blistered.

"Let's go while there's still sun," she said. She wrapped me in an old Pendleton blanket and guided me up the steep block steps. She pushed from behind, supporting most of my weight until I reached the chilly summit.

The sun's light washed over me and pressed into my body. I closed my eyes and tipped my face toward the sun's.

"Thank you, Mama. Thank you for this," I murmured. The baby fluttered a little, moved her hands and feet. "She likes it too," I said. "It really woke her up."

I turned in all directions, searching for a patch of color. "There." My mother pointed to the distant road, which had been cleared by plows. Pushing up from the road's edge were clusters of hardy crocuses, thriving in spite of the cold. They looked like a set of elegant lavender teacups, lonesome for a picnic.

I said, "They're a month early." But my mother didn't seem at all surprised.

"They came out to see you," she told me. "They know how important it is." She held out her hand, offering me a peppermint candy. "Take this in your mouth, and when it melts, we should get back inside."

The descent was trickier than the climb. My mother went ahead of me so I could balance myself by clutching her shoulders. The baby kicked me all the way down, restless, disappointed. *Can't we stay a while longer?* I imagined her pleading. She was furious with me, and by the time we entered the house she had tensed her plump body and was fighting for release.

• • •

It was old Mrs. Elk Nation who told me that my father was buried in the Catholic cemetery. "I pass him all the time on my way to visit Albert," she said. "They'd be side by side except for a good-sized chokecherry tree sprouting right between them. I know they enjoy that fruit."

"What's his name? How do you know it's him?" I asked. I would have shouted at her, but I didn't have the air.

"Everybody knows," she said. She patted my arm with her crippled hand, frozen with arthritis and heavy as stone. "Now you're growing up, it's about time somebody told you. Shouldn't be the last to hear. And you have the mark of sadness on you. I want to wash it away." I didn't know whether she meant my expression or the birthmark on my forehead.

"What's his name?" I asked again. I was whispering now.

"Clive Broken Rope," she said. "Born 1918, died 1946."

"The year I was born."

"That's right. That's all I'm going to say now. You ask your mother about the rest. She's the only one who knows for sure."

Mrs. Elk Nation smiled at me and walked away, hoisted her shawl higher across her shoulders and joined a line of older women dancing at the edge of the powwow circle. They danced close together and matched their movements in perfect time to the drum. I liked the way their shawl fringes overlapped, connecting them like beads strung on a necklace. I made myself watch, to push the name back. Clive Broken Rope. If I weren't careful I would hear ripe chokecherries fall from the tree and strike hollow ground, making my father's bones rattle, his teeth chatter. I think Mrs. Elk Nation meant well, meant to do right by me. After all, I was fifteen years old and it was time I had some of those answers I scratched up my sore arms longing for. But now I was in a deeper hole—in the red, as they say—because those answers had split up into more questions, multiplying like rabbits.

Ask your mother about the rest. I couldn't imagine her telling me secrets. I still saw her the way I had as a child: across miles of cracked linoleum, massive as a statue, part of the great unknown.

I found my mother in the garden, on her knees in the black dirt. She cast a broad shadow across the plants, threatening as a storm cloud. She wasn't tending the vegetables we grew to put on our table but was cultivating the several varieties of weeds, roots, wildflowers, and herbs that were her private pharmacy. Over the years she had taught me the healing properties of each plant, made me recite the cure recipes to test my memory: bloodwort for whooping cough, sweet flag for diabetes, wild onion for bee sting, purple coneflower for rabies or snakebite, fleabane for rheumatism, wild licorice for fever, and on and on.

In a separate plot of land behind our house she grew tall stalks of prairie larkspurs, as high as my waist, the white blossoms sprouting in every direction like a spray of stars.

"Watch out for these," she had warned me once, looking pleased as she pinched an ivory petal. "They can be poison." Beside them she had pointed out feathery bundles of prairie parsley. "If you know how to use this plant you can control weak minds." She broke off the end of one hollow stem and chewed the tiny leaves as if to say she had a strong mind that nothing could bend. I wondered if this was the ingredient with which she captured the affections of young, good-looking men. I could picture her sprinkling their corn soup with the green flakes, watching as, sip after sip, their minds opened to her, peeled back like nutshells to expose the tasty meat. My mother had a trail of young Sioux men go through her bedroom, men just a scratch older than boys, young enough to be the sons she never had. She didn't collect them for long, here one day, gone the next, and I was used to their silent arrival and empty eyes. Used to seeing her clamp her hands on their wrists, fingers tight as shackles, to lead them upstairs. If she won power over them with the herb, it would be the only plant I'd known her to utilize. She had a garden full of remedies, but she never attempted to heal anyone. She could have plucked flat clusters of bloodwort, chewed it to a paste, and prepared a poultice for my sore arms, but the plants remained rooted in soil. *I* could have done it, but somehow I understood that the garden was hers and not mine, her collection of hoarded knowledge. I felt she was as greedy about the shoots and stems as *wašičun*s about their gold. Maybe she counted the buds and leaves and knew exactly what she owned, how much she had coaxed from the fickle ground.

Mrs. Elk Nation was probably still dancing with her friends at the powwow grounds, but I thought I felt one of her rigid fingers jab between my shoulder blades.

"Ma," I said to my mother's hunched back. She still crouched on the ground. She looked up at me. "Ma," I whispered.

The questions nearly choked me; they filled my throat and hammered my teeth. Why couldn't I peel them from my tongue?

"Clive Broken Rope," I said. I blinked then, flinched in anticipation of a big reaction. But my mother's usual, vaguely annoyed expression never changed. She put out her hand, and I helped her up. She slapped her cotton dress to dust it.

"Those biddies must be squawking," she said to herself. To me, she said: "Clive Broken Rope is a long story, and I don't like the way it ends up."

I thought that was all I would hear, and started planning ways to get the information from Mrs. Elk Nation. But my mother surprised me. "I'll make us some horsemint tea, and then I'll tell you," she said.

My mother blew on her tea, and the steam hid her face. She looked like a ghost. "When your father came to me he was a dead man. He wanted me to breathe life into him, jump-start his blood. I met him straight out of the army, when we had an honor dance for all our World War Two heroes. He was in one of those tank regiments that liberated the concentration camps in Germany, and he told me his hair turned white from what he saw, pure white in just a couple of days."

White as the larkspur, I was thinking. I saw his head bobbing like the bell of a flower.

"All I had to do was cook him a meal, let him talk about his experiences, and he was happy. He said it made him a new man. He started smiling after a bit, and then he could laugh again. He tried to make me laugh, but it wasn't easy. The best trick he knew was imitating that Little Tramp from the silent movies, the one with the Hitler mustache. He wore his big army boots and turned them out so he could waddle like a duck. He looked like a drunk, sick bird. I almost wet my pants every time he did that routine. Imagine, a Sioux warrior goofing like that.

"People talked, the way they do, because he was younger. But we didn't care. We married Indian way."

I knew my mother meant *lived in sin,* but she wasn't Catholic like me. She didn't have to go to the Catholic reservation school, where the old-crow nuns pecked our souls to pieces.

"Your father wasn't wounded in the war, but he came back damaged. At first I didn't notice it, I thought he was getting better all the time, but once he found out I was carrying, the holes in him opened up. I think he was afraid what he might pass on to you. I don't know. All I know is, the memories of that war chewed his mind away."

I wished I could tell her to stop. I could see it, all too clearly: my father's skull empty and gleaming, licked clean from the inside. I heard the sound my mother made when she cracked bones and ate the marrow.

"You were afraid of him," my mother told me. "Every time he put his hand out to touch my belly, you flipped over. When you got too big to move that much, you kicked his hand away. You already knew there was something wrong.

"Your father hit me just once, and that was enough. 'That's the last mistake you'll ever make,' I told him. I didn't care if he was half crazy or had left his mind in Germany, blown to bits like everything else. Nobody does that to me, or mine." My mother got up and poured herself more of the smooth tea. It smelled cool and clean as virgin snow.

"Some little thing upset him. I don't remember what. He howled and scratched his face so deep he was bleeding into his collar. I grabbed his hands to stop him, but he knocked me down. When I tried to get up, he kicked me right here." My mother touched her thick middle. "So he kicked you as well. The toe of his boot left that mark on your face."

My hand lifted to the birthmark, massaged the area above

my left eye. It was just a birthmark, nothing more, certainly not the pointed edge of my father's boot, tattooing my flesh with his crazy anger. I knew it wasn't true, but I believed it.

"Your father died a week before you were born," my mother said.

It was all she would tell me.

I stood up and went to the kitchen window for a breath of fresh air. Waving below me in the soft wind were neat rows of prairie larkspurs. Their white faces nodded at me until I became dizzy and had to look away.

I married Martin Lundstrom on March 10, 1964, in a tiny office at the state capitol. I had always been impressed by the nineteen-story skyscraper constructed of smooth limestone, but on my wedding day clouds massed behind my eyes, making the sky look bleak and overcast, transforming the majestic building into a cold tower. I wasn't excited by the rare elevator ride, and I was impatient with employees of the state who gawked openly at us. I reached for Martin's hand, straightened my spine, even tilted my chin at a haughty angle. One pink secretary, fluffy as a lamb in a cashmere dress, stared the longest, her jaw opened so wide I could count her fillings. Just before we turned a corner and left her sight, I flicked my fingers at her.

Martin grabbed my hand. "Don't be bothered. They're just ignorant." He lifted my hand to his lips and warmed it with a soft kiss. "No," he amended, "they're just jealous."

Our witnesses were strangers on a coffee break, and every mouth was set in a flat line of grim disapproval. A storm swept through my head, and it took a great effort of concentration to get through the brief ceremony, hear enough of it to respond properly. Once it was over, the chaos descended: Thunder cracked in my eardrums, and needles of lightning flashed through my skull. Hailstones the size of jelly beans pounded my brain, shattering my thoughts. I leaned against my new husband. I gave up the future to him.

I am a weak vessel, I told myself as I peered out the rain-streaked windows of Martin's Thunderbird.

"The state sure hates to see us go, it's crying its eyes out," he said. He clutched my knee.

I am a weak vessel, chanted in my head, the drone of a familiar prayer.

"We'll hit Chicago tomorrow," Martin told me. "Things'll get better, just wait. How about some music?"

All we could tune in on the radio were gospel shows or music hours filled with mournful hymns, oppressive as dirges:

I'll cling to the old rugged cross, and exchange it some-day for a crown.

Voices soaked with tears of passion swelled in the car, the harmonies strained and nearly collapsed. We drove through a great bath of tears until we reached Minnesota.

"Now we've found the sun!" Martin cried. He rolled down his window and thrust his pale hand into the light. "The sun always makes a difference."

I believe I nodded my head, but really it was a useless gesture. The voice of my thoughts was stuck in a groove; rain or shine, it bumped over the same ground.

I am a weak vessel, it sputtered, over and over again.

Martin and I rented a two-bedroom apartment on Belmont Avenue, not far from the harbor full of crisp white sailboats, webbed with intricate rigging. Thanks to a glowing reference letter written by the manager of the Oscar H. Will Seed Company, Martin was able to secure a position in the advertising department of the *Chicago Tribune*. We were suddenly respectable, saving our money and attending company parties, where only a handful of people seemed aware of our clashing colors.

I was determined to make Martin happy in the small ways left to me. My hair was once again firmly pressed into a flip, and I added depth to my face with a dark brown eyebrow pencil and a tube of coral-red lipstick. I cleaned the apartment regularly and thoroughly, paying attention to even the smallest details. I starched our linen so that it had snap to it and a crisp fragrance, and the snowy white curtains I'd sewn by hand billowed spotlessly at each open window. I scented every bureau drawer with potpourri, scoured the ceilings with a rag-wrapped broom to discourage cobwebs, and I polished our two fluted wineglasses until they sparkled from the recesses of the kitchen cabinet, though we had yet to use them.

Isabel Lundstrom appeared at our front door on the first Monday in June, while I was beating rugs on our back porch, dust and lint powdering me like pollen. I heard the knock and ran through the long chain of rooms, slinging the door open so abruptly that I frightened Martin's mother and even myself. We both started.

"Oh," she gasped, "oh." I had never met Isabel Lundstrom, but I recognized her from a photograph Martin had placed on our mantel.

"Come in, Mrs. Lundstrom, please. Let me help you." She had an alarming number of suitcases and shopping bags scattered around her feet. I wondered how she'd managed the two flights. "I hope you didn't haul these upstairs yourself."

"No, there was a cabdriver," she said. She finally stepped inside the apartment and I wrestled with her bags, carrying them into the spare bedroom. One shopping bag was torn at the bottom, and the contents spilled to the floor with a great clatter.

"Not to worry, it's just the *plätpanna*." She pointed to a massive iron pancake pan I was lucky hadn't landed on my foot. Despite the heat, she was wearing a heavy woolen overcoat, which I helped her remove. Beneath it she wore a brown cardigan and a yellow scarf tied at her throat. When she cocked her head to the side I nearly giggled; she was the picture of a stout meadowlark.

We sat in the narrow kitchen with a view of rickety back porches, our faces hanging over the pot of tea so we could inhale the steam.

"Smells wonderful," said Isabel, but she didn't appear as though she meant it. "I hope a visit won't be inconvenient. Martin is very young, and I want to be certain he's eating properly. His appetite was always poor. It was such a battle to get him to eat any fruit, I sometimes feared he would suffer the shame of scurvy."

Isabel left the table, and I heard her rummaging through her shopping bags. She returned with a sack of oranges in one hand and a tin of brittle gingersnaps in the other. "These are Martin's all-time favorite cookie. I usually make them only at Christmas, but I wanted to bring him something special."

"This is certainly a treat," I assured her.

She decided to take a nap so that she would be refreshed by the time Martin returned from work. "Just a catnap," she said. "Please wake me one half-hour before you think he'll be here. Two days of sitting up on the train, I must surely be a wreck. No, don't tell me different. I'm puffed and strained and creaking.''

Isabel swept into the spare bedroom, and I put my head down on the table. I needed time to digest this new development, this sudden hitch, but I had dinner to prepare and was still covered with a thick layer of dust. In moments Isabel's dainty snores issued forth from her room, whistling in my ears like a tune. I found it impossible to form a single coherent thought. Just as one floated toward consciousness, fragile as a bubble, Isabel's piercing note popped it mercilessly, and I remained bewildered.

Martin's arrival sparked a squall of tears; a typhoon washed over him, embraced him, and only reluctantly let him go. Isabel aged ten years in the time it took him to cross the threshold; her mouth went slack, and her hands developed a subtle tremble.

"She's made such a long trip!" he said, to her, not to me. "Oh, she must be exhausted!"

"Well, yes. My recovery time isn't what it was, but I have only to look at you and all will be well."

This threatened to be a prolonged visit, and I decided then and there that I would be pleasant about it. Isabel would be my penance, my hair shirt, and I willingly shouldered the burden. Foolishly, I hadn't thought to alter our Monday-night menu in honor of Isabel's arrival. I realized my mistake when I set the food on the table. It looked bright and ridiculous: clown's food, fit for a child's birthday party. I served spicy tacos, a bowl of peas, grape-flavored Kool-Aid, and butterscotch pudding for dessert.

Isabel nibbled at the peas and picked a few morsels of hamburger from the orange sauce. "Very nice," she said. "Very tasty."

After dinner she offered to wash the dishes. "The cook mustn't do everything," she scolded. "You need your rest after such a spread."

We struggled over a dish—I insisted she should visit with her son and leave the task to me—and we both relented at the same moment, letting go of the plate, which then crashed to the floor.

"I'll get it!" we both cried, and we nearly knocked heads in our haste to pick up the pieces.

Martin poked his head into the kitchen. "Is everything okay?"

He didn't wait for an answer but limped toward us, his arms spread wide so he could embrace us simultaneously. "It's grand to have everyone together!" he said. And for just a moment I *was* reminded of Tiny Tim, disloyal as that felt. He was beaming, bouncing a little on the balls of his feet. He never noticed the look that passed between his mother and his wife.

My life quickly became one long home economics course. I majored in Smorgasbord and minored in Patience. I learned to make Swedish pancakes with lingonberry jam, potato griddle cakes, spiced red cabbage, fried salt herring, home-cured ham and pork sausage, limpa bread, shortbread, cardamom coffee cake, almond tortes, and walnut meringues. Martin gained five pounds, and one evening before he switched off the bedroom light, he thanked me for being so kind to his mother.

"She's getting old," he said.

"Well, sixty-two," I reminded him.

"That's old for some people, especially when they're alone. I think she's doing better with us than she ever did before."

I kissed his mouth to quiet him and yanked on his cow-licks. Lately they threatened to disappear, so I trained them when I could, bullied them into maintaining their former rebellion.

"Don't ever change," I told my husband.

I discovered an eerie parallel between mother and son. Evidently Martin's reluctance to address people directly was an inherited trait. Isabel wouldn't say anything to correct me when I made mistakes but instead left little notes around the kitchen to guide me. I came to despise her fancy rounded script.

Needs more salt, she taped to casserole lids. *Cake fell!!* she penned, when it was hardly necessary. Or, *I saved this from burning to a crisp.* I even found a note in the bathtub; I had nearly washed it down the drain. *Too much grit,* she admonished, so I switched to another cleanser.

I found her most agreeable when she was dressing her hair for the day. It was a complicated procedure, involving the careful pinning of waves, the arrangement of tortoise-shell combs, and the twisting of fine silver-blond hair. She was solemn and quiet for those twenty minutes and never offered an opinion—written or otherwise—on any subject. I liked to watch her fuss with the waist-length tresses; it was her single vanity. Gradually I came to notice that the ritual was difficult for her, painful. Sometimes her fingers slipped and she'd have to begin again. I offered to help, and for the longest time she refused. It wasn't until autumn, when the damp cold must have penetrated her bones, that she sighed in defeat.

"A simple bun will do," she told me.

"I'm not good at this," I admitted. "But if you help me, tell me what to do, I know I'll get it right eventually."

I think she appreciated the effort, so she made one of her own: forcing herself to speak directions, to interrupt my movements with a helpful comment. We managed best when she sat at a low dressing table Martin had bought from the Salvation Army. We both faced the old warped mirror and watched as her hair was transformed from a tangled mass into a sculpted crown. By December, Isabel allowed me to brush her hair before we pinned it, and I could tell she enjoyed the sensation, for she closed her eyes and her wrinkles smoothed as I applied one hundred tender strokes.

The week before Christmas, Isabel took the brush from my hand as I made ready to fix her hair. She covered my hand with her own, squeezing it. We stared into the mirror, gray eyes finding brown, our hands clasped together and our breathing perfectly still. Her palm was rough from so many years of housework, but the touch didn't chafe; her raw hands felt like silk to me.

"I want to show you something," Isabel said. She opened a little drawer in the center of her dressing table and removed a black velvet box. "My grandmother made this when she first came to this country."

The box opened with a whine, revealing a tiny painted bird's egg, no larger than a thimble. "Isn't it cunning?" she said. She lifted it from the fabric nest and placed it in my hands. "You see, it's a miniature globe." The egg was blue and its continents worked in cheerful vermilion, each line delicate as thread.

"She must have used an eyelash," I said, awed by the careful effort.

"I don't know how she did it. My mother never told me. But there is a story connected with this little egg I'd like to tell you."

"You better take it first," I said. "I don't want to squash it, it's so fine." We settled the egg back in the box but left the lid open so we could admire it from a safe distance. I took a seat on Isabel's bed, and she turned her stool to face me.

"I had twin sisters," she said, and then stopped. She fingered the yarn fringe of her shawl. "Their names were Beatrice and Dagmar, but everyone just called them 'the angels' because they were such beautiful little girls. They had thick blond ringlets like gold coins, and green eyes Mother said were emeralds stolen from Africa. I adored them, plain and simple. They were five years younger, but I never thought they were a nuisance underfoot. I liked to make up stories to tell them late at night, when they had trouble falling asleep. 'Bell,' they called me. 'Tell us something, Bell.' "

Isabel paused, caressed the egg with one finger. "Mother and I always saved the milk for them to drink. The rest of us drank water. The milk cow must have eaten a toxic weed one time, because she suffered like a poisoned thing, thrashed on the ground and took so long to die. We didn't kill her, because we kept hoping she'd recover. Cows were so valuable back then.

"When the girls got sick the doctor came and gave them paregoric for the colic. 'But they're poisoned,' Father spoke up. Doctors were like God in those days, and when our doctor said they weren't poisoned, well, they weren't. The angels died no more than an hour after he left. The end was terrible, but they never let go of each other's hands, and my parents ordered a special coffin so they could be buried like that, side by side."

Isabel pinched her nightgown between her fingers. "My parents were distraught. My mother said there was no life for her without the angels. I was so strange: I couldn't cry. I missed them, but I couldn't cry at all. Mother decided to bury Grandmother's egg with the angels. 'It passes from mother to daughter,' she said, 'and now it is the end of the line.' Mother lifted the white satin coverlet we'd spread over them, and placed the egg beneath their clasped hands. I was set to watch over my sisters while Father took care of Mother. I guess you know I robbed them. It was wrong. But Crystal, I would do it again. It wasn't right for Mother to forget that I existed.''

Isabel rose and shut the lid of the box. ''It wasn't the end of the line, and it still isn't. I pass this on to you.''

I now possessed two objects I prized above all others: Isabel's painted egg and a beaded turtle amulet I kept hidden beneath my slips. I set them both out on my bureau, one beside the other, and meant to leave them there together. I quickly decided against it. There was something about the turtle that unnerved me; it looked so alive, so capable of cracking the egg's delicate shell with its hinged jaws, devouring the globe and its vivid continents and slippery oceans.

I had given birth to a baby girl. I know this because Anna Thunder said, her voice triumphant, ''I *knew* it would be a girl!''

I asked for the umbilical cord so I could slip it in the turtle amulet I wore around my neck. My mother handed the cord to me. ''I'll stitch it up later,'' she said. ''I'm busy.'' But I intended to sew the amulet closed myself.

Then she cleaned the baby with a warm washcloth and wrapped her in flannel.

Now I'll get to hold her, I thought. But Anna left the room with my baby caught up in her arms.

"Mama, what are you doing?!" I cried. She returned moments later with a drink like spiced cider. It soothed me, helped me to relax.

"Everything is fine," she said. "Fine and dandy, just like candy."

Had I heard wrong? My mother sounded foolish, girlish. The world broke apart, and when I tried to fit the pieces back together, I got it wrong. I thought I saw my mother waltzing with the baby. She spun toward the ceiling in defiance of gravity, and I was looking at the soles of her shoes. Then I was flying, or floating, out the window, onto a feather mattress settled in the bed of a pickup truck. Roger Bonnin's face swooped toward mine and then swelled to fill the horizon. I wanted to scream, but my tongue was thick cotton. Snow sparkled in the air; it was crushed diamonds, and its dust covered me until my staring eyes went blind.

Martin found me curled in the backseat of his Thunderbird, empty, wrapped in quilts. When he asked me what had happened, I knew, even though I couldn't remember. My spirit belonged to me, free and clear, for the first time since I grew in the bowl of my mother's womb. But the price was my daughter's soul. Anna Thunder had stolen my child to raise, to cast in her own image so she would never die. My hand shook as I reached inside my nightgown. Was anything left? Then relief washed through me: the beaded turtle was there.

"Where is the baby?" Martin asked me. He was digging through the quilts as if she might be nestled there. I covered his warm hands with mine. I sent a chill through him, because my touch was ice.

"The baby is dead," I told him.

• • •

I do not know my daughter's name, or the shape of her face. In dreams she stands with her back to me, her hair in tight braids, stiff like black ropes.

"Ina," she says—mama—but she is speaking to my own mother, who sits before her and looks at me over my daughter's head. Anna smiles. *Such a good girl,* she says in these dreams, and although she is looking at me, straight into my eyes, I know she doesn't mean me.

Sometimes I wear the turtle amulet Anna made for my baby. Coiled inside the beaded shell is her umbilical cord, a dry piece of flesh that ties me to the small girl with black braids poking down her back like sharp spears. The amulet is meant to guard her from ill health and other calamities, but I have taken it because it is the mother's job to keep a child safe. If I protect the amulet, then surely I will protect the girl. At least this is the story I tell myself when I wake up from those dreams in which my daughter stands with her back to me and will not turn when I call, will not tip her face in my direction so I can see if she looks anything like me.

For as long as I could remember, my mother was pre-occupied with her boyfriends. She had a great hunger that was never satisfied. They marched up her stairs, awkward as puppets, their empty eyes proof of some troubled magic. Those eyes were spilled ink, drained of love and hope. If they reflected anything at all, it was surely fear and not my mother's beautiful lined face.

I understand now that my mother's lovemaking was despair, but when I was little I thought it was her great adventure. The sounds fascinated me: animal cries, the shrill creak of her brass bed, but mostly the *tap tap* of her knee knocking against the wall. I was on the other side of that barrier, and I liked to press my hands against the flaking plaster and feel the vibrations.

I came to believe that her rhythmic knock was a hidden message, a kind of code. In the library I discovered a thick book on a secret language called International Morse Code: a series of dots and dashes, short raps and long thumps. Finally I could translate my mother's most potent signal, her purest magic. The next night I listened carefully at my post, ear against the wall, jotting marks on a yellow tablet. A pattern was forming, a regular series of sounds played over and over like a song with many verses: *Dash-dash-dot / Dot-dash-dot / Dot-dash / Dot-dot-dot / Dot-dot-dot.*

Grass, she said. My mother's knee spelled *grass.* I collapsed with disappointment. Was this the great secret I had so eagerly anticipated? I flung the book to the floor and pulled the covers over my head.

Grass. I couldn't escape the word; its stiff tattoo pounded against my wall. I could not make sense of it until I imagined my mother on the plains surrounded by tall grass, perhaps little bluestem, rising to her shoulder. I could see her move with the stalks, ripple in the wind, her hands in the air and fingers spread like wispy flowers. My mother's roots drilled deep, and she would not be plucked. I thought that if anyone tried, he would tear up the earth, and a tongue of flame would shoot from the core, straight to his heart.

Okay, I told myself. *Mama is the grass.* And me? I couldn't have said as a child. But now I know that I am not like Anna Thunder. I am one of those seeds that will push up tentative shoots wherever I land.

6

A Hole in the Sheets

Anna Thunder
(1961)

JEANNETTE MCVAY'S PERFUME SET THE DOGS BARKING. IT
was Chanel No. 5, and I should know, because I once had
enough of it to fill my porcelain tub. I had a sudden whim
to submerge my flesh in its sweetness and sent my boyfriend of the time, Roger Bonnin—his pockets bulging with
lease money—into Bismarck to fetch me some of that nec-
tar. I went in slow, made it a misery, and when the liquid
closed over me, with just my head poking out like the olive
in a cocktail, I knew I was something spun of gold or mined
from a vein of precious rock. I knew I was special. Which
Jeannette McVay was not, though intoxicated by her own
spirit of misadventure.

"Hello-o-o, there's no be-ell," she sang in a bright voice
too bleakly cheery to hide her fear. I let the dogs—two
fierce brothers named Gall and Crazy Horse—lunge and
scratch at the kitchen door; I could hear claws raking the
screen. Their growls were crushed gravel in their throats.

"Okay, pipe down," I said when I was finally bored.

I didn't let that girl in right away. I'd seen her step out
of Herod Small War's blood-colored Pontiac, which was
bottom-heavy as a matron, and that old criminal was not
someone I called friend. *What's he landed on my door?* I
wondered, not eager to find out.

Jeannette's Chanel fragrance entered my house before
she did. She was wary of the dogs and hampered by the

tallest suitcase I'd ever seen, the sleek texture and color of a shark.

"This isn't a rooming house, despite what you may have been told," I said.

"Oh, I know," she puffed. "I take this wherever I go, because home is with me at this moment."

"You've just told me more than I wanted to hear," I said. I thought it would make her pause on the back porch, but she moved ahead and dragged that monster suitcase into my kitchen. "If I weren't Sioux, I'd walk you through the house and usher you right out the front door," I told the girl. "But as it is, I'm Dakota, and that means I'm going to feed you something first."

She laughed at that, and I stopped to watch her because her mouth was like a balloon releasing air. "I didn't know you had such a sense of humor," she said. I had the idea she didn't mean me personally but was making some vague reference to my people. I opened a can of commodity peaches, letting my little finger trail in the syrup so I could taste it. I placed a bowl of the sweet fruit before her, and a glass of cool water. "This is the best," she sighed. We sat in silence for the next few minutes while she finished that bowl, and a second, and a third.

Jeannette McVay, as she turned out to be, was tall and bony, like a set of wooden rulers tacked together to make a stick-figure girl. She had one brown hair for every blond one, and all of it was pulled back into a limp ponytail, thin as a pencil. She had eyes the color of tarnished nickels and skin that looked stained and yellow like a smoker's fingers, but the balls of her cheeks popped out in bright happy circles, wearing a faint wash of pink as if she'd pinched them.

"What a generous lady you are," she said when the can of peaches was gone.

"You speak too soon," I warned.

"You must be wondering what this is all about, this intrusion." She laughed again, and I could smell the peaches. "Well, let me lay it all out to get you even." Before she began her explanation, Jeannette put on eyeglasses with heavy black frames that swept up at the corners into wings. The glasses didn't fit properly, so she was constantly adjusting them, her cuticle-bitten finger pushing them onto the bridge of her nose.

"What's this?" I said. "You need to see the words as they come out of your mouth?"

"No," she said, all serious. "I want to see *you.*" So I was quiet, and she chattered like a ground squirrel, her head tipped to one side and then to the other, her thin yellow hands pressed between her knees.

"I come from Pennsylvania," she told me. "A little town you wouldn't know, although it has its share of moguls who flatter themselves they're running the world. Well, maybe they are." She paused here and looked at me as if to inquire: *What do you think about that?*

I didn't even blink.

"So this is the boring part," she continued. "My father is a work-obsessed dad who hasn't said more than five words to me since giving me life, and my mother is a country club mental with a waist smaller than Scarlett O'Hara's and a brain pickled in Long Island iced tea. She's said plenty to me, none of it pertinent. The good news is that I spent the last four years of my life at a girls' college, East Coast but *not* Pennsylvania, a place where everything is relevant, an issue. I studied archaeology, and that led to anthropology and mythology. I'm going to go to graduate school, but first I thought I'd do some work in the field, get firsthand experience and go out there to meet humanity rather than just slip it under a microscope or flash slides of it across some institutional-green wall." Jeannette sipped her water and sloshed it in the glass. One tiny swell washed over the lip and spattered her skirt.

"My parents think I'm part of a team of graduates—you know, complete with funding and dorm rooms and ancient chaperones. They think I flew, but I took the bus all the way to Bismarck and then hitched to the reservation, and let me say, that was a thesis in and of itself." Jeannette laughed as she sipped.

"I thought this was going to be a thing about death: dead culture, dead language, dead God. I came out here to record the funeral, so to speak. Collect data on how a people integrate this kind of loss into their souls. And you know what? I found all this activity and vitality and living mythology. I feel like I've stumbled upon a secret."

My daughter Crystal suddenly charged into the kitchen, having just returned from school. She was a freshman in high school, and her canvas bookbag was heavy with texts. I noticed for the first time that her school uniform—a green plaid jumper—was almost obscenely tight; it was a girl's size, while she was nearly a woman. She rinsed her hands in the sink and splashed water on her face. She'd brought the smell of springtime into the warm kitchen, and it made my ankles itch.

"Come meet our company," I said. "A visitor from the East." Crystal looked as uninterested as I felt. She shook Jeannette's hand but quickly backed out of the kitchen and went upstairs. I heard the phonograph hum as it warmed up and then strains of that number I called the oily song because the lyrics were all about slipping and sliding.

"I have to get this down," Jeannette mumbled. "A Sioux girl listening to Little Richard."

I am not considered a patient woman. "You have yet to place yourself in my kitchen," I said.

Jeannette put down her spiral notebook, its metal spine crooked and tortured-looking. "That's right. We're not there yet," she said. She nudged her glasses higher.

"When I first got here and asked about your religion and your medicine people, I was sent straightaway to Herod Small War. He was nice enough, but prejudiced against women. I was barred from his sweat lodge and couldn't take part in his Yuwipi ceremony because I was on my period. When I argued with him and told him about a few little developments, such as a woman's right to vote, he told me I could not vote my way into his ceremony or his sweat lodge. What's the use of studying with someone like that, who excludes me, doesn't recognize me as a full-functioning peer? So I asked about the women, and they told me: you." Jeannette removed her glasses and pulled out the tail of her cotton shirt to clean them. When she repositioned them on her nose, crescents of fog smudged the lenses. Jeannette was a sphere of heat; I could feel the mercury rising.

"I was told such stories—they were legends really, but alive and moving upon this earth. I absorbed the tales, marveled that you were nothing less than Aphrodite, Goddess of Desire, with her magic girdle that helped her spell the other deities and mortal men. But think how wonderful this is, because you're not in some book or reclining on Mount Olympus. You're right here in the kitchen, serving me peaches!"

Jeannette reached for my hand, but I anticipated her move and clasped my hands to form a single fist. The girl pinched the scarred wooden table instead. Steam enveloped her lenses, so I couldn't see her eyes when she whispered urgently: "Anna Thunder, I want to get to know you, understand you, see you in action. You are modern magic and miracles I was raised to think were passé—no, worse than that: were gone forever. In short, I am here because I revere you."

I was no Aphrodite, Goddess of Desire, and I never wore a girdle in my whole life, though I have spread until my sitting end is broad as Texas. I was fifty-one years old, and my face was pleated by early disaster—what people so innocently call "hard times." I was not one to gaze long in the mirror beyond parting my hair in a straight line, and I knew the tips of my fingers were squashed-looking from so many years of beadwork, but my breath was sweet with the taste of wild plums and my eyes were black as those cut into gambling dice, and if I looked into a man I could lower a line so skillfully it would hook his heart. Then I would jerk it right out of his throat. I collected so many I kept thinking I would get my fill of them, but I never did.

Medicine pulsed within me, shot through my veins, and I don't mean the kind a doctor pumps into the body. I didn't practice good medicine or bad medicine, or a weak magic summoned by poems; I simply had potent blood inherited from my grandmother's sister, Red Dress. And there were times when it pained me like a fire, or froze me like a rock, and any weaker person would have crawled toward death.

Jeannette McVay, that little white girl with pennies in her penny loafers and a plaid kilt fastened with what looked like a diaper pin, could see this power in me, and it raised her temperature. Her nickel eyes rubbed against mine, flint striking flint, and sparks shot around the kitchen. *Everybody duck,* I thought to myself, and had to pull a smile through all those wrinkles.

I will be the first to say it: Jeannette McVay appealed to

my vanity. And who *wouldn't* enjoy being admired, quoted, chronicled? One cannot be a pariah without feeling the effects, and the very qualities my neighbors feared were those Jeannette valued. I allowed her to stay in my house for an unspecified period of time, and when I learned that she'd picked up a colony of head lice in her travels, I spent several evenings combing them out with kerosene.

"That feels so wonderful, it's worth the experience of lice," Jeannette murmured as I worked through her hair in sections.

I thought to myself, *This is what it's like to have a daughter,* because my own daughter was increasingly withdrawn, always putting a door between us.

"Crystal, your dinner is ready," I had to call every evening, only to watch her take it upstairs to eat in her bedroom like an invalid. I would have welcomed rebellion, but this was a complicated surrender. If I insisted she have dinner in my company at the kitchen table, she ate furtively, in pecks and nibbles, her brown eyes growing larger by the minute until they looked capable of sliding across her face like runny eggs skidding off a plate.

Two weeks after Jeannette made her appearance, I scolded Crystal, telling her: "You should stick around and listen like this little *wašičun* girl. This is your story I'm telling, not just mine."

"I have a test tomorrow," she whispered, and although she was taller than her mother, she had backed so far into her shadow she seemed small enough for me to settle on my palm. My daughter was the color of a chestnut mare, and her eyes rolled white like a shy pony's to avoid my gaze. It was too easy to dip into those eyes; I looked away. Jeannette was furiously chewing gum—it sounded like a string of firecrackers set off in her mouth—while she studied samples of my beadwork: a few pairs of moccasins and a child's vest.

"Be careful what you throw away," I told my daughter. "Be cautious with your spirit, because it can fill up with the wrong things. I will tell you a secret," I murmured. Crystal flinched, and it was all I could do not to slap her. The scent of plums left my mouth. "Too many people don't believe in their souls, don't recognize them when they feel the spirit twist against their heart or snap across their brain. And some that do believe hand their spirits over to the care of others, just give them blithely away, though they may be tightfisted when it comes to their coins. I own my spirit. Can you say that? How many can say that? How many have fingered that cobweb veil? I've fingered yours. I know its texture. It tastes like bitter apricots."

Crystal stumbled toward the stairs, collapsing into her shadow. "I have a test," she sobbed.

"You will have many," I tried to assure her. But she had already glided up the steps and melted into the walls of her room.

That night I couldn't sleep, though I had plumped the pillows and folded down the quilt, which was too heavy for the mild air. My daughter's thoughts were noisy on the other side of my bedroom wall. Her mind was full of children's voices: a whining, a litany of complaints, a chain of foolish songs. I wanted hinges and a latch worked beneath her hair so I could smother all that noise.

It wasn't until morning that I slipped into a light, anguished doze; every muscle was tense and cramping, my fists strangling the sheets and teeth chewing the pillow. I dreamt it was my daughter's ear caught between my teeth and I was beading her thoughts, picking into her brain with my needle. And oh, the sparkling cells were easy to string!

I am beading you a medallion, I told her. *A new brave heart for you to wear around your neck.* But when I awakened there were no beads, no busy needle, and my daughter's thoughts were scattered throughout the house, uncollected, an explosion of them like shattered glass.

Spring had nearly ended. It was a balmy morning, and I was already seated on my back porch, welcoming the crimson light. I was busy braiding the tassels of wild turnips to chain their bulbs together. I sang an old Dakota song to encourage the sun in its rising:

> *She came in a red dress,*
> *that sacred woman.*
> *She was a warrior in a red dress.*

I had a deep drum voice I could throw for some distance. On this morning I cast it to the ground so it sounded as if my notes came from a hole in the earth. When I saw a storm of dust washing toward me, I thought my song had stirred the creatures from their burrows. But moments later I noticed the mud-speckled blue vehicle ripping through the center of that cloud. It was Calvin Wind Soldier of the tribal police. I continued my work and pushed my voice to drum harder, until I made those spinning tires vibrate. The car barreled down the gravel road, spitting rocks, and looked as though it would crunch its way right through my house. I stood my ground. Finally it rolled to a stop just outside my unpainted fence, nudging it lightly like a horse against its hitching post. Some former boyfriend of mine, whose name has gone down the well, had decided to build that fence, but he couldn't have lasted long, because the pickets extended for about five feet and then ended in space, attached to nothing, leaning this way and that like broken teeth.

Two figures emerged from the car: Calvin Wind Soldier, fresh as rain, his black hair lightly oiled and holster creaking, and Jeannette McVay, naked but for a towel.

"I threw my clothes out the window," she said. "But not my shoes." They dangled from her fingers. "I've got narrow feet, hard to find a good size, so I won't make a statement with these. But the rest went flying!"

Calvin moved past her as if she weren't there. He walked to the porch and rested one foot on the bottom step. "Did you put her up to this?" he asked me.

"I don't know what she's done, but you can tell me over a cup of coffee," I said.

"Can't." Calvin shook his head. "There's a carnival setting up in town, and the crazies will be trailing onto the reservation. She can tell you what happened. I'm not sure I understand. Keep an eye on her. If she's staying here, then she's your responsibility."

I stood up and walked over to Calvin Wind Soldier. I set the string of wild turnips across his shoulder and held out my hand. He shook it lightly, barely touching, which is the proper way. "You take those home," I told him.

Calvin thanked me and patted the turnips. "Soup tonight," he said. He looked into my eyes.

It felt as though the morning went cold, the air became blades sharpening their edges against my skin. I almost trembled. I almost told him: *I forgot what it's like to see eyes clean of fear.* I soaked in that look, and after Calvin drove away, I watched the dust trail him like smoke. I watched it hover, fall, and settle.

Jeannette stalked through the kitchen, her bare feet slapping the dull yellow linoleum. "We heard you, Anna, from way back," she said. "Your voice was coming from everywhere, and even though I was mad, hopping mad, I registered that this was another one of those unaccountable things you do. I wished I had a recording device. I liked the way it surrounded me and filled me up and said, *Jeannette, I am bigger than you and come from someplace you know nothing about.*" The girl stopped pacing to pluck a splinter from the pad of her heel.

"So tell me why you're doing a striptease on the highway," I prompted.

"No, I was already stripped," she said, as if that explained everything. "I was determined to take part in a sweat, to rid myself of the last vestiges of East Coast snobbery and foolishness, of my petty issues, which I well know are nothing compared to the struggles I see around here. But let me point out before I continue that I think it's an accomplishment for me to even realize this. My folks would never get it that a balloon payment on the mortgage, or busted Waterford crystal, isn't the be-all and end-all."

Jeannette dropped suddenly on her haunches to kiss my dogs, which she had won over with baby talk and beef jerky. "I walked all the way over to Herod Small War's place. I know his schedule. I know he likes to start the day off with a sweat. He and Archie Iron Necklace and Bill Good Voice Elk. They got it going pretty good, and their assistant was busy heating more rocks, when I stepped inside there."

"Wearing what?" I asked.

"Wearing me, just me. I took my clothes off at the entrance. But there was so much smoke it wasn't a show or anything."

"They must have liked that," I said.

"You would think that they would finally see my pure

sincerity, the depth of my respect and willingness to learn. But they are blind as my parents. Herod flapped his hand and told me, 'Shoo.' Like I was some fly. 'Shoo. Shoo. Men and women don't share a sweat.'

"I said, 'So if I was some white guy who probably didn't even believe in any of this, you'd welcome me with open arms?' At least he was honest. He said, 'No. If you were a white guy I'd give you a bloody nose.' Then the assistant called Calvin to bring me back here, and I was protesting. I wouldn't budge. They put me in the car and gave me my clothes. They're out there somewhere.'' She waved at the distant road.

I wagged my head at the girl. "Jeannette McVay, why do you need these men?"

"I could ask you the same thing," she said.

Later that day she questioned me: "Why is it that people take their spiritual matters to Herod Small War even though he doesn't have one shred of your control, while your name they speak in whispers? It's a thing against women, right?"

"That's easy," I told Jeannette. "Herod waits for them to come to him, waits for their tears and their sad little stories, their confusion and illnesses, their fear of death. I enter before they invite me in."

Calvin's square face was before me as I worked in my garden. I crumbled soil in my hand and imagined its soft rushing motion was like his shiny hair slipping through my fingers. Straight flat eyebrows stretched across his face like the even line of the horizon, and his eyes rose beneath them like two black suns. I caressed his skin as I collected the tomatoes and said his name in Dakota: "Tate Akičita." I dug with my trowel and planted that name alongside the parsley.

"Anna, I made lemonade," I heard Jeannette call from the kitchen. I left Calvin, and the name buried in my garden. "You've been preoccupied," Jeannette said. "Is it the stunt bothering you? I won't try it again."

I held lemonade on my tongue, cool and sweet and bitter. I shook my head. "I'm just recalling stories."

"Tell me, tell me," she murmured. She pulled her chair closer to me and nearly spilled her lemonade.

"This is an old story, from a hundred years ago," I began. I told her about my grandmother's sister, Red Dress, who had been a woman warrior. "She killed a number of U.S. Army soldiers," I said. Jeannette tittered like a lark sparrow. She hugged her knees to her chest and wiggled her bare toes.

I talked about the love between this woman and a Dakota warrior named Ghost Horse. "That policeman who brought you back this morning, Calvin Wind Soldier, is descended from him. Ghost Horse's brother was Calvin's great-grandfather. Ghost Horse was *heyo'ka,* one of our old-time clowns. Today people refer to them as contraries, because they had to work in opposites." I told Jeannette she better not dream about the thunderbirds who rule the sky, or she too would have to appease them with perverse behavior that antagonized people.

"I think I already do that," she said.

"My stories never have a happy ending," I warned the girl. I proceeded to tell her that the lovers never came together, that some believed they were still searching for one another in the open country.

"It's like Cathy and Heathcliff," she interrupted.

I nodded. "Yes, it is a little like *Wuthering Heights.*"

"You know that book?"

"I knew it once."

Jeannette pressed her thumbnail into her knee. She was curious; I could see the fog creep across her lenses. But I would not say more on the subject. That is a road I left behind me and will not travel again, for anyone.

Jeannette dragged around the house all day, morose. I told her to take a hot shower, that would surely draw Pennsylvania out of her pores, but she didn't even smile.

"We're going to the carnival," I announced, promising: "We're going to cheer you up." I knocked on Crystal's door. I could see her so plainly through the wood grain it was like X-ray vision. I knew she was huddled on her bed, surrounded by books and magazines that did nothing to transport her. "Come with us to the carnival," I said through the door. "We're going to make some mischief."

"No," she answered. "My finals are coming up next week."

Your finals are useless knowledge, I wanted to tell her, but I was suddenly tired. *My blood is somewhere inside you, percolating,* I thought to myself. *It will show in time.* So I let her close up like a box.

The carnival was in full swing by the time we arrived. The rides were lit, streaking neon colors against the night sky. Shells of sunflower seeds crackled beneath our feet, and lean dogs prowled behind the concession stands. Jeannette pointed out two of them fighting over a hamburger bun.

"I've never seen such a people for dogs, they're everywhere roaming loose," she said. "But I thought your tribe liked to eat them too. Have you ever tasted dog meat?"

"I only eat poodles," I said. Jeannette laughed a beat too late.

She pitched tennis balls at tin cans, and I chewed corn

dogs, my eyes scanning the crowd. Finally I saw him, one arm wrapped around his young wife, the other draped over his sister-in-law's shoulder. The women were twin sisters but very different. Calvin's wife, Lydia, was nearly six feet tall, and graceful in her body. She wore her long braids pinned around her ears like a little Swiss girl, and she never wore lipstick or any paint on her face but it was bright with color. Her dark eyes reflected light the way people say only white can. Calvin seemed drawn to their shine; he searched them again and again. Evelyn looked much older than her sister. She was half a head shorter than Lydia, and her body sagged with fatigue. The lashes rimming her eyes were short spikes, and her hair was a dense thicket. I didn't often see her with Calvin and Lydia. She was usually in the company of a rodeo cowboy named Philbert, but their romance was such an up-and-down drama it was difficult to keep current. I was surprised to hear Evelyn laugh. It cut me. I became angry with the three of them: their careless pace, the tangle of their arms, their breezy voices.

I watched as Lydia tucked her slim hand in Calvin's back pocket. *It's empty,* I told that foolish, untroubled girl. *Nothing is there.*

As I walked across the carnival grounds, I was like Moses parting the Red Sea; my neighbors swept to either side, watchful, humming like wasps. The only one to stagger in my path was Chester Brush Horns. He stood with his head down and hands thrust deep in his pockets.

"What is it, Chester?" I asked him.

"No money," he said, his eyes still on the ground. "I could sure use some smokes too."

"I can do that," I said.

I was so weary and blue I took the trouble to collect Chester Brush Horns. It was no triumph, for he was pliant, his mind a crushed bird. I don't remember what the damage was—a car accident, a beating, or a drunken fall from a window. It didn't really matter. He was handsome in pieces, but the placement was all wrong. His features were crowded around the center of his face, orbiting his nose the way darts cluster around the target. But he was strong, and smiling now at the promise of tobacco. And it was so easy to dole out the cigarettes one at a time, stealing a pinch of the shredded leaves and dropping the flakes in my dress pocket.

"I want to ride the Ferris wheel," I told him. I bought two tickets, and Chester's hand was already seeking mine before we lifted into the night air. When our car reached the top and I looked out from our point of light at the dark land, I felt a sudden pull. Gravity sucked at the soles of my shoes, and I was heavy, a lodestone drawn toward the earth. It was a delicious moment. I think the attraction messed up the works, for the Ferris wheel became stuck, with our car riding at the top. Men hollered up at us: "We'll get it going again in no time." But I was unconcerned.

"Entertain me," I said to my companion.

Chester Brush Horns stood up in our car and bowed to me. He placed one hand on the seat and the other on the metal back, and carefully lifted his legs into a handstand. He puffed happily on the cigarette clenched between his teeth, and except for the tension in his arms, he looked peaceful. I heard gasps, but no one shouted.

"Pull him in," someone muttered from another car.

I smiled to myself and tried to spot my house in the distant shadows. I flicked the ash from Chester's cigarette when it burned down. "You could have been an acrobat," I told him.

And then, just to make things interesting, I gently set the car to rocking.

The next morning I woke in a bed of ashes, and my bedroom was gray with a pall of smoke. Chester Brush Horns, whose sense of balance was now legend, coughed himself awake.

"I hear Jeannette making breakfast," I told him. "If you want something to eat, you better get it now." He looked so disoriented I pointed to the door. His hair fell forward, covering his face, and he dressed silently.

"You're a serious smoker," I said. "It's going to get you in trouble one of these days." Chester Brush Horns didn't perch on my bed to pull on his boots, but gathered them, together with his socks, and hugged the bundle against his chest. He crept toward the door lightly, on his toes, as if I were still sleeping. So I said, "I'm awake now, Chester. You can go ahead."

He sprang for the doorknob and nearly dropped his boots as he struggled with the lock. The door flew open, slammed shut, and there I was, obscured by the haze, filling my lungs with acrid air. I knew Jeannette was alone at breakfast, just as I was certain that Chester Brush Horns was running down the gravel-sharp road, barefoot, shirttails flying, still clutching his socks and his boots.

Jeannette opened the bedroom window and beat the air with her skinny hands. "How can you breathe?" she complained. She was wearing crisp cotton pajamas and her winged eyeglasses. I waved her over to the bed.

"That guy took off from here like a bat out of hell," she said.

"I bet he did." I chuckled.

"You made him do that last night, didn't you?" she asked me. "I looked up and saw him rising out of that car. People were grumbling, you should have heard them. I thought they were going to string you up. To defend you, I said, 'He's a grown man.' But by that time it was all over."

"No one's going to string me up," I said with conviction. "You pay attention now," I told Jeannette, my voice low and steady. She scooted closer. "I am going to right a wrong of history." It felt strange to speak my thoughts; I had never announced my intentions before. The room filled with quiet, became heavy; I thought my bones would collapse and settle beneath the rest of me. My heart stopped in that moment, I know it did, until my hand massaged the spot and my voice exploded the silence: "You just watch."

Calvin Wind Soldier, whose name was planted in my garden and whose ancestor had so dearly loved mine, would find his way into my arms. We would close the unhappy circle, change the ending of that story I had been told so many times it seemed like my own life read back to me. Calvin was half my age, but I would live forever. I would never leave him. Already I could hear him calling me, *"Unči"*—grandmother—and we would laugh at how ridiculous that was, because my hands and knees could clamp like vises. I was so caught up in this dream, I felt it was already accomplished. *Not yet, old girl,* an inner voice warned. *Not yet.*

This would take a special skill, a profound concentration. Calvin Wind Soldier would not be trapped by powder in his soup or loose tobacco. He would not slump forward if I clapped my hands, or spend his last penny to purchase some desire I whispered in his ear. I closed myself in the bedroom and walked the floor. Jeannette brought me lunch on a tray, but I didn't touch it. I listened so closely to myself I heard my heart talking. *Simple is best,* it told me. *Plain is powerful.*

At sunset I stood in the yard, breathless, spade in hand. *Look at this wash of colors,* I told Calvin. *Look at how the sky is painting itself.*

How sad, I thought, *that even now Calvin Wind Soldier is oblivious to his coming happiness.* I dug into the ground with my spade, used my foot to plunge it into the mother's dark flesh. When the hole was a foot deep I knelt beside it and placed two objects in its mouth: an old rattlesnake rattle, once used as a baby's toy, and a wild plum that was not yet ripe. Then I covered them with a heavy rock so the dogs wouldn't be able to disturb them, and replaced the dirt.

Tonight I will find him, I said. And an instant later the sun ducked its head.

I sat right on the ground in my housedress, rocked myself to the beat of my heart. At some point I fell over onto my back, and the night sky pressed me down. Was I falling? The stars were spinning and the moon whirled, flat as a dime, and the grass below me grew into the weave of my dress. I heard the rattle hissing in the ground. I smelled the plum. As I clutched dirt in my fists and pointed my feet at the back door, just a few steps away, I journeyed to Calvin Wind Soldier's house. He was sitting out front on a truck tire.

"Lydia is going to paint this," he told me. "She's going to grow flowers in it like a planter."

"Lydia is yesterday," I said. "Anna is tomorrow." My dress had patch pockets, and I raided them now, removed the rattlesnake rattle and the green plum. "My auntie Red

Dress was a friend to snakes," I told the young man. "She wore their rattles in her hair to hear their voices. Your uncle loved her and planted a plum tree in her honor, but the fruit has gone untasted."

Calvin grinned at me, and I did not like to see his white teeth bared that way. I shouted, "Calvin Wind Soldier, I am claiming you!"

He held a finger to his lips. "Lydia isn't feeling well, and she is sleeping," he said. "I don't want your noise to wake her."

The ground trembled then, and the sky was black muslin—I wanted to tear it down the middle. "Where is your respect?" I bellowed. But that was too desperate. I made my voice a song. I crooned: "Wind Soldier, I am here to claim you. Wind Soldier, Anna is here."

"Of course you are," a third voice cackled. "We had a feeling you would come." An old man stepped from the house's shadow. It was Herod Small War, Jeannette's nemesis.

"Old man, you are nosy," I told him.

"Old woman, you are greedy. You go on home now and stop this mischief." Herod smiled, and I could see his back teeth were missing. His white hair glimmered in the moonlight. "I can make a few things," he was telling me. "You're not the only one. See this belt Calvin's wearing? I give it to him a long time ago and told him to wear it."

I looked at the piece of leather threaded through the loops of Calvin's blue jeans. It was snakeskin, not some common cowhide. The scales glistened with oil; I thought I saw them flex.

"You will not make your way past this belt," Herod continued. "Your fingers will slip and fumble and shake, and you will just embarrass yourself. I think you should go on home and leave this man to his wife. Remember who you came from. Your people didn't approve of this kind of fooling around.''

"Enough," I said. "I am too old for you to be lecturing." My daughter would have been surprised at my control. I knew she thought I was a cyclone spinning disaster, losing itself in its own fury. But I was deep calm, the cold dark water you find at the bottom of the sea.

I put away the rattle and the plum, held out my hands to show their emptiness. "You are too clever for me," I said. "Old man, you have more tricks than I thought possible." Herod grinned and shifted his weight. His body ached, the joints giving him pain; I could hear the flesh moan. I nearly felt pity for the aged man and his foolish manipulations, for the young man still seated on the tire, thinking all the time about his sleeping wife and how he would slip into bed beside her.

"I am gone," I said. I had turned my back, but I could hear them smile at one another. I knew the two men would sleep well that night, give themselves up to their dreams. Their hearts were peaceful because they didn't know the thing that powered me.

Later that night, when I came back to myself, I was cradled in my daughter's arms.

"Mama, why are you doing this?" she cried. Her tears fell onto my eyelids and slid across my cheeks. "I thought you were dead when I saw you stretched out on the ground."

I opened my eyes then and saw an oblong patch of light—the gaping back door of my house. Jeannette was standing in the doorway, flanked by the dogs. Her eyes looked strange to me, enormous and unblinking, until I realized I was staring at her glasses. I was in no hurry to move from my daughter's embrace. I reclined there, my empty hands in empty pockets, my eyes loose, rolling this way and that way, my tongue trapped.

"Little spider, let me go," I finally said, and Crystal released me so quickly I doubted I had ever been held. But that was good; I had to be firm with myself. "Fate will never ride me again," I told Crystal. "I broke that horse a long time ago and kicked it with my heels. I had to take my own spirit in hand, or it would have shriveled like gauze held to a flame, been consumed, and my mind would be in too many pieces for me to scrape together. So I am here, working my fate, driving it before it has the chance to drive me."

Jeannette stepped forward, out of the light. She hurried down the back steps. "What was that?" she called to me. "What was it you said?"

I held out my hand to Crystal and, with her help, rose to my feet. I was not a tall woman, but that night I grew. I was flying without leaving the earth. I shot into the darkness, higher and higher, until the clouds circled my breasts, the stars lightly burned my skin like embers falling to flesh, and the planet I stood on was a turquoise stone too small for a ring. I answered Jeannette, though she had disappeared far below me.

"I am Providence," I said.

My people don't always turn out for celebrations—weddings and graduations—but they will travel hundreds of miles for a funeral. A good wake becomes a family reunion, maybe even a political caucus; feasts are spread, matches made, sometimes children conceived, when we come together to honor the dead. So when I heard that old Albert

Elk Nation had departed this life, I became alert as the dogs. I could predict where my neighbors would be that night: congregating in the cavernous paneled meeting hall on the second floor of the tribal agency building. They would converge to shed their tears, eat their food, sing honor songs.

A month had passed since the night Herod Small War turned me away, and in that time I had mapped futures in my head, decided how a number of lives would turn. Jeannette asked me questions: "What will you do? How will it work?" And I answered plainly, letting her document my activities as if this were all a scientific experiment performed in a lab. She was so excited she was losing weight, just the opposite of Crystal, who increasingly craved soft starchy foods that rounded her figure, blurred her edges, made her less visible to my eyes.

But the things I did I managed alone, striding from empty house to empty house, using nothing more than a needle, thread, and a small pair of scissors. When my neighbors had left for the wake, I went first to Calvin Wind Soldier's house, entering boldly through the front door, which in those days was never locked. I found the bedroom in mere seconds and decided that the left side of the bed was his, because when my people dance as couples around the drum, the men are on the left and the women on the right. This was the side I revealed, though carefully, disturbing as little of the coverlet as possible; I would have to smooth the bedding when my work was done.

I imagined what Calvin would look like in that bed, how his body would relax against the mattress. I traced with my finger a small area on the sheet, a space I thought of as the Region of Lust. I crimped the material at its center and, with sharp scissors, snipped a piece of the fabric, such a small swatch my little finger couldn't push through the resulting hole.

Half a mile away, in the bedroom of a clean but flimsy shack, I repeated the process, only this time I worked on the right side of the bed, the woman's side, and repaired the tiny hole I'd just made, with the fabric from Calvin's sheet. It was so easy I was almost disappointed. Both sets of sheets were white, and the damage invisible unless you knew where to look. I had to return to Calvin Wind Soldier's place to mend his sheet with the material I'd taken from the other bed. I cut the thread. I restored order.

Perhaps my hands could not get past the belt he was wearing, perhaps they would remain lonely and never work happiness on Calvin Wind Soldier, but he would soon learn that there were other prying fingers and warm palms ready to touch him.

I was not a witness to the affair I had manipulated. I could only imagine the details. I don't know how many times Calvin Wind Soldier was late coming home to his wife or quick to leave her in the morning so that he could meet her twin sister, Evelyn, in some private spot. Maybe they used the back of his police car, feeling all the while like furtive criminals, or desecrated the top of Angry Butte, where young men went to cry for a vision. The only thing I knew for sure was that I had filled these young people with hurtful desires, changed the course of their destinies, because, after all, I could do it.

As I lay in bed at night, I thought to myself, *Perhaps right now Evelyn's bramble hair is scratching Calvin's face, as he flicks the blunt edges of her eyelashes with his tongue, tastes the tears leaking from her eyes.* I was sure their bodies would be heavy and their mouths would burn, and their limbs would ache and ache because there was no release in all this; the want would start up again as soon as they were apart. Sometimes I spoke to Lydia in the dark: *Isn't it funny how things end up? You're so young and beautiful and, everyone says, sweet, and now your arms are empty as mine. We are widows together.*

Slowly, gradually, like draining batteries, the cheating couple must have lost desire. The wonder of it is, my triumph was only beginning, for there would be a child. And he would have Calvin Wind Soldier's square face and even brow, but his hair would grow in tangled brown waves like his mother's.

Jeannette McVay had given up her perfume and become so skinny her shoulder blades protruded like budding wings. Summer was almost over, but its heat was still oppressive, and Crystal had taken to wearing a towel around her neck. Only Jeannette, whose body temperature must have lowered with her dwindling flesh, looked supremely cool. She was the one who brought the news from town, finding me in the kitchen at my beadwork.

"Evelyn is pregnant," she announced.

"Well, she's been shacking up with that goofy cowboy," I said. I was convinced of my success and didn't have to look for credit.

"You know that baby isn't his," Jeannette said. "She kicked him out months ago, and he's been down in South Dakota ever since." I thought she would crow, but she looked sober, a little troubled even.

"Yes," I admitted, "that child is my creature."

Jeannette shuddered, and it was so hot that day the movement appeared strange. "You really do what they say you do," she finally whispered.

Dakota people have an acute awareness of cycles, the patterns in time. I opened a can of commodity peaches and poured the fruit and the rich syrup into a bowl. I handed it to the girl. She was slow to eat, the first taste no more than her tongue grazing the spoon. But midway through the bowl she gained her appetite and soon asked for another serving, and another. The peaches were gone; the juice glistened on her chin, and she sucked it from her fingers. I realized that on this day, months after Jeannette McVay first entered my house, we had traveled only one step. The girl who came to me eager to discover a modern mythology had not really believed in it any more than she trusted that Aphrodite would show up at our next powwow wearing nothing but a dance shawl and her magic girdle. I don't know what finally convinced her. Everything that happened in my life could be explained in those bland terms that comfort the faithless. But there was no mistaking the pure fear I saw in her eyes.

"I am not a bedtime story," I told her now. "I am not a dream."

I was suddenly angry. I reached out and pinched what little flesh remained on her arm. "Feel that? Feel me? Remember Pennsylvania and your college in the East, and the buses, all the buses you took to get out here?" She nodded. "That is all a legend from the past, and here you are where things happen. It is so real now it is a nightmare, am I right?"

Jeannette was still and silent. The warm air was like broth; it didn't move. We were caught in a spell of dense lethargy, and it was Crystal, emerging from her upstairs bedroom, who finally ended the painful moment.

"Tell her," I said to Crystal. "Tell her that what happens in this house is not imagined."

Crystal's lips trembled. "Oh, Jeannette," she stammered. "You aren't asleep, and this isn't a story." She stopped there. She squeezed Jeannette's shoulder with her hand.

I looked at the girls, my girls, and nodded. "It's about time," I scolded. "Now we're all starting from the same place."

The next morning Jeannette dragged her shark-colored suitcase down the stairs and left it at the back door. "Herod Small War's coming to pick me up," she said. "I guess he's forgiven me, or maybe he just thinks I'm a lost cause and will be glad to see me go. Anyway, he said he'll drive me into town and then he has some relative there who will get me to the bus."

I knew all this, I had heard her make the call, so I just smiled placidly. "I could have driven you," I said.

"Oh, no. You've done so much for me already. It's a terrible cliché to say so, but honestly I don't know how I'll repay you for taking me into your family the way you did. My parents would never do something like that for a stranger."

She jabbered on this way, nervous, glancing out the window for plumes of dust signaling Herod's arrival. I was so calm and certain of the future; I remember humming to myself. I called to the dogs: "Get out here and say good-bye. Your little friend is taking off." They came to lick her hands and roll their eyes with great sadness. "So dramatic," I teased. "I don't know which they'll miss more. You or the beef jerky."

Crystal failed to appear, but it didn't surprise me. "Don't mind her," I told Jeannette. "She's at that moony age when everything is a little purple. She won't get her mind back for a couple of years."

Herod Small War didn't come up to the house, and I didn't step outside. There was danger between us, and though it didn't frighten me, I thought it best to leave that package unexplored.

"Good-bye," said Jeannette. "Good-bye, good-bye." She was chirping with relief, and new strength gathered in her arms—she lifted the heavy suitcase as if it were packed with feathers. We shook hands in the doorway, my expression solemn while she descended the steps, walked to Herod's car, then disappeared into the Pontiac.

I felt the smile break after Herod drove away. Laughter gripped me, exploded from my diaphragm, shook and shook until my body convulsed. I fell to the floor. I cried weak tears, lost control of my bladder, burned myself with all the salty fluid from my body, and still I laughed.

That girl left so lightly, so certain of her escape, she didn't feel my thumb on the crown of her head. "It isn't good to be a sound sleeper in this house," I told her now, wheezing. I thought of her narrow feet, their difficult size, and the prized penny loafers she tucked so neatly beneath her bed. I remembered how the night before, anticipating this betrayal, I had crept into her room and borrowed those shoes. I pried up the insoles with a screwdriver and sprinkled loose reservation soil inside the loafers. I glued the insoles back in place and returned the shoes.

Jeannette McVay might make it to town, but there would be no bus. She would find herself incapable of leaving the reservation. She would struggle with herself, would probably cry. She would pack and unpack and live out of a suitcase. She would take a lover and every night tell him, "I am leaving." But she would never get very far. I laughed in my kitchen, already hearing the question that would rise to her lips again and again: "Why can't I leave when I long to leave?"

I was ready with the answer she would never hear. "Because I have willed it. And I am not a fairy tale."

7

Honor Song

Lydia Wind Soldier
(1964)

THERE ARE THOSE WHO WOULD SAY I CAN'T POSSIBLY have memories of the womb. But I do. I remember my twin sister, Evelyn, speaking to me as we curled side by side. She had plans even then.

"I'm going to get out of here first," she told me. And indeed, she did. She muscled past me, day by day, positioning herself, getting ready. Her birth was an explosion, while mine, hours later, was a slow, careful migration into the light that was my mother.

My sister was born with two inches of black hair and was nearly twice my weight. But in her terrible rush to conquer the world she spent herself; her straight black hair became frizzy in texture and faded to brown, and her bones stopped growing before mine did, so that eventually I stood six inches taller.

My mother frequently told Evelyn: "Slow and steady wins the race," pointing every time at me. I would shake my head and wriggle my shoulders because I didn't want my sister to change. I admired her fierce energy, her loud voice that carried from one room to the next, giving away all her secrets. It was, therefore, a surprise to all concerned when I became a woman first. I was twelve years old, and the blood horrified me. I hid inside my mother's small cabin, refusing to go anywhere. Evelyn was fascinated by the commotion and tormented me with so many questions

I finally said: "Look after your own womanhood, little girl. I'm too old for you now."

She squinted at me, and her lips pressed together. It looked as if her whole face was clenching into a fist. That night she came by her own blood, although our mother quickly discovered that she'd cut her thigh with a small paring knife.

"What will we do with you?" my mother scolded. "Such a character. Say your rosary and thank the Lord for letting you remain a girl for a little while longer. Don't rush His hand. He knows what He's doing."

I heard Evelyn cry that night for the first time in my life. She hadn't cried when our favorite puppy was carried off by an eagle, or the time our mother had a dangerous fever and in her delirium held a hunting rifle on us for several hours, thinking we were agents from a boarding school intent on stealing her children. Evelyn hadn't even cried when two days after an appendectomy her stitches ripped open. She'd only looked surprised. But now she sobbed, and her shuddering body made our bed vibrate. I touched her shoulder, but she rolled violently away.

"You've left me behind," she wailed.

"I haven't gone anywhere," I said. I wrapped my arm around my sister and held her against me so that we folded together as we slept, looking more like one egg than two.

Over the years I heard what people whispered: "Lydia is the beauty. Lydia is the one with the face of our ancestors." But whenever I looked at my sister, her face was so lively it overwhelmed me, and her brown eyes fascinated me like amber—that brittle resin I'd looked through, only to find trapped insects from another time. Surely this was beauty. Not just height and straight black hair long and heavy enough to give me headaches. For the most part, the boys at our school saw Evelyn the way I did. She always had more beaux and became expert at setting them against one another.

"Meet me behind the chokecherry tree at lunchtime," she told both Jimmy Pleets and Truman Keeps Eagle, and when all three converged on the spot, she stepped back to see how it would come out.

"That's how I decide between them," she said when I chided her for starting trouble. "Whoever's left standing is the one."

Evelyn and I grew up strangled by our mother's rosaries and scapulars. She practiced a complicated form of religion, a stringent program combining Catholicism and traditional Dakota customs. I heard so much about chastity, which was highly prized in both cultures, I found it difficult to touch my own body, even to bathe, and made certain to scrub my flesh with brushes rather than caress it with a cloth. Evelyn, who could be counted on to filter out half of what she was told, took long baths I thought of as sinful, sponging her body so gently you'd think she was soaping antique china.

I expected her to leave home first, to fling herself into a relationship or take to the road, teach someone else to touch her flesh generously, carefully. I looked forward to her adventures as if they would be mine. I waited for developments. And then my own life happened when I wasn't looking.

I had been out of school for a year, working as a cook at the same high school I'd attended. Actually, I was an assistant to the cook, a Winnebago grandmother named Pearl, who had married into our tribe twenty-five years earlier but was still somewhat baffled to find herself in Sioux country. We worked well together because I was quiet, fascinated by her stories of Wisconsin, which, as she told it, was not only the center of the universe but the place where all life began. We baked special treats for the students at every holiday, working late into the night, and so it was my mother occasionally let me borrow her car, a machine that had been rebuilt so many times we no longer remembered its age or the company that had produced it. It ran like a train, a profusion of smoke and noise and rocking, and the headlights would work only if switched to bright. There were holes in the floor, and someday, I expected, the bottom would fall out, but it was part of our family, like a favorite pet, and we thought of it as courageous because it worked so hard to get us from one place to the next.

I'd spent the evening before Valentine's Day in 1960 at work, baking heart-shaped cookies and cupcakes coated with pink frosting. Snow was falling, and the air was so cold it seemed flat and heavy, layers of pressed metal like the cookie sheets I slid in and out of the oven. But inside the kitchen it was warm and fragrant, the windows white with steam as if they'd been sugar-glazed. I tasted everything, pinches of batter and frosting, until my lips were sweet as candy. I reached impulsively for the vanilla extract, and when Pearl wasn't looking, I dabbed a few drops behind my ears and at my wrists. I laughed in surprise, and Pearl stared at me.

"Don't mind me," I said. "It smells too good in here, and I'm feeling tasty myself."

Pearl grinned. "Good thing it's only me," she said. "When you start talking like that, it's time for Confession."

By the time we had finished preparing the desserts and cleaned the kitchen, it was nearly midnight. The snow had stopped, but the air was even colder, dangerous because without a wind it seemed mild. I drove Pearl home, her legs straddling the hole in front of the passenger's seat. The heat didn't work, so for the duration of the ten-mile trip she slapped her arms and occasionally reached over to pound mine. Pearl hopped out quickly when we reached her yard, but she leaned inside the car to tell me: "Go straight home as fast as you can. You could freeze in there."

"I sure will," I told her. I was just fifteen miles from my mother's cabin, but it seemed a treacherous distance. The bright headlights blazed across snowdrifts; it was like staring into the flash of a camera. The snow had been sculpted by the wind, and the dramatic frothy crests seemed permanent, perfectly preserved now that the drafts were gone. The tires rolled across a road that looked to me like row upon row of starched white shirts, crackling in their paper. I mowed them down and nearly plowed through a dark boulder in my path. The brakes were loose, which probably saved me. The car shimmied, shook its rear in a slinky dance. I was able to skirt the lump in the road, but the car spun in a smooth circle; when it stopped, I faced the direction I'd been traveling. The boulder moved in the glare of my headlights. It opened up, sprouting arms and legs and a head that wagged like a pendulum.

"Oh, my God! I nearly killed you," I breathed. I rushed out of the car to help the person and discovered he was no stranger. "Calvin Wind Soldier." I called to him, trying to penetrate the cold, and my terrible cramping fear, and the man's ears, which I noticed were a little black at the tips.

"Umm," he said. His lips cracked. I watched them split in perfect lines, flesh unzipped, but there wasn't any blood. I imagined it, blue and frozen, gone to slush like a Sno-Kone. I placed his arm around my neck and lifted him to his feet. His body creaked as it unlocked, and I heard a series of small clicks as he moved his feet one careful step at a time. I walked him to my car and helped him fold onto the seat.

I planted his legs on the floor, saying: "Don't move your feet, or they'll slip under the car."

"Umm," he answered. He tried to lick his lips, but his tongue seemed to adhere to the side of his mouth. It pained me. I thought of freezer burn.

"I'll get you right home," I told Calvin Wind Soldier.

He lived just a few miles down the road, but I was shivering when we arrived, because Calvin chilled the car. He was so still I checked repeatedly for the stream of smoke that left his lips with each breath. He was a glacier, not a man. I didn't want to touch him again, to help him out of the car. But he was motionless.

"Here we are," I said. I willed myself to open my door, walk to the other side of the car, and raise Calvin from the seat. "Left and then right, left and then right," I chanted as I moved him gently through the snow. His feet were clumsy, great chunks of rock, but he punched them into the ground until we stood on the threshold of his patchwork shack.

"It's unlocked, I guess," I mumbled. I didn't see a knob or a space for a key, so I just pushed the door with my shoulder. It was heavy, but it moved. I took Calvin's hand and tugged him indoors. Moonlight spilled inside, spread like a carpet beneath our feet. I soon found the kerosene lamp in the center of Calvin's table. I lit the lamp. I had never been in this place, although years earlier I'd imagined coming here while Calvin was out, letting myself in and then producing such a pleasant change I was sure he would propose to me just moments after his return. It was tidier than I'd expected, with a military order to the tightly made bunk, the ironed shirts hanging from a peg on the wall, and the chipped plates neatly stacked on a wooden shelf above the dry sink. There was just one room, dominated by a potbellied stove and a muddy tarpaulin covering the dirt floor. I started a fire in the stove and set Calvin on his bed, where he perched, immobile, even his eyes frozen in their sockets. As I fussed over him, I relaxed, not in the least bashful to find myself alone with a man I had loved as a little girl, because I thought his mind was cloudy from the cold, insulated by frost.

"Okay, Calvin. Let's see if we can thaw you out. Find the handsome man I know is in there somewhere," I said flirtatiously. I opened his coat and dragged it off; his arms were so stiff it was like working a doll. Finally he was stripped to his long underwear, which was a brilliant white and smelled of soap. As the air warmed, becoming thick and pungent like a sticky molasses, I shed my own coat. Calvin Wind Soldier had been colorless and odorless when I found him, an ice sculpture uniform in its elements. Now the whites of his eyes spun crimson threads, and the stench of stale beer rose off his body in steady waves. I looked into those eyes, concentrating on the black marble irises. The brume cleared; I could see the man's thoughts move.

"You're back," I said. He nodded—a ragged drop of his head. "I'm glad." My coat was draped on the back of Calvin's only chair, and I reached into the pocket. I'd kept one of the Valentine's Day cookies to give to my sister Evelyn, but now I fished it out and broke it into small pieces. I fed them to Calvin, watching closely to avoid rushing him. When the cookie was gone I noticed stray sugar crystals on his lips. My finger brushed them off, and the touch surprised me. His mouth was like stone.

"So cold," I murmured. "Still so cold."

And that was how it started, a swell of pity, the desire to lead this man back from some gelid, lonely place. I was aware of myself for the first time; I felt tall and strong, filling space, sweeping the air with movement and the wash of my sweet breath. I was a blanket, a robe. I was the firm shore beside water. The curves of my body were a mountain range like Paha Sapa, the Black Hills, and my long hair was the nest of roots digging into the earth.

"Lydia," I said to Calvin Wind Soldier. "Lydia Many Wounds," I repeated. I was telling him, *Here, here I am,* in this cautious way. I had never presented myself to the world.

Then I burned through the frost. Everywhere he was cold, and everywhere I was warm. I took his fingers into my mouth, one at a time. I held his generous earlobes between my lips. I breathed across his brow, licked his lips and the straight row of teeth, solid as a wall. I tucked his feet beneath my sweater, the arches curving against the soft swell of my belly. I moved across his body, inch by inch, until it hurt to touch him. His flesh burned.

"Lydia." It was Calvin's voice now, and I was the one to be comforted, to be rescued from the heat. I swirled into what felt like an illness, a fever, a drowning.

"Am I dying?" I asked Calvin, my voice choked with rocks.

"No, Lydia." He spoke against my throat. "I'll never let you do that."

And then we spun away together.

There was no shame in me when I drove up to my mother's house the next morning. I emerged from the car and stood straight as I could, pausing to smooth my hair. A ring had been promised me, already, as soon as I opened my eyes and blinked at the sun washing through Calvin's window. I wondered for a moment at my sudden spontaneity, the way I hadn't hesitated to accept Calvin's proposal. After all, I hadn't found him in the best condition the night before. Some could say his prospects looked bleak. *Where is the old Lydia?* I asked myself. The one who would have shied from any new development. *She is banished,* I decided, which settled everything.

Calvin insisted upon a ring, though I knew it would be hard for him to come up with the money. As a temporary offering, in its place, he'd given me a Silver Star.

"From the Korean War," he'd said simply, as if it had nothing to do with him and the terrible ways he'd risked his life. That star was pinned to my sweater; I could feel its comfortable weight. I stroked the medal through the heavy fabric of my coat.

"Here she is!" It was Evelyn's voice, skidding across the packed snow. "You were at Pearl's, right?" She asked the question with little interest. I could tell no one had worried about me, assuming the snow had kept me at the school or at my friend's. We didn't have a phone and neither did Pearl, so there had been no frantic dialing.

I wanted to say, *You wouldn't believe where I've been,* collapse against Evelyn, and whisper the story urgently, sister to sister. But that would have been handing the experience to someone else, and I was greedy. I didn't want to share it. I was honest, but not forthright. I told my mother and Evelyn: "I nearly ran down Calvin Wind Soldier last night, on my way home. He was passed out in the road and half frozen. I got him back to his place, got him settled. I saw him through the night."

Again, there was no suspicion. I was Lydia, the good girl who confessed every Wednesday and took Communion each Sunday, Lydia who spoke fluent Dakota to the elders while Evelyn stumbled through "Hello" and a few simple phrases. As my mother was fond of saying, I was the good from both sides, though it was my impression it bored her, this circumspect behavior. I let the women believe what they would. It was enough that I'd thrilled myself. I said nothing more about that night until I had the ring.

"So you're going to marry him after all?" Evelyn teased me a month later. "You dreamt about it so many times, you wanted it too much. I guess I thought those were the things that never happen. The world is never that kind." My sister surprised me with this musing. She was usually too intent on having fun to step back from experiences and consider their meaning.

"Well, it's sure been kind to me!" I shouted. This time she was surprised. I wrestled my sister to the ground, straddled her waist and tickled her until she sobbed.

My mother stuck her head in the door. "Get off your sister," she scolded. "What's come over you?"

My mother didn't know how earnestly I'd planned this coming wedding when I was just a little girl. I was ten years old when Calvin Wind Soldier enlisted in the army. He and two other Sioux boys, none of them over eighteen, were shipped to Korea together. I organized a group of girls into a support unit, mailing care packages to our tribesmen. I made certain to include a strand of my hair or to mark an object with a carefully pressed fingerprint, so there would be something of myself in the box, some essence of Lydia traveling the many unimaginable miles, passing through so many hands, to be delivered to Calvin Wind Soldier, discovered by him. I wasn't attempting spells; it was pure longing. I was spinning daydreams. I never imagined the battles: the noise and fear and dying. The devastating guilt. When I thought of Calvin in Korea he was dancing—I made him do that. I made him remember the graceful steps I'd seen him perform at countless powwows. He was moving past flags, across enemy lines, fascinating the troops on both sides with his imitation of the eagles. I could hear the soldiers call to him, telling him to fly; surely he could fly, even in that sweat-soaked uniform. The feathers would sprout, and he would soar beyond the trouble.

When I was ten years old my wishes didn't work, they weren't able to lift Calvin out of war and into my scrawny arms. But they were powerful now.

Two months after I nearly crushed him beneath the wheels of a car, I married Calvin Wind Soldier. Father Zimmer performed the service at Saint Mary's, the tiny weather-beaten church behind the high school, so windblasted its paint was forever peeling. My mother was there, and Evelyn, even Pearl, surrounded by her Sioux children and grandchildren, who didn't understand the threats she made in Winnebago.

Herod Small War, Calvin's close friend, stood beside him at the altar and nimbly managed the slim rings. He was my mother's generation and liked to tease her for being such a devout Catholic, since as a Yuwipi man he prayed to Wakan Tanka rather than Jesus Christ.

"There aren't any Indian angels in heaven," he often told my mother. "You fly up there on your eagle wings and they'll say, *Wrong kind, you got to have those pigeon feathers.* And then they'll spot the moccasins you're wearing in case of a good powwow, and show you the door. You got to go barefoot or wear sandals in that place."

Herod was solemn on this occasion, however, and nodded politely at my mother.

Ghosts were there, though I didn't see them. I was a horse with blinders, and ahead of me in full view was Calvin, his square face and the widow's peak that softened the lines, the crest of black hair that was so thick it suggested defiance. We were the same height and could look straight across at one another without raising or dipping our faces. Calvin wore his uniform from the service, and I wore an eggshell-white dress that barely covered my knees. The ribbons streaming from the bridal bouquet were longer than the dress. I was so conscious of my daring, of my exposed legs, I didn't hear the ghosts file into church and settle themselves in the back pews. But my husband must have noticed them, because on our wedding night, as we squeezed together on his narrow bunk, he shouted in his sleep, called names I'd never heard before. There was one name I recognized: Čuwignaka Duta—Red Dress. When I heard it I was instantly jealous, though the lady was long dead, a legend, really, from another time. I didn't want this woman reaching for my husband as he slept, so I shook him awake.

"Bad dreams," I told him in my mother's soothing voice. "Let go of those bad dreams."

My husband and I didn't live in his shack for very long. Calvin had stopped drinking, was hired as a member of the tribal police force, and was soon building me a house, a real house with electricity, indoor plumbing, and a phone line. I wanted tiles in the bathroom, a double sink in the kitchen, and a picture window. I wanted shag carpeting and a brick fireplace that didn't even have to work. I was greedy not for things, but rather order. I thought I could organize happiness through careful housekeeping, matching plates and flatware, tasteful drapes, and a vacuum cleaner. Maybe I thought I could eradicate the past with disinfectant or the sucking hose. But it clung to my husband, spawned cells in his blood.

"Tell me the worst thing," I urged him. "Tell me all the bad parts you remember, and they'll let you go." He never did. He said the images and nightmares would only pass to me, a fearful gift, and he wouldn't allow it. The most he said was that he served as a scout in the war.

"The COs always made Indian boys scout for them. It went back to the movies, I think, to Custer's Last Stand and all that. They told us, right to our faces, that we could track like bloodhounds and move so quietly we might as well be invisible. That our vision was so sharp it was supernatural. They said this without looking at our files. Pulled it out of every story they'd heard. Scouting was dangerous business."

I knew that of the dozen Dakotas who had served in Korea, Calvin was the only one to return. I could picture the boys advancing on their own, young and frightened, but proud too, determined to make the stereotype valid, trying to convince themselves the officers had read their hearts and were speaking from wisdom rather than ignorance. It hurt me to think of them dying alone.

But these were not the bad things, the memories that seized my husband when his mind opened to dreams. He was haunted by the Silver Star and what he had done to merit the award, the terrible work of his own hands that he wouldn't describe for me, no matter how many times I insisted, wishing to free him.

"What about Red Dress, then?" I prompted. "Tell me about her."

We had moved into the new house, fragrant with the

smell of fresh lumber, when he finally told me the story. We faced one another across the kitchen table. My hands smoothed the Formica, stroked it possessively.

"It will sound crazy in this house," Calvin said. I understood. The overhead lights were bright, illuminating every corner of the room, and the house was so well insulated it swallowed the noise of the wind scouring the plains. Certain things weren't possible in a house like this.

"You already know about the legend?" Calvin asked me.

"Of course. I think everybody on the reservation has heard some piece of it."

"They say she hasn't left this earth," Calvin continued. "She died so long ago, but she's all wrapped up in her descendants and still looking for her lover." I nodded to encourage my husband, but I kept my eyes on the new table. "That lover was an ancestor of mine," he said. "A great-uncle, or two greats, I forget. I'm the last of that line, so I think she has her eye on me."

I looked at him now.

"Not in an evil way. I think she's concerned and wants to keep me out of trouble. She has that crazy relative, you know, that niece who stirs up so much trouble."

I knew he meant Anna Thunder, who was the subject of so many rumors I didn't know whether to fear her or pity her. I was skeptical about magic, and when I heard people whisper that she was a witch, I was relieved to be in the twentieth century, where a hanging wouldn't follow the accusation.

"How do you know all this?" I asked my husband. "How do you know the motivation of a spirit?" Calvin leaned back in his chair; his fingers drummed the table, and

I picked out the pattern of an old Dakota song honoring warriors.

"My dad was still alive right before I shipped out to Korea. He was so proud of me, but worried too, and wanted me to call on everything possible to get myself through what was coming. He told me to call on my ancestors for help, because they can get lonely and miss hearing their names. He made me promise to go for a vision. He talked about it day and night until I finally agreed to do it. I wasn't thrilled with the idea of that ordeal."

Calvin stood and paced across the linoleum, squashing the design—crisp black dots resembling tiny spiders—with his boots. He told me the story of his vision, the most private communication. I felt privileged to hear the words. But his conversation made him nervous, so he moved around me as he spoke, stepping away from the images he sketched with his tongue.

"I guess I thought the whole adventure was a little corny," my husband confessed. "The last thing I wanted to do was spend four nights alone on Angry Butte, standing in a vision pit dug into the earth, not allowed to eat or drink water for the whole four days. But it meant everything to my dad, so I did it. The only thing I changed was that I was supposed to stand in the pit with just a blanket wrapped around me, but I insisted on wearing clothes."

Calvin played with the change in his pockets, gathered the coins and released them. He was hypnotized by the memory. I think he was back in the vision pit, standing upright with only his head aboveground. He could smell the tobacco ties staked around the hole's perimeter; he heard the wind comb through the grass.

"There was a light rain," Calvin said, "and it soaked my head and my arms. It was cold in the ground. Worms wriggled into my pants pockets, and gnats were trapped in the sweat under my collar, but I didn't remove them. My dad told me it was a time to accept everything that came to me. The second night I slept a little, standing up. It wasn't too bad, because I leaned against the dirt wall and carved a niche with my shoulder blades. What woke me up was the moonlight settling on my face. I realized how hungry and thirsty I was, so I put a pebble in my mouth—my father taught me that trick—and sure enough, my mouth worked better, wasn't so dry. I was getting restless for things to happen and almost didn't believe anything would, except maybe me catching a cold and losing some weight. I think I complained. Said something like, 'I don't see any spirits.'

"*That's because you are impatient,* a voice answered. It was a woman's voice, and the strange thing was, I could swear she spoke in English and Dakota simultaneously. Not translating, but two messages at once." Calvin shook his head, moved behind my chair, and rested his hands on my shoulders. "The part of the voice speaking Dakota was low, from deep in the throat, and the part speaking English was breathy and high, the *s* sounding like a hiss. I couldn't say anything, my teeth were probably chattering like one of those telegraph machines."

Calvin walked over to the generous kitchen window above my double sink. He stared into the distance. "The voice became a figure," he continued, "a woman standing on the ground above me, about ten feet away. She was wearing a long buckskin dress and matching leggings, the hide painted red and decorated with rows of elk teeth. She had thick black hair, like yours, but it fell unbraided all the way to the ground and dragged behind her like a train. It was alive with sound, coming from the dozens of rattlesnake rattles tied in her hair. She wore a bull snake around her waist for a belt, but it wasn't dead and skinned. I could see it squeeze and then release her. That woman's eyes were silver-black. She was so beautiful it was hard to watch her face.''

Calvin leaned against the sink, his body suddenly heavy. "She held up her arms so I could see what she was carrying. In her right hand was a war shield of buffalo hide, and in her left hand were the rope ends of three nooses.

"*My name is Red Dress,* she told me in both languages, *and this is evidence of my success.* I knew then who she was, the one who tangled with army soldiers way back. I liked her confidence and was beginning to feel safe, when she twirled the nooses so they spun separately above her head. With one quick throw she lassoed me and pulled the circles of rope tight. I was caught by each wrist and the throat. *I'm not going to hurt you,* she said. *I just want your complete attention.* There was no question but she had it.''

Calvin returned to the kitchen table and took a seat. My mind was swirling with ropes, the image of snares unleashed, and to calm myself I looked around the kitchen—the most important space in any Sioux house. Now it was even a place of revelations.

"She warned me then," Calvin said. "She told me that her niece was confused, and determined to confound everyone else. She didn't want to see me trapped by that one's scheming. *She'll come after you,* Red Dress said. *You be ready for her.*

"I felt bad for that woman," Calvin whispered. "Before she left she jumped into the pit beside me. We were pressed tightly together, and I could feel the bull snake squirming at my waist. *You look so much like your uncle,* she cried in her two voices, and then she kissed me. She tasted like wild plums. She pulled the breath from deep inside my diaphragm, the way old men inhale their pipe tobacco, until I fainted.

"When my dad came to get me after the fourth night, he was so pleased to find me standing in that pit, singing to the spirits, stronger than ever. But he looked worried when he saw the rope burns on my wrists and circling my throat. 'The spirits were hard on you,' he said. 'Not so bad,' I told him."

Calvin reached across the table to take my hands. "I didn't do anything about that spirit's warning. I didn't think Anna Thunder could get to me in Korea, and after I came back I didn't care one way or the other. But things are different now. I went to see Herod Small War right before we got married, and he made me this belt I've been wearing every day."

It was fashioned of handsome snakeskin, and I liked to touch it. The texture was somehow satisfying, and when I fingered it, I found it difficult to pull away.

"Is it supposed to protect you?" I asked.

"He's pretty sure it will work," Calvin said. "Red Dress was fond of snakes, she learned things from them and kept them close. This is almost like her seal, her mark of favor, and if that niece of hers comes looking for me, she won't get far with her pranks, because she can't stand up to her ancestor: it would be like crushing her own spirit.

"This is all too much," my husband whispered. "I feel like I've pulled you into a tornado. I should have said something before, to give you choices."

I glided across the terra-cotta floor, that solemn color reminiscent of dried blood. I pulled my husband to his feet and fit the two of us together, we were so evenly matched. Impulsively I began to turn, bringing him with me. It wasn't a dance, though we rocked on our feet. We circled faster, spun on our heels, on our toes. We made ourselves dizzy, and I heard my voice shout: "I give myself up to the tornado!"

My husband should have hushed me, but he was young, not yet thirty, and we were standing in a kitchen that could have been featured in a commercial. How could there be room in such a place for spirits and their grim alarms?

My mother and my sister Evelyn were infrequent visitors to the new house, which was an L-shaped ranch structure with a carport—the only one of its kind on the reservation. My mother said it made her uncomfortable because the floors were too big; I suppose she meant spacious. My sister liked the house just fine, but she was preoccupied with her own relationship. Her boyfriend, Philbert, was a champion bull rider who did a lot of traveling.

"He just takes off," Evelyn confided, clearly enthralled with the idea. "He travels the rodeo circuit, goes clear up to Canada and even to Chicago for some exhibitions." When I thought of them together, I saw my sister perched behind Philbert on a bucking Brahma bull. She wasn't grasping her boyfriend around the waist but kept her seat by clenching her knees. Somewhere in the picture Philbert was tossed to the ground, but Evelyn clung to the animal's back like a wood tick, dug in, ignoring Philbert's waving arms and shouts for her to let go. The scene was so vivid in my mind I asked Evelyn once if she'd ever ridden a bull.

"I thought about it," she admitted. "Sometimes Philbert makes it look easy and I can see myself doing the same thing. But I'm only crazy for a second."

I kept working at the school and turned over the paychecks to my mother. She was aging rapidly and had to give up the job she'd held for so many years, cleaning the church and Father Zimmer's spartan living quarters.

"We've got to watch out for Mama," I told Evelyn.

She said, "Mama will be going strong when we're gumming our meat and can't remember our names."

I knew that in my sister's view of the world our mother was the sun and we were satellites, and the young men who swept across our paths so fervently were nothing more than transient meteors destined to burn themselves out. Evelyn had recognized us in a science textbook, and decided I was shimmering Venus while she was hot little Mercury. "The spitfire," she'd bragged. I wasn't as certain as Evelyn that our lives would continue unspoiled by change, but I wasn't ready for what followed either.

A year after marrying Calvin Wind Soldier, I was plagued by a nightmare. It was the same every night, and no matter what strategy I devised to divert my thoughts, hoping to trigger happier dreams, it washed over me again. Once asleep, I found myself staring at a purple sky, bright with stars hanging heavy as ripe fruit. Then a voice rasped, *Little sister, let me in.*

I despised that voice and wasn't fooled by its softness. When I looked up, there was always a cottonwood tree, the down floating from its branches. There were other voices, huskier than the one I dreaded: male voices hoarse with sorrow, calling, *Love me, love me.* Hanging from thick cottonwood branches were three soldiers with shiny boots and oiled mustaches. Their swollen tongues protruded, but still they said the words: *Love me, love me.* Their hands dangled uselessly at their sides. "Grab your swords and cut yourselves down," I shouted at them. But I don't think they heard me.

I looked away and noticed the figure of a woman approaching from the lavender horizon. Her face was covered by a buffalo-hide shield, and as she walked I heard the rattle of snakes. *Little sister, let me in,* she coaxed. And when she reached my side she leaned close to me, her words pricking my ears. *All the way in,* she demanded.

I was weary of the dream and somewhere in the long chain of nights exerted my will. This time when the woman joined me I said, "Red Dress, why are you doing this? I thought you wanted to help my husband." The figure recoiled and pulled the shield so close her nose must have pressed against its hide. I snatched the shield from her hands to face the demon. But it wasn't Red Dress I exposed. The face was stitched with wrinkles, and the hair was a tangle of blunt wires.

"Anna," I said. "What are you doing in my dreams?" Her startled expression collapsed into a smile. *Just a little scouting expedition.* She laughed. *Chasing after my own Silver Star.* I watched her toss the shield into the tree, where it caught on the toe of one soldier's boot. I pinched myself awake, more unsettled now than on all the previous nights.

Anna Thunder came for my husband a week later. I missed the event, since I was down with the flu. I was seldom ill but always slow to recover, because I fought so hard to ignore the bug and maintain my schedule. Calvin insisted I get my rest; he even asked Herod Small War to drop by and scold me. The old man tried to be serious. He said, "Lydia, who are you trying to impress? We know you're tough. We're all pretty stringy around here, hey?" A moment later his lips peeled into a grin, and he pressed his hand to my forehead. It was the softest touch of anyone's, his flesh like tissue. I fell asleep with his gentle fingers rubbing at my thoughts.

When Anna materialized in the yard I regularly fertilized and watered, wanting so much for it to become a lawn, Calvin was shaken. "I didn't see her walking up the road or crossing the open fields. It's like she stepped from a hole in the sky," he later told me.

Herod emerged from the house and tried to shame Anna. "She took it pretty well, too," Calvin said. "She gave us our due and walked away, but I only saw her take a few steps. It was dark by then, so maybe she just slipped into the dusk, but it was eerie the way she was there and then gone."

I never told anyone about my nightmare, and it hadn't returned since I confronted the older woman. I embraced the safety I now felt, and spoke of children and the future. My dreams were no longer haunted by hanging men and vindictive women but crowded with infants, their round faces a plump version of my own or Calvin's. I taught myself to knit, following directions in a book, and produced a tiny blue poncho that curled up at the edges because I hadn't yet learned to make fringes. I prepared dishes no respectable Dakota had ever tasted—Welsh rarebit and chilled gazpacho soup—because their foreignness made me feel even safer.

I was slow to notice my husband's absence. He was a hard worker in a demanding job, so it was a while before I saw the truth. My mother recognized it first.

"I'm worried about your sister," she told me. "I think she's lost herself in something unhappy." She was purposely vague, I think, wanting only to set my mind in motion.

Later, when I believed that my husband and my twin

sister had come together as a result of sinister medicine, I cannot say their actions grieved me less. It felt as if the veins had been stripped from my arms, or my hair was lit, burning to the roots, promising to scorch my memories. When I was little I'd seen a group of traditional elders prepare a dog for a sacred feast. The slaughter was a careful ritual, humane, almost graceful, and then the fur was singed. I remember the acrid smell so clearly, and it came back to me as I struggled with betrayal. It filled my nose for several months, flavored every meal, seeped from the bottle of my perfume. The stench began to fade after my husband came back to me, his eyes resuming their former intelligence, the spell shaken from him. It had finally disappeared, when I learned that Evelyn was carrying Calvin's child. The odor of singed fur did not come flooding back at the news. Instead I lost my sense of smell and the ability to taste, and these two faculties were never to return.

I can't say I lost more than my sister. I saw her erect gates and fortress walls in her mind, close off some areas, only to retreat into the corners. After she gave birth to Duane, it was as if he never existed. She put him out of her body, her heart, her mind. She thought of him as my son, and then everyone else did too. I was the only one clear on his origins, always mindful and a bit resentful. I held him too much, could reach him before he uttered the first cry, because his wavy brown hair didn't charm me and I found his precocious agility unnerving.

"You're a climber," I teased in a soft voice, hiding my irritation when he tried to scale my dress. People commended me for being such a good mother to the child. Even Herod Small War said, "This is how it should be. Your ancestors would be proud of you." But surely they could read my heart and must have pitied my nephew.

I will never harm you, I promised Duane silently. *You will always have a home with me.* But I couldn't promise love, no matter how much he deserved it. Some things cannot be willed.

I blanched when Duane first called me "Mama." I worked frantically to teach him "Daddy" and must have confused him, because for a while he looked at me whenever he said "Mama" or "Daddy." Calvin was initially nervous when Evelyn refused the child and we brought him home. But I think it was just his concern for me, because he quickly warmed to Duane. He took the boy for rides in his police car and introduced him to horses before Duane could walk. On Saturday mornings the two of them could be found on a borrowed pony, Calvin enveloping his son, towering above him like a shelf of rock.

I was both happy and sad to see them together. I wanted Calvin to care for his son, but I was jealous for our unborn children and worried that this first child, spawned by vengeful magic, would be his father's lifelong favorite and my own sons would be shadows beside him. I wrestled with these thoughts; it was my way of handling the pain and confusion. I tried to squelch my base ideas. But when I learned I was carrying a child, my selfishness excluded all reason. I began to think of the infant Duane as Anna's offspring. I saw a sudden resemblance between them, and when the boy watched me I was uneasy, thinking it was Anna peering into my soul. Each day I was kinder, petted him more, smiled at him dozens of times, but these were meaningless gestures. I hoarded love the way deer mice gather earth beans; passed it through the placenta like every other nutrient. I pretended to sing for Duane as he crawled from one end of the kitchen to the other, but really I was singing for the baby curled inside me.

I became moody; no matter how many times Calvin told me he was eager for the delivery and would celebrate this birth, my thoughts kept grinding. *He feels strangled by responsibility,* I fretted. *Too many children all at once.* The baby became my secret ally, supporting every decision I made, agreeing with my conclusions. We were a family unto ourselves.

A month before I was due, Duane developed a hacking cough and fussed unless I bounced him in my arms. By nightfall my limbs dragged heavy as petrified wood, and my feet were swollen stumps. Still Duane screamed when I tried to put him down for a nap. Calvin attempted to comfort him, but the boy held his arms out to me. I walked through the house, covering miles, and at one point Duane nearly fell through my hands because I was slick with perspiration. Calvin sponged my arms, my face, the back of my neck.

"You're lucky," he told his son. "You have the best mother."

Late that night I slumped into a chair, numb from exhaustion. Duane sputtered quickly to life, a wail building in his congested lungs. His chubby legs shot into my lap, swift kicks that made me gasp. *The baby,* I thought. *He's trying to hurt the baby.*

Duane and I erupted together. He cried until his coughing choked him, and I shouted for his father. "Get him out of here!" I hollered. "I need him out of here for a while!"

Calvin scooped the boy into his arms. "You'll scare him," he chided. He looked stunned. "I know it's been rough tonight, but just hold on."

"Out!" I cried, my voice harsh, the word scratching my throat. "Please take your son and get out of my hair."

Calvin dipped his head. "We'll go for a drive." He spoke so gently I was momentarily pacified. But then I realized he was speaking to Duane. He grabbed a blanket from the crate he'd transformed into a child's bed, sanding off splinters and fitting it with a mattress of feathers and sweet grass. He draped the small quilt over Duane's shoulders and left the house.

I wanted to call him back, but I wasn't lonely enough. After all, I had the baby.

I had no premonitions, no sudden flash of knowledge. I didn't hear about the accident until Herod Small War came to my house and told me.

"You will find your own comfort," he said. "Just know that I am here."

Father Zimmer and my mother emerged with their shiny rosary beads and listed my blessings with precision. Evelyn sent a sympathy card from her refuge in a big city.

The night my husband and nephew were killed, I became ashes. My throat burned and my tongue swelled. They said a drunk driver was responsible for the tragedy, but I knew it was my anger and the terrible power of my voice.

Sometimes I will sing for my husband when the drummers play a good honor song. It can be a song for warriors or lovers, because Calvin Wind Soldier was both to me. But I do not speak to the people around me. I won't unleash the killing voice, even to soothe my son, who is the only blessing.

And so I have become another person, the one who sits on her tongue. I answer to Lydia, but when I think of myself, I use another name: Ini Naon Win. Silent Woman.

8
Red Moccasins

Anna Thunder
(1935)

MY NIECE BERNARDINE BLUE KETTLE, THE ONE I CALLED
Dina, was thirteen—too old to be sitting on my lap. But
there she was, her long legs draped over mine and her feet
scraping the ground. Our fingers were laced together, both
sets of arms wrapped around her pole waist. My four-year-
old son, Chaske, was sitting on the floor, drumming a pillow with my long wooden cooking spoon. He covered one
ear with his hand and twisted his face to imitate the Sioux
singers he worshiped, old men who singed their vocal cords
on high notes. He pounded his music into the pillow, making the Dakota lullaby sound energetic as a powwow song.

"Dance for me," I told Dina. I wanted her to play along
with Chaske. Dina left my lap and danced around her
cousin as if he were a drummer at the powwow grounds.
She was a serious dancer, aware of her posture, light on
her feet, tucking sharp elbows into her sides. Max, my son's
pet burrowing owlet, watched Dina circle the room. He
bobbed forward on the offbeat from his perch atop the mantel clock. My husband had discovered him wandering
through a prairie-dog town.

"Look at Max," I told the children. "You've got him
dancing too." But Max quickly tired of the game and used
his long legs to turn himself around, so all we could see
were his feathered back and hunched shoulders.

I clapped and clapped when the song ended, and Chaske

gave up the spoon so I could stir his supper, another batch of the watery potato soup we'd been eating for weeks.

It was 1935, and a good portion of North Dakota had dried up and blown away. Grit peppered our food, coated our teeth, and silted our water. We heard that cities as distant as Chicago and New York were sprinkled with Plains topsoil. I thought it was fitting somehow. I imagined angry ancestors fed up with Removal grabbing fistfuls of parched earth to fling toward Washington, making the president choke on dust and ashes. We prayed for rain, and when it did not come, when instead we were strangled by consumption, many people said the end of the world had come to the Sioux reservation. I was not a doomsday disciple. I wouldn't let the world end while my son Chaske still had so much living to do.

"Bet you can't guess what's for supper," I teased Chaske, who was perched on Dina's shoulders.

"Potato soup!" he shouted, delighted to be suddenly taller than me. Dina rolled her eyes but didn't say anything. She bounced Chaske up and down, stooped over and then lifted on her toes—a horse rearing on its hind legs.

They looked like two opposites, like people with blood running from separate rivers. Chaske, whose baptism name was Emery Bauer, Jr., after his German father, was sturdy and tall for his age, his powerful calf muscles bulging, little crab apples under the skin. His hair was creamy yellow, the color of beeswax, and his eyes were a silvery gray, so pale they were almost white.

I couldn't trace Chaske's Sioux blood or find evidence of his father in his features and coloring. It was as if he came from his own place, having sidestepped all the family tracks laid out before him. Dina, on the other hand, was a blueprint of the women in our family, long-legged and graceful, thick braids grazing her narrow hips. Her little heart-shaped face was dark brown, the color of a full-blood, and her eyes were black as onyx studs. Dina had been with me when I delivered Chaske, holding my hand while old women assisted me. Dina was the one who brought him to my arms, and I remember thinking, as she held him, that he looked like a bundle of sunflowers, yellow against her dusky skin. I put the children together in my mind, couldn't imagine one without the other.

After supper Dina washed the dishes. It was so easy; it was like a game to her, because in my modern house, fit for a white woman, she could pump water directly into the kitchen sink and watch it drain away. She didn't have to go outside and haul buckets. I pulled out my sewing basket and let Chaske play with a jar full of buttons.

"Have you finished my dress?" Dina called over her shoulder.

"You'll be the first to know," I said. I laughed because she was so impatient, more impatient every day. I was sewing Dina her first traditional Sioux dress. Ordinarily a mother would do this, but Dina's was the next thing to useless. Joyce Blue Kettle had never gotten close enough to a needle to stick herself, let alone sew a costume. As a child she'd been restless and boy-crazy, so she never learned to tan hides or do beadwork. If her mother scolded her, saying, "Look at your little cousin. Look at her fine beadwork," Joyce would puff out her bottom lip and squeeze round tears onto her flat cheeks. She would say, "You know I can't see right," pointing to her left eye, which was crossed, permanently focused on her nose. Of course, she managed to see well enough to paint her face and read movie magazines she swiped from the Lugers' store. Joyce and I were first cousins, which in our tribe made us sisters.

When Dina finished stacking the clean plates, I called her into the sitting room. "I'm almost ready to start your moccasins," I said. I traced the outline of her foot onto a scrap of cardboard so that the soles would match perfectly her fine narrow feet.

"Will you make me rattlesnake hair ties?" Dina asked. I dropped the paring knife I was using to cut out the pattern.

"Where did you see hair ties like that?" I was careful to leave the blade in my lap, because my hands were shaking.

"I've dreamt about the Red Dress woman," she confided. "And she had rattlesnake rattles tied in her hair. She shook them at me. She told me I could wear my hair like that."

"You can't," I said. I knew I sounded too angry. "When she comes after you, turn the other way."

"Have you seen her?" asked Dina, staring at me.

"Yes. But I discouraged her from coming." I didn't tell my niece that at her age I had dreamt about Čuwignaka Duta, Red Dress, my grandmother's sister. I had heard her insistent voice, crackling with energy, murmuring promises of a power passed on through the bloodlines from one woman to the next. I had seen her kneeling beside a fire, feeding it with objects stolen from her victims: buttons, letters, twists of hair. She sang her spells, replacing the words of an ancient honor song with those of her own choosing. She doused the flames.

"Could she really control people?" Dina asked.

"That's what they say. But it didn't do her any good. She spelled one too many, and he killed her."

My niece held her unfinished dress in her hands. She

stroked the blue trade cloth and tugged on the cowrie shells sprinkled across the dress and leggings. I'd hidden the beaded belt and flour-sack cape covered with inch-long bugle beads, to surprise her with later.

There was a knock at the kitchen door. Dina's father, Clifford Blue Kettle, poked his head into the room and waved at me.

"Come on in," I said. He shook his head and twisted the doorknob as if he was trying to wring it loose. Black bangs hid his eyes.

"Dina here?" he asked me, so whispery he had to clear his throat and ask me again. Dina stepped into the doorway between the sitting room and kitchen. "Your ma says to get home now," he told her.

"He's so shy around you," Dina said, laughing softly.

I waved off her comment as if I disagreed, but she was right; my cousin's husband had feelings for me. When we were children, he had followed me everywhere, helping me with my chores and bringing me little treasures he'd discovered: seashells, fool's gold, ripe chokecherries. One time he brought me a round glass eye he'd poked from the socket of his sister's doll. It was too much for Joyce. She intercepted the gift, snatched it from the palm of my hand as I studied the green iris. She took Clifford over the same way, ordering him around, demanding his attention, and because I didn't love Clifford, I let her keep him. It never seemed to occur to him that he could protest. He was amiable and slow-minded. He longed to please. Even now he brought me little gifts or fashioned toys for Chaske, like my son's first baby rattle, and I could see he had something for me. One hand was hidden behind his back.

"What have you got there?" I asked. I walked to the

door and tried to peek over his shoulder, which made him grin.

"Got these in a giveaway. Know Joyce can't use them." He handed me a mason jar full of red beads tiny as poppy seeds. I spilled a few of them into my hand and admired their rich color, scarlet as a fresh wound sliced into my palm. I poured them back into the jar.

"Thank you. I can put these to good use."

Having given me the gift, Clifford appeared relieved. He kicked the back steps with the toe of his boot. "Come on now," he called to his daughter.

Dina kissed Chaske's round cheek before she left, and he smiled at her, kissing his fist and popping it against her arm.

I meant to stay up late to finish sewing Dina's leggings, but Chaske started coughing. He clenched his hands over his chest as if he had captured something between them, a sawing cricket or fluttering moth. I knew the odd gesture was a way he dealt with pain, trying to hammer it down. I carried Chaske to my lumpy brass bed and curled beside him. His coughing finally tapered off, and he murmured, "Max."

"Max is fine," I said. "Go to sleep." I rubbed Chaske's back, my hand moving in circles, unable to relax while I listened to his breathing. His hair smelled like sweet grass, and his little body, changing too quickly from plump to wiry, warmed the bed. I guarded his sleep, forcing my breath into a perfect rhythm as if I could breathe for him, and in the morning I was weary but triumphant, having kept the world in orbit.

I had been a widow for two months, since the end of November. Dr. Kessler, a notorious alcoholic but the only doctor on the reservation, had diagnosed Emery as consumptive and told him he should go to the white sanatorium in Rapid City.

"I better not," my husband said, terse as always. But after seven years of marriage, I could practically read Emery's mind. He didn't want to split up our family. If I became ill, I would never be admitted to the hospital Dr. Kessler had suggested; I would be sent to the inferior sanatorium, the one for Sioux, where few patients recovered. And our son Chaske wasn't really an appropriate candidate for either place. Who knew where he would end up?

"We'll take our chances," Emery said, and so we did. Emery remained at home, where I was to keep him well fed and well rested. Consumption was rampant by this time, hitting nearly every family on our reservation, and no attempts were made to isolate the sick from the healthy. My husband was a successful rancher, in partnership with his two brothers, and I couldn't keep him from work for very long. In the end, it wasn't consumption that killed him, but a wild horse he called Lutheran. Emery's two brothers brought my husband's body to me, stumbling beneath his bear weight. They were crying, promising me they would shoot the devil horse that had thrown Emery and broken his neck.

"No!" I said, and they looked wary. They grabbed my arms as if they expected me to pitch forward. "That horse did him a kindness." I wanted them to leave, so I could comb Emery's hair and wash his face. "He didn't waste away from the consumption. He went quickly."

Later that night I sat on the edge of Chaske's cot. I told him that his sleeping father, laid out in the next room on our brass bed, was having such good dreams he didn't want to wake up.

"Is he dreaming about Max?" my son asked me.

"Yes," I said. "He's dreaming about all of us."

I panicked that night when I realized I didn't own a single photograph of my husband. It wasn't my memory I worried about but Chaske's. He was so young I couldn't trust that he would remember Emery, the shape of his black beard, his tremendous wingspan and silent laugh. As Chaske slept, I told him about his father, chanting our history until it became a song-story I hoped he would follow in his dreams.

I told him about the day I met Emery Bauer. It was the winter of 1928, and I was eighteen years old. I had been snowbound for several days in my family's cabin and was desperate to be outdoors, where I could work the cramps out of my legs and fill my lungs with fresh air. I went for a long walk, fighting through high drifts, pausing only to search for landmarks.

I wandered onto the leased land of the Bauer ranch, thinking I was heading toward town. I came to a shallow frozen pond. The ice was uneven, marred by tangled clumps of weeds, but I noticed a man skimming across it as if on a smooth pane of glass. He balanced on silver blades slim as butter knives, propelling his barrel body forward and then magically backward, skirting the weeds and chiseling the ice with his skates. I had heard about ice-skating, but I'd never seen it done. I'd never seen a man spin like a top. I hunched beside a frozen bush, hoping he wouldn't notice me. But I was framed in white and difficult to miss. The graceful man skated toward me, and stopped so quickly his blades spit a spray of ice. He towered over me, smiling, alternately fingering his black beard and tapping the heavy work boots slung around his neck.

"You like to dance on water?" he asked me. I shook

my head. I didn't know what else to do. "I'm Emery," he said. He waited, staring directly into my eyes, which made me uncomfortable.

"I'm Anna Thunder," I finally answered.

"Now *that's* a name to live up to." He clapped his large hands together. "Come here, this will be fun." Emery removed his skates, which I saw were metal blades screwed onto a pair of work boots. He donned the boots he'd been carrying and knelt in the snow. Even down on one knee he was tall.

"Give me your foot," he said. He was the only white man other than the doctor and the reservation priest I had ever spoken to, but I trusted him. Strangely, I think it was his size that calmed me. He was such a giant he seemed uncomfortable in his body; his posture was an accommodating stoop, and his gestures apologetic. Off the ice, he shambled awkwardly. So I did as he requested. I watched him stuff one of his mittens in the toe of each boot and then fit the skates on my feet. He held my hands and pulled me across the ice. At first I was rigid and tottered on the slippery surface, but eventually I relaxed and pushed off, cutting the ice with confident strokes.

"God made you to skate," Emery breathed in my ear.

Our courtship was an ice dance, and Emery's wedding present to me was my own set of silver blades he'd ordered from the Sears catalogue. He attached them to a new pair of ankle-high laced boots cut out of fancy thin leather.

Emery and I married despite disapproval from both sides. Joyce Blue Kettle protested the loudest, flapping her tongue so much I thought she might wear it thin as a hair ribbon. Joyce had been married for several years by that time and was already a mother, but she was jealous.

"People will say you're greedy," Joyce confided to me the night before my wedding.

"What do you mean?" I only half listened, distracted as I was by the last-minute details of polishing my shoes and combing my damp hair with a clump of sage to scent it.

"They say you're marrying him to get things. What about the seven new dresses he bought you, one for each day of the week? What about the horsehair sofa and brass bed? Didn't he even build you a house?"

Earlier that day I had taken Joyce on a tour of the new house, a neat clapboard structure made of planed lumber. I felt guilty as we moved through the rooms, the number of my possessions suddenly overwhelming me. All my life I had been taught that material goods were dispensable, things to be shared with friends and family. We were not supposed to have more than we needed, so there were endless rounds of giveaways at our dances, where people unburdened themselves of accumulated objects. But Emery was not Sioux, and his affection for me resulted in lavish offerings.

Let them say what they want, I decided. I repeated this aloud to my cousin Joyce, who was pinching the ivory-colored velvet fabric of my wedding cap.

"They know Emery has different ways," I told her.

"Whatever you say." Joyce shrugged, and the next day, when I pinned the elegant cap to my newly bobbed black hair, I noticed sharp creases in the pile, which no amount of smoothing could repair.

On our first wedding anniversary, Emery and I gave a feast for my Sioux relatives. I'd thought time would set things right for Joyce, but she remained bitter about the match. She trailed after me at the feast, and pretended to help me in the kitchen, where she sat idle, letting her mouth do all the work.

"Čuwignaka Duta was really looking out for you." She fought a sly smile. She was referring to our grandmother's sister, Red Dress. Joyce liked to tell people that Emery hadn't fallen for me but for the old magic I had used to spell him. I ignored her, knowing that I'd never tested these powers. If they really existed, I figured, they must have atrophied like an unused muscle. Besides, I'd heard people say the same thing about Joyce and her conquest of Clifford. I struggled for something pleasant to discuss.

"That Bernardine's getting smarter every day, and Clifford looks like he's doing real good."

"That's because I keep him happy." Joyce passed a narrow hand across her wiry hair.

"You know, it works differently in my house," I said. "Emery comes up with so many ways to please me." I ran my own narrow hand from my waist to the round edge of my hip.

Later I forgave Joyce, because when she heard about my husband's death she sent Bernardine to the house to watch over Chaske. Clifford accompanied his daughter, offering to take Emery's personal stock of two horses and one cow to his place, where he could tend them. I was grateful to my cousin for letting her family assist me.

Before his brothers buried him, I bathed Emery's face and trimmed his beard. I filled his pockets with the lemon drop candies he favored and the deck of cards we used for gin rummy. Then I packed both pairs of ice skates in the coffin so that he would be waiting for me by a shallow frozen pond, ready to strap skates on my feet and take me ice-dancing.

• • •

The first day of February was mild, so I opened the windows to air out the house. I'd traded two of my dresses for a scrawny chicken, and I was relieved to be cooking something other than potato soup. Max pecked at the chicken's liver, winking at me from his perch beside the stove.

I overheard Chaske talking to Max. *"Atewaye"*—my father—he called the young owl. I understood then that this was Chaske's way of keeping his father alive. *"Atewaye,* look at this," he said, holding up a blue-and-white-swirled marble. He chattered for a long time, disturbing Max's meal, until he started coughing. I moved to hold him, murmuring, "You aren't sick," because his eyes looked afraid, round as the owlet's.

He was racked by coughing fits most of the day, and his cheeks were flushed. By the time we finished supper, I considered bundling him up and trying to get him to Dr. Kessler's, three miles away. But the wind changed. The sky turned a heavy gray, and it seemed to be lowering itself, ready to flatten our reservation. Without the horses, I was afraid to set out on foot.

"Close the windows!" I shouted, and felt foolish. I was the only one who could heed the command. So I sealed our house against a kicking wind and a crushing mantle of snow. Chaske and I went to bed early. I slept through the night for the first time in many weeks.

Chaske was worse the next day. The pain in his chest made him cry. I gave him castor oil, which Dr. Kessler had recommended for my husband, but it didn't seem to help. No one I knew had a phone, so I put on several layers of clothes and started to walk the half-mile to Joyce's place, thinking someone there could contact the doctor. But I realized it would take quite a while to make it through such deep snow. I couldn't leave Chaske alone for very long.

I told him stories to take his mind off the pain. I even unpacked the baby rattle he'd given up years before, the rattlesnake rattle Clifford had made for him. I shook it beside his ear, punctuating my singing with its sliding rasp. I sang him funny songs, even dirty songs, and when the pain had exhausted him, I sang the Dakota lullaby he had so recently performed. He was too weak to raise his own voice, but he wielded the wooden cooking spoon in his hand and banged it against the wall. The brass bed rocked with our desperate rhythm; we churned the air with our noise. For a moment I wondered if I could save Chaske myself, summon a healing magic. But I remembered Joyce's futile attempts to cure her crossed eye, the hours she spent as a child pointing her finger at the offending organ while staring at her reflection in a cracked mirror. I knew we did not have the healing touch.

The house was dark and my voice was almost gone, when I heard a knock at the front door.

"Coming!" I croaked.

It was my cousin Joyce, standing on the porch. I could see Emery's sorrel mare at the gate and Dina seated on my slender palomino. I waved to her.

"I came about the dress," Joyce said. At first I didn't know what she was talking about. "There's that powwow tonight," she continued, "up at the hall. Dina was hoping her dress was ready so she could wear it."

"I haven't been able to finish it," I said. "Chaske is real sick. He needs the doctor. Could you stop at Dr. Kessler's and tell him to come?"

Joyce promised to fetch him. She patted my arm.

I returned to Chaske, warm with confidence. "Everything will be okay," I crooned, my voice clear and strong again. I rocked Chaske in the brass bed, held his body against mine as if I could absorb the tearing coughs. At least an hour passed. I was sinking into the dark and feeling hope drain away. I could actually *feel* it, a trickle of heat on my hands.

All this time I pictured Joyce driving the horse through wet snow as high as its chest. I could see the horse swimming across the snowfields to reach Dr. Kessler's. But the picture changed. I saw my cousin and her daughter break through snow walls, pound the flakes to slush beneath the horses' hooves, but only as far as the community hall. They were inside that flat building, their cheeks pink and fingers warming in their jacket pockets. They were dancing together around the drum, their feet moving in perfect mother-daughter symmetry. Then it was Dina—graceful even in baggy overalls—dancing alone as her mother watched from the sidelines, tracking the girl with the eye she could control. Her lips were tight with satisfaction, she held herself stiff and straight in the wooden folding chair, proud. The picture dazzled my eyes as I sat in the dark room, burned itself against the back of my eyelids. I imagined I could even hear the song that moved Bernardine's feet. It swept across the snow and spilled its notes against the bedroom window. The glass shrieked.

Finally I lit the lamp. I saw my reflection in the windowpane and noticed new lines etched in my face, drawn from nose to chin. I lifted the lamp high to regard the rest of the room. I nearly dropped it. Patches of brilliant red speckled the walls beside my bed and the faded quilts. My own hands were covered with blood from Chaske's lungs. His eyes were truly white now, as if his spirit were the only thing that had given them pigmentation. I knew I had lost him. But before I moved to wash his body, I poked my finger in his mouth, deep in a pool of black blood. I swal-

lowed the fluid, because wherever he had gone, I wanted
to follow close behind.

My son's coffin was carried to town and stored in an
icehouse. The ground was frozen, so we couldn't bury him
just yet. Joyce Blue Kettle showed up at my door with wet
eyes, and small pails of food. She said Dina was so upset
she couldn't get out of bed. I didn't let her inside the house.

"Get away," I told her. I refused to open the door wider
than an inch.

"I'm just sick about it. I didn't know how bad he was."

"You were dancing, weren't you? You were dancing."

Her eyes sparked and lit like a flash fire. "Who do you
think you are? If Dina was sick, you know that doctor
wouldn't lift a finger to make it over here. He'd tell me to
bring her in. What makes you think he'd come for yours?
Is yours better than mine?"

I left the door cracked open and went to my room. I
removed every dress from the wardrobe, even stepped out
of the blue calico I was wearing. I rushed down the stairs
in my cotton slip.

"Here!" I said, throwing the dresses at my cousin, who
waited, curious, on my front porch. "You always wanted
them. Take them! Take them!" She caught the dresses and
draped them over her arm.

Joyce backed down the steps and hurried away. She
nearly tripped over the skirt of one dress, the one I had
worn at my wedding. I watched her run across the frozen
yard, my dresses clutched to her chest.

I was frozen as the ground, frost on my upper lip, my
tongue a chunk of ice. My mind was numb, but my fingers
still worked. I dug out the red beads Clifford had given me.
Originally I'd planned to find dark blue beads as well and
decorate Dina's moccasins with the two contrasting colors.

But now I just wanted to finish the slippers.

It took me three full days to bead the moccasins. I beaded the upper part, the sides, the leather tongue, even the soles, using all but a handful of beads. The moccasins were pure red. In those three days I didn't eat a single morsel of food. I kept my stomach filled with water. The pump had frozen, so I had to drink gritty melted snow. I let Max pick at the meals the community had cooked for me.

I remember the night I finished beading Dina's moccasins the way I remember stories I have read in books—from a distance, from behind a barrier, perhaps a sheet of ice. I folded Dina's outfit and placed the moccasins on top. Then I wrapped the bundle in a pillowcase. I dressed to go outdoors, wearing Emery's work boots, and fastened Chaske's baby rattle to my braid with a leather thong. I tossed the braid over my shoulder and heard its warning rasp. It was after midnight, but I didn't take a lantern; the moon was a chilly night-light. I picked up the package and was about to set off, when something stopped me, a sudden prick of heat deep inside my body. The snow attracted my gaze when I paused in the doorway. It looked clean, as though it could deaden the spark. So I covered my head and arms with snow, molded it to my thighs. I didn't feel the chill or the moisture. I moved on like a snow queen.

I can still hear my footsteps crackling through the drifts. I stopped several feet from the door of the Blue Kettle place.

"Čuwignaka Duta, you help me now," I implored. I hunched in the snow.

Bernardine, I called with my mind. *Bernardine.* I didn't speak aloud, but my head buzzed with her name, the syllables filled my throat. My teeth clicked her name. *Bernardine.*

She was wearing the flannel nightdress I'd given her for Christmas, and she was barefoot. She came right up to me. *We must dress you,* I said, still silent. She was obedient, her eyes glazed and swollen from crying. She lifted her arms so I could remove the nightdress. Her skin shriveled in the cold, but she didn't shiver. I dressed her then, in the trade-cloth dress and leggings. I tied the belt around her waist and slipped the cape over her head. I smoothed her thick braids. Finally I knelt before her and fit the beaded moccasins on her feet. I tied the laces.

"You dance," I hissed. The words were white smoke in the air.

No one will ever know how many hours Bernardine danced in the snow. She danced herself into another world. Clifford found her the next day about a mile from their house, at the edge of a circular track she'd worn through high snowdrifts. People said she was frozen to a young hackberry tree, embracing it as if she had given up on her powwow steps and commenced waltzing.

I heard that Joyce wanted someone to remove the shreds of leather and beads, all that remained of Dina's red moccasins. But the pieces were fused to her daughter's skin. One old woman started to cut them off, slicing into flesh— which was the moment Joyce stumbled out of her mind. So they were left on Dina's feet.

For two months she and my son Chaske rested side by side in the icehouse. People avoided me and my cousin after an initial round of visits. But everyone turned out for the joint burial.

Joyce and Clifford and I stood near the open graves. I noticed everyone else had pulled back. I don't remember a single word uttered by the Catholic priest. I don't even remember walking to the tiny cemetery behind the church. But I can hear the sound of Joyce's laughter. She giggled into a white handkerchief, tears rolling down her flat cheeks. Her short hair was patchy, singed in several places; I guess Clifford had tried to set her hair with a curling iron. She looked years younger, her face smooth and empty, so different from my own face, which I hardly recognized anymore. My skin was parched and lined as the bottom of a dry creekbed.

That spring, after the children were buried, I discovered that magic let loose can take on a life of its own. I had made my niece dance, and there was no one to tell her to stop. Bernardine Blue Kettle was still dancing, this time around my pretty clapboard house. I didn't actually see her; I was too afraid to look, afraid I would see Chaske riding on her shoulders. But I heard the stamp and shuffle of her steps. She never visited at the same hour, teasing me with her unpredictability, and there were no footprints in the dirt. But each time the noise ended and I found the courage to step onto my porch, I saw the flash of red beads that had fallen on the ground. I didn't touch them. I kicked the dirt to hide their gleam.

I noticed that even the magpies, always greedy for shimmering objects, scavenged in some other yard. They did not covet the sparkling red beads scattered outside my house.

9
Snakes

Red Dress
(1864)

FATHER LA FRAMBOIS WAS ANXIOUS TO BAPTIZE ME IN the Missouri River, to change my name from Čuwignaka Duta, or Red Dress, to the holier appellation Esther. He was an energetic old man and vivid in color, his cheeks so brightly red they looked slapped, and his eyes a dark blue like the night sky, although sometimes dimming to black in moments of anger. I would not be coaxed into the Missouri, not even to repay him for the hours he spent teaching me to read, to write, recite, to form my thoughts into plain, desolate English until I could speak in terms more lovely than could the priest. He bribed me with stories of heaven and eternal life, told me it was within my power to transform my soul from a black crusted thing into a white snow goose with silken wings. When that failed, he bribed me with sugar, and silver crosses that I could wear dangling from my earlobes. I wore the crosses to test their potency, expected Christ to whisper his message directly into my ears. And when he was silent I knew that the silver crosses were really symbols of the morning star, the same image we painted on our buckskin clothes. But I did not tell Father La Frambois, because it isn't polite to point out to an elder person that he is mistaken.

The missionary priest traveled alone throughout Dakota Territory, perched on a tall American horse that routinely charged our ponies and had to be led through the village

239

with a blanket covering its head. The priest arrived year after year in the fall, noticed first by Šunka Gleška, Spotted Dog, who would race in circles around my father's lodge, occasionally pausing to howl. This clever companion was a pumpkin-colored dog with wiry fur and white speckles on his muzzle. He could respond to commands made in either Dakota or English, which greatly impressed my father. Once alerted by Spotted Dog, the village would turn out to welcome Father La Frambois, moving toward him like an errant wave from the river. We became accustomed to his annual arrival at our winter camp, familiar with the heavy black dress he wore falling awkwardly from his crooked shoulders; he resembled a turkey vulture with broken wings. He would remain with us until spring, drill me in my lessons and study my careful penmanship. He taught me to write the name Esther so that I would be ready to claim it once I had saved my soul; and although I refused the name, I liked to draw it, managing the ink so that it would flow gracefully without bleeding, and fashioning the *E* with dramatic flourishes, curved into the shape of a lush bear heavy with winter fat.

Perhaps I should have told the Jesuit directly: "I will never be the convert you desire. I am Red Dress, beloved of snakes." I know he would have found that statement foolish. He had no patience for spirits, dreams, or animal totems, despite his self-proclaimed ability to transform wine into blood and a crisp wafer of bread into living flesh. That is why, although I listened quietly to his stories and studied Scriptures, translated his teachings into the Dakota language so that my curious father, Bear Soldier, and his seven sub-chiefs could decide for themselves the merit of Father's words, I never told the priest my own legend.

My mother was Black Moon, the lady whose long fea-

tures threatened to slip off her face until she smiled, beautifully, lifting them back into place. In her care I came to know myself, and her memories of me became my own. I recall being set out to play on a vast buffalo hide, then, made drowsy by the sun, tipping over and sliding into sleep. My mother was visiting with friends a short distance away, her hands busy with quillwork. She didn't notice the two rattlesnakes gliding onto my infant's shadow, where they coiled together, joining me in a nap. I remember their chalky smell and graceful movements, the feel of their cool glossy skin. As I slept, I clutched a serpent by the tail and shook it like a baby's toy. The rattler never struck, was patient with me even when my mother and her friends hovered, horrified, above his twisting head.

"Don't move," the women whispered to each other. They pulled my mother back and made her sit on the ground. "Look at how they are claiming her," one woman said. Eventually my grasping fist released the viper, and he and his companion left the buffalo hide. I think I cried for them to return, but my mother crushed me into her arms and I grabbed her braids, thinking they were black snakes.

"That one charms the snakes," people have whispered all my life, but they have it wrong. The snakes charmed me.

The final winter of my friendship with the priest was 1864 by his reckoning. Father La Frambois was determined to impress, to introduce us to that deity he called the True God. He told me to inform the village crier that he would be saying mass on the prairies.

"The vaulting sky is my cathedral," he fairly shouted at me. His arm swept the horizon. "Everyone must attend. Everyone must be given this opportunity to hear the word of God and discover the life everlasting.''

His skin was slick with the heat of his emotion; I thought of melting tallow. Pity pricked my heart, and when I opened my mouth to tell the crier what Father had said, scheming words emerged. ''Tomorrow Father La Frambois will dance for us on the grass.'' It was a minor deception I felt would bring the people rushing, curious, to the level floodplain Father had selected for his impromptu church. Even the older warriors—dispassionate, believing they had seen everything worth noticing in the world—would surely turn out for such a spectacle.

''You will be my voice,'' Father said that evening, ignorant of my treason. ''You will be the instrument of your people's salvation.'' His bright cheeks were flames; he looked ready to burn.

I had often wondered why the priest chose me, an unwilling acolyte, for his pupil. Why not my younger brother or little sister? Why not a patient child whose mind was untroubled, so rarely did she question what she heard? I asked him now, ''Father, why am I your voice?''

I received the answer that is no answer: ''It is God's will.''

The next afternoon four hundred people assembled on the level plain to witness Father's dance. He received everyone—even the crawling infants—with a handshake and made the people stand in straight rows. ''These are pews,'' he said. When everyone was settled, he faced the orderly group and began to speak: ''Welcome to your grass church. The Lord is all around you—let Him into your hearts. You have been a stubborn people, a great challenge to me. I have come this year, and in past years, because your souls are in jeopardy and I care about you.''

Father paused, waiting for me to translate. I told my

tribesmen: "Welcome, friends. The past winters we spent together have been very pleasant. I've learned a great deal from these visits and I have respect for you. You are a strong people."

The warriors nodded, breathing, "*Ohan,*" and several of the women trilled the *wičağadata* cry of approval. "They say you are making sense," I told the priest. He spoke for an hour about the necessity of cleansing our spirits, until I began to think of the soul as a garment I could rinse in the river and then spread on a smooth rock to dry in the sun. Mind you, when I translated inaccurately it was not out of carelessness or spite. Father was tactless, but he had been a friend to me. It was loyalty that led me to overlook his indelicate remarks and speak in a voice of my own.

All during Father's sermon the rows held. No one faltered in the chill air or stamped his feet. None of the children squawked. Afterward Father removed his ornate thurible from a velvet-lined casket and lit the incense. He paraded in front of the patient families, swinging the thurible up and back, and then in a full dramatic circle. The cloying scent of burning incense blew into their faces. He marched past the people, behind them, surrounding them with smoke. Spotted Dog trailed after him, imitating the priest's dignified pace and inspecting his tracks with something like suspicion. I moved to signal the dog but never completed the gesture. A tall figure lunged into the neat lines Father referred to as pews. The intruder clapped his hands and doubled over, his shoulders shaking with laughter.

"Šunka Wakan Wanaği," people murmured. They were whispering his name, Ghost Horse. The community pulled back and watched as he rolled on the ground like a mad colt; he brayed with laughter and tore the grass with his white teeth. Father La Frambois moved to stand over Ghost Horse. The thurible still rocked in his hands.

"The poor boy is deranged," Father said.

"No, he is *heyo'ka*. He dreamed of the thunderbirds," I tried to explain.

"Stop there, stop there!" Smoke coiled from the thurible like pale ribbon snakes dancing on their tails. I couldn't see Father's face, but I could hear his tongue clicking sharply in his mouth. "I thought we were progressing. I believed you were beyond all this."

Father La Frambois, his posture collapsed in defeat, trudged back to his guest lodge. Spotted Dog trotted behind him, snapping at the threads of smoke and coughing whenever he swallowed the rich vapor.

Disappointed with the program, the people quickly dispersed, until only Ghost Horse remained, thrashing at my feet. He quieted, sat up, and dusted his graceful arms. White streaks of lightning painted his arms and legs, and his face was striped with vertical lines in black and white. A bunch of switch grass was tied to his forelock, hiding eyes I knew were clear and black as polished buffalo horns. A cold wind was blowing from the northwest, the place winter came from, but Ghost Horse didn't shiver. He fanned his face and complained of the scorching heat.

After dreaming of the giant thunderbirds who could shoot lightning from their glimmering eyes, Ghost Horse had become *heyo'ka,* a sacred clown. His behavior was perverse: he wept at social dances, laughed at solemn events, shivered in the hot summer sun, and sweltered in frigid temperatures. He rushed into battle ahead of other warriors, treating war as play, and he always said the opposite of what he meant. I sensed he was lonely, burdened by his powerful dream, which obligated him to appease the thunder-beings through public humiliation.

Ghost Horse stood and shook his limbs as if to rouse himself. I stared at the ground, polite, demure, my legs trembling beneath my dress. "I disappointed the priest," I finally said. "He doesn't understand the way we do things."

Ghost Horse was silent a long moment. Then he told me: "He understands everything."

That winter, as in years past, Father La Frambois failed to secure a single convert. "I've made headway with other bands. Why are you people so obstinately, willfully blind?" he asked me.

I shall say here what I couldn't tell Father La Frambois: His stories did not make sense to us. Bear Soldier, head chief of our band and my own father, was a logician whose counsel was solicited by other leaders. He listened to the anecdotes I dutifully translated for the priest—Cain slaying Abel, Abraham's willingness to sacrifice Isaac, Joseph delivered into slavery by his jealous brothers—and shook his head. My father wanted to know, "Why are his people so determined to kill their relatives?"

So I asked Father, "Why did Cain murder his brother?"

Father pointed at me and shook his finger. "Because he didn't have faith."

I told my father, "When the priest's people don't believe in the higher spirits they go crazy."

"Then we'll pray for them," he said.

My father had seen other bands trade with white people, succumb to diseases, and grow dependent upon their superior goods. He decided that we would trade only with our traditional sources: other bands and friendly tribes. Our arrows were tipped with filed bone, not metal; to cook our meals, we used the stomach lining of a buffalo rather than shiny kettles; we rejected mirrors, flour, coffee; and we used quills and paint to decorate our clothing, rather than the colorful beads from Europe. I felt it would be rude to tell the priest his teachings were just another import for us to resist. Instead I told him, "We will not be degraded."

Father's mouth fell open, and his tongue flicked out and then back in, like an alert frog's. He swallowed the words he was about to deliver. I quickly apprehended. In Father La Frambois's view of the world, we were already a degraded people, whom he intended to elevate, single-handedly, into the radiant realm of civilization.

I dream of that place where the North Platte River crosses the Laramie, a place of soldiers, treaties, and immigrant trains. I've never been there in waking life, but I still recognize Fort Laramie. I've heard that in springtime this area is a green blanket of lush buffalo grass, yet in my dream the ground is dead white. I am walking through a field of—what? My legs push through tall stalks of limp parchment paper, shredded, tattered, a grim harvest sprouting from chalky soil. Death crackles beneath my moccasins. The grass is gone, and the wildflowers and delicate lacewings, the plump grasshoppers, the cottonwood trees, the lively killdeer. As far as I can see—squinting in every direction—the paper spreads, licking across the land like a prairie fire out of control. I want to leave this nightmare. I look at my feet and notice that each step I take leaves a stunted patch of pale, dry grass, struggling to grow.

I am here for a reason, I tell the wind, and it whips the paper, threatens to tear it from the white plains. *I am the uneasy voice of the grass.*

• • •

My life, like Ghost Horse's, was altered by a dream. It was decided that I would travel to Fort Laramie after the spring thaw. No one knew what would happen once I arrived—assuming I completed the treacherous journey—least of all myself. Father La Frambois had said the Lord called him into service, and this is how I felt: directed by the spirits. All winter I suppressed a nervous euphoria, vacillating between fear and anticipation.

My brother Long Chase was two years younger than I was, sixteen, but had already brought down buffalo bulls and accompanied war parties on raids against the Arikara. Long Chase told me: *"Tanke"*—older sister—"I am coming with you. You can tell me not to, but I'll just follow anyway. Get used to it."

Father La Frambois left before I did, to visit more promising bands: Indians who pressed their lips to the large crucifix dangling from his belt, who could chant prayers in Latin. When he departed, his horse seemed aware that the village was watching, and it minced across the prairie, lifting its stocky legs higher than was necessary.

I had written the priest a formal farewell message to show off my elegant script, and signed it "Esther," as a final act of kindness. But nowhere in the missive did I mention Fort Laramie or the dream or my coming trip. For years I had thought I was shielding Father La Frambois from information I felt he would never understand, would in fact find disturbing. It was only as I watched his bent figure diminish to a speck that I realized my motives were suspect. I had been protecting myself, refusing to speak aloud the legends and ideas I thought would sound absurd in bare English. I nurtured secrecy to avoid derision. Perhaps this was why the dream came to me. A rare opportunity for redemption.

The day before my journey was to begin, I climbed the top of Angry Butte to pray. I added my prayer—a heavy flat rock—to all the others. They formed a neat pile that rose to my waist. I was careful not to brush my fingers across the other invocations; this place was so powerful I thought I could hear the stones speak. My foot slipped on a round stone, and I fell on my back with such force that the wind left my body. I looked for the stone, with angry intentions. I found it touching a second one, its duplicate, and scooped them into my hand. They were perfectly round and unblemished. I lifted one to my cheek; it was impossibly smooth.

"They are twin sisters," my mother told me when I showed them to her. "You were meant to find them." I painted them red, the color of life, and wrapped them in soft buckskin.

The stones move with a purpose, I told Father La Frambois in my thoughts, though the purpose was a mystery to me.

The next is hard to say, the picture is so vivid. Bear Soldier and Black Moon stood in front of their lodge, their hands fastened on my sister's frail shoulders. Walks Visibly winced in pain. She anchored them there; she was too young to follow me as Long Chase would. No one cried. It would be disrespectful to the spirits who had planned this course of action, but the family must have feared it would never see me or my brother again.

This is what we looked like as we slipped into the unknown: One pony carried our household goods, our water, fire horn, pemmican, and jerky. The other carried a small lodge, the smoked hides lashed onto the poles. Long Chase carried a compact short bow and would ride ahead. We had both packed moccasins stolen from enemy tribes—Crow and Arikara—to wear in their territory so our tracks wouldn't give us away.

Spotted Dog shivered with excitement and sat down, only to jump up and run between the ponies' legs. "You'll get kicked in the head," my brother warned him. "Settle down." The dog sighed and crouched impatiently.

The last face I saw was partially hidden by a clump of switch grass. Ghost Horse moved quickly past everyone else, his arms and legs flashing, a lightning storm in our midst. He chuckled as he handed me a smoked shield of tough buffalo-bull hide. I turned it over to inspect the front: a picture of a woman in a red dress clutching an arrow of lightning in her hand. She seemed fierce, unfamiliar. Twenty-one rattlesnake rattles dangled from the bottom edge of the shield, so with each step I sounded like a den of restless snakes.

Ghost Horse grinned at me, baring his perfect teeth, but the one eye I could see beneath cords of grass was so red he could have been weeping blood. I clutched the shield as I mounted my pony, tried to still my shaking hands. Ghost Horse seized the bridle and for one moment tossed the grass from his forehead.

"I will never miss you," he said.

That day there was a white sky. Clouds choked the horizon and crowded the sun. The sky was so low we were in the sky, we were air, we were something other than what we had been before.

"*Tanke,*" I heard my brother whisper. "The spirits are all around us."

We traveled southwest behind Spotted Dog, who glanced

back at us every few steps to be certain he was heading in the right direction.

"You're not fooling us," my brother called to him. "You're not in charge."

The pale sky sapped my spirits. I was glad when the sun burned through the clouds and searing light peeled back layers of mist. We rode into a valley of trembling flowers; the lacy petals fluttered in the wind.

"Butterflies," Long Chase breathed. Indeed, the flowers were actually swallowtail butterflies, their pale wings edged in blue. I had never seen so many in one place. There were enough of them to bend stems of grass; they dripped from the stalks.

"The ancestors are watching us," I said. "Look at how many we have."

The butterflies lifted then in a rippling cloud and took over the sky. My brother stopped his pony to watch what looked like a snowstorm in reverse, the drifts banking heaven. "This is an odd day," he finally said.

Father La Frambois was frequently in my thoughts. How would he have explained what happened next? I would have told him: *Father, we stepped into a dream, into a world governed by the spirits. Father, for two weeks we never saw another person: no tribesmen, no enemies, only passing herds of elk and antelope.* My brother carried his short bow and I held my shield and Spotted Dog pretended to lead the way, his tail straight as a flag, and we marched across the territory as if we were the only creatures in the land. We covered the distance in two weeks and camped within sight of the fort, dazed and exhausted. Even Spotted Dog collapsed in a careless sprawl.

"What happens next?" Long Chase asked me.

"Tomorrow we visit the fort. One thing at a time."

He looked at me, and I saw the boy in his face, the deep pucker of dimples on either side of his mouth, which he tried so hard to smooth. The edge of one thick braid was clamped between his teeth, rolled back and forth to produce a wet squeak. He caught himself and spat the braid from his mouth. He trusted that I understood what had brought us here. I didn't. But as the older sister, I flashed a smile and told him: "Tomorrow will be an adventure. Your friends would be jealous."

That night I noticed that Spotted Dog crept beside Long Chase and slept with his forepaws against my brother's chest. All night their hearts beat together.

Upstream from the fort was a village I would later hear the soldiers refer to as Squaw Town. This was the place we visited first. The people who lived there were our cousins—a different band of the same tribe. Their leader was a man with a name I have forgotten because I thought of him as Death Shirt, and when my brother and I spoke of him, that was the name we used. His cloth shirt was decorated with tiny metal snuffboxes—sinister as coffins—pierced and sewn so closely together he jangled. He wore a soldier's forage cap squashed low on his head and ragged moccasins shedding beads. He blinked at me and then at Long Chase. We were wearing our ceremonial clothes, our finest buckskins. My dress was painted red and decorated with elk teeth, and my brother's shirt was dyed blue and stitched with quilled stars—he was a piece of the sky.

Death Shirt shuffled his feet. He asked us: "Are you the ghosts of our ancestors?"

"No," I said. "Where we come from we still dress the old way."

He passed his hand across his eyes, and I noticed three

parallel scars on his chin. "Come with me," he said.

We were led through the village, and several times I heard Long Chase draw breath too quickly. He stepped close to me and whispered in my ear. *"Unšika."* Pitiful. The children were barefoot, chewing their fingers, and their mothers stood with long hair unbraided, tangling in the wind. Many of them wore fabric clothes that were coming apart at the seams.

"These ones come from a long time ago," Death Shirt told the village, gesturing at the two of us.

Some of the women were crying, but silently, tears running quick as water. Gifts were pressed into our hands: pebbles, berries, a handful of earth beans and another of parched corn. "We give what we can," an older woman said. She lifted her arm like a hunter wielding a lance and trilled in thunderous rolls; she could have had a thousand tongues. My brother and I shook hands with our cousins and packed the gifts in parfleche containers strapped to our ponies. We handed out presents of our own: moccasins, jerky, and our last cake of pemmican. The women continued to praise us with their voices, even after we rode away. By the time we reached Fort Laramie, the noise was a sad drone, like bees singing in our ears.

Fort Laramie was little more than a hodgepodge of buildings scattered across a plain. Mismatched structures of whitewashed adobe and blond wood cluttered the area, dwarfed by Laramie Peak some fifty miles to the west. The soldiers smelled of rancid butter and looked uncomfortably warm in their uniforms. When I introduced myself as Esther and Long Chase as Joseph, and tilted my head so the silver crosses I wore fell forward, we were told that the post chaplain, a Reverend Pyke, would be most eager to meet us.

"He's convinced the Sioux will never be real Christians," the private said.

We were led beyond the parade grounds to a cluster of cottonwood trees hunched together like old men. I saw the giant's back and smelled his malodorous top hat of poorly tanned beaver hide from several yards away. He was shooting at a tree, I thought, until we were close enough to see that he had nailed a dozen bull snakes to the trunk and was methodically firing at their heads. They were still moving, rippling against the wood. I had to look at the ground. My brother touched my arm to comfort me. His fingers felt like five smooth serpents wrapped around my wrist.

Reverend Pyke turned, and I looked into his eyes. They were a remarkable color, somewhere between green and black, charred, like burnt grass. A broad forehead dominated his features, and his brown beard wasn't on his chin but below it, like a thick strip of bear fur stuck to his throat. His red skin was peeling in several places, and he fingered the patches as he stared at me. He didn't seem to notice my brother.

The first words he spoke were: *"Mine enemies are lively and they are strong, and they that hate me wrongfully are multiplied."* In unison we continued: *"They also that render evil for good are mine adversaries, because I follow the thing that good is."*

Pyke thrust his fingers in his beard and scratched the hidden flesh. "Do you follow the thing that good is?" he asked me.

"I would if I knew what that was," I replied.

He nodded his great head, substantial as a cannonball. "You are of upright conversation," he said.

• • •

As easily as that I attached myself to the fort, becoming a kind of personal secretary to Reverend Pyke. "I want to know what my left hand is doing," he bellowed on that first day. He called me Esther Left Hand. I passed myself off as the Christian whom Father La Frambois had tried so long to create. I relished the irony and would have been rather smug if not for the fact that each day was a step into the void. I was no closer to understanding the purpose of my mission.

My brother and I camped between the fort and the village of our cousins, and went in opposite directions for most of the day. Long Chase had befriended several young warriors, and together they trekked north to find game. "You're a good influence on them," I told him one evening. "You're already so capable." He ducked his head, shy of my praise.

Long Chase had instructed Spotted Dog to watch over me, so every morning the dog led me to the fort and settled in a corner of the patched windowless lean-to Pyke referred to as his study. A vast mirror hung above his desk, its gilt frame a horror of twisted vines and sharp leaves, angry-looking foliage. I thought of it as Eden Lost. The first occasion I was alone in that room I stepped to the glass and touched my reflection with a finger. It was the only time I'd seen myself in a mirror, but the glass was so wavy I could have been staring into water. I was struck by how my mouth tipped downward in a child's pout, and I hadn't realized that I watched the world through my eyelashes. I didn't observe myself for very long. My eyes were the same shape as my mother's, curved like wings; watching them made me lonesome.

I transcribed Pyke's sermons, my hand dipping into ink like a bird pecking at water and then sweeping across the page to keep pace with the rapid language. I knew the Bible well enough to catch when Pyke departed from his own words to quote Scripture. One passage he returned to again and again, while his fingers wandered over the silver revolver he kept on his blotter: *"The wicked have drawn out the sword and bent their bow, to cast down the poor and needy, to slay such as be of upright conversation. Their sword shall enter their own heart, and their bows shall be broken."*

Pyke often raged in the study, his lecture becoming personal, perhaps more revelatory than he intended. "I'm a child of the wilderness," he told me. "God's child. I sprouted from the earth like a bean. No mother, no father, no strangling ties to come between me and the Lord."

Pyke was never without his smelly top hat and on the windiest days managed to keep it glued to his enormous head. His fingers were strangely flat, and pale as grubs, except for the rim of dirt under the nails. I observed that while his flesh was none too clean and, I believe, his clothes had never been scrubbed, he was fastidious about his space. His cherrywood desk was so well polished it looked as if crimson flames burned beneath the surface; his books were regularly dusted, and arranged by size so that the shortest books led to the tallest; and the planks forming the study floor—though gapping and uneven—were soaped and buffed to reveal the wood's golden heart. Insect life wasn't safe in his presence; he crushed what he could. And Pyke said there was nothing natural about the natural world; it was an evil disorder requiring the cleansing hand of God. When he came across a spider's sac of eggs nestled in the folds of his heavy jacket, he squashed it with his fingers and licked them clean.

"I've swallowed the spit of Satan," he announced.

He watched me as I worked. I kept my eyes on the papers before me, but I could feel him staring, and I could smell the sour decay of his hat. I marveled that his fingers never grabbed me by the braids, tearing me from the earth so that I too was no longer part of the natural world, but his creature, a lifeless polished trophy like the preserved prairie dog mounted on a block of wood and serving as a doorstop. Instead he fingered the beard at his throat or the silver revolver, and I labored to set down Pyke's vision of America: a place where animals were bred for food behind neat fences, mountains were leveled, valleys filled, rivers straightened, and grass trained with a ruler.

"Man is the organizer," he said. "Adam named the creatures, mastered the elements, and answered to no one but the Lord. This is the legacy we must claim for ourselves."

I scratched the words onto stiff paper but had the sudden urge to yank the land from beneath Pyke's feet like a slippery rug.

On Sundays I sat in the back of the low-ceilinged hall Reverend Pyke borrowed for his services, and tried not to envy Long Chase his freedom. Pyke's voice didn't have anywhere to go in the small space—even the thick wool uniforms couldn't absorb the fierce syllables—so his commotion penetrated my ears like a great clanging bell. I watched the congregation through my eyelashes, practiced stillness and control of my heart, which I thought of as a fist-sized Indian pony, all kicking legs and twitching tail. I slowed its gallop to a walk and measured each step it took. *I run my own body,* I thought.

The handful of officers' wives sat together toward the front, surrounded by their husbands. I couldn't tell if the women were fenced in or the men shut out. I was fascinated by their pallor, a shade so light it was tinted blue, like thin milk. Their clothes squeezed the breath from them and rendered their bodies taut as bowstrings. I longed to reach out and pluck them, play their one quavering note. The laundresses from Soapsuds Row and the housekeepers sat behind them, decidedly healthier in complexion. These ladies had tired feet that looked to be planted for eternity, and darting eyes. I don't know how many of Pyke's words they digested; they seemed intent on soaking up the subterranean sounds of people trapped together: the rustles, coughs, whispers, sighs.

One lady was, like me, without a group and sat to the far right of the congregation. She was so diminutive her feet didn't touch the ground. Pyke had said she was a recent widow, which would explain why her black dress was still crisp and tidy, unlike those of other widows, who turned them inside out after a time, to get more wear. The color pinched her even tighter than her corset, and in profile she nearly vanished, like the flat of a sword, except for her breasts, tiny and round as ground-cherries. I soon noticed that while this lady always wore black, she also managed a spot of color, perhaps a folding fan, a ribbon pinned beneath her brooch, a nodding sunflower threaded into her bonnet. I thought of these items as her intentions peeking through.

One morning at dress parade I found myself standing beside the widow. She interested me more than the mechanical movements of the soldiers who stretched across the horizon, their white gloves gleaming like teeth.

"Oh, look at the guidons," she murmured. One open hand covered her pulsing throat and the other dabbed at her upper lip with a square of delicate lace. The flags streamed behind the soldiers, pulled taut by the wind. The sky was

pasted with the company colors. Sweeping gusts took most
of the sounds—the orders being called, the jingling of spurs
and harnesses, the indignant snorts of cavalry horses—so
the parade became an eerie drama of tremendous silent activity. I was unimpressed with the display, which struck me
as the kind of thing Pyke would have dreamed up in his
hankering for artificial order, simulated grace. But I said
something appreciative to the widow, to make out I was
enjoying the spectacle as much as she was.

When the soldiers were given orders to retire and began
leaving the field, the widow turned to me. Her eyes were
light brown and unusually bright; they reminded me of the
nuggets of fool's gold Father La Frambois carried in his
pocket. "I'm Fanny Brindle," she said. "You've been
watching me."

I must have started, because she touched my arm with
one finger. "That's not a complaint, it's an observation."

Fanny Brindle removed her hat. Her dark blond hair was
pinned up but seemed to strain against the combs; soft curls
rolled across the slopes of her head like miniature tumble-
weeds. She had a tight little face and a sharp nose that
pointed downward, steady as a compass.

"Are you a woman alone?" she asked me.

"No." I shook my head. "I have my brother, Joseph,
and my dog, and—" Here I should have said something
about the Lord, to continue my pose as a Christian Sioux,
but I forgot myself. "And my ancestors are looking out for
me," I said.

Fanny didn't notice. "I am alone," she said. "My husband was Sergeant Guy Brindle, but he died three months
ago from scarlet fever. I dosed him with potassium chlorate
and ordered him not to leave, but you see the good it did
me." She wrenched a tall sunflower from the ground and

tucked it into her belt. "Not to worry, though. It wasn't a love match. I came here as a governess, and he offered me an easier life than that. I think it's the reason Polite Company won't breathe in my direction. I used to enter their rooms by the back door.

"We should be friends," Fanny told me. She laughed and nudged the dirt with her toe. "I can't get any lower."

Fanny's artlessness—some would have said thoughtlessness—was part of her charm. I began to think of her as a sunflower, all open face and spitting seeds. She liked to stroll from one end of the fort to the other, her slender twig of an arm hooked through mine. She was eager to share the latest gossip gleaned from Bailey Roe, the enlisted man who had worked for her husband as striker and still offered some occasional assistance.

"He is a man of remarkable hearing and recall," she confided. "His word is gospel."

It was early October, Čanwapekasna Wi, the moon when the leaves rustle. The buffalo grass was a drab brown, and winter's breath swirled across the plain. Pyke was working on a treatise titled "Laramie, the Lord's Outpost" and didn't release me or the watchful Spotted Dog until the sun was well into its downward arc. On these days Fanny met me at the door of Pyke's study, quickly taking my arm and heading in the direction of the river. Fanny wasn't one to stifle her curiosity. She came right out and asked me: "Does he pay you for the work you do?"

"I don't think he makes much more than the enlisted men," I said. "But he takes me to the sutler's store every now and then for supplies."

"Well, he should." Fanny sniffed.

I had a habit of addressing Fanny and Pyke and the oth-

ers at the fort in silence, speaking in my head. The truth
had to let itself out some way, or I would have confused
myself. What I said in the secrecy of my thoughts was:
Fanny, mazaska—*the white iron you call money—is useless to me. Even the goods I take from the sutler's store,
the flour, coffee, sugar, and tobacco, the knives and blankets, are things I do not want. I give them to my cousins
who live upriver.*

Fanny squeezed my arm impatiently—perhaps she saw
these ideas moving across my forehead—and said: "Do
you know what they're saying about you? That you're a
princess." I didn't react, but she nodded in affirmation.
"Yes, a Sioux princess with the light of the world in your
heart, and a devotion to Jesus Christ that is so pure, your
soul is white as cream. I think it's because of your remarkable English," she mused to herself. "They can't conceive
of it as anything but a miracle, and it is, you know. It is."

I smiled at Fanny, assured her that I wasn't a princess,
and thanked her for complimenting my speech. But what I
really said to Fanny was: *Koda—friend—look at this sullen
brown grass, dispirited because winter is coming to punish
it. This, to me, is English. It is little pebbles on my tongue,
gravel, the kind of thing you chew but cannot swallow.
Dakota is the lush spring grass that moves like water and
tastes sweet.*

By November, *Waniyetu Wi,* the winter moon, Fanny
could not be persuaded to go on long walks but remained
in her room, wrapped in a heavy shawl. I visited her there,
though it shamed her to have company, even mine, in such
a place. After her husband died, a new lieutenant had
claimed his apartments, as a superior officer was entitled to
do. Fanny had been ranked out of her home and into a
narrow hallway of the same quarters. The young lieutenant

was sensitive enough to her plight to avoid using the hall-way; he left and entered his rooms via the window.

An overstuffed divan pushed against one wall served as her couch and bed, and she told me that she washed and dressed in the huge walnut wardrobe that took up so much of the hallway one could barely squeeze past it. Sergeant Brindle's photograph dominated a table inlaid with mother-of-pearl, and while he may have looked bright and hopeful if you saw the picture alone, the drumming clock placed beside it cast a shadow across his face that made him appear wistful, aware of the coming fever.

"He wasn't very handsome, was he?" Fanny said. It had been decided, so I knew better than to respond. "But he wasn't cruel or petty. You can see the kindness, there, in his mustache." Fanny pointed to meager wisps of hair sprouting above a plump lip.

I ventured a question of my own. "Do you think you'll marry again?"

"I hope to," she said, without any breath or pause. "Oh, it would be a shame to be here, so outnumbered by men they're thick as fleas, and not claim another. I work on it a little." Her face flushed, becoming a red mask. "I go to all the hops, and dance and dance until I lose my feet, forget my toes were ever there. I just float in the officers' arms and turn into a cloud." She laughed. "A rather black cloud. Well, they have fair warning, then!" Fanny looked at her little feet, tapped her heels together, and grinned so broadly her eyes squeezed shut.

Fanny's reference to fleas proved timely. The fort suf-fered a terrible infestation of the pests, which flourished despite the cold weather. The enlisted men blamed a recent shipment of blankets, and the sutler blanched and swore whenever this possibility was mentioned. I washed my skin and Spotted Dog's fur with buffalo grease and ashes, so we didn't suffer, but Pyke, the soldiers, and even the fine ladies were patched with welts and scabs from zealous scratching.

Fanny decided to organize a theatrical to take everyone's mind off the plague.

"I want to be distracted, don't you?" she asked. When I didn't answer quickly enough, she said, "Oh, you. You aren't bothered in the slightest. I can see it. They don't like that Indian blood, do they?" No, I had to admit, they didn't.

The next day she tacked up a neat sign on the porch of Old Bedlam—the unmarried officers' quarters—announcing the staging of *Macbeth*.

"You have to help me with this," she pleaded, so I became her assistant.

I had read the play aloud under the tutelage of Father La Frambois and was curious to see what Fanny and the soldiers would make of it. I thought Reverend Pyke might disapprove of the scheme, but he supported it and in fact landed a role—three to be precise, since he would play all of the witches.

"Measured fun is a holy pleasure," Pyke blasted that Sunday to a chorus of nodding heads.

A stage only slightly larger than an oven range was erected in the front parlor of Old Bedlam, and auditions were held in the evening between Stable Call and Retreat. Pyke was cast as the three witches because there simply wasn't room for more people onstage. Many of the roles were combined and speeches cut. Fanny insisted we would get to the meat of the story and trim the rest, and by the time the officers in the company had their say, the scenes were mostly swordplay, complete with uncorked sabers and plumed hats. One of my jobs was to prompt the actors in their lines, what lines remained, and the text became as familiar to me as Scripture, until I began to confuse the two and would quote Shakespeare as readily as passages from Ecclesiastes.

Long Chase was curious about my activities and asked me what I was doing. There was no term in Dakota for "assistant director," so I said I was helping the *wašičun*s tell stories. Then I told him about the fleas and vaulted onto my pony to imitate the soldiers' odd canter, how they leaned forward in the saddle to scratch their ankles. Long Chase collapsed on the ground, clutching his ribs and rolling with laughter. Spotted Dog jumped over him, barked, thrust his wet nose into Long Chase's face.

"That was good," my brother said when he could finally speak.

During the two-week rehearsal period I became acquainted with several of the officers I'd previously thought of as faceless. The three I came to know best were those with the largest roles, which meant they needed the most prompting. It was my opinion that Fanny had miscast them, each being woefully unsuited to the part. Lieutenant Royal Bourke, who would play Macbeth, had sky eyes and blond hair like moist honey dripping to his shoulders. He was polished, without being insincere, and had the smoothest voice; really, it was like the bolt of silk I'd seen in the sutler's store. He never failed to notice the lurking Spotted Dog and spoke to him so gently the dog came forward, bowed his head, then, in perfect Dakota etiquette, lifted one pumpkin-colored paw to shake hands. And this man would play the irresolute tyrant? I would have chosen Captain Philander Merritt, the handsomest of the three and the most inscrutable. His pale skin glimmered against hair that was thick and black as my own, eyes brown as acorns. His long eyelashes fluttered before he spoke, and white teeth perched prettily on his bottom lip when he smiled, but I saw tension in his face and shoulders, lines in his young forehead that made me question his friendliness. His body was compact but dense, and as the betrayed Banquo, who returns a ghost to haunt Macbeth, he was ineffective, too solidly in the world for me to ever imagine dead.

Finally, the bold, heroic Macduff, who so capably vanquishes Macbeth, would be portrayed by Lieutenant Lemon Van Horn, youngest of the officers and the one whose questions frequently went unanswered because no one heard him. I could tell that his uniform had been altered to hide a wispy figure, but his face was round, plumped out by soft jowls too smooth for whiskers. His face was fairly red with freckles, and his hair red-gold, though lusterless, like his spirits. People seemed to either confuse or tire him, and when he mocked Macbeth during the play's climax, charging, "Turn, hell-hound, turn!" it was with great drawn-out sighs.

Lady Macbeth proved to be the most difficult part to cast, since the ladies felt it would be undignified to participate, and Fanny couldn't cast herself. At the last minute she convinced a recent arrival to the fort, Melody Kendall, the young wife of a noncommissioned officer, that she should step into the role. The young woman could recite well enough but had to be dissuaded from wearing hoops and the latest gown from Boston, decorated with fabric roses large as cabbages. "Ringlets will never do," Fanny scolded gently. She pointed to the tight clusters springing above Melody's ears.

The night of the performance, Fanny was in a generous mood. She ushered me to a seat near the front, just behind the commanding officers and their carefully coiffed wives, who surreptitiously, or so they thought, scratched beneath smooth waves of hair, behind spread fans.

"You've made a hit," Fanny whispered loudly in my ear. "Just look at you. Old Bedlam will never be the same."

"What do you mean?"

"Oh, you. Everyone's half mad with love, or maybe lust." Here she pinched my forearm so hard it hurt.

"No, no," I demurred, quite sincerely.

Fanny sat down beside me, and her small forehead worked itself into a web of lines. "Don't you know you're beautiful?" she asked. I felt Spotted Dog shift against my leg. Fanny picked up one of my hands as casually as she would a teacup. "Look at this, look at these long delicate bones, nails glossy as porcelain. I can't stand it." She dropped my hand and fell back into the chair in one motion. "I think it's that curl of a smile that finally does them in— partway between a sneer and a laugh. Makes them work to impress you.

"I thought you knew," she concluded. "I thought it was a manipulation."

I could only shake my head at Fanny, my friend, who was surely carried away by the night's festivities and her own complicated flirtations.

A brocade curtain rigged up by Fanny's striker, Bailey, lifted to enthusiastic applause and so much squirming I thought I could see a fog of fleas rise up and redistribute themselves. Pyke's witches were in good voice; he thundered spells, while energetically stirring soapy water in one of the laundresses' borrowed tubs. When he came to the familiar chorus—"Double, double toil and trouble; fire burn and cauldron bubble"—there emerged a dozen witches, as soldiers in the audience shouted the lines with him.

Too often the actors absentmindedly raked fingernails through their beards or across their flesh to discourage the biting fleas, but since the spectators were similarly afflicted, it was overlooked. Lady Macbeth, as it turned out, was determined to be fashionable, and her hoops took up the entire stage; the actors sharing her scenes were forced off the platform onto the floor, gazing up at her as they recited lines. Her ringlets bounced with passion, eliciting titters from the crowd, and one man snickered loudly when she scratched, rather than rubbed, the imagined spot of blood on her hand, all the while wearing elbow-length kidskin gloves and twirling an open parasol.

The final battle, an exchange of blows that went on for nearly half an hour, was performed vigorously. But when the curtain plunged to the ground, we clapped at the effort, and the parlor was filled with a happy buzz. The ladies produced eggnog, and I was about to leave, when Lemon Van Horn—Macbeth's cloth head still tucked under one arm—handed me a glass of the creamy liquid.

"You aren't leaving?" he said in his weary voice.

Surrounded by Lemon, Royal, a handful of other officers, and even the wary Merritt, I saw truth in Fanny's observations. I felt stifled by attention and sought comfort in Spotted Dog, who rested at my feet. I spread my fingers through his coarse fur and felt the regular rhythm of his heart pulsing beneath my fingertips. He occasionally rolled his eyes to meet mine and wouldn't look away until I smiled.

What can they possibly want from me? I wondered. A midnight rendezvous in Squaw Town? Something furtive and shameful, to be quickly forgotten? The eggnog left a sour taste. I ran my tongue across my teeth and nearly gagged. I sat as straight as I could and smiled, or sneered, however they chose to read my expression. I was careful not to look into their eyes, so there would be no message.

The men chattered, told anecdotes, and in the telling staggered or waved their arms, jumped onto chairs, pounded their comrades on the back, punched shoulders. The room became a blur of sound and movement I associated with the smell of curdled cream. Somewhere during the mayhem I slipped my hand into the quilled pouch dangling from my waist. My fingers searched for a sliver of the bitter muskrat root that would quickly change the taste in my mouth. I touched something else. Two smooth stones clicking together, released from buckskin wrapping. I cupped one in my palm to be certain of the object. Earlier that evening, when I left the lodge I shared with my brother, these stones had been buried in a shallow hole beneath my pallet. Some hidden force had pushed them through the ground, propelled them through the air, and tucked them into my bag, where they nested like crimson eggs.

The stones move with a purpose, I told the officers. But in my private way, which was no warning.

I am leaving Old Bedlam, which has lived up to its name on this occasion. Men watch me as I travel lightly down the steps. Now I am a dark figure, a shadow moving across the yard. I bend smoothly to place the stones beneath a clump of weeds, not knowing I will do it. Every step, every gesture, is natural, spontaneous. I am inevitable as light or darkness, steady as rain. I push out my breath to match the wind, and soar in the direction of my brother's sleep. Spotted Dog is ahead of me, grinning to himself as he leads the way.

I'm coming, I sing to him. *I'm coming.* But now I think I'm telling the ancestor-spirits who have waited so long for me to move, as I am moving now.

Upon arriving, I don't enter the lodge but sit outside, my arms and legs carefully folded. Spotted Dog leans into my side, lets his weight fall against me. For once I am the alert one, impervious to chill winds and tired feet, to hunger and thirst. "You rest," I tell him.

Later I will find myself standing beside the river, drawn to the battered cottonwood tree once blasted by a revolver. I am utterly alone. I will hear the man before I see him. He is not so graceful; his stumbling feet churn the dry grass. *Whiss. Whiss.* He is the sleepy one with red hair and freckles, the one whose voice is easily lost. He walks to me without hesitation and doesn't flinch when I reach for his hand. The stones are there, clenched in the fist I peel open one finger at a time. I return the stones to my pouch and pluck a strand of hair from my head. I lean into the man as I wind the thread of hair around a brass button on his jacket; the slow circles enchant us both. He wears the rope across his chest like a cartridge belt. I tell him what to do. I look into his eyes for the first time and see only myself. I have forgotten their color. I leave him to his work, stand with my back to the man and the tree.

I will return to Long Chase and Spotted Dog, sidestepping their dreams as I make my way to the buffalo hide I use to cover myself. I will not see how the man, so recently a boy, climbs the tree and coils the rope as tenderly as I wound hair around the button beneath his heart. He will be graceful as he steps into black air, the night space, flying for a long moment. And when he is forced to land, I will not see the color of his face. The sudden emptiness.

• • •

It was Pyke, prowling the perimeter of the fort on his early-morning reconnaissance with the Lord, who came across Lemon Van Horn hanging from a cottonwood tree. His boots were only a few inches from the ground, and for a moment it must have looked to Pyke as if Lemon were just standing in front of the tree.

"He has thrown his soul to the dogs," Pyke growled in his study that day. "He will languish in Purgatory for what he has done. Quick, Esther, take this down. I will address the subject on Sunday."

I had noticed before that any mention of the loss of human life filled Pyke with a peculiar dread. I don't mean the inevitable sorrow, or the rage one feels when a loved one dies, but a terrible fear penetrating his thoughts, drilling his bones.

"Man is close to almighty, he should not be cut down. And to tear himself out of the world—this is an abomination!" Pyke stamped across the floor, his arms flung open and fingers trembling. "I am unsettled," he said. His candor took me by surprise. He tore at the strip of fur beneath his chin and strode past me. He left the study and didn't think to shut the door.

I observed Pyke closely to escape my own feelings, which were heavy as a hundred stones. *I am at war,* I told myself, knowing it was more complicated than that. I was also at war with myself.

I do not know whom the stones will claim next. They are red eyes that can see everything. Moonlight washes over me like a graceful blessing. This man is silent as he approaches the river, carrying a coil of rope. I can't hear his steps or the rope slapping against his thigh, but I can feel the force of his will. His black hair fades into the night, so the fair skin beneath that dark crest is like a torch. This man's body shudders, his mind attempting to surface. The shaking stops him in his tracks. I move forward gently as a pulse of air and take the stones from his hand.

He is gasping as I wind a strand of my hair around his jacket button. This I do more tightly than before, longing to be finished so I can release him. His eyes are burning at the core, the pin of light at the center of his black pupil. He would like to kill me, but he cannot will his hands to do it.

"You are another one we won't have to fight," I tell him, but it isn't enough. I am forced to watch. The tree is hard for him to climb; several times he slides down the trunk. His movements are slow, reluctant. But the rope nearly twists itself.

A week before Christmas, Fanny Brindle organized a skating party. "This will lift our spirits," she declared. Most of the officers and their families turned out, grateful for the distraction, though Pyke was conspicuously absent.

After Philander Merritt was found dangling from the same tree where Lemon had cast his rope, Pyke took an ax to the tree and not only felled it but chopped it into kindling. He said it would produce an evil smoke, so he tossed the chunks of wood into the river, watching grimly as they swirled away. I knew he was probably brooding in his study while we gathered beside the now frozen river, carefully avoiding the forlorn cottonwood stump.

"I am lost in a mysterious world," he had told me just the day before. He even grabbed my hand as I made ready to leave, kneading it with his flat paws. "Death is chaos," he said.

I was happy to be on the river, where the cold wind drew

tears from my eyes and whipped my mind clean. Several of the soldiers had crude blades strapped onto their boots and were moving across the ice like delicate insects skimming water. Their weight shifted from side to side in an elegant rhythm, hypnotizing me as I stood wrapped in a small buffalo-calf robe.

The ladies without skates were being pushed in wooden chairs, whirled quickly on the ice, letting out cries of pleasure. Fanny was there; her skirt was tucked around her legs and her hands inside a muff of beaver hide. She waved to me, then nearly lost the muff as she grabbed for her chair's back. Her face spun away.

Royal Bourke approached, his sky eyes wide with happiness and his shoulders sparkling with snow. "Why are you standing here?" he asked me. "Why aren't you laughing?"

I avoided his blue gaze by counting his brass buttons. "I like to watch," I said.

"That isn't good enough." He extended his arm and I took it, as lightly as I could. He settled me in a sturdy ladder-back chair and then pressed me forward into currents of bright air: a place without breath or sound. The sky was a wheel as I twirled on the ice, the clouds streaming together and the sun becoming a long string of suns. I smiled, I bent over to laugh into my hands. The chair stopped.

"What's wrong?" Royal asked. He knelt on the ice. I shook my head and laughed a little more. "Oh, good. I thought you were dizzy." He chuckled.

"I was. But it was nice," I told him.

When I thought Royal must surely be tired of the game— though he protested he could push me straight to Canada— I joined Fanny beside a table set with steaming mugs of cider.

"Wasn't it wonderful?" she asked. "It breaks my heart to go back to my hallway. I tell you, I wake up with frost on my eyebrows, hugging nothing friendlier than a can of yeast. To keep it warm, you know, or it would freeze like my potatoes. They're hard as rocks." Fanny sipped the cider tenderly, her lips nearly forming a kiss. "How do you make out in just a tent?"

I told her how Long Chase and I had built a willow stockade around our tipi, with a small runway for the ponies to protect them from night drafts. I worked the smoke flaps so we could build a fire in the lodge, and the flames kept us warm all night. "And Spotted Dog warms my feet," I said. His ears flicked forward at the mention of his name.

Later that night I told Long Chase about my dizzy ride. "I wish I'd seen that. You must have looked funny," he teased. "We were playing too," he continued. "I made those kids a sled out of buffalo ribs, and we took it up there." He pointed to a distant coulee.

"That was a good thing," I said. I was proud of my generous brother, who spent so many hours with the children of our cousins, teaching them to do things the old people in their village only talked about. But it was not our way to fuss over one another; my terse praise was enough.

I looked forward to sleep that night, having exhausted myself the way children do. I checked beneath my pallet, as I did every night, for the sacred stones I had collected from Angry Butte and transported to this place of dying grass. My fingers anticipated their sleek texture, stretched eagerly to graze their faces. I marveled at the warmth they emanated, even packed in frozen ground. I scratched the dirt, eventually turning my hands into claws that raked the earth. But it was useless; the stones were gone.

• • •

The sentries are sleepy by the time I reach the fort's perimeter. One dreams with his eyes open, and the other is crushing the snow with his boots to make animal figures. I brush past them, first one and then the other, mad with potent energy, determined to be invisible. I take chances because I think I am the wind. The tree is gone. There are others, but I know better than to head in that direction. I move toward Old Bedlam and mount the stairs leading to its second-story porch. I sway at the top, flinging my head back to count the stars. *I will give them officers' names,* I think. *I will send them soldiers.*

I hear footsteps and reach out to grasp the railing. He steps onto the porch and carefully closes the door behind him. He is not drowsy and he doesn't resist. I think if I told him to fly he would spread his arms and leap at the moon. He hands me the stones before I look for them and lifts the rope in his hands. It is a coarse snake wound between us.

''Give me your hair,'' he whispers, complice to this act. I wrap the button, but only once or twice. The strand floats free, and I don't snatch another from my open braid. He moves to the railing, his steps like a dance, and ties the rope in ugly ways. He slips his head in the loop, and I put out my hand for him to catch. There is a twitch of a smile on my lips because I have called him back. But he is suddenly a golden bird risen from the deck. He flies away.

Fort Laramie was a place of death—I had seen that in my dream—but now it was a place of ghosts, some of them living. Pyke retreated like a turtle, studying tracts for most of the day, the reading material in one hand and his revolver in the other.

"You can't help me," he said when I knocked on his door.

Rope was confiscated, put under guard, and more soldiers assigned watch duty. Royal Bourke had sky eyes, but now he was buried in a shallow grave laboriously chipped out of the frozen earth. People walked with their heads down, moving briskly to get somewhere. Even Fanny was reclusive, seldom in sight. So I took it upon myself to pay her a visit, bringing her a piece of salt pork Long Chase had received from our cousins.

I rapped on her door, but there was no answer. I opened it a crack to slip the package inside and was stunned by what I saw. Fanny Brindle was no longer a woman alone. She lay on the divan, pressed into it by the weight of her striker, Bailey Roe. They seemed to have sprouted additional arms and legs and were flailing them about. They resembled tangled crabs.

I chucked the salt pork into a corner and fled the room before the two could find their voices. I nearly stepped on Spotted Dog in my haste, for he lingered at the door. I was short with him. "Move," I snarled. We walked slowly away from the fort, Spotted Dog beside me, rather than loping ahead. Perhaps he noticed the drag of my feet. My limbs were heavy and cut deep tracks through the snow. Loneliness swept across me until I thought my heart would disintegrate like dust. Fanny Brindle was a woman from the other world, but I would miss her. And I had understood, from the moment we latched eyes, that Fanny would never forgive me what I had seen.

Long Chase's warrior friends told him that a small buffalo herd had been spotted thirty miles to the north.

"*Tanke,* we're going to bring some back for your soup,

so you'll have something to talk to the corn,'' he said. He rubbed the lodge's skin wall, the smoked hide so worn it was becoming transparent. ''We could use some new walls too. We're like a lantern at night.''

Long Chase set off the next morning, wearing his buffalo-hide shirt with the coarse hair against his skin. I knew that before he turned his pony into the fleet stream of buffaloes, he would shed the garment. My brother, inured to the cold through careful childhood training, could ride like that, his flesh exposed to temperatures that would have claimed a soldier's fingers and toes with frostbite. He washed in the snow each morning, joined by Spotted Dog, who thought it was a romp. I had seen them dive headlong into the powder as if it were the river back home.

Now I clasped my brother's hand and looked up at him settled on his horse. I didn't tell him to be careful, I didn't tell him anything at all, because the child was missing that morning, replaced by a smiling man. He squeezed my hand and gave it back to me. I watched him ride away. I knelt on the ground beside Spotted Dog, my arms wrapped around his neck. The dog looked forlorn, upset to be left behind. He knew where Long Chase was headed after hearing ''tatanka,'' the term for ''buffalo.''

''You don't want to leave me all by myself,'' I scolded him. And for a moment he lifted his eyes from my brother's receding back to look at me. His tongue rolled out, a sure sign of forgiveness, so I left him there and moved to tidy our camp.

I was visited that night by a bear. Not *mato,* our fierce brother whose claws are greatly prized, but a human bear bundled in furs. Reverend Pyke entered my lodge without a greeting, looking like a man of snow.

''Good evening,'' I said, polite though his abrupt en-

trance was rude. I gestured toward the caller's space to the
left of my sputtering fire. "Make yourself comfortable," I
told him.

Pyke's legs were stiff as tree trunks; his head grazed the
wall. "I am not calling," he said to me. "I am not here."
I looked at Spotted Dog as if he had an explanation. "But
the Lord is here," Pyke continued. "The Lord suffuses my
soul and expunges the wickedness he finds there with a
flick of his tongue."

I was motionless before the raving giant, my senses as-
sailed by his reeking hat and loud voice.

"The Lord told me that I was blessed," he continued.
"He bade me *replenish the earth and subdue it, and have
dominion over the fish of the sea, and over the fowl of the
air, and over every living thing that moveth upon the earth.*
You will not work your ways on me," Pyke thundered. "I
made you and fostered your demon intelligence. I will un-
make you." And the one I had not spelled or visited with
sacred stones brought his flat hand out of the fur wrappings
strapped to his body. He raised his silver revolver, aiming
it at my heart. The gun's barrel was a black eye, and when
it exploded, a streak of bright color rose to meet the bullet.
Spotted Dog fell at my feet. I knelt beside him and stroked
his back. I rubbed the loose skin behind his ears.

"You are a brave dog," I murmured in Dakota, speaking
the language I told myself he preferred. His blood spilled
across my hands, and it was while I struggled to catch each
precious drop that the tent exploded a second time.

I had turned my back on the giant; he loomed somewhere
above me.

"*Mičeȟpi,*" I called, but not to him. "*Mičeȟpi.*" My
flesh.

• • •

I fell into a river of liquid smooth as the cream *wašičun*s favored, and in that warm bath drawing me through Ina's— the mother's—heart, I was unperturbed by my own death. The recent events were banished from my mind, and I was free to indulge my sensibilities in ways forbidden me in life. I was raised to believe that discipline and self-control were signs of maturity, necessitating the suppression of individual desires. My feelings swept over me now; I was in a womb of my affections. Music penetrated the fluid and my wandering soul, a piercing sweetness from our Dakota courting flute. It was a tune composed by Ghost Horse, the thunder dreamer, a melody he played when I carried water from the river or collected wood for kindling. This was in the days before our dreams—so devastating in retrospect— set us upon divergent courses. My spirit throbbed in anger. I was like an old woman weeping for her children. Ghost Horse and I were victims of utter faith, I realized. We were Job, lonely and afflicted. Chosen. Only the music could stir me from my sudden brooding. I let it move through me until it became the words I couldn't speak and the tears I could not cry.

You will think that I was borne away, but in fact I was a witness to what followed. I tracked Reverend Pyke in the snow as capably as a coyote. He hadn't gone far from the lodge; the ancestor-spirits had trapped him in the drifts, and he was half buried in snow. My sight was sharper than before, and I could see into his deep pockets, where twin sisters with red faces clacked together. The sacred stones had moved for the last time. Pyke's revolver had loosed a final shot, taking him by surprise, I think, for he looked puzzled and his left hand was latched onto his right wrist, as if there'd been a struggle.

My brother Long Chase returned hours later with enough

buffalo meat, tallow, and winter hides to last us through the winter. He sang for me and for Spotted Dog, gashed his arms and legs to wear his grief, and let it pour out of him. He removed the note Reverend Pyke had pinned to my dress. My brother couldn't read the words but knew it was some work of spite. I read the lines, curious as I had ever been: *"Upon thy belly shalt thou go, and dust shalt thou eat all the days of thy life."*

I shook my fists and smiled to hear them rattle. Was it madness, I wondered, or a crystal sanity that led him to write these words?

Long Chase quickly discovered Pyke after I nudged him in that direction. I didn't want him seeking vengeance. *You see, it's already done,* I told my brother. And then I whispered, *Go home.*

The return was a trek of heartbreak and exhaustion. Long Chase trudged through the snow and rarely looked ahead of him, so defeated our enemies were the least of his concerns. I scouted for him, and the few times I spotted distant trouble my spirit made a nuisance of itself, torturing my brother's adversaries with flung rocks and snowy twisters until they changed direction.

Grass was beginning to poke through melting snow when Long Chase reached our winter camp. He emerged from a cloud of horses and was met by Father La Frambois, out for a stroll. My brother walked past him, numbly discourteous, and when the priest moved toward the body the ponies dragged behind them on a bed of furs, Long Chase caught his arm. No words passed between them, but Father La Frambois soon gathered that he was shut out of the proceedings. He would not be allowed to handle my body or baptize me posthumously. His blessings and masses were politely refused. He never learned that in death, I finally became a bride.

Ghost Horse brought my father three sturdy ponies he'd captured from the Crows. "I have fulfilled my obligations as *heyo'ka*," he told my parents. "And I am free to take a wife. Your daughter never watched me, sent me messages, or stepped away from herself, but she was in here anyway." He tapped his chest. "I have these feelings that are only pitiful grains, but they are planted in my blood and growing." He held out his arms and stared at the veins as if he expected to find bold spikes of grass.

"I request the honor of marrying your daughter's spirit, mourning her as a devoted husband would grieve."

Ghost Horse did not bury me in the ground or build a scaffold, but settled me near the crown of a majestic burr oak tree. I was cradled by its spreading branches, rocked in its stout arms. My husband stood beside me in the tree and looked in every direction.

"You will see the world," he said. He ate the fruit of a dried plum, and when its meat was gone, he very gently placed the pit in my mouth. It was the most intimate gesture that ever passed between us.

Before he left, my husband lifted the shield he had given me just a year earlier. "I want you to see what I've done," he told me. He pointed to fresh tracks of blue paint drawn across the tough bull hide. "I recorded your accomplishments," Ghost Horse continued. "You are a warrior, and this is your shield."

I peered at the blue marks, my spirit slow to recognize the figures. Comprehension came in a rush, and when my hands flew to cover my eyes, I stirred a powerful wind. My husband nearly fell from the tree. I shrank from the paint, from the woman in a red dress wielding lightning. The jagged bolt was sharp at its tip, and three blue figures—men in uniform—were impaled by it, collected like beads strung on a needle.

Ghost Horse turned the shield, to face this fierce woman. ''We honor you,'' he said. He threaded his arm through the handles to wear the shield and rolled his arm in quick circles, making the rattlesnake gourds hiss. My spirit was tangled in the tree, dismayed and bewildered. *Who is this woman?* I wondered, and didn't want the answer to come to me. But the rattlesnake gourds produced a soothing sound, and my heart lifted when I saw the creatures emerge from their dens and hiding places. Serpents flowed toward the tree, forming creeks and rivers of writhing motion. They washed over one another, rising and then falling; they became a single unit of grace.

The snakes are dancing, I murmured. And when they surrounded the tree, my spirit fell into their midst, prostrate. We danced together.

Ghost Horse kept my spirit for one year, the most onerous form of grief. His younger brother, Wind Soldier, agreed to help him, and together they prepared my spirit lodge and collected goods to be distributed at the culminating feast. But when the year had passed and the village assembled for my spirit release ceremony, it was unsuccessful. Ghost Horse did what was expected of him, said the words, and gave away his last possession, but he did not loose me from this earth. His heart was a stone room without doors.

My husband sought death on the battlefield, and it wasn't long before a bold Arikara complied. I did my best to deflect the arrows, pushed the air with both hands to send them swerving harmlessly away. But the Ree's horse wouldn't stumble when I leapt for its legs. It carried him so close to my husband that the Ree's shot was deadly, and by the time I reached Ghost Horse he was on the ground.

I thought he might see me, now that his eyes were focused on the next world. I held his head in my arms and spread his long hair across my thighs. *Old man,* I teased, *are you ready for this old lady?* But he was silent, and his polished eyes were stones.

I didn't see him leave, yet it was like him to instantly accept another adventure. He moved on to the place our ancestors inhabit; there was no one living to capture his spirit as he had captured mine.

"You went without me!" I cried. I shook him by the shoulders. My spirit stubbornly clutched his body, which made it hard for his uncles to lift him. "We go together!" I shrieked in their ears. I finally departed when Ghost Horse's pony spooked and almost flung his body back to the ground. The uncles were horrified and scolded the horse, but I understood its terror. It didn't want me on its back.

At least a hundred years have passed, and the plum pit in my mouth has become a grove of trees. I can smell the fruit when it ripens, and my breath makes the leaves rustle.

I am hitched to the living, still moved by their concerns. My spirit never abandons the Dakota people, though sometimes all it can do is watch. I was there when the army confiscated our horses to cut off our legs. I stood behind the Ghost Dancers, and when they fainted in desperate, useless ecstasy, I blew a refreshing wind into their faces. There have been too many soldiers and too many graves. Too many children packed into trains and sent to the other side of the country. Many times I ran alongside those tracks and waved at the bleak copper faces. *You are Dakota,* I called to them. *You are Dakota.* One time I stood in front of a chuffing engine and tried to keep it from moving forward, but it blasted through me. I saw the language shrivel, and though I held out my hands to catch the words, so many of them slipped away, beyond recall. I am a talker now and chatter in my people's ears until I grow weary of my own voice. *I am memory,* I tell them when they're sleeping.

I prefer to watch the present unravel moment by moment than to look close behind me or far ahead. Time extends from me, flowing in many directions, meeting the horizon and then moving beyond to follow the curve of the earth. But I will not track its course with my eyes. It is too painful. I can bear witness to only a single moment of loss at a time. Still, hope flutters in my heart, a delicate pulse. I straddle the world and pray to Wakan Tanka that somewhere ahead of me He has planted an instant of joy.

10
Swallowing the Birds

(1981)

CHARLENE THUNDER DREAMED SHE WAS BEING PRESSED.
She had read of the practice in a book on the Salem witch
trials, and now she blamed the book. *If I hadn't read that
thing, this wouldn't be happening*, she told herself. She was
aware it was a dream, but she still found it difficult to
breathe. A large door rested on her abdomen, chest, and
thighs, placed crosswise rather than covering the length of
her body.

Pumpkin stood on the door, keeping to the middle so
that it didn't tip like a seesaw. She was resplendent in her
grass-dance costume, a shimmering red-gold flame. Charlene noticed that the long fringes cascading past the dancer's shoulders and hips no longer were yarn but had become
ribbons of light. Pumpkin danced on Charlene's chest, yet
it was the girl beneath the door who whispered in a
squeezed voice: "I'm sorry."

Pumpkin stopped dancing and opened her mouth to
speak. Charlene hoped for words, but again, as in her other
dreams, only tiny black birds tumbled soundlessly from
Pumpkin's throat. The miniature birds were so perfect in
every detail, so precious, Charlene hated to see them fall
lifeless to the ground. Soon there was a small pile of them,
enough to fill a dustpan. Pumpkin looked at Charlene when
the last bird had fallen. There was no anger in her eyes,
only sadness. She stepped off the door and Charlene cried

in pain, for with the dancer gone, the crushing weight was more than she could bear.

Waking was not the relief she expected. The burden she felt turned out to be her grandmother's sturdy hand resting on her heart.

Mercury Thunder could no longer go upstairs. Her boyfriends had built a ramp descending from her back door to the yard so she could wheel herself in and out of the house, but the second floor was inaccessible to her. Charlene secretly gloated, thinking this would finally give her some privacy, but Mercury insisted her granddaughter sleep on the first floor and spend as little time as possible upstairs. It was only when Mercury entertained one of her young men that Charlene was allowed to reclaim her room, close the door, and escape from the old woman.

Her grandmother seemed to need very little sleep these days and preferred to spend the night seated in her wheelchair. It unsettled Charlene to awaken stretched out on Mercury's prickly horsehair sofa, her grandmother's eyes staring into her own, Mercury's hand—smelling unaccountably of soil (she could no longer garden)—pressed to the girl's heart.

Is she giving or taking? Charlene wondered, neither option offering much comfort.

"I love you to death," the old woman told her one morning, and Charlene made herself sneeze to conceal her shudder. School was a refuge, but homework was never an excuse Charlene could raise against Mercury Thunder to secure time alone. When she told her grandmother that she needed to study for senior-year midterm examinations, Mercury said: "The only tests you need to pass are my own. And you won't find my courses in books."

Charlene decided she would get to school early the next day to prepare, but once there she discovered that her grandmother had raided her textbooks and torn out half the pages in each volume. Charlene picked up her pen and scrawled in the margins. She wrote "Why?" in large script, then printed the question in tiny block letters. She traced "Why?" with her right hand and then with her left. She wrote the word a hundred times because, of course, she knew the answer and needed this distraction to keep the truth from penetrating her thoughts. The idea emerged despite her careful ploy: *Grandma has shut me out of the world. She wants to keep me to herself.*

Charlene Thunder wept over her trigonometry textbook, half of it missing, probably burned in her grandmother's fire. She could borrow replacements for all her books but knew she wouldn't.

"I'm shrinking," she said, to no one, to herself.

On Columbus Day the sky was streaked with slender clouds, their lines crisp and straight as jet vapors. The air was unusually warm for mid-October, and Mercury told Charlene to open the windows on the first floor of the house. As the girl stood at the sitting room window, she noticed a skunk waddling across the yard. It took its time, rolling from side to side like a bowlegged cowboy. Its markings fascinated Charlene: white fur crowned its black head and trailed the length of its body.

"Looks like it's wearing a warbonnet," she murmured to herself.

"Skunk in the yard," Mercury called from the kitchen.

"How can you tell, Unči?" Charlene asked, startled.

"I can smell those glands even when they're not on active duty," Mercury said. "Leave it to its business. We've got cooking."

Charlene baked a macaroni-and-cheese casserole, enough to fill an enormous pan. She used fresh tomatoes and tangy green onions, and sprinkled paprika on the fine golden crust.

"It's all ready," she told her grandmother, who was sewing clasps on the daisy-chain bracelets she'd beaded earlier in the day.

"How much should I ask for these?" questioned Mercury. "I think three dollars apiece," she answered herself.

Charlene didn't understand why Mercury went to the trouble of packing the beadwork. The function they were preparing to attend was the annual Stomp on Columbus, an informal potluck supper and dance, something like a cheerful wake. There would be only local people, neighbors who could work their own beads and who wouldn't buy from Mercury Thunder even if they had the money. But Charlene wrote the price on a square of cardboard and placed a small folding table, which would serve as Mercury's sales table, in the trunk of her grandmother's car. She carefully set the casserole on the floor of the backseat to keep it from sliding, and helped her grandmother step out of her wheelchair and into the car.

"Where's my shawl?" Mercury asked as Charlene tucked the skirt of her grandmother's dress around her spindly legs. The girl ran inside the house and emerged with a shawl that was red on one side and navy blue on the other, a peyote shawl, even though Mercury had never eaten the star-shaped buttons or prayed with the Native American Church. Mercury insisted on wearing the shawl because, she said, "it shows my two sides: the red for my heart and the blue for my spirit."

Charlene had once made the mistake of responding: "We could all say the same thing, Unči. Doesn't everybody have a heart and a soul?'' The old woman's face was still, impassive as granite, but her eyes snapped to life, and surging within their brown depths Charlene swore she could see the graceful predatory movements of two red-tailed hawks.

"My spirit is complicated," Mercury had told her. "I was one person and now I am another, like two layers of rock." Charlene had nodded but found it difficult to imagine. She could think of her grandmother only as Mercury to the core, a solid mass. Even if she took a chisel to the old woman's outer flesh, she thought, it would be impossible to find another Mercury Thunder, a woman perhaps young, perhaps sweet, as confused and lost as Charlene felt herself to be.

There is only one of you, she had told her grandmother in her thoughts, and Mercury had swiveled her head to stare at the girl, as if she'd heard.

Charlene handed the shawl to her grandmother. "Is that everything?" she asked. Mercury nodded, looking straight ahead through the windshield. Charlene settled in the driver's seat and stoked the car's engine with a few gentle taps on the accelerator.

The new function room at the tribal agency had a lighter shade of paneling than the old one, which made it more cheerful, and a high ceiling that gave the singers' voices somewhere to go. Two long tables at the back of the hall were already covered with food: potato salad, fried chicken, corn soup, berry pudding, fry bread, pies. On a separate table were two enormous coffee urns and a pitcher of tepid Kool-Aid. A drum was set up in the middle of the room, and the singers lounged in a circle around it, smoking their way through a carton of cigarettes.

Charlene wheeled Mercury toward the back of the room,

behind a row of folding chairs, but her grandmother reached down and set the brake. The chair stopped so abruptly it almost tipped over.

"Take me over there," Mercury said. She pointed her lips at a prominent part of the room, the empty space beneath a portrait of Sitting Bull. "I want to sit near the Old Chief," she said. "He might have something to tell me."

I only wish he did, Charlene thought to herself. She set up her grandmother's sales table beneath the painting of Sitting Bull and brought her a plate of food and a cup of coffee that was half milk and sugar. After eating a serving of her own casserole, Charlene told Mercury, "I'm going to help out in the kitchen." She wandered in that direction.

The older women clearly had things under control. Charlene squeezed past them and opened the back door for a breath of air. She stood on the threshold; an easy wind tousled her hair. She relaxed, smiling to herself, but a shrill bark interrupted the peaceful moment. An orange comet streaked across the parking lot, flying toward her. Charlene groaned. "Not the creature again." She waited until the pinched muzzle belonging to Chuck Norris was inches from her ankles; then she pulled back and slammed the door.

Chuck's sharp claws scraped the barrier and he growled enthusiastically, but the noise was pitched almost comically high—the rasp of wild rice poured into a coffee can. Charlene pressed her lips to the door. "Chu-u-uck," she crooned. "Come on, boy. What's stopping you?" The dog must have hurtled his slight body at the door, which bounced suddenly, cracking against Charlene's nose. She retreated from the kitchen.

Harley must be here somewhere, she was thinking, and moments later she saw him enter the large hall with his mother. Lydia was carrying a pan covered with tinfoil. She stood very straight, her black hair pulled into a single long braid. Charlene felt her own back stiffen in imitation, she grazed her flat cheekbones with blunt fingertips. Lydia looked to her like a queen, though she was wearing nothing fancier than blue jeans, scuffed boots, and a shiny windbreaker. Lydia glided across the floor, passing Mercury without a sign of recognition. The sight thrilled Charlene. It was a rare insult. Everyone else made sure to shake her grandmother's hand, murmur a few polite words. They might not purchase her beadwork, and probably checked their shoulders for stray hairs before approaching the old woman, but they didn't dare offend her.

Charlene watched as Harley sat down in a chair just inside the front door. He set a small suitcase on the floor between his feet and leaned so far back in the chair the front legs lifted off the ground. Charlene seated herself beside him.

"Hey, Harley," she said. He looked at her then, but it took a few seconds for his eyes to focus and stop looking through her.

"Charlene," he said simply. His eyes slid off her face.

"I keep meaning to say I'm sorry about your friend," Charlene said. Harley's look was quick and penetrating; his chair thumped back on all four legs.

"Did you know her?" he asked. He leaned forward, his hands clasped between his knees. He watched Charlene's face.

"No, not really. But we had a conversation."

"What did she say?"

"Nothing I remember."

"I do," he said.

"What?"

"I remember."

Charlene had forgotten the activity around her, and the surrounding noise rushed between them. "What do you remember?" she prodded, to feel alone with him again.

Harley's knees jiggled nervously, and his hands gripped them as if struggling to keep them still. "She was different from everybody else. Pumpkin was really Indian. She was the best grass dancer I've ever seen. But there was this other side." His voice faded to a whisper. "It was like she knew all our secrets, but we didn't know any of hers." He tossed the hair out of his eyes. "I better get moving," he said, slapping his knees and rising from the chair. Harley picked up the suitcase and walked to the men's rest room.

When he emerged, nearly half an hour later, Charlene shivered. She cradled her elbows in the palms of her hands to quiet the shaking. Harley had donned a grass-dance costume, not the more traditional outfit he previously wore to dances. He had selected Pumpkin's colors—red, yellow, orange, the shades of fire—and strings of gold beads looped below his eyes, framing them. He moved silently, yarn cascading from his knees instead of the usual ringing bells.

He walked to his mother and tapped her on the shoulder. He didn't speak—perhaps Lydia's silence had captured his own tongue—but he held out his arms as if to say, *There, how do I look?* Lydia adjusted his beaded cuffs; their design reminded Charlene of a brilliant sunrise.

He's dancing to honor his friend, Charlene said to herself. *But who will honor me?* She glanced then at her grandmother. Mercury sat behind her table, the colorful bracelets spreading from her in a semicircle; she was like the sun, and they were beams of light radiating from her waist. Sitting Bull was suspended above her head, and to Charlene it seemed that he watched her grandmother, his expression mournful, eyes wrinkled in confusion.

The drummers sipped coffee to clear their throats of smoke, and began to sing. Many people danced that evening, but Harley was the only one wearing a dance costume. Charlene observed for nearly an hour, unmoved by the music, remaining in her chair. She thought that Harley danced with a graceful sincerity, but he didn't have Pumpkin's skill. He was not the spirit of grass, a stalk trembling in the wind and whirling from the ground. His feet rolled, as they would have if he had been surrounded by grass, covered to the waist, and had to thresh it with his legs. He danced to get the job done, stepping with fierce concentration until sweat poured into his eyes.

Charlene finally jumped out of her seat and went to speak to her grandmother. "I'm going home," she told Mercury. "Can you get a ride?"

Mercury nodded and smiled. She held out her hands, and Charlene was surprised to see how smooth the woman's palms were, hardly lined at all, as if the fate once etched there had been wiped clean.

"I know," Charlene murmured. "The pickings are good."

She left the hall, passing the tables of food on her way out. They were nearly empty now. She looked for Mercury's pan but, when she couldn't spot it, decided to collect it another day. As she pulled out of the parking lot, she noticed Harley's dog near the kitchen door.

"Still there?" She chuckled. Charlene trained her headlights on the dog, but he didn't look up. His front paws were planted in the macaroni casserole Charlene had baked. Two neat squares—the servings Charlene had carved for her grandmother and herself—were missing, but the pan Chuck Norris attacked was otherwise full. *They must have thrown it out,* Charlene thought. *And it was good too.* Tears pooled in her eyes, but she squinted fiercely to keep them from spilling down her face.

She stepped on the gas, and the smell of burnt rubber filled the parking lot. Charlene sped down the main road, which led from the tribal agency building up into the hills. Her foot was heavy on the accelerator, and her hands drummed the steering wheel, tapping out song after song. The car was quick and light, a hurtling bullet. She loved the snub-nosed green Maverick, even the rust that blossomed on its sides and reminded her of the jagged lightning people sometimes painted on sports cars. She pushed the car to move faster than ever before, ignoring the red needle of the speedometer as it moved wildly toward the higher numbers.

''I can be different too!'' she yelled in the car, and that is what eventually stopped her. She knew this wouldn't be different, but more of the same. Another Indian dead on the highway, another totaled car finding its way into someone's yard. Charlene halted the car in the road and opened the door. The air was cool and black, a dark ointment smoothing her skin. She smelled nothing but dust and feathers, as if she had wandered into an abandoned nest. Charlene didn't cry. She launched into an old Patsy Cline number, ''Walking After Midnight.'' By the second chorus a coyote had joined her, his sorrowful voice an octave above her own.

Over the next few days the Indian summer continued, but Charlene didn't notice. She was busy collecting her dark eyelashes in a plastic pillbox. She rubbed her eyes several times a day and then looked into a compact mirror to search for any delicate strands she may have brushed loose. Finally she had gathered a dozen lashes. She spilled them into batter and baked six chocolate cupcakes. She prepared a separate batch for her grandmother to eat, so there would be no questions.

The next day Charlene carried the moist cakes to school. Her first class was homeroom, an hour for students to check their homework or study for tests. Charlene sat in the back of the room, surrounded by restless boys who were quick to smell the fragrant treats packed in a paper bag. The boy next to her, Bennett Little Soldier, whispered, "Hey, Thundercloud, I'm hungry."

She patted the air with her hand, a signal to hush. "Later," she whispered. During the five-minute break between classes, she distributed cupcakes to the young men at the back of the room: Bennett first, then Larry Crow's Ghost, Franklin Hairy Chin and his cousin Thomas, Jerry Grindstone, and Mert No Heart.

"No fair," she told them. "None for me. Wait, give one back." Franklin Hairy Chin started to divide his cake, but Charlene stopped him. "I'm just kidding," she said. "You're doing me a favor by keeping it out of my mouth and off my thighs."

The boys left in a cluster, their mouths full. They all turned at the door to wave. "Thanks," Larry Crow's Ghost said. "Yeah, thanks," the others mumbled in a ragged chorus.

"No problem," Charlene answered.

That was easy, she thought, but it didn't make her smile. She hadn't expected the boys' immediate trust, and it touched her. *Maybe they don't lump me with Mercury after all,* she mused. But it was too late now. There was no giving back their naive faith, no calling off the medicine Charlene sensed rushing through her veins, a thick serum that made her feel both nervous and drowsy. *At least it isn't Harley,* she told herself.

Throughout the day Charlene was aware of a growing tension; admiring eyes followed her thick figure, hearts pounded, fingers were busy writing her love messages. She had never been one to receive valentines, but now the poetry erupted; her features were praised, her disposition was complimented. It was fun for a few class periods, but eventually it became depressing.

Don't think about it, Charlene scolded herself. *Don't fight it.* Charlene imagined she had peeled Mercury's shadow off the walls and draped it across her own round shoulders. She shrugged, but the shadow didn't slip; it became a second skin.

After school six boys waited for Charlene by her locker. There was jostling, friendly at first but increasingly violent. She stepped into the clump of long legs and lank black hair, gently touching each boy on the shoulder.

"Let's go somewhere," she said to Bennett, and he nodded eagerly. The others did too. "Just you," Charlene ordered, but the boys moved as a unit, as if their limbs had been braided together. In doubting the success of her venture, Charlene realized she'd overplayed her hand.

"What the hell," she finally said. "You can all go." Charlene and her classmates piled into one car—Thomas Hairy Chin's station wagon, with the crunched back fender and the dragging muffler. The car stopped at Mert No Heart's place for the sweet bottles of muscatel his uncle had buried in the backyard for his coming birthday celebration. Then the group drove beyond the hills to an abandoned house bearing the legend of Frank Pipe on its spray-painted walls.

• • •

Charlene could no longer feel her lips; her face was numb, and her legs were loose as rubber bands. She remained seated on the floor. "I never knew you were so much fun," she told the boys, laughing at everything they said.

"You have to do what I tell you," she reminded them, and so far they had been obliging. She felt safe in her power, certain of her control. "You're only puppets," she said.

But the puppets were bound to her so tightly they begged to be set in motion, launched into their awkward dance. Soon they were no longer boys but hands, too many pairs of hands petting her hair, smoothing her clothes, lifting her with two fingers each, as if it were an evening of slumber-party games. The hands covered every inch of her body, so that Charlene was unaware for several minutes that her clothes were gone. When she did notice, Charlene began to cry, but her tears were wiped away by someone's fingers. The hands claimed her, moved across her and inside her. She lost track of her limbs, couldn't tell her toes from her ears. Sometime during that night of eager magic, Charlene Thunder forgot her name and believed she was one of six boys, became each of them in turn as they claimed her cold body pressed into the splintered floor.

I am Bennett, she thought. *I have a ragged ear.*

No, I am Larry. And my left eye is sleepy.

Hold on, I am Franklin, and my teeth are beautiful—a seamless white fence.

I see myself now: I am Thomas. I never noticed before how the cluster of moles at my temple forms a five-pointed star.

How could I forget? I am Mert, and my hair covers my eyes so I can't see anything.

I recognize myself. I am Jerry. I remember my crooked nose, which was broken twice.

Charlene came back to herself only after the hands released her. She had been dressed carefully, her hair patted smooth, and the tears swept off her face. An enormous jacket was draped across her shoulders and a set of car keys was in the palm of her hand. The boys were gone; they had fled the house on foot at the first fingers of light.

Charlene shut her eyes and curled her body into a lonely ball of sore muscles and injured flesh.

The sun was like a hand washing Charlene's face. It covered her mouth, filled her nostrils, and crept into her eyes. She sat up feeling tired and queasy. Goose bumps rippled across her skin. *I'm not alone,* she quickly grasped. Charlene scanned the room with her eyes; she didn't want to turn her head, which was heavy with pain. Two women were watching her with great interest: a stout white woman with silver hair, whose fingers were busy plucking a chicken; and a tall Dakota woman in a red buckskin dress, wearing a wriggling bull snake for a belt.

"She's awake," said the white woman, shaking the strangled bird.

Charlene blinked, too exhausted to muster anything like fear. The Dakota woman approached her, fluid as a snake, her silver-black eyes like polished hematite, clear and friendly.

"Good morning, niece," she said. Charlene couldn't be sure if the language was English or Sioux. "You had quite a time."

"She found what she was looking for, I guess," the other woman added from her seat, a plush wing chair that hadn't been there the night before. "But it was terrible to watch."

"I didn't want this," Charlene whispered, her voice breaking.

"What's that?" The Dakota woman knelt beside the girl. Charlene reached out and caressed the bull snake with her finger. "The old lady brought me here because she was worried and she knows you are my relation. I'm your aunt, Red Dress, if you haven't already figured it out."

Charlene mouthed yes.

"I'm going to say this only once, so you better sober up and listen." Red Dress covered Charlene's hand with her own, but all Charlene could feel against her skin were flower petals moist with dew. "You misused the medicine because you have a bad example. If you are selfish with it, someday it will be selfish with you. We do not own the power, we aren't supposed to direct it ourselves. Give it up if you don't understand my meaning. Put the medicine behind you. Will you do that for yourself and for your people?"

Charlene cleared her throat and answered, "Yes." One crystal note.

"Good. There is only so much a spirit can take, and you put this poor old woman through an ordeal last night." Red Dress gestured toward her companion, who worked steadily, producing a blizzard of feathers.

Charlene covered her eyes with a clammy hand, kneaded her aching head with her knuckles. And when she had pushed the pain back a little, she peered into the room. It was empty and silent.

I'm probably just waking up, Charlene thought, but she knew better. The room was thick with the perfume of wild plums, and the fragrance followed Charlene all day, even as she entered Mercury's house.

• • •

Charlene had expected her grandmother to fuss about her absence, but Mercury was subdued, almost deferential in her treatment of the girl.

"How about some cinnamon toast?" she asked Charlene, and before her granddaughter could answer, Mercury was wheeling through the kitchen to make breakfast.

"Nothing for me, Unči," Charlene said. "I want to sleep for a hundred years."

With sudden boldness, Charlene mounted the stairs and entered her old room. She quickly fell asleep, but even in her dreams could not escape the cloying scent of ripe plums.

On Monday morning Charlene reported not to her homeroom class but instead to the office of the guidance counselor.

Jeannette McVay welcomed her: "We haven't had a good visit in so long. How are you doing?"

Charlene sat in a metal folding chair. She shrugged.

"How do you like my new digs?" Jeannette trailed her fingers across the smooth expanse of her varnished desk. The room was empty of decoration except for framed photographs of Gloria Steinem and Betty Friedan, and a poster picturing Chief Joseph of the Nez Percé. Printed beneath him were his famous words: I WILL FIGHT NO MORE, FOREVER.

"Spartan, isn't it?" Jeannette smiled. "I learned that from all my years on this reservation. Siouxs aren't impressed by *things*, are they?"

Charlene lifted her hand and offered her palm, noncommittal.

"Well, let me shut up and give you the floor." For a confused moment Charlene wondered if Jeannette was going to pry loose the drab industrial carpet. "What brings you here? Not that you *need* a reason," the counselor prompted.

Charlene looked into the woman's eyes and found herself able to talk. Since the last time Charlene had taken the trouble to notice her, Jeannette McVay had transformed herself. She no longer dyed her hair a dense artificial black that seemed to drain light from any room she entered, but had colored it a warm brown with henna highlights. Her gray eyes were now hazel, no doubt the result of tinted lenses, and she'd gained a few pounds, which softened her face.

"I need to change," Charlene said. Jeannette nodded encouragingly. "I mean, I need to change homerooms. Could you put me somewhere else?"

"That depends," Jeannette responded.

"On what?"

"Why you want the transfer."

Charlene tucked her hands beneath her thighs until she was sitting on them. "It was a bad weekend," she eventually said. "Things happened. There are people I don't really want to see again."

Jeannette stood up and walked to the back of her office. Charlene had to crane her neck to watch. For the first time she noticed a small Navajo rug on the floor, surrounded by tobacco ties and clumps of sage. Jeannette carefully picked up her feet, one at a time, and stepped on the rug. She lifted her skirts. She moved as if she were wading through a creek. "Give me a second," she mumbled. "Clear your head and I'll clear mine. I have to think."

Long moments passed. Charlene turned her back on the counselor, concentrating instead on pressing her fingers into the metal seat. The pain comforted her.

"Okay," Jeannette piped cheerfully. "I've decided I don't need to hear what happened. I'm going to give you your space and privacy. I understand you're a laconic people. I mean, you don't have to tell me more than you're ready to." Jeannette returned to her seat. "But I *am* ready to listen. Is there more?"

Charlene shook her head.

"I'll send you next door, then. That's your new homeroom. How's that?"

Charlene whispered, "Thank you." Her hand was curled on the doorknob, when Jeannette called her back.

"Maybe it will be easier if we share. I'll tell you a secret."

Charlene dropped her hand but remained near the exit.

"I'm marrying Alex Holy Hand next week, and by New Year's we're going to be adding to the population of this reservation."

"Congratulations," Charlene murmured, reaching again for the door.

"So you can tell me anything, anytime."

Charlene turned to face the counselor. "I know," she said. "I really do." Then she fled, before the woman could share even more.

At the end of the week Charlene was given a present. It was waiting for her at her new homeroom desk, folded inside a plain white envelope addressed to her. The script was elegant, a little old-fashioned, like sample penmanship traced from a book. Inside the envelope was a newspaper clipping. The graceful handwriting was in evidence here as well, looping above the article. It read: "*Dakota Times*, October 29, 1981." The piece had been printed just the day before.

BEADING DA VINCI, the tiny headline proclaimed. Charlene read the text without interest: "An enterprising couple in Chicago have turned beads into gold! Martin Lundstrom and his Dakota wife, Crystal Lundstrom, née Thunder, former residents of North Dakota, spent the last three years bringing da Vinci's vision of the Last Supper to life in a new form." The article described in detail how Martin Lundstrom had sketched the pattern of the famous tableau for his wife and how she rendered the scene in beadwork, using a massive loom of her own design. The final product was a beaded tapestry twelve feet long and six feet high, weighing forty-five pounds. Crystal had used approximately 1.8 million beads in 120 different shades, and it was all held together by eleven miles of nylon thread.

"Clearly you are a pious woman," a reporter had said.

"Not really," Crystal Lundstrom had responded. "I just wanted to do something of consequence."

Charlene didn't know what to make of the story until she saw the photograph below the columns of print. A smiling couple stood beside the beaded tapestry, which could have been a paint-by-number canvas, its lines were so precise. The woman fascinated her.

Her face is flat like mine, Charlene thought, her fingers drifting from the features in the photograph to her own profile, and back again. She held the paper to her face and squinted into the woman's eyes, tiny as the head on a pin. They were wide-set like her own. *This is what I'll look like someday,* Charlene mused. Her inspection was so focused she didn't notice the two long tears spilling in straight lines down her cheeks. The drops of water horrified her, as they fell onto the photograph, obliterating first the noble visage of an apostle and then the pleasant face of the woman's companion.

Charlene opened her loose-leaf notebook, oblivious to the classroom around her, unable to hear the ticking clock on the wall above her head. Her heart drummed, a song without music; her fingers were awkward and could barely hold the pen.

This is my mother, Charlene wrote. It took such effort that her teeth were sawing her tongue, and tart blood trickled down her throat. *My mother is alive. My mother is in Chicago.* Each sentence was more difficult to produce than the one before. Charlene pressed the pen into the paper, tearing through the top sheet and the sheets below.

These are the facts, she said to herself. *Nothing but the facts.*

Charlene Thunder responded automatically to the bell that signaled the change of classes. But rather than keep to her schedule, she fled to the school library and hid in the stacks. Charlene intended to sort through her thoughts but was so thoroughly lost in the dense silence of her refuge that she fell asleep instead, her feet tucked in the Biography section and her nose grazing a Biology text.

Charlene awakened an hour before school ended, refreshed and ready for pure action.

She found herself in Jeannette McVay's office for the second time that week, but she felt years older now. She presented the article to the guidance counselor. "Show me how to call Chicago," Charlene said. "I need to find a number."

Jeannette barely glanced at the slip of paper. "I knew your mother," she said.

Charlene dropped into the metal chair. "Don't tell me." Her hands covered her ears. "I'm taking this one step at a time, and if I hear too much, or think too much, it might stop me."

Jeannette dialed information for her but let Charlene make the request herself. "Do you have a listing for Martin Lundstrom?" she asked. A number was read to her, but when she tried to write it down she froze, and Jeannette had to take the phone from her and write the number.

"Here's what we'll do," the counselor said. "I'm going to let you use my office. You can try them now if you want. It's still work hours, so maybe no one's home. But it's worth a shot, don't you think?"

Charlene's head dropped in a reluctant nod.

"I'm going to be right outside the door, meditating in the hall. You need anything, let me know." Jeannette squeezed Charlene's shoulder and then left the room.

Charlene picked up the phone without hesitation. She was determined to act, rather than allow her thoughts to spin. "Be tough," she muttered through clenched teeth. "Your people are tough."

The phone was ringing and ringing, the shriek of a torn muscle, and then a woman's voice broke through the clamor: "Hello?" A tentative question.

The words came so easily Charlene could have been reading them from a prompter. "I'm calling from a reservation in North Dakota," she said. "We're collecting money for our orphans and neglected children."

There was no response, only the gentle static of an open line.

"No, that's a lie," Charlene said firmly. "This is Charlene Thunder, and I'm calling for somebody named Crystal Lundstrom because I think she's my mother."

Again, there was silence. Charlene focused on the barely audible white noise.

"I'm Crystal Lundstrom," the other voice breathed. "I'm your mother."

It was Charlene—so empty and so full, the calm at the eye of the storm—who kept the conversation moving forward. There were no tears or accusations. She told her mother: "I know why you did it. We don't have to go through all that. I think I would do the same thing to get away."

Charlene could hear when Crystal covered the mouthpiece to smother her sobs. "Don't cry," Charlene said. "Tell me about my father. Tell me who he is."

"Your father is an artist, and he can capture anything in his sketches. He drew me once. That's how he got me." After a pause, Crystal told Charlene: "You have a grandmother too."

"Do I ever!"

"No, I mean another one. Your father's mother. She's a good woman. You would like her. Tell me, when are you coming here?" The question was so simple.

"Now that I found you, you want me to come?" It was Charlene's only reproach.

"I've always hoped you would find me."

Plans floated back and forth across the line, until Charlene remembered a loose end. "What about my father? Does he know I exist?"

The answering silence was more terrible than the previous pauses. "He thinks you died at birth," Crystal admitted. "None of this is his fault. He had no idea."

Charlene felt love for him already; her blood warmed. "I'm not going anywhere until you tell him," she said. "And I want to make sure I'm not stepping into a battle zone. I want it to be okay between you. Not launching a divorce or something."

It was growing dark when Charlene returned the receiver to its cradle and joined Jeannette McVay in the hall. "I owe you a fortune,'' she told the counselor.

Charlene sat beside Jeannette on the floor of the dim hall, her back pressed against the lockers. "She's telling him," Charlene said. "My mother is telling my father that I'm alive and I'm seventeen years old, and I'll see them if they're not going to kill each other. She promised to call me back."

Jeannette reached for Charlene's hand, and she let her counselor take it because the hall was so dark they were only shadows.

Charlene curled in her seat, careful not to brush against the man beside her, and watched the plains rush past like roiling brown water. She clutched the stub of her bus ticket because it was her only possession.

"*Don't* go back to the house," her mother had ordered. Charlene wondered at how quickly authority had entered her voice. "That woman will figure you out and own you again." So Charlene had spent the night in Jeannette McVay's office, unwilling even to travel on the reservation roads.

Her guidance counselor had packed a bag of sandwiches for Charlene, given her money for a one-way ticket, and called a friend to take her to the depot. "I don't go into the city, otherwise I'd take you there myself," Jeannette explained. It was her fiancé, Alex Holy Hand, who turned up at the school to start Charlene on her journey. He smelled of bitter coffee but was sweetly cheerful and didn't stop smiling once during the forty-five-minute drive.

"You know my woman a long time?" he asked Charlene.

She told him yes.

"You're lucky, then. I didn't meet her soon enough."

He pointed to a set of scars trailing down the right side of his face. "Look at all this fighting I did." He laughed. A mile later he said, "So you're a Thunder woman. I better look out, or maybe this car will lift off the ground and I'll have to fly it like a plane."

Charlene laughed now. "That's right. I'm going to fly us all the way to Chicago." She was giddy by the time they reached Bismarck, and hungry too. She sat in the depot eating a peanut butter sandwich, counting the minutes before her bus left the capital, and the state of North Dakota, and Mercury Thunder, whose powers, she hoped, were like a television signal: fading at a distance, dribbling away to nothing.

Charlene's seatmate was snoring, and she wondered if her father made those bull sounds in his sleep. She didn't think so. His voice had been gentle and patient when he called, just minutes after Crystal had broken the news to him.

"Hello," he had said. "I am the father. It's all right. I'm glad she is my daughter." He sounded tongue-tied, tripping over his words. "I am not crazy," he said. Then he spoke to Crystal: "Tell Charlene I am not crazy."

Crystal echoed her husband. "He's not crazy, Charlene. He just has problems talking to people directly. I've worked up a theory over the years that he's so careful when it comes to people, he has to step around them. He's a good man.

"You are too," she told him when he protested.

Even his mother had joined the conversation, telling her granddaughter, "I'm old, but I guess I can't kick the bucket for a while. I have a lot of raising to do, sounds like. Seventeen years' worth of work. You're going to listen to me now, when you get here. We have a lot of ground to cover.''

Crystal had retrieved the phone. ''Don't let her scare you. Mostly she's talking about cooking.''

Charlene closed her eyes and decided to keep them shut until the bus had left North Dakota. *She's getting smaller and smaller,* Charlene told herself, imagining Mercury shrinking, reduced to a speck, an amoeba, visible only with a microscope. But her mind played tricks. She could also see her grandmother growing, expanding until her flesh filled the house, her feet broke through the windows, her hands tore down the chimney. The house exploded as the old woman rose and wheeled across the debris, her colossal wheelchair carving canyons in the backyard. Charlene was beginning to imagine Mercury's telescope eyes finding her, when she fell asleep. The telescope eyes collapsed, blind as jelly.

Charlene Thunder was startled to find the roof of the bus gone, sliced away. The wind roared in her ears, and her hair was whipped in circles. Charlene looked to her right, beyond the missing window, and noticed Pumpkin dancing alongside the bus. Her steps weren't rushed or frantic, yet she managed to keep up with the speeding vehicle. Pumpkin waved to Charlene, and it was more than a greeting: a stylized movement that became part of the dance. Pumpkin opened her mouth to speak, and Charlene flinched, dreading the beautiful little birds, which she knew would leave the dancer's lips only to die. This dream was different. The birds emerged, the same as always, but this time darted away. They were a neat flock, so miniature and close together that they looked to Charlene like a school of fish. Her mouth creaked open in surprise. Quickly, easily, the birds flew past her teeth, entering the cave of her jaws.

Charlene coughed, but the birds coasted down her throat, tickling her with their fluttering wings.

It was a terrible moment, and then it was sweet. Charlene tasted licorice candy, and words rolled off her tongue. Pumpkin's words, at last. It was so odd to see the dancing girl move her lips but hear the voice rising from another source.

It wasn't your fault, Charlene heard. *These things happen. There was nothing you could do.* She laughed, the relief lifting her out of her seat. She danced up and down the aisle, from one end of the bus to the other. She swallowed the birds and heard them sing, *It wasn't your fault,* over and over again. But because the noise came from her own throat, she couldn't tell if it was Pumpkin who forgave her, or Charlene forgiving herself.

11

The Vision Pit

(1982)

HEROD SMALL WAR WAS PRESIDENT OF THE OUTSIDE Committee, which organized the annual North Dakota Prison Rodeo in cooperation with the Inmates Committee. This year, in addition to a dozen rodeo events, there would be an evening powwow—all of it taking place within the brick walls of the state penitentiary. The second weekend in June was hot and dusty, the wind a warm blast scattering loose soil. Harley Wind Soldier, Frank Pipe, and the rest of their class at Saint Mary's High School had graduated three weeks earlier, in a subdued ceremony that seemed about endings more than beginnings; few of the students would be attending college. But the Prison Rodeo promised to be a well-attended distraction for the graduates, their families, and of course the inmate population.

Mercury Thunder was one of the first to arrive on Friday morning, conveyed there by her old friend Roger Bonnin— of all her previous boyfriends, the one who genuinely cared for her. He had built Mercury a portable arbor, complete with whitewashed latticework and plastic roses threaded through the bower. He took care with its placement, finding a spot already shady but central to the action. Mercury maneuvered her chair inside the recess and settled a slim board on the armrests to fashion a table. A burrowing owlet no larger than a tennis ball perched on the woman's shoulder, bobbing rhythmically forward and, if startled, plunging its

beak in the stiff nest of her hair. Mercury never went anywhere without the bird, its delicate talons hooked onto her
dress, but people could not discover its name. When asked,
Mercury would say, "It's a secret," or, "It doesn't have a
name," or simply, "Nothing." So her neighbors took to
calling the bird "Nothing" behind her back. And when
they noticed the woman's flesh collapsing to the bone and
her eyes sinking into their sockets, the people's fear turned
to pity, and they said: "Look how Mercury Thunder has
been left with Nothing." But there were others, who were
more cautious and wondered if Mercury Thunder wasn't
kin to the clever killdeer—the shorebird festooned with a
double-strand black necklace and known as an accomplished actor, simulating a broken wing only to fly safely
away, its mocking call ringing in a predator's ears.

"Look out," they warned their children and grandchildren. "That one is more dangerous now that the nest is
empty."

Several babies had been brought to the Prison Rodeo and
were handed around from one relative to the next, only one
of them carried in a traditional Dakota cradleboard: Jeannette McVay's five-month-old daughter, Gloria Betty Holy
Hand. Gloria Betty had caused a small sensation at the first
powwow she attended, a month earlier, for she looked like
a full-blood, more Sioux than her Sioux father and without
a trace of her mother's lineage.

"That's what determination will get you," Herod teased
the mother. "You must have sat there with a spoon and
skimmed off the white cream. This baby is pure Dakota."
He became serious. "But Jeannette, she needs to know both
sides. Otherwise she'll stand off-balance and walk funny
and talk out of one side of her mouth. Tell her *two* stories."

Jeannette had promised, her tinted eyes lowered in respect. Now she stalked across the prison grounds, the baby strapped to her back. Gloria Betty stared from the lofty perch at her surroundings, black-pearl eyes wide with the world. She smiled at Frank Pipe as he ran past, and he responded with a salute.

Frank was the assistant to the arena director and had spent the morning delivering messages and lending a hand wherever necessary. His straw cowboy hat was gray with dust and sweat, and the ends of his long braids were tucked in his back pockets to prevent them from swinging in the way of Frank's work. On a break, he bought two hot dogs wrapped in fry bread, then gave one to Aljoe Big Nest, the chute boss, who was so skinny it looked like his back met his front.

"What's it like in here?" Frank asked his cousin.

"Not too bad." Aljoe held the hot dog gently, as if it were a flower, and barely nicked it with his teeth. "There's more classes than I had in school."

Frank had finished his meal in three large bites. He wiped his fingers on the brim of his hat. "My grandfather says you're born again," Frank said.

"Amen." Aljoe became animated. "My soul was muddy, and they dipped it in Clorox. I can feel it now against my ribs."

Sure you can, Frank was thinking. *You can probably feel your spleen and liver rubbing up against your sides.* "How come you went that way?" Frank questioned.

"Well, I'll tell you." Aljoe was chewing on his bony thumb rather than his hot dog. "It seemed so organized it didn't scare me. Herod, now, he talks to spirits. He sees things walking across the hills and flying through the air that other people don't. He's *in* the spirit, and I've seen him collecting the secrets of the world all my life. I think

I like a God who owns all of the power and doesn't share."
Aljoe grinned, which made him look years older than
twenty-two, because his top front teeth were missing.
"That's a less confusing situation, you know?"

Frank plucked the straw hat off his head and waved it to
stir a breeze. "That's what Tunkašida told me, something
like that. He said the Christian God has a big lantern with
the kerosene turned way up, and the people pray to Him
for help, for guidance, and He lights the way. Now, Wakan
Tanka, when you cry to Him for help, says, 'Okay, here's
how you start a fire.' And then you have to make your own
torch.''

"You got it," Aljoe said, pulling on his ear. "They got
to walk me through this life. I'll admit that to anyone." He
held out his hot dog. "You finish this. I can't eat in the
morning." Aljoe left to check the restless stock.

Frank rocked back on the heels of his boots and looked
at the sky. He could feel power in the wind, sense mysteries
stitched inside the frothy clouds. The dense simplicity of
the horizon and the rich complexity of the soil beneath his
feet filled him with satisfaction. He was beginning to ap-
preciate his grandfather's vision, an attitude of wonder, ex-
ploration, and acceptance. He thought his grandfather's soul
wasn't inside the old man but outside, so that you touched
the filament if you shook his hand, or grazed it if you
bumped his elbow.

Herod Small War had told Frank that if he wanted to
assist his grandfather and learn his religion, it would become a life way. "It won't stop at the end of a ceremony,"
Herod had warned. "It will follow you to bed and to breakfast, it will be there at a basketball game or a powwow.
All the time."

Frank wasn't positive yet that he could live his life receptive to the world, his own soul turned inside out, vulnerable.

"Do you think I can do it?" he'd asked Herod.

"I saw the possibility in you from the first," his grandfather had told him. "That's why I kept you so close. Otherwise I wouldn't teach you, even if you begged."

Frank Pipe watched the rodeo clown paint his face and wondered what had been in his cousin Aljoe, or what had been missing. *Why is he afraid under the weight of the sky?* the boy asked himself. His cousin had once made a living by stealing to order. He went from house to house on the reservation, compiling an inventory list:

"You want a thirteen-inch Sony Trinitron?"

"You need a Panasonic tape deck?"

"You want some size-fourteen Nikes for your son?"

"You want the *Sports Illustrated* swimsuit edition for your husband's birthday?"

His prices were reasonable, and he would handle trades. When the state police finally caught him, many families on the reservation felt that his absence was like the loss of a local K Mart franchise.

Before the trouble with the law, Frank remembered seeing Aljoe in the boys' bathroom at Saint Mary's, getting high on the fumes of correction fluid. Frank was five years younger than his cousin—eleven at the time—but he knew the dangers of the practice.

"You'll kill your lungs," he whispered in Aljoe's ear, careful not to embarrass him in front of his friends, who were drawing deep breaths from their own crumpled bags. "They'll get hard and stop, and you won't be able to breathe."

"Cool." Aljoe's smile was beautiful; his teeth hadn't been knocked out yet by an encounter with a steering wheel. "That's so cool. They'll be paper for somebody to write on, and I'll stop breathing."

Frank Pipe now watched his cousin inspect the rodeo stock. Aljoe was easygoing but thorough, paying close attention to details—which is why he'd been so good at theft. Frank wished him well and decided he'd better get back to work. He took a few steps and then stalled, his left pants leg stapled by a set of sharp teeth. Frank squatted and scratched Chuck Norris behind the ears, then pushed him over to rub the dog's round belly.

"Where's your buddy?" Frank asked him. "Did you let him come along for the ride?"

Harley Wind Soldier appeared from behind Frank. "So you've figured out the boss of this operation," he teased. He gently poked the squirming Pomeranian with his foot.

Frank straightened. "Where you been?" he asked his friend.

"Nowhere." Harley tucked his hands in his back pockets and tipped his head until he was looking beyond the penitentiary wall.

Frank wondered what Harley could see. "I talked to Aljoe," Frank said. "He's really got religion. Well, I guess whatever works. It's just weird hearing him talk about it."

Harley shrugged. "What's the big deal? It's all a scam." He strode away, his long torso tilted forward, like a person walking into the head of a stout wind.

Frank jogged after him. "I don't get it, man. Why all this doom and gloom? It's been a year since the accident, and you hardly knew that girl. Just one night, *koda*."

Harley flung his arms to the sides as if the answer were physical, something clenched in his fists. He moved away quickly, Chuck loping behind him on three legs, the fourth limb useless, out of sync.

Frank squinted at Harley, determined to see his friend's heart as clearly as his grandfather would have seen it.

Harley Wind Soldier had become a person of swift gestures and abrupt departures, not because he felt he had places to go, but rather because he felt he had circumstances to leave behind. The dark silence that had blossomed inside him as a small child had both expanded and compressed, become a leaden weight branching everywhere, even to his fingers. Harley imagined he was pure surface, taut skin covering emptiness. But what frightened him most was discovering that even a person flush with dreams and goals, a synthesized soul, such as Pumpkin, who had been learning to reconcile contrasting impulses, could be shaken out of the world.

What good are you? he taunted himself. Harley didn't think he was particularly interesting or talented. He couldn't dance like Pumpkin, no matter how hard he tried; he didn't play basketball with the same intensity as Frank Pipe, who could outjump taller players and defend so tenaciously he earned the nickname "Mosquito Wičaša"— Mosquito Man. Harley couldn't sing like his mother, pray like Herod Small War, or regard the world with blithe optimism like his school guidance counselor, Jeannette McVay. He couldn't even express himself as effectively as Chuck Norris, who made plain his desires, his preferences.

"I could learn from you," Harley growled at the dog. Chuck Norris halted in his steps, dipped his head, and then raced past Harley, longing to be chased. He slowed in disappointment when there was no pursuit.

Harley leaned against the brick wall, which was warm as heated stones. His pinched muscles relaxed. The institution was nearly a hundred years old, although Harley remembered that this was not the original wall. Heavy pine planks had once encircled the inmates, and he was curious about their stories, could almost see generations of prisoners wandering in the yard. He was so hypnotized by the images his mind conjured that he didn't recognize the one firm gift he possessed: his imagination. Harley assumed that everyone who stood upon a historic battlefield could see the dreadful skirmishes replayed, that anyone who looked up at the moon would understand what it was to travel there, to leave footprints in lunar dust. Harley Wind Soldier watched a parade of ghostly horse thieves and con men, bootleggers, murderers who looked gentle as children—recalcitrants of every ilk. Harley transformed the men from dim shadows into creatures of precise detail. He noticed a missing eyebrow, toes breaking out of shoes, one man nibbling a stalk of grass, another naked to the waist and plunging his nose to the ground in smooth push-ups. Harley's breath was uneven, strained, because sometimes a figure passed too close, treading upon his toes.

Harley Wind Soldier was nearly trampled by ghosts but wholly unaware of how remarkable his vision was.

The rodeo began at noon and ended at suppertime. The contestants were all inmates, there to entertain the public. The first event was the Mad Scramble, followed by Bareback Bronc Riding and Calf Roping, Saddle Bronc Riding, Steer Wrestling, a clown act, and the treacherous Bull Riding, in which prison cowboys dared one another to mount the meanest of the bucking bulls: Yellow Jacket. The finale was a Wild Horse Race that kicked up so much dust it looked like smoke from a blazing fire rolling through the arena and the stands.

Chuck Norris worried the stock with his courageous

lunges in their direction and his piercing barks, until finally a prison guard threatened to shoot the dog. Harley scooped him up and carried him to the truck. He noticed that Herod Small War and Frank Pipe were setting up for the small evening powwow, cleaning the arena, spreading sawdust, designating locations for drum groups. Harley was planning to dance later, but the flurry of activity suddenly depressed him.

"Let's get out of here," he said to Chuck. The dog's smile was crooked but sincere. He leaned against Harley, his weight so insignificant that the boy didn't notice its pressure.

Lydia Wind Soldier had been working on a traditional Dakota dress for several years. No one knew of the project except her son. She had tanned the buckskin hides the old way, using cow brains and then a scraping stone, and she beaded the yoke of the dress following a design in a photograph that had belonged to her mother: a faded picture of the dress that Lydia's great-grandmother once wore to important ceremonies and that currently languished in Chicago's Field Museum, untouched, unworn. An expanse of blue beads formed a brilliant sky, and streaming through the glittering air were the slender forms of Dakota women waving to their husbands, warriors on horseback leaping across death, and shaggy, tireless buffaloes that were never brought down. Lydia made leggings that resembled the American flag, the familiar stars and stripes depicted in beads, because this too was part of her story. The moccasins were replicas of her mother's wedding slippers, as close as Lydia could get to the original pair working only from memory: the crimson roses just opening, their petals outlined in black.

The dress materials had been expensive; Lydia squeezed money for beads from the benefits she'd received since her husband's death and from her paychecks earned in the kitchen at Saint Mary's. There had been times when she ran out of beads and was forced to put the work aside for several months until she saved enough money to buy more.

Lydia donned the dress, leggings, and moccasins for the first time to wear to the Prison Rodeo powwow. The dress was heavy, but Lydia held her back straight as she braided her long hair. She stood at the sink so she could wet her fingers to tame wayward strands. She flickered as she walked, the beads reflecting light, but she wasn't entirely pleased with the outfit. She realized it needed a belt. In the bottom drawer of her husband's dresser, a snake rested in coils. Lydia withdrew the snakeskin belt Herod Small War had made for Calvin so long before and wrapped it around her waist. She then opened a snuffbox packed with the crimson carmine she'd prepared with her own hands. She drew a red streak down the part in her hair and two bright circles on the knobs of her cheekbones.

Now I am ready, she thought with satisfaction. The woman's labors had nothing to do with vanity—though her entrance would cause a stir—and everything to do with embracing her past. Lydia would never use her voice to tell Harley what he needed to hear. She would offer a story he could read with his eyes.

We will dance together, she said to herself. *He will finally know me and understand where he comes from.* The memories Lydia wore that evening were a gift to her son.

Harley Wind Soldier sat in the bed of his pickup, running a thumb across coin-sized patches of rust and spilling warm beer down his throat. He had the idea he was filling something up, challenging the perceived emptiness, but he couldn't tell if it was working.

"Slow down!" he shouted, ignoring the fact that the truck was parked in the concrete lot behind Saint Mary's. Chuck Norris whined nervously. The little dog nipped gingerly at Harley's hand.

"Geez, lemme alone!" Harley cried, and with the offended hand sent Chuck skittering across the metal bed. The dog crept back cautiously, an inch at a time. Harley leaned against the cab of the truck, his head cracking the thick pane of glass. He wouldn't feel the pain until the next day. He swallowed foam and golden fluid; he thought it was moonlight swirling through his mouth. He threw back his head and bayed. Chuck Norris retreated, his eyes bulging like black marbles, but eventually lifted his voice to join Harley; his tail wagged tentatively in a start-and-stop pattern.

"Man, am I shit-faced," Harley said when his throat clenched. He tossed the last beer can, empty now, onto the ground and promptly fell over the side of the truck as if diving after it. "Better get ready," he mumbled, and staggered to his feet.

Harley changed, as best he could, into his grass-dance costume. He stared into the rearview mirror to paint his face and didn't recognize the red eyes, the foolish grin. He was reminded of a clown and decided to use the *heyo'ka* design that belonged to his ancestor Ghost Horse. The jagged lightning streaks were blurry, because of his unsteady hand, but the lines were close enough. Harley drove the pickup onto the road, unable to feel the pedals with his numb moccasined feet, leaving Chuck Norris in the back of the truck, where the little dog slipped from one side to the other, thrown at every bend in the road.

Drugs, alcohol, and intoxicated participants were strictly prohibited at the rodeo dance, so Harley entered as swiftly as he could, waving casually to the guards. His knees throbbed with the beat of the drum. He decided he was having fun. One of the rodeo clowns perched on a fence surrounding the arena. He was wearing his loose pants and a red rubber nose. Harley approached and shook his hand.

"One clown to the other," he said.

The man laughed. "Feeling no pain, brother? Right on!" He plucked the bulbous nose from his face and presented it to Harley. "Go for it," he said. "The whole nine yards."

Harley slapped it on. "Thanks, man." He raised his fist. The rodeo clown raised his and laughed so hard he slipped off the fence.

Harley Wind Soldier staggered into the arena, his movements exaggerated in the way of powwow clowns. He leaned to one side, almost far enough to fall, and at the last moment caught himself, only to lean the other way. He released blasting war whoops and danced counterclockwise, against the stream. He played the fool.

Harley didn't notice his mother in her priceless regalia until she stood in front of him. Lydia shamed him. She trailed her eyes from the feathers on his head to his moccasins shuffling in the dirt. She inhaled the fumes of his malt binge and smeared the greasy lightning on his cheek with her finger. Lydia moved back, as if to leave, and slapped her son's face. The blow jerked him off his feet. Lydia stepped across Harley's prostrate form, walking directly to Frank Pipe. She pointed at Harley with her lips.

"Don't worry, I'll take him home," the boy said.

Lydia gathered her things and left, taking Chuck Norris along with her.

Harley awakened in Herod Small War's cramped pantry; his grass-dance costume hung from a nail on the wall above his feet. The colors were too bright for him, and he quickly shut his eyes.

"Coffee," Alberta Small War called from the kitchen.

"Mmm," Harley groaned.

The old woman poked her head in the pantry and said, "Sit up and drink this. Then go to the sweat lodge. My old man wants to see you."

Harley choked down the bitter brew and with great care made his way to the dome-shaped lodge. He peeled off his clothes. Heavy blankets were draped across bent willow poles, and Harley pushed them aside to enter. The heated stones hadn't been shoveled in yet, so he didn't replace the flap. The lodge interior was dim, but Harley gradually recognized the occupants as Herod Small War, Frank Pipe, Archie Iron Necklace, and Bill Good Voice Elk. He watched them furtively, too ashamed to look directly into their faces.

"We're going to draw the sickness out of you," Herod promised as the stones were passed into the structure and a bucket of water poured over them.

Harley forgot everything but the steam; his eyes burned, breath scalded his lungs, his mind melted. After four sweats the men emerged, scrubbing their bodies with sage.

"You can go home now," Herod told Harley. "You're clean enough to face your mother." Harley dressed and was ready to begin the short hike to his house, when Herod tapped him on the shoulder. "There are ways to learn what is inside you. We have all cried for ourselves a little, that's natural, but don't let it go on for too long. That is a child's way. I think you want to be a man?''

Harley nodded; his hands opened and closed in his pockets.

"Frank can help," Herod confided. "He's just learning too."

Harley Wind Soldier stood in the same deep pit his father had occupied thirty years before. Harley was more cooperative than Calvin had been, and wore only his gym shorts and a blanket. He clutched Herod Small War's pipe against his chest and watched the four flags staked at the perimeter of the pit rise in the wind. His mother and Alberta Small War had made the long string of tobacco ties that encircled him.

"I don't know how to pray," Harley mumbled, but he dismissed the idea. *I will learn,* he told himself.

He remembered the preparatory petitions Frank Pipe had made on his behalf: "Tunkašida Wakan Tanka, my friend is ready for the *hanbdeč'eya.* He wants to send you his voice so you will notice his prayers. But he might not have the strength to stand up and speak to you, so I am asking you to help him." Frank Pipe expressed himself in Dakota, finding the words so effortlessly his grandfather nodded. Harley's pulse quickened. His friend was in the spirit, and the sight of it moved Harley, gave him a spark of hope.

But now he was alone on Angry Butte, beneath the face of the sky. "I have to stand up for myself," he said aloud. He tried a tentative prayer: "Tunkašida Wakan Tanka, you know everything, you made my heart. Let me look into it for the first time."

Harley taught himself to pray from a hole in the ground.

It felt appropriate to be simultaneously buried in the earth and thrust into the air, a lone figure exposed to the elements. Hours passed, and it was suddenly dark, as if a woman had thrown her shawl across the sky. Harley shivered in his blanket, already exhausted on this first night. His eyes fluttered, and he slept on his feet until he heard horses speaking to each other in soft nickers. He looked up at the bright moon and noticed four men on horseback descending a broad beam of light, a lunar road. They were Dakota warriors, young men just a few years older than Harley and so confident, so easy in the saddle, their dignified postures could be mistaken for arrogance. They lifted their hands in greeting from high above Harley's head, moving gracefully toward him, in no rush.

"Cousin," they called, when their horses' hooves touched on solid ground. "Come ride with us!" The smallest of them charged up to the vision pit and hooked his arm through Harley's. The youth was whirled into the saddle behind the rider. He could see over the shorter man's head as the horses plunged down Angry Butte, galloping noiselessly across the open plains.

The men laughed; clearly they were friends. "Our cousin says we are too slow," one of them shouted.

"He says we don't know how to ride," another called.

The man who'd plucked Harley into the saddle said, "He is telling me our horses are on their last legs." Even the ponies snorted at his words.

"Cousin, are you ready for an adventure?" the warrior beside him asked.

"*Hau*," Harley answered in Dakota. Yes.

The warriors rode into the valley where as a young boy Harley Wind Soldier had searched for the medicine hole.

The ponies halted at the torn lip of a crevice in the valley floor.

"This is it," Harley murmured. "This is what we were looking for."

"Are you sure?" one of his guides asked.

The short Dakota grinned. "Cousin, you will have to go on alone. Crawl through the tunnel to the other side."

The ponies jostled one another, restless. Harley slipped off the horse and patted its warm silken haunches. "I'll never forget this ride," he told the warriors. Then he lowered himself into the medicine hole.

Harley crawled on his hands and knees for what seemed to be hours, certain he would never be able to unfold his body and stand tall again. He smelled of the grave and was covered with tiny spiders; he could feel them marching across his back and through his hair. The tunnel descended for a time and then climbed upward, curving so sharply in places that Harley thought he might be traveling in circles. The end of the passage came as a surprise, around a hairpin bend. Harley blinked at the flickering brightness, which turned out to be firelight.

"Welcome to the council fire, *takoja*." Small hands pulled him from the tunnel and brushed the dirt and spiders off his body.

"Unči!" Harley cried, clasping the woman's hand.

Margaret Many Wounds led her grandson closer to the light.

"I saw you!" he told her. "When I was little I saw you on the television—I mean, on the moon. You were beautiful, Unči, and dancing." Harley hadn't recalled the event until this moment.

"I know it," she said. "I felt you were there, watching. You have to keep that picture with you," she scolded softly. "It can be of great comfort to know that such things are possible."

Harley thought that his grandmother was radiantly old, each line on her face a curious thread of light. "I didn't think people could be old in heaven," he told her.

She laughed, her hand covering her mouth. "This isn't heaven," she said. "Who wants to go there? This is the edge of the world, which is really not so different from what you know. Time keeps moving, it can't help itself.

"You see." She plucked a young man forward. Harley hadn't noticed him there before. "This is your brother, Duane. I believe he's three years older than you."

The brothers shook hands. "You're taller than me," Harley said.

"But you look stronger." Duane clapped his brother on the shoulder. The two gazed back and forth, their eyes hungry for details. Their faces were the same square shape, but Duane's hair was a wavy brown and his skin a lighter shade.

"You're a pretty good-looking guy," Duane teased.

"You too," said Harley.

Margaret pulled another man forward, and Harley recognized his father. He held back in awe and fear, but the older man claimed him, pulling him into a rough embrace.

"You're doing real good," Calvin Wind Soldier whispered. "I saw you learning to pray. You're doing better than me." He shook his son's hand.

"We have to be careful what we say, because you're supposed to find your own answers. But you are my son."

Harley wouldn't release his father's hand. He was mesmerized by the face that was like his own, the firm chin that managed to be kind.

"There is someone else," his grandmother interrupted. Calvin squeezed Harley's hand, and the boy let go with a brief nod. "This is your uncle," Margaret said.

The most beautiful man Harley had ever seen stepped out of the fire. His eyes were black torches, his mouth a straight line beneath the perfect triangle of his nose.

"Nephew, I am Ghost Horse," he said. "You come from warriors who would give their true heart to their people. Let me shake your hand so you will know this." Ghost Horse's touch was gentle; he barely grazed Harley's hand. "You see? A warrior is not what you think."

Ghost Horse didn't smile, but Harley warmed to him. He had never felt such trust before. *I could put my life in his hands,* Harley thought.

"*Takoja,*" Margaret called to her grandson. "You don't know it, but you've been with us for three days."

"It was so quick!" Harley protested.

"When you remember this vision in the future, you'll realize that it was long. You have seen many things. How can you take it all in? Think of us over the years, and I promise you will learn something new every time you turn us in your mind."

Margaret walked Harley to the medicine hole. He swiveled his head in every direction, but the firelight was so dazzling he couldn't see his relatives.

"You have to go back to your prayers, *takoja,*" Margaret said. "There is someone else who wants to see you." He felt the pressure of her fingers in the small of his back, and had no memory of the return trip. The touch of Margaret's hand became a bump in the wall of the vision pit, a slight protuberance that dug into his spine.

•　•　•

Harley closed his eyes and slept, and in the morning prayed with renewed strength. At dusk he felt a rare burst of joy. *This is the last night,* he thought to himself. *I've almost made it.*

"Almost, but not quite," said a voice out of the darkness. A young woman appeared above him, her moccasins just inches from his nose. She knelt in the dirt to look into his face. Harley knew he was visited by Red Dress. His tongue swelled in his mouth, and he longed to touch the river of hair that poured onto the ground and snaked into the pit.

"I have seen you dancing," Red Dress said in two languages, two distinct voices. "There is something you should keep in mind when you tie the grass to your shoulders and your knees and step as if you knew something about that kind of movement." Red Dress stroked a rattlesnake gourd that was tied in her hair, so tenderly it didn't make a sound.

"Do you know what the grass represents?"

Harley shook his head.

"But you are even one step further from the truth, because the grass has become yarn, a replacement for a replacement." Red Dress trailed her finger along the rim of the vision pit, loosening the soil at its edge. "This is not a pleasant thing, but then, you aren't a child. A long time ago, when we vanquished our enemies in battle we would hold a victory dance and flaunt trophies of war—the long hair of our adversaries. So when you move through those old steps, remember that you are dancing a rebellion and that the pretty fringes are hiding blood and flesh and captured hair."

Red Dress rose, her train of rattles hissing. "One final

question," she said. "Did you see your uncle?"

Harley answered, *"Hau."*

Red Dress sighed. She looked at Harley and reluctantly stepped away. "I want you to be happy, because I know what it is to be sad." Red Dress turned to leave.

Iyotiye wakiye, echoed in Harley's ears. *I am sad.*

The woman's form quickly blended into the darkness. Harley thought she was gone, but a final message carried across the earth: *You are dancing a rebellion.*

Harley Wind Soldier was eager for the dawn, his legs quaking with exhaustion and his throat so dry it felt as though he were swallowing needles. He thought he would never be able to speak another prayer.

Color bled into the sky with agonizing care; it was too protracted a process for Harley on that particular morning. At last he heard the drum approaching, its pounding song supported by the voices of his community, which was ascending the hill to collect him. He recognized his mother's singing first and was suddenly lonesome for her. Next he heard Herod Small War, croaking like a bullfrog, and Frank Pipe, nasal as a magpie. He could even hear the frantic yelps of Chuck Norris, who had been locked in the house for four days to prevent him from joining Harley.

The honor song swelled in Harley's ears, and the united voices comforted him, lifted him up so that he stood tall in the vision pit. He would spot them any minute now, cresting the flat top of the hill: his friends and relatives. None of them strangers. But a powerful new voice that was unfamiliar to Harley disturbed his ears. Who was this unknown singer? He became a little angry, thinking to himself that after such an ordeal as the *hanbdeč'eya,* it wasn't right to bring outsiders into the circle.

Harley listened carefully, his hands curled into fists, and it was only as the song neared its end that he realized the truth: What he heard was the music of his own voice, rising above the rest.